Going the Distance

Going the Distance

CHRISTINA JONES

ORION

First published in Great Britain in 1997
by Orion
An imprint of Orion Books Ltd
Orion House, 5 Upper St Martin's Lane,
London WC2H 9EA

A CIP catalogue record for this book
is available from the British Library

ISBN 0 75280 510 X

Typeset by The Spartan Press Ltd
Lymington, Hampshire

Printed in Great Britain by
Clays Ltd, St Ives plc

Dedicated with all my love
to the memory of my parents,
Fred and Aimee Wilkins,
who gave me the gifts of love
and laughter, freedom
and imagination.

"No Regrets"

Acknowledgements

To Jane Wood and Selina Walker at Orion who guided me gently and skilfully through the quagmire and made it so much fun.

To Sarah Molloy, my agent, for her perception, kindness and friendship; for always being there when I needed her and never minding me asking incredibly silly questions; and for her ready acceptance of my tendency to scamper around like a giddy squirrel.

To Hilary Johnson of the R.N.A., not only for her generous advice, constant support and encouragement, but also for making me laugh.

To Pat Powell, my best friend for ever, for making the research a never-to-be-forgotten experience.

To Hilary Lyall and Carol-Ann Davis who always believed in me.

To Dorothy Hunter with many thanks.

To Gill Boucher, Corinne Rees and Jane Clark for being such true friends and giving me all those lovely nights out when I never stopped talking.

To Rob and Laura for loving me, for being my inspiration, and for never once complaining about it being beans on toast again.

One

She was sure her suspenders were showing. Twisting round, craning her neck to check in the mirror, Maddy grinned. They were covered. Just.

Even with the breath-taking aid of Fran's second-best basque, Maddy had always known the dress was going to be too tight and far too short. Resignedly tugging the borrowed grey crêpe shift over her head, she gazed dolefully at her wardrobe. She couldn't wear the green velvet again – which left an exciting choice between the black skirt and the black trousers, either of which would need a suitable party top . . .

With a sigh, she hurled Fran's dress on to her bed, where it hovered for a moment before slithering to the floor amidst several discarded newspapers and an empty tub of Slimfast. A week ago she had vowed she would live on nothing but Slimfast. She was going to slink into tonight's party looking svelte and toned and seductive, and Peter would wonder why he had ever left her for Stacey, the bow-legged stick-insect.

Of course, she hadn't reckoned on the Slimfast being quite so moreish – especially when mixed with condensed milk and a dollop of Cornish ice cream . . . Maddy kicked the diet plan under the bed and decided to seek consolation in a chocolate Hobnob. It was only the insistent chirrup of the telephone that prevented her from polishing off the remains of the packet.

'How was the dress?' Fran's voice was that of the eternal optimist. 'OK with the corset, was it?'

Maddy pulled a face. 'No. It wouldn't have been OK with steel girders. The basque helped a lot – but I still looked like a lumpy pillow.'

'Pity.' Fran giggled. 'It always has the desired effect on Richard.'

'That's probably because I'm two sizes larger than you – or because Richard is turned on by lumpy pillows. Thanks for trying, Fran, but it looks like it'll have to be the black skirt again – if I can find a top.' She shrugged. 'Maybe I'll give the party a miss.'

'Oh no.' Fran became school-marmish. 'Maddy Beckett, you are not a quitter. You'll shimmy in there tonight – as we planned – and hit Peter right between the eyes.'

'My chest'll probably do that,' Maddy said. 'Always supposing that the thighs don't get him first.'

'Good girl. A man likes a sense of humour, although why you're attempting to waste it on Peter, God only knows. Especially after the way he—'

'Fran.' The word was heavy with dire threat.

'OK. OK. You loved him – you still love him.'

'No I don't,' Maddy protested. 'I want to prove that I've survived and prospered without him. That there is life in Milton St John without Peter Knightley. And life in Maddy Beckett . . . It's just that if he's got Stacey in tow I'll feel like a beached whale.'

'Which, as I recall, was what he likened you to.' Fran's voice dripped ice. 'The bastard.'

'Well, I am a bit overweight.'

'Nonsense,' Fran said briskly. 'You're curvy and pretty and sexy. Peter Knightley was a prat.'

'People always say hurtful things at the end of a relationship.' Maddy was beginning to shiver inside the basque. She really must remember to ask someone to look at the boiler. It slept soundly all day, conserving its energy for sporadic bursts of tropical heat at about three in the morning. 'I'm sure I was just as unpleasant. Anyway, it's all history. I'll drop your things off tomorrow on my way to work.'

'Goody.' Fran's voice was smiling again. 'I'll get the kids out of the way and the kettle on – and open a new packet of chocolate fingers. I shall want to hear every detail, mind. All of it. And Maddy?'

'Yes?'

'Borrow a top from Suzy. That white one she wore to the Cat and Fiddle last week should render Peter speechless.'

'Brilliant! Fran, I love you!'

A toe-amputating draught was screaming under the front door as Maddy replaced the receiver. Having had to become energy conscious since the last heating bill, she tugged at the mat which had got caught between the door frame and the step, but it held fast. Irritably, she opened the front door, kicked the mat back into place and smiled at Mr Pugh from the Village Stores, who was wobbling past on his bicycle. She was closing the door when Suzy came tearing up the path.

Maddy dragged her sister inside. 'Oh, good. You're just in time. Fran's dress was hopeless. I want that white top thing of yours, Suzy. The one that drapes . . .'

'Holy hell!' Suzy's heavily kohled eyes blinked in astonishment. 'You didn't, did you, Mad? You opened the door – like that? I wondered why Bernie Pugh's bike was more shaky than usual. And for heaven's sake come away from the window. You'll frighten the horses. Why,' Suzy sniffed with all the superiority of a seventeen-year-old sister over one ten years her senior, 'are you dressed like a tart?'

'It's a long story,' Maddy sighed. 'And can I have that white blouse for tonight?'

'Nah, 's in the wash.' Suzy was tugging off her mud-caked boots. 'You can have the pink one.'

'I can't wear pink!' Maddy wailed. 'I've got red hair!'

'So have I – sometimes. Of course you can wear pink. Where are you going, anyway?'

'Diana and Gareth's drinks party.'

Suzy arched an eyebrow. 'Really? I wouldn't have thought you had the right number of hyphens in your surname for one of Diana's parties. What's the catch?'

'No catch. Diana thought I'd enjoy it.'

'Can't imagine why.' Suzy had removed most of her riding clothes and was striding through to the kitchen. Maddy watched her waif-like figure without envy. Although it was thoroughly sickening to be faced with a pert size eight – especially when it was related and lived in the same house – there were compensations. Suzy favoured voluminous jumpers and stretchy tops. Maddy borrowed them at every opportunity.

She sucked in her breath. 'Because Peter is going to be there.'

There. She'd said it. She waited for the explosion. It wasn't long coming.

'Holy hell, Mad!' Suzy paused in the middle of slapping golden syrup on to a chunk of bread. 'Have you got a death wish? Are you going to let Peter the Perv perform another public execution?'

'Don't call him that – and no. I'm not. I'm going because I want him to see how well I've done without him. He's thinking of coming back to Milton St John, Diana says, and she thought—'

'She thought she'd make you look a complete fool. Diana James-Jordan is a cow. Look what she did to Richard and Fran. I thought they were your friends?'

'They are. Fran knows I'm going. I've promised not to say anything about Richard being jocked off in favour of Newmarket's golden wonder. And, after all, Diana does put work my way.'

'And loyalty to your friends takes a nosedive because she's invited Pete to snuffle in her trough!'

Maddy groaned. Sometimes she despaired at Suzy's coarseness. It was mixing with all those stable lads that did it, her mother had said. Maddy was pretty sure that Suzy could teach the lads a thing or two about colourful epithets. She really didn't want to get dragged into a discussion on the ethics of race riding – or Peter Knightley. Suzy was very strident in her views on both.

4

'Look, I'm freezing here and I'm going to be late. Where's your pink blouse?'

'Under the bed,' Suzy mumbled through a mouthful of golden syrup. 'On the left – the clothes side, not the shoes . . .'

Suzy's bedroom made Maddy's clutter look pristine. Ignoring conventional furniture, Suzy kept her entire life beneath her bed. Maddy fished around with trepidation, and eventually emerged triumphant with a handful of pink lace.

Suzy had descended on Milton St John in general, and Maddy in particular, the previous May. Maddy, at that time still smarting from Peter's rejection, had welcomed her younger sister with motherly delight. It hadn't taken long to discover that Suzy didn't need mothering. Suzy, Mr and Mrs Beckett's menopausal mistake, had been given her head and it showed.

Maddy, planned for, cosseted and protected, had still been in ankle socks at twelve. Suzy had been fierce and fearless, Maddy timid and unsure. A late developer, Maddy reckoned she'd gone through puberty at about nineteen. And then there was the question of a career . . .

Suzy had always known she would be a jockey. This was not a childish dream engendered by pony clubs and gymkhanas, but an obsession with horse racing bordering on the unhealthy. At the age of seven, Suzy could work out odds, read form and pick winners. Maddy, struggling with A levels, had been highly in awe of this talent. She was even more in awe of the fact that Suzy knew at primary school exactly what she was going to do with her life. Maddy had a vague notion of going to university if her results were good enough, but after that she didn't have a clue.

There had been loudly voiced reservations from her parents about this wild child of their middle-age pursuing such an unladylike vocation – especially as Maddy had been something of a disappointment – but Suzy had taken no notice. As soon as Maddy moved to Milton St John, she wrote begging letters to every trainer. As Maddy was well known in the village, there had been some speculation about Suzy's ability to achieve riding weight, and Maddy had been forced to admit that Suzy took after the bone-thin side of the family. So far, it had worked out very well. It was like having a whole second wardrobe.

Maddy hurried across the hall to her bedroom. As it was too late to have a bath, and there would only be half an inch of hot water at this time of the evening anyway, she squirted herself liberally with Body Mist. Deciding to make the most of the basque and stockings, she pulled her black skirt over the top of them, and struggled into the pink blouse.

The result was less disappointing than she'd expected. Peter was hardly likely to fall panting at her feet – not that she wanted him to, of course – but neither would he recoil in horror. With make-up on, she squinted into the mirror. She might even pass as glamorous . . .

Suzy wandered into the bedroom eating a pork pie as Maddy applied haphazard blusher. 'What shall I do with my hair?'

'Put it up.' Suzy perched on the bed. 'It sort of tightens your face.'

'Cheers.' Maddy wrenched her abundant auburn curls on top of her head and anchored them with several clips. 'So? How do I look?'

'Surprised.' Suzy slid from the bed in search of more food. 'No, really Mad, you look super. Very pretty. Everyone will fancy you rotten. Oh, and guess what I heard today? Someone has bought Peapods at last.'

Not Peter, Maddy thought in panic. She had only just got used to the idea that Peter was back in Milton St John. She really couldn't cope with him living just across the road.

'Who?' She tugged on her black suede boots.

'Oh, some foreign geezer. Well. Welsh, or something. He's going to use it as a stables again. He's been training flat horses somewhere or other and he wants to move on to a

6

mixed yard. I think his name's Dermot – Dermot MacAndrew.'

'That is neither foreign nor Welsh.' Maddy applied scarlet lipstick and wished she had time for matching nail varnish. 'It sounds like a fairly good Celtic cocktail. Still, it will be nice to have Peapods running as a stables again – the health farm was a disaster.'

'Yeah.' Suzy poked her head round the door. 'Especially when it employed people like Stacey . . .' She managed to duck the lipstick as Maddy lobbed it towards the doorway. 'And take the car tonight, Mad. Don't rely on Pete giving you a lift home. It looks so tacky to be hanging around hopefully at the end.'

'Won't you need it?'

'Nah. I'm walking down to the pub with Jason and Olly. It's karaoke tonight.'

'OK. Fine.' Maddy scooped up the car keys from the dressing table. 'I'm off. Wish me luck.'

'I'll wish you whatever you wish yourself.' Suzy looked at her sister fondly. 'Just don't go breaking your heart – again.'

But of course, she hadn't, Maddy thought, as she drove towards the white curve that passed as a main road in Milton St John. Broken her heart, that is. Peter had. Peter with his golden hair and his golden skin and his honeyed voice. Peter Knightley, who had left her fifteen months three weeks and two days ago – not that she was counting – for Stacey the bimbo stick-insect. And he hadn't even told her. He'd just gone – and written a letter two weeks later.

She supposed Fran and Suzy were right to be anguished about his equally abrupt return, but then they hadn't known him like she had. It had taken Maddy only moments to fall in love with Peter, to fall in love for the first time in her life. It had been an intense and all-consuming passion. For nearly four years Peter Knightley had been her life. More important than her work, more important than Suzy or her parents,

7

more important, God help her, than her friends. When Peter had ended their relationship and left Milton St John he had not only taken her heart, he had practically taken her entire existence. That was why it was vital that she should make a survival statement tonight.

She drove slowly as she always did, as every resident of the village did, knowing its horsy population and being aware that each rounded bend might reveal a glossy string of racehorses worth a king's ransom. Not a confident driver, Maddy used the car only for sorties such as these within the village, where a safe thirty miles an hour was speed of Schumacher proportions. For journeys farther afield she relied on the good local minibus service, or caught the train at Didcot.

Peter had laughed at her when she'd tried to explain to him how flustered she got by incomprehensible road signs and the aggressive roar of the motorway. 'You're an anachronism, Maddy. You don't like fast traffic, you don't know how to work the video – you don't even completely understand the microwave, for goodness' sake.' His caressing voice had taken the barb from the words. He'd made it sound like a compliment rather than a criticism. 'You'd've been much happier in the 'fifties than the 'nineties. You really will have to drag yourself into the present, love. You'll never survive waging a one-lady war against progress.'

She turned the car into the tunnel of lilac trees that heralded Diana and Gareth James-Jordan's training stables, remembering with painful clarity how she had tried to protest that she was really quite content with the 'nineties, merely finding technology rather difficult to understand, and Peter had smothered the explanation with his lips and his arms, and told her that he loved her anyway – and always would. And she, gullible fool that she was, had melted in delight. Then he had left her.

And now he was back.

'Maddy! Angel! You look gorgeous.' Diana opened the

door herself, which was encouraging. It signified that this really might be "just a little get-together before the season takes hold and we're all too busy, darling", as Diana had said when she'd issued her invitation.

As she clashed cheeks with her hostess Maddy was overcome by a waft of Chanel's finest. 'Diana . . .' The greeting ritual was complete.

She followed Diana into the hall, where walnut and rosewood gleamed, and parquet flooring looked as though it was about to hold a skating spectacular.

'You do look lovely, Maddy,' Diana cooed over her shoulder. 'New top?'

'Yes.' Well, it was. To her. And Suzy had only had it a month or so.

Diana, of course, was groomed and curry-combed to parade ring perfection. Everything sleek and stark and shining. Was there really no other woman in the whole of Milton St John, Maddy wondered, who battled with plump thighs and a chest that always threatened to explode from its confines? Just because it was a racing community where the horses were slender and tight muscled, and the majority of the men were, by necessity, the same, surely not every woman had to be honed to near-anorexia? Even Kimberley Weston, Milton St John's token female trainer, who had to be at least a size eighteen, managed to look as though it was all solid flesh with not a wobble or wrinkle in sight.

'Gareth is seeing to the drinks – and of course, you know everybody, I think.' Diana continued to chat over her shoulder.

Maddy smiled. 'Yes, of course.'

There was no way on earth that she was going to ask about Peter. If he was there, she would know. Without even seeing him, she was sure she would know.

'Hello, Maddy. Pretty as a picture as always,' Gareth James-Jordan boomed from his great height just inside the door, sounding like the kind of children's entertainer who would send even the bravest playground thug scuttling behind his mother's skirts. 'What are we drinking?' Whatever it was, Maddy thought, it appeared that Gareth had had quite a lot of it already.

'Just a mineral water, please.' Maddy kept her back to the crowd she could hear humming. 'I'm driving, but I'll maybe have something alcoholic later.'

'That's the spirit,' Gareth roared, peering at the non-alcoholic selection on the sideboard. 'Er, which ones are minerals, Maddy? My eyes only focus on brandy.'

Laughing, Maddy helped herself. She liked Gareth. Despite his loudness, he was a nice man, and a good trainer. The brains and the money came from Diana. And Diana never hesitated to trample all over people to achieve her ends. Hence the fall-out with Fran and Richard.

She moved away from the sideboard, anchoring herself between an elm bookcase and a table she had always admired with claw feet that were the very devil to dust. He wasn't in the room.

'How's tricks?' John Hastings, the trainer who employed Suzy, paused on his way to refill his glass, his eyes skimming over Maddy's cleavage. She wasn't insulted. John Hastings always cast a professional eye over horses and women with the same detachment. Horses excited him more. 'Your Suzy tell you about that thing of Sir Neville's, did she? Smashing little filly.'

Maddy wasn't sure whether John was referring to her sister or the horse, but chanced it was the latter. 'No. We didn't have much time to talk about work this evening. It's very kind of you to promise her some good rides this season, John. I know she appreciates it.'

'So do I.' His leer was practised. 'I've always had an eye for a decent apprentice. I hope to get her on the racecourse by the end of the month.'

He continued talking about horses and entries, about viruses and weights, and Maddy nodded and said 'oh, yes' and 'of course' and 'no, really?' in what she hoped were all the right places, and all the time her eyes were fixed on the door.

Diana was right. She knew everyone in the Small Room – a drastic misnomer as it stretched into infinity between linen fold panels and beneath carved ceilings, and would have swallowed up Maddy's entire cottage in one gulp. Trainers, jockeys, villagers, jockey's wives, trainers' secretaries; all friends or at least nodding acquaintances from Milton St John; all gathered to discuss the ending of the jump season and the start of the flat. The same as dozens of other gatherings she had attended in the time that Milton St John had been her home. With one exception. Peter wasn't there.

Maddy joined groups that splintered off into other groups, and talked about The Derby and the new Chinese in Newbury and The Oaks and the price of the bungalows in the next village and The Guineas and about Richard being jocked off.

'Not really Diana's fault, eh?' Barty Small piped through the general murmur of sympathy. 'If the owner wanted the golden boy from Newmarket to ride, then what could Diana do?'

'But Richard is her stable jockey. It's his first season with her. He'd been banking on it.' Maddy was fiercely loyal, even though she had promised Fran she wouldn't get involved. 'And Fran is your secretary. And—'

'And the owners pay everyone's wages. The owners call the shots, Maddy, as your Suzy will tell you. Of course,' he moved closer so that his nose was almost lodged on her bosom, 'you wouldn't really be affected, would you? After all, racing isn't in your blood.'

Maddy resisted the urge to flick his nose away from her chest. Barty Small had a weasel's face and piggy eyes and straw-coloured hair with a pemanent indent around the crown where his trilby lived. 'Maybe not, but it's in my heart,' she said doggedly. 'And it was a slur on Richard's ability.'

'Not at all.' Barty was bristling. 'It all comes down to money in the end.'

'What about friendship and loyalty? What about repaying good service? What about—'

'All dead and gone.' Kimberley Weston smoothed down her well-boned frock. 'Sadly, Barty's right, Maddy. Racing is an industry and is as fragile as any other in these mercenary days.'

Maddy was irritated. Not just because she couldn't give full vent to her feelings for fear of insulting her hostess, not just because Peter wasn't coming and she'd rehearsed being cool and uninterested until her teeth ached, but also because the basque was cutting into her, and she was starving.

'Oh, scrummy!' Kimberley's brown eyes zoomed towards the doorway. 'This must be who we've been waiting for. Diana said she had a surprise up her sleeve.'

Maddy froze. Her hands were sweating. She wished she'd rubbed Body Mist into her palms. She wished her third glass of mineral water contained a pint of gin. She wished she was a stone lighter.

She arranged her face in careful anticipation. She would turn and smile, a pleasant 'Oh, lovely to see you again. How long has it been?' smile, and her legs wouldn't wobble at the golden hair and the golden skin and the big blue eyes that looked like a hurt child's but masked a business brain as sharp as a laser. She turned round.

'Maddy, Kimberley, Barty. I'm sure you'll be pleased to meet—' There was a crash and an oath from the far side of the room, followed by Gareth's braying giggle. Diana frowned. 'Excuse me a moment . . .' and she left her charge at their mercy.

Maddy felt as though she'd walked into the wrong film at one of those multi-screen cinemas. All geared up for the heart-stopping delights of Peter Knightley, the man standing beside her was something of a disappointment. Not, of course, that he wasn't attractive. He just wasn't Peter.

Kimberley, who must have been the archetypal head girl, made neat and brief introductions. He nodded at each one, spending just the right length of time meeting eyes and shaking hands. His face was nice, Maddy decided as he released her hand after a firm squeeze, it looked like it laughed a lot. With you, not at you. His hair was dark and his eyes weren't. He was somewhere between thirty and forty, and a complete stranger.

'As Diana seems to be otherwise occupied, I'll have to make my own introductions.' He had the sort of voice that would soothe without boredom, and command without being abrasive. 'I'm Drew Fitzgerald.'

It was probably the anti-climax of him not being Peter that pushed Maddy's mouth into gear before her brain had time to put on the brakes.

'Goodness, what a coincidence. It must be the time of year for Celtic cross-breeds . . .' She was aware of Kimberley and Barty holding their collective breath, but didn't heed the warning.

'I beg your pardon?' The tawny eyes flashed slightly.

'Your name . . .' Maddy tripped on. 'My sister was telling me earlier about a Welsh-Scottish-Irishman who has bought the stables opposite our cottage. He's some sort of trainer from out of town. I don't suppose he'll make a go of things.'

'Why not?' He sounded interested.

'Oh, the place is really run down. It needs a professional to lick it into shape if it's going to be a successful yard again.' Maddy was beginning to lose her thread. Why didn't Kimberley or Barty join in the conversation and let her off the hook? 'It's been empty for over a year, and according to my sister, the new owner wants to turn it into a mixed yard. Far too ambitious for a new starter . . . Are you in racing, Mr, um, Fitzgerald?'

'Darlings, I am so sorry.' Diana appeared at Maddy's other elbow. 'Gareth got a bit carried away with the Glenfiddich. Nearly drowned poor Mrs Pugh. Now, have we all introduced ourselves?'

They all nodded dutifully.

Diana beamed. 'Good-oh. You will probably be seeing loads of Drew, Maddy darling, as he's going to be a close neighbour of yours. Drew has just bought Peapods.'

Two

It would have been easier to laugh, blush, die at his feet. But Maddy had never been one to take an easy option.

'Oh, so you must be Dermot MacAndrew? That is, you're not. I mean, you're the person I was just telling you about. Only I'm sure you'll make a success of Peapods, of course. You obviously know exactly what you're doing and—'

'Maddy,' Diana spoke quietly, 'I think perhaps Drew would like to engage in horsy talk with Kimberley and Barty. Maybe you'd like to chat to Mrs Pugh, she's looking a bit lost, poor love.'

'Yes, of course.' Maddy's tongue seemed to have glued itself to the roof of her mouth. She gave Drew Fitzgerald a scant smile of apology. 'I'm sure we'll see more of each other, as we're going to be neighbours.'

'I'm sure we will.' Drew Fitzgerald made it sound like a hanging offence.

Bronwyn Pugh, co-owner of the Village Stores, was mopping the remains of Gareth's Glenfiddich slick from her paisley frock. Maddy approached her with a smile of sympathy. 'Diana told me. How's it drying out?'

'Nicely, thank you,' Mrs Pugh hissed. 'Although I'll smell like a distillery.'

'Not a bad thing to smell like.' Maddy's smile had stretched to manic. 'Mr Pugh not with you tonight?'

'No.'

Trawling round for scintillating party chat, Maddy said, 'I hope he's not ill. I saw him earlier and—'

'Maddy,' Bronwyn Pugh stopped mopping, 'Bernie isn't

here this evening because he had a little accident. It left him very shaken.'

'No! Oh, poor Bernie. What happened?'

'I think you know very well, Maddy Beckett. You were dressed up like one of them stripperamas, Bernie said. It shocked him. He fell off his bicycle. Now, I'm not one to gossip – as you well know – and what you gets up to in the privacy of your own home is your affair. But,' Bronwyn Pugh took a deep breath, 'I do not want you enticing my husband, you understand?'

Maddy was stricken. 'I wasn't! The door mat had got caught up and I just—'

Bronwyn frowned fiercely. 'That's as maybe. But my Bernie is spoken for.'

Maddy bit her lip. 'Oh, but I'm not after him, I can assure you. I wouldn't want your husband if he was the last man in Milton St John. No, well – I don't mean . . .'

But it was too late. With a sniff and a glower, Mrs Pugh marched away towards the door. She'd been right. She smelled exactly like a distillery. It didn't go well with Tweed. Maddy closed her eyes. It was one of those days.

'Grub's up!' Gareth yelled. 'Form an orderly queue! No shoving at the back!'

Maddy's stomach rumbled. Not even an evening of un-mitigated social disasters could disguise the fact that she hadn't eaten properly since breakfast. She'd just grab some-thing to eat and then sneak away. No one would notice.

The food was laid out in the alcove, a mouth-watering array of squishy temptation. Maddy hung around until people had borne away piled-high plates and then crept in for the leftovers. Gareth James-Jordan had the same idea.

'Still plenty here for the workers,' he roared through a generous portion of salmon roulade. 'I say, you look pretty miserable, my dear.'

'Thanks,' Maddy said mournfully, helping herself to prawns in flaky pastry and sautéed goat's cheese balanced on dangerously thin slices of rye bread. 'I'm in the doghouse.'

'Me too.' Gareth tried to balance chicken liver parfait on top of his glass. 'I dropped a bottle of malt on Mrs Pugh.'

'I told Mrs Pugh that I wouldn't want her husband if he was the last man on earth. And I told the new man at Peapods that he'd never make a go of it because he was too inexperienced.'

Gareth looked impressed. 'God, Maddy. A double whammy. That's not like you. You're usually so kind to everyone. I thought I was the only person in Milton St John who could put both feet in my mouth at one go.' Gareth patted her shoulder in a vague gesture of sympathetic solidarity and drifted back to his drinks.

Maddy stared out across the darkening gardens and distractedly scooped up a handful of leek brioches. Diana had ordered far too much food considering the vast majority of the guests were weight-watching. It was one of the joys of Milton St John's social life. There was always plenty to eat.

Heaping her plate, Maddy hunched into the window seat and tried to become invisible. Not for the first time she wished she had Suzy's lightning reflexes in moments of disaster. Suzy would have flirted with Drew Fitzgerald and told him that he'd have to prove her wrong. Suzy would have assured Mrs Pugh that her balding, buck-toothed Bernie was the sexiest thing in Milton St John. Suzy would never have blushed and stammered and apologised. It was thoroughly demoralising to have a seventeen-year-old sister who had been born grown up.

Naturally, she was munching her way through a prawn tartlet when Peter Knightley arrived.

'Maddy!' His seductive voice was straight out of her dreams. 'Maddy! How wonderful to see you again. How are you?'

'Fine . . .' she mumbled, trying to swallow. 'Hello, Peter . . .'

The fifteen months three weeks and two days hadn't taken their toll on Peter. He was still gloriously golden.

'You've lost weight.' Peter was helping himself to salad, ignoring the dressings. 'It suits you. You look super.'

'Thanks.' Had she? Did she? Maybe the Slimfast had worked after all.

She was trying to lick traces of mayonnaise from the corner of her lips as Peter turned from the table. 'Very provocative, Maddy.' The blue eyes crinkled and so did her stomach. She still fancied him. And her body wanted him with an urgency that hurt.

'Diana said you'd be here.' Her voice was squeaky but at least she'd swallowed. 'Did things not work out in London?'

'Things worked out brilliantly.' Peter lodged himself beside her on the window seat. He was only inches away. 'That's why I'm back.'

He wanted her to ask why, so she deliberately said nothing. He left if for thirty seconds then, with only the merest trace of irritation, said, 'I'm here to share some of my good fortune with Milton St John. After all, the village was very good to me. I want to return the favour.'

He was obviously itching for her to gasp girlishly, to hang on his every word, but she damn well wasn't going to.

'Yes, well, I'm planning to invest some of the profits from the health and fitness clubs into a little project the whole village can share.' He turned and looked at her. 'Aren't you going to ask me what, then? You were always so interested in what I did.'

She picked up a nearby napkin and wiped her fingers. 'But that was before; when we were together. Now we're not. I've got other far more important things to think about.'

God! Suzy and Fran would be so proud of her.

'Maddy, I simply don't believe you. You're teasing me.'

'I never did that.'

'No, you didn't, did you? You were quite a little demon.' He stretched out one long slender finger and stroked her cheek. Her skin flamed. Why did one's body have to behave at direct odds with the instructions from one's brain? She hadn't loved him for over a year.

'We've all come in for seconds,' Kimberley's voice barked across the alcove. 'Oh, good heavens. Hello, Peter.'

Maddy gave Kimberley, Barty and Drew Fitzgerald a smile of relief. Peter was pumping hands. Maybe she could walk away now while they were all reintroducing themselves. She slid her boots to the ground, hardly able to feel her feet after curling in the window seat for so long.

Peter barred her exit. 'You never told me you had a new neighbour, Maddy. And a famous one at that.'

'We hadn't actually got round to village small talk, had we? And I didn't know he was – famous, that is.'

'I'm not.' Drew Fitzgerald didn't seem to want to look at her. She couldn't blame him.

'Oh, but you are.' Peter was adamant. 'As soon as I heard your name, I knew who you were. And I'm so glad that you'll be putting Peapods to good use. I used to own it, you know. I ran the Knightley Health Studio.'

'I'd heard.' Drew turned away and accepted a plate of leftovers from Kimberley who appeared to be drooling. 'I shall probably keep the smaller of the gyms for my own use – and that of my staff, of course.'

'There!' Peter beamed at Maddy. 'You can just pop across the road and use Drew's gym. Maybe you won't feel so intimidated by hordes of stable lads. You never came near the place when I was running it.'

'And I don't intend to now.' She shot Drew another look of apology. 'I shall be far too busy. I do have my own business these days.

Peter's eyebrows climbed up his golden forehead. Drew, with creditable good manners, managed to look interested.

'Shadows,' Maddy said with pride. 'It's been running for twelve months and it's been very successful.'

'Diana mentioned that you did some kind of work for her.'

Drew deserved a gold star for his attempt to resurrect the social niceties. 'What does Shadows supply? Secretarial staff to the stables?'

'Maddy's a treasure!' Kimberley giggled like a sixth-former. She was definitely flirting with Drew. 'So are Elaine, Brenda and Kat. They work for Maddy. They're all treasures!'

Drew and Peter gave Kimberley a look of profound doubt.

'Shadows provides cleaning staff,' Maddy explained. 'Most of the houses in Milton St John are huge, and need someone "who does". Those who don't have their own housekeepers – and so few can afford live-ins these days – use Shadows. We have regular contracts with some places, and work as-and-when with others.'

'You're a char?' Peter choked on his roquette. 'Maddy, that's perfect! Who better? You were never happy with those office jobs you used to flit in and out of. And, of course, you had such good training.'

'Exactly.' Maddy spoke quickly before he told them how he'd met her. 'It's something that I do well, a job I enjoy doing, and something that is always in demand.'

'Though unless you've changed a good deal, you certainly don't take your work home with you.' Peter grinned in a very familiar way. 'You used to live in virtual squalor.'

'I didn't!' she protested hotly. 'I'm a bit chaotic, that's all.'

Rescue came from an unexpected quarter.

'I'm sure if I spent all day mucking out other people's houses,' Drew said, 'the last thing I'd want to do when I got home was start on my own. They always say cobblers' kids have bare feet, don't they?'

Maddy beamed at Drew. Peter nodded thoughtfully. 'True enough.' He looked at Maddy. 'I'm surprised that you're making a success of it, though. You used to be such a scatterbrain.'

'I used to be a lot of things.' Maddy looked directly into Peter's eyes, challenging him to contradict her. 'I've grown up

– a bit late, admittedly, but I couldn't let Suzy be the only career woman in the Beckett family, could I?'

'I'd heard from Diana that Suzy is cutting a swathe through the apprentices – in more ways than one.'

'Suzy is determined to be the top apprentice this year, and champion jockey in five years' time. She'll probably make it.' She turned to Drew, deliberately changing the subject, reluctant to lose the high ground to her sister. 'Maybe I could come across and speak to you about Shadows some time? Peapods is a huge house, and you might be able to use us.'

Drew nodded. 'You'll have to speak with Caroline about that. She'll be organising the domestic side of things when she gets here. She's still over on the island at the moment.'

'Caroline? The island?' Kimberley had bounced back into the conversational volley.

Drew smiled again, a pale imitation of the previous one, but nice nevetheless. 'My wife. Jersey. It's where we've moved from.'

Kimberley deflated before their eyes. Maddy felt desperately sorry for her. It was typical of Diana to have neglected to mention that there was a Mrs Fitzgerald.

'That would be great.' Maddy was being professional now. 'I'll be pleased to discuss rates and hours with her. We're very reasonable. You can't miss my cottage – it's the one with the sloping green roof opposite your drive.'

'The one that looks like a bijou Nissen hut.' Peter laughed.

Maddy shot him a surprised look. That was exactly how Diana always described her cottage. How come Peter, who had been out of circulation for so long, was quoting Diana James-Jordan? She joined in the laughter along with Kimberley and Barty. Drew was surveying them all with some doubt. Maybe they had a different sense of humour in the Channel Islands.

'I could probably use Shadows, too.' Peter clung tenaciously to the conversation. 'When I've found a suitable property.' He moved closer to Maddy. 'Maybe you could come and discuss your rates with me?'

'Yes, of course. You aren't going back to your flat, then?'

'Heavens, no! I've moved onwards and upwards. I'm hoping to buy one of the houses by the church.' Millionaires' Row. Maddy was suitably impressed. The Knightley Health Studios must have made a bomb out of the flabby thighs and sagging bottoms of the rich and famous.

'Well, as soon as you're settled, I'd be delighted to discuss business with you.'

'Just business?' Peter's breath was warm on her cheek.

'Just business.' She edged about an inch away from him, her knees quaking. Damn stupid physical attraction. It was over. Her brain knew it, and so did her heart. It was a pity her hormones were so slow on the uptake.

'Spoilsport,' Peter teased, making the words sound like 'take your clothes off, I want you – now.'

Fortunately she was spared the need to respond to this onslaught. With admirable timing, Drew dropped his plate of leek and mushroom tart down Peter's elegant cream trousers.

'I'm most frightfully sorry!' He looked anything but. 'I don't know what happened. Here, let me mop you down . . .'

'No, no.' Peter was backing away, flicking at clinging pieces of moist grey-green filling. 'I'll go and sponge it off in the cloakroom. If I'm quick it won't stain.'

'You must send me the cleaning bill of course.'

Drew was smiling as Peter rushed out of the alcove. He really did have the most delightful smile. Kimberley and Barty were refilling their plates and hadn't noticed. Maddy bit her lip. 'You did that on purpose.'

'Of course I didn't. It was a complete accident. I was so enthralled by his conversation that I simply lost my grip. I do apologise if you and he are an item.'

'Were,' Maddy said, watching with admiration as Drew adroitly scraped the remains of the leek and mushroom tart from Diana's Chinese silk carpet. 'Peter left Milton St John – and me – over a year ago. Although after my garbled introduction earlier, you probably think we're admirably suited.'

'A match made in heaven,' Drew agreed. 'And has he returned for you?'

'God, no! According to the grapevine, he's come back to the village to set up some new venture.'

Drew stood up and shoved the tart's remains and an expensive linen napkin into the depths of an ornate urn. 'I trust it'll be slightly more in keeping than his attempt at a health studio. The first time I looked over Peapods I thought the decor and fitments were down to Cynthia Payne.'

Maddy's giggle suddenly died as Stacey, the bimbo stick-insect, shimmied into the alcove. She was wearing a leopard-skin Lycra dress, and her legs, encased in the sheerest black, disappeared into stilt-high heels.

'Hello, Maddy. Where's Peter?'

'He's had an accident. With his trousers.' Drew was straight faced. 'He's in the cloakroom cleaning up.'

'Oh!' Stacey's glossy lips pouted into a perfect O. 'Is he hurt?'

'No. It wasn't that sort of accident. More a mishap.' Maddy smiled, hating Stacey with all the ferocity of a woman made to feel like a lard mountain. 'I didn't realise you were with him tonight.'

''Course I am. Petie and I are inseparable. I was out in the yard. I persuaded Diana to show me her sweet little horses.'

Drew choked. Maddy grinned at Diana and Gareth's multimillion-pound string of Classic contenders being described as children's hacks. Then she had a sudden vision of Peter's gloriously athletic body entwined with Stacey's fragility in the throes of passion and felt sick.

'If you'll excuse me,' she picked up her glass of tepid mineral water, 'I need a refill.'

On cue, Peter made his appearance. 'Oh, don't go yet, Maddy. We've still got so much to talk about.'

'I'm sure we haven't.' Maddy threw back her head in an attempt at haughtiness and immediately wished she hadn't. The basque gave an ominous groan. 'We can discuss Shadows

23

when you've found a suitable property. You know where to find me.'

Peter narrowed the blue eyes. 'Are you with someone?'

'Don't be so unflattering. It's not that hard to believe, surely? Actually, I'm not tonight.' Anger surged through her. 'By choice.'

'Really?' The eyebrows started their upward climb again. Then he spotted Stacey. 'Hello, sweetie pie.' He encompassed Stacey's slender waist with his arm. 'Did you miss me?'

She obviously had by the way she immediately started nuzzling his ear. It was with infinite pleasure that Maddy noticed the very distinctive damp patch across the crotch of Peter's cream trousers.

'Oh, this is nice!' Diana wafted in to join them. 'All catching up on old times, are we?' She turned to Drew. 'Peter and Maddy were something of a fixture at one time, you know. Now he's got dear little Stacey, and Maddy darling has been so civilised about it. I always say one should try and be on friendly terms with one's exes. Especially in a small village like this. After all, relationships are a bit like musical chairs here, aren't they, Maddy?'

Maddy frowned. Diana made it sound as though Sodom and Gomorrah could take lessons from Milton St John.

'Oh, I couldn't agree more.' Drew nodded in time with his hostess. 'Everybody should stay friends with everybody else and share the children round at Christmas.'

'Have you got children?' Stacey gave Drew a ten-second bat of her false eyelashes. 'I'm sorry, I don't know you, do I?'

'No, you don't.' Drew shook his head, smiling his pussycat smile and not attempting to enlighten her. His eyes were momentarily cold. 'And no, I don't have children. Peter obviously likes them, though.'

The remark bypassed Stacey and landed on Maddy who looked at Drew Fitzgerald with renewed admiration.

'Oh, yes. We want to have hundreds. Don't we, lambkin?'

Lambkin! Maddy bit her lips until her eyes watered.

Peter cuddled Stacey closer. 'I understand Maddy is your

cleaner, Diana. Very creditable of you – inviting the staff to your parties.'

'Naughty boy.' Diana tapped his arm playfully. Maddy suddenly wondered whether Diana and Peter had had a walk-out. And if so, when. 'Maddy is one of my dearest friends, as you well know. Shadows is a super idea – and very highly thought of in the village. She's come on in leaps and bounds since you left Milton St John, you know.'

'So it would seem. She looks gorgeous and she's running her own company . . . What's the uniform, Maddy? Curlers and wrinkled stockings?'

Stacey giggled. Peter had loosened his grip and Diana had moved between them. There was definitely something there, Maddy thought, suddenly wanting to be as far away from this party as possible.

'If you don't mind,' she said to Diana, 'I really think I should be making tracks. I've got an early start in the morning.' She turned to Drew. 'It has been very nice to meet you – and again, my apologies for the misunderstanding earlier.'

'Don't mention it.' Drew was party polite again. 'And when Caroline arrives, I'll ask her to contact you about Shadows, shall I?'

'Please do.' Maddy took Drew's extended hand. A familiar tingle started to spread through her veins and she wrenched her hand away.

'Do you need a lift home, Maddy?' Peter hadn't missed the rise of colour in her throat. 'Stacey and I won't be long leaving.'

'No thank you.' She didn't dare look at Drew who was now talking to Barty Small. 'I've got the car. Diana, thank you so much – it was delightful,' and with a return match of cheek-clashing she made her exit to the usual goodbye sonata.

This was something of a record, she thought as she circled the jungle of guests still prowling the Small Room, to discover that she could madly fancy two men at the same party – neither of whom was remotely interested in her.

She was still grinning when she reached the car.

Three

Milton St John looked glorious at this hour, Maddy thought as she cycled dreamily along the high-banked lane. The acid-green lace of Goddards Spinney spread uphill from the stream which gurgled beside the main road, and Maynards Orchard with its froth of pink and white blossom, looked like a peeping petticoat against the bare brown legs of the peaty downland. There was a sort of misty promise about the early morning, as though solutions to problems would rise like the sun through the gauziness.

Horses were hard at work already. The gallops were full of swift-moving pin-prick creatures streaming along the brow of the hill; first lots making their way back to their stables with steaming nostrils; second lots clip-clopping sedately out of yards. April was a transitional month in the village; the jumping stables were celebrating or otherwise over Cheltenham and Aintree, while the flat racers were bursting with anticipation about The Guineas, The Derby and Ascot.

Maddy waved greetings as she cycled past St Saviours and the Village Stores. Mrs Pugh was putting out litter bins and ignored her. Maddy, en route to her first cleaning appointment of the day, knew she had to apologise to Bronwyn as soon as possible. The Cat and Fiddle, standing in an oasis of empty crisp packets, was tightly shut. So was the betting shop.

Jumping from her bicycle outside Fran and Richard's bungalow, she pulled the Tesco carrier bag from the basket and hurried up the path. Fran was her closest friend in the village, blissfully married to Richard, and loyal to the death.

Maddy pushed the kitchen door open. The children, as Fran had promised, seemed to have made an early departure for school, leaving a clutter of trainers, discarded folders and sweet wrappers in their wake. Their father, Fran's first husband, had been killed in a riding accident when they were only babies, and Tom and Chloe had welcomed Richard riotously when he and Fran had married two years ago. The whole village knew how much Fran now longed for Richard's baby to complete their noisily cheerful family.

'Kettle's on and there are chocolate fingers in the tin,' Fran called as Maddy stepped inside the kitchen. 'Pour me a cup of coffee, Mad – black and no sugar. I'll be with you in a sec.'

Maddy did. Fran's kitchen was smaller than hers but at least it had the advantage of being kitchen shaped. Maddy's was a maze of odd angles and dark corners. Fran hopped into the kitchen wearing one court shoe, still managing to look efficiently secretarial in a straight black skirt and striped blouse. Maddy's working uniform was leggings and voluminous T-shirts in summer and leggings and voluminous sweaters in winter.

Fran looked at the carrier bag. 'Oh, thanks for returning the dress and corset. I've heard all about the party.'

'You can't have.' Maddy passed Fran her second shoe. 'It's too early.'

Fran wrapped her hands round her mug of black coffee. 'Not for a jockey's wife. Richard has three rides for Diana and Gareth today up at Haydock. Gareth was on the phone begging a lift – seems his hangover was a killer and he didn't want to drive. Diana, of course, is taking the prestige meeting at Kempton. Anyhow, Gareth spilled the beans.'

Maddy, wondering which beans, sank down at the breakfast bench and built bridges with the chocolate fingers. Fran scuttled round collecting her car keys, cigarettes, make-up and shopping list from the various surfaces. 'Of course, being a man, he left out the interesting details. Like, how was Peter and more importantly, how did you react.'

'Peter was as glorious as ever. You'll be pleased to hear that I'm definitely out of love with him – but maybe not so delighted that I still fancied him like mad.'

'Oh, God. But you stuck to your plan? You made him aware that you are now an independent career woman who doesn't need a man? You did, didn't you, Maddy?'

'I think so. Anyway, Stacey was with him, which made it easier to be cool and distant.' She looked at Fran. 'Stacey calls him lambkin and wants to have his children.'

'Jesus!' Fran looked quizzically at Maddy. 'You haven't eaten any of those biscuits. You're just playing with them. What's up?'

'Nothing.' Maddy quickly dismantled the chocolate finger bridge.

Fran paused in the middle of shrugging into her secretarial jacket. 'Gareth told me about your gaffe with the new man from Peapods. What's he like?'

'Very nice – extremely attractive – but married to Karen or Carol or someone, who is still living in the Channel Islands but will be joining him shortly. I'm going now before we're both late for work.'

'Sit down! You can't leave it at that.' Fran gulped at her coffee. 'I've heard all about Drew Fitzgerald – he's absolutely gorgeous by all accounts and he's famous and he's bringing some pretty prestigious horses with him and—'

'Peter said that he was famous, too,' Maddy mused. 'What for?'

'Oh, he used to be an amateur jump jockey, Kimberley said. He won some major race fairly spectacularly. I think it must have been abroad . . .'

'And when did Kimberley ring you?'

'This morning, after Gareth.'

Maddy shook her head. The jungle drums had been red hot. She stood up. 'I really do have to go, Fran. Oh, did Kimberley tell you that Bronwyn Pugh thinks I can't be trusted with her Bernie?'

Fran shook her head, her eyes wide.

Maddy smiled. 'Good – at least I've got some secrets left.'

'Maddy! What the hell did you do to Bernie?' Fran was torn between finding out every last detail and risking Barty's wrath if she was late. 'Oh, come on, Mad. Bernie'll keep – he's a minus on our lust scale – but at least tell me about your run-in with Drew Fitzgerald. We always tell each other everything.'

'I have told you. Everything. He's attractive, charming, funny – he's also married. And I've got to dash . . .' She let herself out and ran down the path, then looked over her shoulder at Fran glowering in the doorway. 'Oh, and he's got the sexiest smile in the world.'

The morning passed quickly, as they always did. Maddy had three regular cleaning jobs on Thursdays and spent two hours at each. Monday and Tuesday were given solely to Diana James-Jordan and John Hastings, who owned the largest houses and the largest yards in the village. Wednesday afternoons were also fully booked, and Friday was paperwork day. She fitted her own life into Wednesday mornings and weekends.

She was proud of Shadows – and of herself. Unlike Suzy, her teenage ambition had come late in life, but now Shadows was a proper business, with employees and an accountant and headed notepaper, and she was a proper woman. That was what she had hoped Peter noticed. Nothing physical. Just the late emergence of the real Maddy Beckett.

She smiled to herself as she cycled back to the cottage to grab her usual lunch of a haphazard sandwich and coffee before starting her afternoon rounds. Shadows filled her life. If she'd had a lover, he'd have to have been slotted in on Wednesday mornings. But then – she crashed the bike against the scrubby box hedge – as she didn't have a lover, and hadn't had one either before or after Peter, the problem didn't arise.

She unlocked the door, using her shoulder at just the right moment to free the hall rug, and remembered Peter's amazement at her virgin state.

'Do you mean –' he'd rolled over on that huge bed amidst all those creamy lace pillows and widened his choirboy eyes – 'that this is the first – the only – time you've been to bed with anyone?'

And she'd tried to explain, wrapping herself in the flimsy sheet, embarrassed then by her nakedness, that yes, it was. Oh, there had been several early fumbling and groping attempts at parties, and for a time at university she'd gone out with a history student with a car and her legs had been covered in door-handle bruises as she'd wriggled away from his ardour. But she had never made love with anyone, simply because she had never been in love.

'Maddy . . .' He'd always said her name like a caress. 'You don't have to be in love, darling. Not these days. If you want it, grab it.'

It had been difficult, curled against him on the bed in the hotel room with her striped cleaner's overall discarded on the floor, trying to explain that she didn't think like that. Old fashioned as it may be, making love had to be just that. A physical act to express pure and deep emotion. That she couldn't just leap into bed with anybody; she had to be in love.

She slammed the cottage door and padded into the kitchen to make coffee. Now Peter was back, and obviously planning to make his home once more in Milton St John. She bit into a Mars bar that Suzy had left on the draining board. After last night she knew she could cope with Peter in the village. She had at last outgrown him.

Maddy sighed. Of course, a new man in her life would be nice . . . as a friend, a partner, a lover in the proper sense; but she was pretty sure that sort of man didn't exist outside the covers of romantic novels. She wasn't going to find a Heathcliff, a Rhett Butler, or even a Mr Rochester in Milton St John.

She looked down at her hands in horror. She had demo-
lished the entire Mars bar without tasting it. She'd be talking
to herself next. Scrabbling the wrapper into a guilty ball, she
sloshed hot water on to the coffee granules in her mug and
headed for the rubbish bin.

Because the cottage had such a peculiar design, the kitchen
was in three parts – a tiny square bit with a sink and cooker
and three cupboards, leading to a long narrow bit with a
table and chairs and an ancient refrigerator. This then turned
a right-angled corner into what had at one time been the
scullery, and now housed the washing machine, tumble dryer
and the bad-tempered boiler.

She had rented the cottage from Diana when she first came
to Milton St John. That had been one of her few wise moves
in those early days. Peter had had a flat in the High Street,
and on those heady afternoons in his hotel room when they'd
first met, he'd begged her to come and live with him. Maddy,
hopelessly in love, had desperately wanted to be close to him
but had had some sixth-sense warning to remain independent.

They'd compromised eventually on her renting the cottage.
At least they were in the same village, Peter had said in his
candied voice, twisting her red curls round his fingers, which
meant so much more variety. Two bedrooms . . . two
beds . . .

'Of course, I can't ask you to pay very much rent,' Diana
James-Jordan had gushed on their first meeting. 'It's practically
derelict, and I'm certainly not going to throw money away on
renovations. I used to put my lads in there, but,' and she'd
actually shuddered, 'they've all got notions of bungalows with
central heating and double glazing and built-in kitchens . . .'
She'd paused, hoping to elicit some sort of sympathy vote from
Maddy over the inflated dreams of the lower classes. Not
receiving one, she'd charged on. 'So, if you want to do it up a
bit, my dear, that's entirely up to you. I'll charge the merest
peppercorn for it. You are working, I take it?'

Maddy had said well not exactly yet, but she had some interviews in offices in Reading and Newbury coming up, and her savings would certainly pay Diana's rent in the meantime.

'Oh!' Diana had arched exquisite eyebrows. 'I understood you were with Mr Knightley – Peter – in his venture. Is that not the case?'

Maddy had said no, it definitely wasn't the case. Mr Knightley – Peter – and she had been together for some time, but she wasn't in any way involved in his health studios. And then she'd signed a lease to be renewed every twelve months, and parted with her cheque, and the cottage had become her home.

She lifted the lid on the bulging rubbish bin, reminding herself to empty it that evening, and screamed.

There was a dead person under the boiler.

A pair of legs, tightly clad in faded jeans, tapered into large feet encased in disreputable desert boots. The rest of the body was out of sight beneath the boiler's innards, but not for long. With a curse, a noise that sounded like skull on metal, and a further, far more colourful oath, the body, much to Maddy's relief, began to wriggle.

Why a strange man should be tinkering with her boiler was not the thought uppermost in Maddy's mind. She was riveted by the sight of a strong, well-muscled and healthily suntanned torso appearing slowing across the none-too-clean floor of the scullery. Drew Fitzgerald emerged, tugging his sweater down over the fleetingly revealed body, and frowning.

'Heavens!' Maddy was stunned. 'What on earth are you doing?'

Drew sat up, rubbing his head and examining his fingers for traces of blood. 'Why did you scream? I could have knocked myself out.'

'Sorry. I thought you were dead. Well, I mean, I could only see your legs and I thought that—'

'That I'd been the victim of a hit-and-run heating system?'

He pulled himself to his feet, brushing his hair from his

eyes. He looked much younger and more tousled than last night, Maddy thought. And angry.

'Sorry I screamed. But I wasn't expecting to find you prone in the scullery. I mean, it's not the normal way my visitors arrive.'

'I'm not visiting. I'm mending your boiler.'

Maddy tried to remember. Had she told him about the boiler last night? Had she issued him an invitation to sort out the vagaries of her heating system? Had she told him where the back door key was hidden for him to gain access? 'I don't understand . . .'

'Your sister came across to Peapods this morning.' Drew was piling workmanlike tools into a box. 'She introduced herself. A very friendly girl. Is that her own hair colour, by the way?'

'I don't know. What colour was it?'

'Sort of apricot.'

'No, then. So Suzy asked you to fix our boiler?' Maddy was horrified. 'I really am so sorry. She shouldn't have—'

'Will you stop apologising? I offered. When she arrived to introduce herself I was checking out those peculiar steam bath things the health studio had, and wondering whether I could use the sauna pool for my horses. She, er, Suzy said the horses were luckier than some humans – at least they got warm baths. It went on from there.' He snapped shut the tool box. 'I said I hadn't really got much on. My furniture won't be arriving for days, my horses aren't due for at least two weeks, I can't interview any staff until I know just who I've got coming over from the island. I was at a bit of a loose end, so I said I'd have a look at your boiler. She told me the key lived in the wisteria. So,' he shrugged, 'here I am – and it's fixed, by the way.'

'Really?' Maddy beamed. 'You mean we can have heating when we want it and baths at any time? God, that's luxury. It's never worked since I moved in five years ago.'

'Your landlord should have fixed it for you.'

33

'Diana's my landlord, and I pay such a piddling bit of rent it seemed like a cheek. And then when I asked heating engineers for quotes they were far more than I could afford . . .'

Drew smiled for the first time. A slow, devastating smile. 'I assume you had this cottage when you and Mr Knightley were together, so why couldn't he have fixed it for you?'

'Oh, Peter never lived here – and he didn't do practical things. He just dreamed up schemes, had meetings, made money. He didn't like getting dirty.'

'Somehow I'd guessed that. No one who likes getting dirty would wear designer cream trousers in a horsy village. He probably won't again anyway – not if we're going to be in the same social circles.'

'You disliked him, didn't you?'

'That's a bit unfair.' Drew leaned against the tumble dryer. 'I hardly know him. I'd heard of him, naturally, as he'd once owned Peapods. He seemed very proprietorial towards you. I'd already decided that you were a nice lady. I thought you might need rescuing.'

'Not from Peter.' Maddy could have bitten off her tongue. She sounded as though she was defending him. 'I mean, he behaves like that with everybody. He thinks he's irresistible.'

'So I gathered.'

It was a pity that Drew hadn't thrown his food at Peter for her sake. It was sad to realise that he would have done the same for anyone.

'Thank you so much for mending the boiler. How much do I owe you?'

'Nothing.' Drew moved towards the back door. 'I was pleased to be able to help. Once the horses arrive I probably won't have that much time to be neighbourly. And I haven't forgotten about your cleaning company, either. I telephoned Caroline this morning and she will definitely discuss it with you when she comes over.'

'And will that be with the furniture?' Maddy questioned artlessly. 'Or with the horses?'

Drew shrugged. 'Caroline could just turn up this afternoon if the fancy took her. I hope it'll be sooner rather than later.'

Damn! Maddy thought. He was missing her. 'I'm looking forward to meeting her. The village can be a bit cliquey. I mean, I expect Diana will be all over her, but Kimberley Weston would be a better friend. Sometimes it's handy to know these things.'

'Naturally. And you don't like Diana much, I take it?'

'No . . . well, it's difficult. I mean she's always been very nice to me, like you would be to a stray dog or something, but I'm sure she thinks I am very unmaterialistic and naive. I was very much so, when I first came to Milton St John. Still, as I live in her cottage and work for her, I can't really slag her off too much. It's just—'

'Yes?'

'Oh, she's got the current Derby favourite in her yard, as you probably know. Saratoga Sun. And my friend's husband Richard, is Diana's stable jockey this season. He's been a jockey for ages, but this is his first shot at the big time.' Her voice rose indignantly. 'He's ridden Saratoga in all his previous races. Now the owner wants a different jockey, and Diana just jocked Richard off. She didn't even try to persuade the owner to change his mind.'

'Trainers are at the mercy of their owners,' Drew echoed Barty's words of the previous evening. 'I doubt if there was anything Diana could do.'

'She could have put her foot down. Said that Richard had been brilliant on the horse – which the owner knows – said that if Richard didn't ride then she wouldn't train Saratoga any more. It's just because Richard isn't particularly glamorous, and Newmarket's golden boy is.'

'Luke Delaney?' Drew asked. 'He's ridden for me a few times. He's good, as well as marketable. And no trainer is going to risk losing the Derby favourite at this stage of the season. I don't see that Diana had any choice.'

'Well, I do,' Maddy insisted crossly. 'But then I'm an outsider. You trainers are bound to stick together.'

'Ouch!' Drew grinned at her. 'You do have claws in there, then. Anyway, I mustn't keep you. You're obviously busy.'

Suddenly Maddy didn't want him to leave. 'Have you got time for a coffee? It's the least I can do if you won't take any money – to say thanks for fixing the boiler, and for being so pleasant about last night's goof. I was feeling rather on edge . . .'

'About the reappearance of the divine Mr Knightley?' Drew's eyes crinkled at the corners. 'Perfectly understandable. I'd have felt the same in your position. Not a pleasant prospect.'

Maddy giggled. 'I'm sorry I can't offer you any lunch. I've only got bits and pieces. Suzy might have left another Mars bar somewhere . . . '

Drew considered the invitation, then smiled. 'A Mars bar would be great.'

Maddy was mowing her patch of grass with an ancient sit-up-and-beg machine, enjoying the weak evening sun that filtered through the tangle of jasmine and honeysuckle, when Suzy arrived home.

'Did Drew fix the boiler, Mad?' She leaned out of the kitchen's skew-whiff window. 'Can I have a bath?'

'Yes and yes.' Maddy puffed to a halt. 'You shouldn't have pestered him though, Suzy. I nearly died when I came in at lunchtime and found him sprawled on the kitchen floor.'

'Thought it was your birthday and Christmas rolled into one, huh? I mean, he's as old as the hills, of course, but he's still pretty damn sexy.'

'I honestly can't say I'd noticed,' Maddy lied.

'Nah – well, you wouldn't. Not if you've still got the hots for Pete the Perv. And why haven't we got any food? I'm starving.'

'Oh, er, I haven't managed to go shopping today.' Maddy

said quickly. Bugger. She'd completely forgotten her intention of apologising to Bronwyn Pugh at the earliest opportunity. 'I wondered if you'd drive into Newbury and get some stuff at Sainsbury's for me. We could stock up then, and not keep spending a fortune at the village shop.'

'If you like,' Suzy said goodnaturedly. 'But I'm going to have a bath first. Won't it be lovely, Mad? Water up to your neck. Bloody hot water at that. And at normal times, instead of getting up in the middle of the night. Oh, and John Hastings sends his regards.'

Suzy's head disappeared from the window, and almost immediately the peace was broken by an earsplitting blast of AC/DC. Maddy continued to shove at the mower. She loved Suzy dearly, enjoyed her company – and her clothes that fitted – and wouldn't dream of asking her to move out, but sometimes she wished she was a little quieter.

'That was orgasmic.' Suzy wandered out into the garden half an hour later swathed in two bath towels and Maddy's quilted dressing gown. 'Totally bloody orgasmic.'

'I'm so glad you enjoyed your bath.'

'Don't be prim, Mad. It doesn't suit you.' Suzy sank down on to the fallen tree trunk that served as a garden seat. 'So how was Mr Twice-Knightley?'

Maddy picked a cowpat of dried grass from the mower's gnarled blades and luxuriated in the heady scent. 'We exchanged civilised social chit-chat as people do at parties. I still don't know why he's come back to Milton St John. I didn't ask. You and Fran would have been proud of my disdain and lack of interest.'

'Real?' Suzy started gouging at her purple nail varnish.

'Yes, real. I am well and truly over Peter Knightley. I wouldn't care if I never saw him again.'

'Oh good.' Suzy removed the towel from her hair so that her head was surrounded by a halo of apricot spikes. 'Does that mean you'll be available for the dishy Drew, then?'

'No.' Maddy felt the blush creep into her cheeks. When on

earth was she going to be too old for blushing? 'He's married. And I don't need a man.'

'Everybody needs a man.' Suzy rose gracefully to her feet and headed towards the back door. 'You can't just shut yourself away from them all because Pete the Perv treated you like cack. You're bloody pretty, Mad. A bit fat here and there and disgustingly old of course, but people still fancy you.'

'They do? Who exactly?' Maddy asked, but Suzy was out of earshot. She resumed her grass-cutting with a wry grin. Maybe it was better not to know.

Four

Caroline Fitzgerald arrived three weeks later, after both the horses and the furniture had been installed in Peapods. These had been observed, reported on, and approved by most of the villagers, who were now anxiously awaiting the appearance of Drew Fitzgerald's wife.

As it was Friday, Maddy was frowning over her paper-work, calculating the weekly pay for Elaine, Brenda and Kat, half-listening to the *Breakfast Show*. The sun sliced through the window, illuminating the dust motes that danced in the golden shaft. Maddy played with her pen. Dust, like every-thing else, looked so pretty in the sunshine. It would be a pity to disturb it. She took no notice of the constant cars stream-ing in and out of the drive opposite. Drew had had builders working in Peapods for ten days now, so the dark blue Mercedes was of no special interest.

'Any chance of a coffee for old times' sake?' The smooth voice stopped her dead. She dropped her pen and half-rose to her feet. The voice had reached the kitchen. 'Maddy? Where are you?'

She hadn't seen Peter since Diana's party. Village gossip said he'd made an offer for Milton St John Manor. Village gossip also said that he was planning to turn it into a fast food restaurant, a laserdrome, and ice rink, and a bowling alley. Maddy guessed this all depended on the vividness of your imagination and whether you thought Peter Knightley was the best thing since Richard Branson or a darned nuisance.

'I should have phoned.' He smiled, assuming she would

forgive the unheralded arrival. 'But I've been so busy. I had a few moments spare in my schedule this morning and I happened to be passing . . .'

'I was going to stop for coffee, anyway,' she lied, pouring water into the kettle. 'Friday is my day for doing the books – it's the only time you'd catch me at home.'

'I know. I made enquiries.'

She wasn't sure whether to be flattered or annoyed.

'We can be friends, can't we?' He had pulled out one of the mismatched chairs and sat down uninvited. 'No hard feelings?'

'None at all.' Maddy rinsed mugs under the hot tap. 'And of course, if our paths cross, I can't see any point in screaming like banshees. Is that what you came for?'

'More or less. And I've missed you.'

'No you haven't,' she hissed, her throat dry. 'Any more than I've missed you. Don't waste your sweet-talk on me, Peter. I know you too well. Sure, if you're coming back to live in the village I'm quite happy to accept that. And of course we can be polite to each other when we meet. But that's all.'

He took the mug of coffee, nodding. Maddy was furious with herself. She'd remembered that he took it black and without sugar. It would have looked far more cool to have asked him.

'You really have changed. You've grown up. Diana told me I'd see a difference in you. And I have missed you, Maddy. No one could ever make me laugh like you did.'

'You'll have to employ a court jester then, won't you?' She rested her back against the refrigerator. 'As a replacement. After all, I've heard you're intending to be Lord of the Manor.'

The golden eyebrows arched. Damn. It sounded as though she was interested in what he was doing. She shrugged. 'So, now that you've found your new home, have you come to ask me for a quote on cleaning?'

'I wasn't being serious about that. I couldn't employ you, not after—'

'Why on earth not? We're supposed to be friends, aren't we? I don't see the problem.'

Peter spread his hands in a helpless gesture. 'Stacey and I are getting married.'

'Is she pregnant?' God! Now she sounded just like her mother.

'No.' Peter's laughter bounced off the walls. 'Not yet. Maybe we should have got married, Maddy . . .'

'And added to the divorce statistics in record time? Hardly. I don't think marriage was ever mentioned, was it?' Maddy hoped her face had retained its expression of polite cynicism. If it had, it was a miracle of mind over matter. She felt, perversely, like bursting into tears. 'Well –' she placed her half-finished coffee on the table – 'thanks for coming to tell me your news. Give my best wishes to Stacey – I'm sure she'll need them. When's the big day?'

'Not until September. You'll get an invitation. I wanted to tell you first, before the grapevine got hold of it. I owe you that much – especially because of the way I treated you when I left.'

'Don't even think about it. It's in the past, Peter. We're different people now.' She was secretly pleased that he'd told her. Maybe Peter had grown up too.

'Maddy . . .'

He had stood up. She'd forgotten how tall he was when he was close to her. And how persuasive those wide blue eyes had always been. She could smell him; warm, clean, the expensive cologne reawakening a million memories. His hands were on her shoulders. She could feel the insistent pressure of his fingers though the thin T-shirt.

'Just for old times' sake?'

'I thought that was the coffee?' She tried to sound joky and failed. 'Don't, Peter . . .'

'Don't' still didn't appear to be in Peter's vocabulary. He kissed her. Maddy's beleaguered senses registered relief. It was a kiss of friendship, his lips skimming lightly over hers.

For an instant. Then he pulled her against him, coaxing her lips apart, using his mouth to undo every ounce of resolve. Oh God! It was bliss to be kissed by him. It always had been. And she hadn't been kissed properly for months . . .

His fingers fastened in the tangled fall of her hair, his knee edged its way between her thighs.

'Excuse me? Is anyone at home? I tried the front door but no one answered. Oh!' A darkly glamorous female face was framed in the skew-whiff window. 'I'm most awfully sorry.' The voice was laughing although the beautiful face was composed. 'I did ring the front doorbell. It didn't seem to work. Look, shall I come back when it's, er, more convenient? I'm looking for Maddy – Maddy Beckett.'

'And you've found her.' Peter had transferred instant charm to the woman outside the kitchen window.

'The back door's open,' Maddy gulped, pushing her hair out of her eyes. 'Please come in.'

'I can call back later if this is a bad time . . .'

'No, I'm just leaving.' Peter's voice had resumed maximum huskiness as he looked at Maddy. 'Aren't I?'

'You are.' She was hotly disgusted with herself. He had always been able to do it to her – but never again. Never, ever again.

The dark woman was hovering uncertainly in the dog-leg bend between the scullery and the kitchen.

'I'm Maddy Beckett.' Maddy extended a damp hand.

'Caroline Fitzgerald.' The hand was taken in a cool grasp.

'Peter Knightley,' Peter grinned, 'and I'm just leaving.' He turned to Maddy. 'I'll ring you some time.'

'No, don't. Just give Stacey my condolences.'

Peter was still laughing as he closed the door.

'I'm terribly sorry.' Maddy indicated the chairs. 'Please have a seat. Can I make you coffee?'

'Would it be awful if I asked for tea?' Caroline sank gracefully into the seat Peter had vacated. 'I'm simply gasping, and we've got the water cut off at Peapods. In fact I think we've got everything cut off. That's why I came over now. The place is swarming with builders, Drew is tearing about calming the horses, and I can't find anything.'

Maddy gave her a smile of understanding. She was going to like Caroline Fitzgerald.

As she made the tea, Caroline explained that Drew had written a sheaf of notes for her and left them on the kitchen pin-board. 'Shadows – Cleaning – Maddy Beckett – Cottage Opposite – Green Roof' had sounded like a very good idea in the middle of the mayhem. 'Although, of course, it obviously wasn't the ideal time to call.'

'It was a perfect time.' Maddy's voice was fervent as she placed the teapot on the table. 'Peter came to tell me he was getting married.' She felt she owed Caroline some explanation for the wanton behaviour. It seemed very civilised, discussing it like this over tea. Caroline would never know that Maddy's body was still pounding.

'Oh, and is that the traditional form of congratulations in the village?'

'You must think I'm depraved.' Maddy slopped tea into her saucer. 'I really don't make a habit of it. We're old friends . . .'

'I'm not owed an explanation. I shouldn't have been peering in the window.'

'And I definitely shouldn't have been kissing Peter Knightley. He's strictly off limits.'

'Very attractive, though.' Caroline's little finger crooked unselfconsciously as she lifted her green cup. 'As is all forbidden fruit. Tell me, Maddy, do you see much of my husband?'

'Practically nothing,' Maddy answered quickly. 'We met when he first arrived, but since he's been having the alterations done and the horses arrived, I've only seen him from a distance. Er, did you want to have cleaning done on a regular basis?'

Caroline nodded. 'I think that would be best. I want to get

all these things organised. Drew's hopeless at domestic arrangements.'

Maddy was going to say he had been red-hot at fixing her boiler and immediately thought better of it. She smiled. 'I'll just fetch the diary.'

They settled on an hour each morning, and two on Friday afternoons. Maddy could spread it out between Brenda, Elaine and Kat, and would be able to do Fridays herself once the books were done as it was just across the road.

Caroline seemed pleased with the arrangements and the cost. 'I won't always be here.' She accepted a refill of the green cup. 'I don't know if Drew told you. I shall still be running my own concern in the Channel Islands. I'll get over to Peapods as often as I can, of course, but it'll be a relief to know that at least he isn't living knee deep in dirt while I'm away.' She cast slanting green eyes round Maddy's kitchen and smiled again.

'I'm a bit behind . . . Peter . . . caught me on the hop . . .'

'Of course.' Caroline smiled sleepily like a cat. 'That's understandable.'

'So, are you over here for long this time?'

'As long as possible. I want to help Drew settle in. I'd like to vet his new staff, too. I was never really involved in the stables in Jersey – we preferred to keep our business lives separate. It became obvious that he'd gone as far as he could in the Channel Islands, and he was desperate to expand. This seemed the ideal solution.'

'And you don't mind living apart from him?' Maddy couldn't imagine anyone not living with Drew if they had the chance.

Caroline laughed. 'No. You clearly don't know much about Drew. He's best at a distance. He lives and breathes, eats and sleeps, horses. Always has.' She stopped. 'Anyway, it's been lovely to meet you. When we're straight you must come over for drinks.'

'Why don't you come to dinner?' Maddy spoke impulsively. 'You and Drew? Tomorrow night? About eight?'

'Are you sure? I mean—'

'Absolutely. Tomorrow the whole village will be at New-bury racecourse. It's the Greenham – the Derby trial. I'll just throw something in the slow-cooker for when we get back. Do you want to ask Drew and get back to me?'

'No need.' Caroline stood up. She was slender and elegant, and moved with feline grace. 'Drew would love to have a proper meal instead of microwaved pizza. Thanks – we'd be delighted. You're very kind.'

'I'll ask some friends.' Maddy's mind was racing. 'We'll have a party.'

She waited until Caroline had crossed the road and then telephoned Fran at Barty Small's. She didn't mention Peter's visit, or his news.

'Brilliant, Maddy. Richard'll be on a real downer seeing as Luke Delaney's riding Saratoga in the trial. I don't fancy spending the whole evening with him feeling gruesome at home, and I'm dying to give Drew Fitzgerald the once-over. I'll sort out a babysitter. Count us in.'

The freezer didn't offer much hope. There was not enough of anything to make a decent-sized portion for one, let alone feed a dinner party. Maddy sighed. She'd have to drive into Newbury. Sainsbury's stayed open late. She'd leave it until after the rush hour.

Brenda and Elaine arrived for their wages. Middle-aged and interchangeable with their perms and their rainbow shellsuits, they were the backbone of Shadows, cleaning like demons. She told them about the new job at Peapods, joined in some gossip about Diana, said yes, she'd ordered J-cloths and a carton of Mr Sheen, and agreed with their decision to have a few bob on Saratoga the next day. Kat, who was nineteen and already had two children, collected her money on Saturday mornings. As soon as Brenda and Elaine had pedalled away, Maddy checked the car. Elderly and unreliable, it always needed coaxing. Without switching on the engine, she sat in the driving seat and clutched the steering wheel. Her mind, as always, drifted.

Peter... She traced the outline of her lips with her forefinger. She shouldn't have allowed it to happen. But it had been blissful. She may be independent and happy in her career, but she hadn't realised just how much she'd missed being kissed. And Peter Knightley was a seriously professional kisser...

She didn't hold out much hope for Stacey and Peter's marriage, not if Peter was still prepared to seduce at the drop of a hat. Strangely, she didn't feel any jealousy. She really didn't want Peter back in her life, and he might as well be married to Stacey as anyone. He had always had the power to arouse her, and always would have if she was stupid enough to let him get close enough. She'd have to be more careful in future.

She leaned her chin on her hands, transferring her wandering thoughts to the activity at Peapods. Caroline's attitude had been odd, Maddy considered. Still, she knew nothing about the Fitzgeralds. Maybe Drew was a complete bastard. Maybe he was moody and uncaring. Maybe he was a wifebeater. She shook her head. Not that. His eyes were too kind – and he'd been very sweet over the business with the boiler. Still, you could never tell.

She turned the key. Nothing. She tried again. The engine didn't even whimper. There was a strange buzzing noise. Pushing her ear against the dashboard, Maddy cursed. Suzy had left the radio on all night. The battery was as flat as squashed hedgehog.

'Bugger!'

There was no one she could ask for help. She wasn't sure if she needed a battery charger or jump leads, and if she'd had them she wouldn't have had any idea what to do with them. She could hardly go and interrupt them at Peapods, and Suzy wouldn't be home until late. And she'd promised Caroline Fitzgerald a dinner party! With two beefburgers, one small pizza and a packet of kippers.

Of course, there was a solution, but was she brave enough

to face the glacial Bronwyn Pugh after all this time? She really should have apologised straight away. She slammed out of the car vowing to kill Suzy. She'd just have to be brave enough . . .

Bronwyn Pugh was stacking freshly cut blocks of cheese into the chiller cabinet when Maddy pinged open the door.

'Won't keep you a mo,' she called. 'I'm nearly done. Ah, there we are.' She straightened up and the smile of greeting died 'Oh! You're something of a stranger. We haven't seen you in here since—'

'No,' Maddy said quickly. 'I meant to come in straight away and apologise, but the longer I left it the more difficult it became. Like putting off a dentist's appointment . . .'

Bronwyn's frown was a killer. Maddy gulped. 'No, I don't mean . . . oh, look, I'm really sorry. I honestly didn't mean to insult either you or Bernie. My mouth was out of control.'

'And not only your mouth.' The lips had turned practically inside-out.

'Mrs Pugh – Bronwyn . . .'

'I think it better be Mrs Pugh, don't you? Under the circumstances.'

'Mrs Pugh, please listen. I'm having a dinner party. Tomorrow night, and . . .' Suddenly Maddy had a surge of inspiration. She almost clapped her hands. 'A dinner party, for you and Mr Pugh. To say sorry. To apologise for my behaviour.' She hurled in her trump card. 'I've invited both the Fitzgeralds from Peapods.'

'Both?' The eyes glinted. 'Is she over, then? I didn't know that.'

Maddy sensed victory. 'She – Caroline – only arrived this morning. I told her that you and Mr Pugh were the hub of this village and that she really had to meet you. She was very enthusiastic. Mrs Pugh, you can't let her down.'

Maddy held her breath. The eyes softened. The mouth became less harsh.

'Oh, well, in that case . . .'

Maddy wanted to turn cartwheels. Instead, she left the shop, her credit limit extended, with everything she wanted, and two dinner guests that she didn't.

'We'll be there at eight,' Mrs Pugh called as Maddy balanced the carrier bags on her bicycle. 'And just to show that I'm not one to bear a grudge, you can call me Bronwyn.'

Maddy unloaded the shopping and began a concentrated cottage clean-up. It had been ages since she'd entertained, and tomorrow night's guests were going to be a pretty mixed bunch. She'd be the odd one out again. She'd have to ask Suzy to stay in and make an even number.

The dining-room doubled as her office, and it took nearly all the afternoon to make it presentable. It wasn't even a proper room, just a corner of the sitting-room that had a curtain across it. Maddy surveyed it. She'd drag in the kitchen table and the mismatched chairs, and with two stools and the ottoman there would be enough seats. The overhead lighting could cause a bit of a problem, especially with that crooked shade that cast an obscene shadow. What had she got that would give a soft, romantic glow? Candles, of course, Maddy thought happily, candles stuck in empty wine bottles. There were loads of those outside the back door. She'd coerce Suzy into bottle-washing as soon as she got home – that would be fair retribution for the flat battery – and cutlery washing, and plate and glass washing. After all, it was Suzy's fault that the Pughs were coming to dinner.

If she peeled the vegetables tonight, and threw everything into the slow cooker before she and Fran left for Newbury in the morning, that only left a starter and a pudding. Some sort of dip would be a good idea – then she could just do extra vegetables for the crudités, and an apple pie. That was it. Organised. She really couldn't see why people got into such a flap about entertaining. The phone diverted her from worrying about a tablecloth and napkins.

48

'Maddy?' She didn't recognise the voice. 'Maddy, it's Drew. It's very kind of you to invite us tomorrow night. I was ringing to see what veg you'd planned to go with the Mars bars.' Drew laughed in response to Maddy's giggle. It was a husky, toe-curling laugh, and for the life of her Maddy couldn't imagine why Caroline would want to let it out of earshot.

'I also wondered if we were to bring wine? I know it's considered a social no-no in the higher echelons.'

'God, bring whatever you like. When you're as skint as I am, all contributions are grabbed with both hands.'

'Great. That's how I see it, too. Caroline was very pleased with the Shadows arrangements, by the way. She liked you.'

'I liked her, too. Are you going to Newbury tomorrow?'

'I hope to. I haven't got anything running, of course, but it would be a great opportunity to size up the opposition. I might see you there – if not, at eight o'clock tomorrow. And Maddy, thank you.'

She was still staring dreamily at the telephone when Suzy nearly took the door off its hinges.

'Mad!' Suzy thrust the *Evening Post* under Maddy's nose. 'Read the racing page!'

She started to, but Suzy jabbed impatiently at the declarations for the next day's Newbury meeting with a silver nail. 'Holy hell, Mad! There! The Arlington Stakes! Fourth horse down! What does that say?'

'Dancing Feet, trained by John Hastings . . . So?'

'So? Dancing Feet doesn't have a jockey listed, does it?'

'No, but a lot of the runners don't have jockeys sorted until the actual race day.'

'Dancing Feet has now!' Suzy's grin spread from ear to ear. 'Me! John's putting me up. He's just told me. It's my first ever real ride on a racecourse, Maddy! My first ever!' And she promptly burst into tears.

Maddy gathered her laughing, crying sister into her arms and banished all thoughts of flat batteries as she hugged her.

'I'm so proud of you, Suzy. God, it'll be wonderful. I'll scream myself hoarse! Well done, darling.'

Suzy wiped her eyes on the cuff of her denim jacket, leaving smears of kohl across her cheeks, and clung to Maddy. 'Should I ring Mum and Dad? Or should I leave it 'til tomorrow night just in case I cock it up completely?'

'Oh, no. Tell them now.' Maddy could imagine her parents' excitement. 'They'll be able to watch you on telly then, and Dad's bound to have a huge gamble on you winning. They'll be so thrilled. Ring them now. I'll put the kettle on.'

Ten minutes later, Suzy, still beaming, sauntered into the kitchen.

'Well? Are they going to have every television tuned into you tomorrow? Are they going to hock the family silver for a massive bet? Come on, Suzy, what did they say?'

'They're coming to watch me!' Suzy grabbed Maddy's hands. 'They're so proud of me, Mad! They're going to drive straight down to Newbury in the morning. I said it was too far for them to do both journeys in one day, so they're going to stay here tomorrow night! Won't that be brilliant?'

Five

'It's not as bad as all that, surely?' Fran looked up from her race card. 'They're only your parents, after all.'

They were leaning over the parade-ring railings at Newbury, prior to The Arlington Stakes. The horses, coats glossy in hazy afternoon sun, stalked round in front of them.

'Are they here, then?'

'Over there.' Maddy nodded in the direction of the new stand. 'Talking to John Hastings and Kimberley Weston. Suddenly, Suzy being a jockey isn't a subject to be discussed in hushed whispers. They think they've spawned the next Lester Piggot.'

Fran laughed and looked across the heads of the crowds. 'Your mum's got a mighty posh hat. And your dad looks really nervy. I've always liked them.'

'I know. They're both lovely. I just don't want to have to entertain them tonight. However Suzy does this afternoon, I'm going to be held up as an example of how not to achieve anything worthwhile in life.'

'Maddy? You're not jealous of Suzy, for God's sake?'

'No – well, yes. A little bit. I always have been. I love her to bits, of course, now. But I was a spoiled brat of a child when she arrived. I'd been an only child for ten years. She got all Mum's attention when she was a baby, and then she turned into this determined scary kid who had no fear of anything. She always knew exactly what she wanted to do – and did it. I weighed things up, dithered, and then missed out. Mum and Dad are bound to draw very loud comparisons, especially tonight.'

'With the mixed bunch you've invited I shouldn't worry. They'll be lucky if they're heard over Richard slagging off Luke Delaney and the Pughs spilling the village gossip. It should entertain Caroline Fitzgerald no end. Is she here?'

'I haven't seen them.' Maddy flicked through her race card. She didn't want to see Caroline and Drew together. She'd got used to Drew being alone. The gorgeous Caroline would only remind her that he was not up for grabs. She concentrated on the horses. 'Dancing Feet looks as if he's got anything but. What's Richard riding?'

'According to him every horse he rides today should be called "Lukes Leftovers",' Fran sighed. 'It's hell at home. I'm simply not used to him having the grumps. And the kids are worried sick about him.'

'Can't you seduce him out of it? I thought that was your cure-all.'

'It isn't working this time. He just hunches over and stares at the floor. He's really depressed. This Derby ride was probably his last chance to haul himself out of the also-rans and make it big-time. He wanted to win so that I could finish work and try for a baby.' She sighed. 'Not much chance of that at the moment.'

Maddy squeezed Fran's hand. There had to be something she could do. She hated people to be unhappy. It was typical of Diana to cause this sort of problem.

'Think of the devil,' she muttered as Diana, magnificent in yellow and black, swanned from the member's bar. 'And who's she with?'

'The tall one is Saratoga Sun's owner, Mitchell D'Arcy,' Fran squinted. 'And the dwarf is the bane of my life – Luke bloody Delaney.'

'You can't call him a dwarf!' Maddy grinned. 'He's fairly tall for a flat jockey – taller than Richard.'

'I know. That's something else he's pissed off about. Luke Delaney is drop-dead gorgeous. My Richard, much as I adore him, could hardly be described as that.'

'They're both very attractive.' Maddy nodded grudgingly, watching the two dark and handsome Saratoga connections fawning round Diana James-Jordan. 'They look like Hollywood's idea of Mafioso hoods. No wonder Diana is squirming over Saratoga's owner. And of course, if she gets Luke as well, it's like double top.'

'Don't be disgusting.' Fran laughed. 'I'm sure Darling Diana's motives are as pure as the driven snow.'

A whisper rustled through the crowd. The jockeys, like a fallen rainbow in their iridescent silks, spilled into the parade ring. Maddy's heart nearly stopped beating. Tears sprang to her eyes as she watched Suzy walking proudly towards John Hastings and Dancing Feet's owner in the middle of the grass. She looked so frail, so very tiny, in the white breeches and the red colours. This was the moment Suzy had dreamed of for ten years. Maddy felt a pang of envy. She would never realise a dream like this.

'She doesn't look like a girl.' Fran gulped, overcome by emotion. 'She looks just like Richard and all the others.'

'She looks so young. Bless her.'

They held hands tightly. With her spiky hair tucked out of sight under the scarlet cap, no one could have guessed Suzy's gender.

At the bell, the stable lads led the horses in towards the centre and the jockeys were practically thrown up into the saddles. Maddy wiped her eyes as horses and jockeys circled the parade ring. She grinned up at Suzy as she passed. Suzy, white faced and grim lipped, gave a sketchy smile in return. There was no sign of the ebullient, confident, streetwise teenager that Maddy knew and loved.

'She's scared.'

'Of course she's scared.' Fran blew a kiss to Richard as he rocked past calmly on his equally serene mount. 'She wouldn't be natural if she wasn't. How much have you put on her?'

'Two pounds each way on the Tote.'

'Such confidence!' Fran laughed. 'Don't tell her.'

'Dancing Feet is thirty three to one for heaven's sake!' Maddy protested. 'We all know she hasn't got a hope.'

As the runners for The Arlington Stakes filed out of the parade ring for the gallop to the starting stalls, the crowds round the fence immediately began to drift away towards the grandstand.

'I'll see you in the stand in a minute.' Fran smiled. 'I'm going to make myself scarce. You're having a parental invasion.'

'Don't go!' Maddy said in desperation, but Fran was already flying towards the members' gate.

'Isn't this just wonderful?' Mrs Beckett peered out from under the brim of the hat she had worn for weddings for as long as Maddy could remember. 'This is the proudest day of my whole life. You look nice, Maddy, dear. You've lost weight. I hope you're eating sensibly.'

'Hello, Mum, Dad.' Maddy kissed her parents. 'It's lovely to see you.'

'We couldn't have missed this, could we?' Mr Beckett squeezed his daughter's shoulders. 'And it was about time we came to visit you. You never seem to get up to us.'

'No.' Maddy was instantly guilty. 'I'm so busy. Maybe in the summer . . .'

'We do understand, dear.' Her mother smiled. 'We're very proud of you both, you know.'

'Are you? Really?'

'Of course,' Maddy's dad said. 'You've got a good little business going by all accounts – and now Suzy . . . We reckon we've got two daughters to shout about.'

Again, tears prickled under Maddy's eyelids. Why did she have to be so emotional? She hugged them both. 'Come on, then, we'd better hurry if we're going to get a good view of this first Beckett triumph.'

They squeezed into the stand reserved for owners and trainers and assorted visiting dignitaries. Fran was with John

Hastings and Kimberley Weston. Diana was clinging to the handsome gangster who owned Saratoga. Luke Delaney was not in evidence. She could hear Gareth's braying laugh somewhere in the crowd. Poor Gareth.

The whole of Milton St John seemed to be poured into the various grandstands, with the exception of Peter and Stacey. Of course, this was no surprise. Peter had no interest in horse racing. His interest had always been in the bank balances of the horses' human connections.

'There she is!' Mr Beckett passed the binoculars to his wife. 'Up there behind the starting gate! There's our Suzy!'

Maddy thought she was going to cry again. Every ounce of emotion was squeezed into a tight ball in her throat.

Drew Fitzgerald appeared at her side. 'I thought we'd missed it. Caroline couldn't decide what to wear.'

Maddy smiled at them both, and as Drew smiled back, the ball of emotion bounced down to her heart.

'Drew tells me your sister is riding,' Caroline said. 'Which one is she?'

'In red. She's riding Dancing Feet.'

Caroline lifted expensive field glasses and scanned the horizon. Maddy shook her head. Until that moment she had felt fairly smart in her going-out costume of baggy black trousers and long black jacket with an emerald silk shirt. Caroline's outfit in navy and fuchsia screamed Designer.

'Only two more to load,' the commentator barked. 'That's it! All in! They're off!'

Maddy closed her eyes. The roar from the grandstands rocked her senses. She could hear the screams of encouragement from her parents, could sense the pricking of a million nerve endings. She opened her eyes. The tiny red dot bobbing along towards the back of the field looked hopelessly outclassed.

'Oh, God.' Maddy prayed. 'Please don't let her be last. Anything but last.'

'There's still over a mile to go,' Drew spoke reassuringly. 'She's well positioned.'

The multi-coloured river flowed along the brow of the hill, turned as one, and poured relentlessly downwards. The commentary was lost in the roar of voices. The red dot was nowhere to be seen.

'She's fallen off!' Maddy yelled. 'Where is she?'

'Middle of the chasing pack.' Drew was calm. 'Moving up nicely. She's got style, your sister.'

Maddy glowed. It was a secondhand compliment, but she accepted it gratefully on Suzy's behalf. Maybe, one day, Drew would say it about her.

They were easily visible now, streaking past the three furlong marker. Then the two. The red dot was cruising through the field.

'Jesus!' Maddy grabbed the sleeve of Drew's dark green jacket. 'She's brilliant!'

Drew covered Maddy's clenching fingers with his hand. The roar was deafening. Suzy finished third.

Maddy buried her face in Drew's shoulder. Slowly, he lifted her face. She smiled at him in absolute happiness and kissed him.

His lips seemed surprised at first, but only for a second. Suddenly, Drew Fitzgerald was kissing her back with the sort of passionate urgency that should be reserved for four-poster beds and spilled champagne. Trembling, Maddy pulled away from him. He was smiling. Caroline wasn't.

All explanations were cut short as Mr and Mrs Beckett, John Hastings and Fran, caught her up in their mad dash towards the winner's enclosure.

'Richard won!' Fran glowed as they fought their way through the pushing, pulling crowds. 'He won! That should spice up our love-life a bit! And Suzy was amazing – that horse was a no-hoper! Oh, come on, Maddy! Run!'

Maddy ran.

Crushed beside her parents, she watched with brimming pride as John Hastings hugged the slender red and white figure in the unsaddling enclosure. Suzy grinned at the applauding crowds, high on the powerful cocktail of adrenalin and success. Maddy clapped as vigorously as anyone, feeling as though she were having an out-of-body experience. She was looking down at herself, standing between her parents, proudly acclaiming Suzy's success, and all the while her body and brain were reeling with the arousing sensations of Drew Fitzgerald's kiss.

Caroline, in the space of twenty-four hours, had watched her kiss two men who belonged firmly to other people. And she'd invited her to dinner . . .

The rest of the afternoon passed innocuously enough. Drew and Caroline were glanced occasionally through the crowds, but not at close quarters. This was probably why Caroline didn't want to live with Drew on a permanent basis, Maddy realised. Drew Fitzgerald was the sort of womaniser who would relegate Peter to the second division. She grinned guiltily to herself. As a kisser, Drew made Peter look like a rank outsider. It was a revelation.

Suzy, once back in her jeans and T-shirt, had kissed everyone expansively, hugged her family, and floated off with Jason and Olly and the other Milton St John apprentices to celebrate her success.

'Bloody great ride your Suzy gave that 'orse!' Brenda and Elaine with their equally interchangeable husbands and children, grabbed hold of Maddy's arm as she queued at the Tote's pay-out window. 'We did 'er each way.'

'So did I.' Maddy said, collecting a very welcome thirty-two pounds. Obviously the Tote punters hadn't given much for Dancing Feet's chances either. 'Big celebrations at the Cat and Fiddle tonight?'

'Too right.' Brenda nodded her perm vigorously. 'Specially if Saratoga wins the Greenham.'

Maddy hoped he wouldn't for Fran and Richard's sake. She hoped that Luke Delaney would ride like a sack of potatoes and saw the horse's mouth off. Of course, he didn't.

'Sod it.' Fran sighed as they again stood in the stands, this time to watch the Derby trial. 'He not only looks sensational, he rides like an angel. I bloody hate him.'

'Richard's doing OK, though. He's in second place.'

'Second place on Diana and Gareth's second string,' Fran moped. 'And going backwards.'

They all were. Luke Delaney was cruising along the undulating green carpet, merely using hands and heels, not once touching his whip. Saratoga Sun was an outstanding horse and Luke Delaney was an outstanding jockey. Grudgingly, Maddy thought Diana had a point.

There were wild celebrations over Saratoga's win. The whole of Milton St John seemed to have remortgaged their houses. Maddy hadn't had a bet, out of solidarity with Fran and Richard, and now the odds would be hopeless for The Derby. Diana was kissing Mitchell D'Arcy and Luke Delaney and anyone else that came within range. Gareth looked cross-eyed.

'We won!' He attempted to pat Maddy's cheek and missed. 'We bloody won. I think we've just seen the Derby winner there.'

'So do I.' Maddy shot a quick glance at Fran. 'Congratulations.'

'You've made this very nice, Maddy.' Mrs Beckett looked around the cluttered sitting-room. 'A bit, er, bohemian, perhaps, but that was always your taste.'

'Yes, I like it. Do you want a drink, Mum? Dad?'

They both shook their heads and said they'd prefer tea.

'And you're sure it's not putting you out? With sleeping arrangements and everything?'

'Not at all. I've put you in my room. It's got a double bed.' She'd spent until the early hours making it respectable. 'And I'll go in with Suzy.'

'But with all your friends coming tonight . . . We don't want to be in the way if it's a dinner party.'

Maddy laughed. 'It's very informal. It's to welcome the new couple across the road.' She savoured the memory of Drew's kiss for a delightful moment, then swallowed. He'd probably ring and cancel now. 'Otherwise it's only Fran and Richard, and Mr and Mrs Pugh from the Village Stores. They're your generation. You'll like them'.

'And Suzy? Will she be joining us?'

'Eventually. If we can ever get her head out of the clouds. Now, do you want a cuppa first or a bath? There's loads of hot water.'

They opted for tea. Maddy waltzed out into the kitchen and filled the kettle. There was something missing. Something . . . There was no mouth-watering aroma. With a scream she lifted the lid on the slow-cooker.

She'd forgotten to switch it on.

Determined not to panic, at least audibly, she gnawed her fingers. If she hooked the carrots, onions and celery out of the pot and rinsed them off they could bulk out the crudités. The apple pie was safely in the larder. She wondered if Caroline Fitzgerald had ever been invited to a Jersey society supper where they'd skipped the main course. She somehow doubted it. It was just after six. She had two hours to stage a salvage attempt.

Carrying her parents' tea through to the sitting-room, her brain was working overtime. Mr and Mrs Beckett were watching a slow-motion replay of Suzy's race on the video and didn't look up.

'Mum . . .'

'Yes, love.'

'Mum, those pasties you used to make . . . How long do they take to cook?'

Scooping the brasing steak and vegetables from their icy grey gravy in the slow-cooker, and cubing them with manic determination, Maddy watched the clock. She'd slapped together a mountain of haphazard pastry which was now sitting in the fridge, and defrosted two loaves of bread in the microwave. She certainly didn't have time to peel potatoes. Fat pasties and chunks of bread . . . She'd pass it off as peasant fare. Caroline was practically foreign – she'd never know the difference. If she even turned up.

'Can I give you a hand, love?'

'No!' Maddy shrieked at her mother. 'Er – no, thanks. Why don't you and Dad go through and have your bath and get ready. I've got everything under control here.'

Mrs Beckett cast a professional eye round the kitchen's devastation but wisely made no comment.

'All right then, if you're sure.' She suddenly kissed Maddy's cheek. 'Well done, Maddy, love. It's lovely to see you doing well. Making such a success of your business. And looking so good on it, too.'

Maddy could have cried with pleasure.

The dining-room looked passable enough in daylight, and by the time they sat down at around nineish the curtains would be closed and the candles flickering. It would soften the edges. As her only tablecloth was grubby, Maddy had covered it with a square of net curtain and was very pleased with the effect. She had dragged chairs across from the bedrooms to seat her parents, and although it looked a bit crowded, she hoped that they'd all manage to eat without stabbing each other.

At quarter to eight Maddy poured herself at least four fingers of whisky and headed for the bathroom. It was a shame there was no time to luxuriate in the oceans of hot water which now belched from the boiler, but she splashed around quickly in the scented foam, wrapped herself in the only dry towel left on the towel rail and dived into Suzy's bedroom.

Her long green velvet dress was laid out on the bed. As it was fairly low cut she twisted some green glass beads round her throat, ran her fingers through her hair so that the curls cascaded wildly, drew two lines in black round each eye, mascaraed like a maniac, bolted the whisky, and was in the sitting-room by a minute past eight.

'You look like a gypsy queen.' Her father beamed. He was halfway down the whisky decanter. 'And which young man are you going to introduce us to tonight?'

'No one.' Maddy poured herself another drink and topped up her mother's sherry. 'Both your daughters are a bit slow in the son-in-law stakes, I'm afraid, Dad.'

'Oh, there's years yet for Suzy.' Mrs Beckett was resplendent in royal blue. 'But if you want to have babies, Maddy, you ought to look to your laurels. Thirty isn't that far away, and it's all downhill from there.'

'Thanks. I'd better start advertising for a man, then.'

'Whatever happened to Peter? I liked him.'

'Oh, he's . . .' Maddy floundered. She didn't want to say that he was back in Milton St John or about to marry the bimbo stick-insect. She didn't want to discuss Peter with her parents at all. 'He's still wheeling and dealing, you know.'

A commotion in the hall prevented any further explanations.

'My first guests.' Maddy drained her glass.

'Not unless all your friends have front door keys,' her father said wisely. 'Perhaps it's our Suzy?'

'I'll go and see.' Maddy got as far as the sitting-room doorway.

Our Suzy was swaying unsteadily in the hall, her T-shirt rapidly descending from one shoulder, and with purple love bites beneath each ear.

'Hi, Mad . . .' Her smile was diamond bright. 'We've been having a bit of a celebration. Not too late, am I?'

'No. Just in time. But for God's sake wear a polo neck. Mum and Dad'll have a fit. Oh Jesus!'

Suzy looked over her exposed shoulder and beamed almost soppily. 'Luke came back with us. He's a bit pissed. He can't drive back to Newmarket like that so I told him he could stay to dinner . . .'

Six

Don't panic! Maddy thought. There was a padded stool in the bathroom. And Luke was so thin, he surely couldn't eat more than one pasty, could he?

She held out her hand. 'It's lovely to meet you, Luke. Please come through and have a drink while Suzy's getting changed.'

Luke took her hand in a cool grasp and smiled directly into her eyes. 'Thanks, I'd love to, but I won't stay if it's inconvenient. Suzy said you were entertaining. I don't want to intrude.'

'Not at all. It's just a few friends round for the evening.'

At this rate she'd have the whole of Milton St John playing sardines in the sitting-room. She poured Luke a mighty gin and tonic and introduced him to her parents, who immediately thought he was Suzy's Young Man, and began twenty questions.

A scuffling at the front door heralded the next arrivals. Maddy opened the door, reminding herself to get the bell fixed. It was so inconvenient for people to have to squat down and rattle the letter box.

Fran, wearing the grey shift Maddy had to reject for Diana's party and looking gorgeous, ushered a very subdued Richard into the hall. Maddy kissed them both.

'He's still down about Saratoga,' Fran hissed. 'I couldn't even get him into bed.' This was a serious depression. Fran and Richard's marathon love-life was legendary in the village.

'You were brilliant today, Richard. You had a winner – and you came second in the Greenham.'

'Which is where I'll come in The Derby, if I'm lucky.'

Richard's normally cheerful freckled face was pale. 'I hope you've got plenty of booze tonight, Maddy. I just want to drown my sorrows.'

'Oh, loads. Most of it left from Christmas but still drinkable.' Maddy was smiling brightly. 'You go in and meet my parents – my dad'll tell you how much money he's won on you over the years. That'll cheer you up.'

'The only thing that'll cheer me up is that shit Delaney breaking his legs.' Richard headed for the doorway.

Maddy swallowed. She jerked her head at Fran.

'What?'

'There's a bit of a problem . . . Luke Delaney's in the sitting room'.

Fran dived after Richard and linked her arm through his. 'Why don't you stay and talk to Maddy, darling? I'll go and get some drinks.'

'You want me to stay in the hall?'

'Yes.' Fran had thrust him back against the bathroom door. 'Maddy wants to ask you something.'

'Do I? Oh, yes. I, er . . .' Maddy floundered as Fran disappeared into the sitting-room. 'I wondered what you thought of Suzy's performance today?'

'Brilliant.' Richard was twitching. 'Why do we have to discuss this out here, Mad? Couldn't we talk about it over a drink?'

'Bit crowded in there. My parents – I, um, didn't want them to hear if you thought Suzy was rubbish or anything, you know . . .'

'Here we are!' Fran was beaming like a mother soothing a recalcitrant child with an ice cream. 'Gin. Double.'

Richard leaned against the bathroom door and gulped at his salvation while Fran sent murderous eye signals across his head. Maddy shrugged helplessly and was rescued by a further rattling of the letter box.

Bronwyn and Bernie Pugh were dressed for Going Out. They were also carrying two bottles of sweet sherry and a box of chocolates. Maddy fell on them.

'How kind! Thank you. It's lovely to see you both.' She checked downwards in case her chest was escaping. She couldn't risk another scene. 'Please go through to the sitting-room and meet my parents.' The Pughs squeezed past Fran and Richard.

'Why can they go in there and we can't?' Richard squinted through his gin.

'They're the older generation – like my Mum and Dad.' Maddy was sweating. 'They'll probably want to talk about Radio Two and pension plans. Fran, get Richard a refill . . .'

Suzy tumbled from her bedroom wearing a black polo-necked sweater that just covered her bottom, and red Doc Martens. With a hazy smile at Fran and Richard, she wandered into the sitting-room.

'Is she going to talk about pension plans, too?' Richard looked bemused.

'Probably.' Maddy nodded, wondering if Suzy was wearing anything at all under the polo-necked sweater. 'She's, er, very concerned about her future.'

It was nearly half-past eight. Drew wasn't coming. Maddy knew she'd have to usher her odd assortment of guests through the curtain towards the dining table before long. Richard was smiling through a gin-induced haze which augured well. She'd have preferred him comatose before he realised Luke was under the same roof, but it would do.

The letter box rattled again. Maddy pulled open the door with trembling hands.

'So sorry we're late.' Drew smiled a distant smile. 'Caroline couldn't decide what to wear, again.'

'No problem.' Maddy held the door open wide. Drew looked gorgeous in a pale blue shirt and black trousers. 'I'm just so pleased to see you. And it's my fault – I should have made it clear that it was informal.'

'Formal, informal,' Drew shrugged, 'she still wouldn't have known what to wear. You women are all the same.'

Maddy wanted to say that no they weren't. She had the

black trouser suit for racing, and the black skirt and the velvet dress for parties. Choices were made for her by necessity. It must be bliss to have so many clothes that it caused a problem.

She kissed Caroline's proffered cheek. The delay had been worth it. Caroline was wearing a dress that by its simplicity indicated its cost. It was like a cobweb caught on a dewy morning.

'Sorry.' Caroline smiled. 'I drive Drew mad when we go out.'

Drew handed Maddy two pints of Glenfiddich, a bottle of Krug, and three bottles of Valpolicella. 'I wasn't sure what we were having. I thought these would cover everything.'

'You're wonderful! I mean, they're wonderful. Thank you. It's more than generous. Er . . .'

Drew laughed. 'Just put them somewhere safe. Shall we go through?'

Caroline didn't enquire why the party was taking place in the hall, or why Richard was sliding down the bathroom door, but shook hands politely.

'Now, through here we have . . .' The introductions were made. With relief, Maddy realised that both Caroline and Drew knew Luke. It might come in handy later.

At quarter past nine, unable to put it off any longer, she led the way through to the dining-room. It looked cosy and inviting in a gothic sort of way.

Richard, his arms around Fran, squinted at Luke. 'I've had too much to drink. I'm having hallucinations about bloody Delaney.'

'Shut up!' Fran hissed. 'It *is* Delaney. He's here with Suzy. You don't have to talk to him.'

Maddy, having to ignore convention, had placed her parents and the Pughs at either end of the table, with Caroline, Fran and Richard along one side, and Luke and Suzy, herself and Drew along the other. She really hadn't deliberately put Drew as her neighbour, but it was the only way she could keep the diagonal length of the table between Richard and Luke.

The dips had been a brainwave. A real ice-breaker. Everyone leaned across the table in the candlelight, clashing carrot sticks and being polite about 'after you with the blue cheese' and 'is this the one with the garlic, Maddy?'

The candleglow sparkled on the glasses, making them look like crystal rather than the petrol station freebies that they were. Maddy filled them at every opportunity. Her guests were mellowing nicely.

'You look absolutely gorgeous.' Drew crunched celery without inhibitions.

'So does Caroline. Drew, about this afternoon . . .'

'What about this afternoon?' He turned and looked at her with deceptive innocence. Because of the snug seating arrangements he was so close that she could see the freckles smudged beneath the tan on the bridge of his nose. 'It was a thoroughly enjoyable time. Saratoga Sun is a brilliant horse and Suzy is definitely going to be a star. I might even have some rides for her next season when I'm up and running with my flat horses.'

Was he letting her off the hook, or had the kiss meant nothing to him? Maddy's surge of lust was instantly dampened.

She noticed with some panic that Luke and Suzy had dispensed with the crudités and were happily sucking dips from each other's fingers. She tried to distract her mother.

'Mum. Has Caroline told you that she and Drew have moved from Jersey? You and Dad had some great holidays there, didn't you?'

Caroline was soon chatting across the table and Maddy relaxed again. Richard was waving a spring onion wildly in Luke's direction but was having too much trouble focusing for it to be a threat.

Mrs Pugh leaned across towards Maddy, 'It was so kind of you to put all this on for our benefit, Maddy dear. Bernie and

I are thoroughly enjoying it. Aren't we, Bernie?' Bernie was watching Suzy and Luke with a glazed expression and nodded.

Caroline turned her head. 'I hadn't realised that this was an arranged function, Maddy. I thought yesterday that you invited us on the spur of the moment. I do hope we haven't intruded.'

'Not at all.' Mr Beckett was splashing Valpolicella into everyone's glasses. 'I understood it was all in aid of you and your husband, myself. With you being new to the village.'

'No. No.' Bronwyn Pugh noisily sucked a bread stick. 'It was Maddy's way of saying sorry for a little misunderstanding. Wasn't it, Maddy?'

'Er, yes . . .' Maddy wanted to sink beneath the tablecloth. All eyes were riveted on her. She shook her head.

'Least said, soonest mended,' Mrs Pugh said smugly. 'It was all a mistake, wasn't it, Maddy?'

'Mad went outside in a basque and suspenders.' Suzy grinned at her parents. 'You know how forgetful she is. Bernie was cycling past and got excited and fell off his bike. I think Bronwyn felt it was a seduction attempt.'

The silence was awesome.

Everyone started to talk at once. Maddy, blushing from her toes, scooped up an armful of dishes and hurtled to the kitchen. She'd kill Suzy. Slowly. Inch by bloody inch.

'Can I help?' Drew, carrying the rest of the plates, appeared in the doorway.

'No! Go away. Oh, I mean, thanks for clearing the table – now go away.'

'So that story about Bernie Pugh was true?'

'Yes. Sort of. You don't know what I'm like. Things just happen to me.'

'They do a bit, don't they?' Drew had put the plates on the draining board. 'It's OK, Maddy. They're all laughing. They think it's hilarious. Except Richard of course. He's past laughing. I honestly thought Suzy was joking about you, um, disporting yourself and Bronwyn taking umbrage.'

She stood up from lifting the trays of pasties from the oven and pushed the heavy fall of her hair away from her flushed face. 'I'm not a tart.'

'I don't think anyone ever suggested that you were.'

'No, but with this afternoon and everything, you must think . . .'

'What I think,' Drew looked at her steadily, 'would probably get me thrown out of here. And why are we having pasties? Didn't you say something about the slow-cooker?'

'I forgot to switch it on.'

Drew laughed. Not unkindly. Maddy turned away from him. 'If you want to help, you could take these baskets of bread in.' She reached up to the cupboard for clean plates. 'It'll sort of prepare them for the fact that this course isn't going to be conventional. Will Caroline mind?'

'Why should she?'

'Because she's so perfect. So elegant. She's how I'd like to be if I ever grow up.'

'Don't do that. Not if it means you'll change. And Caroline won't care if she eats crisps from a spoon. She can't cook to save her life – and even if she could she wouldn't.'

Maddy placed the pile of plates slowly on the top of the smaller cupboard. There was loads of room in the kitchen now that the table was in the dining-room. Maybe they could have dancing later. It was nice to know that there were flaws in Caroline's perfection.

'I didn't mean to kiss you.'

'Yes you did.' Drew put down the bread. 'Or at least, I hope you did. Because I certainly meant to kiss you.'

She had been right. He was a womaniser. And heartless.

'It was just the emotion of the moment. I got carried away.'

'Not carried away enough. Although being in a crowd of thousands probably had something to do with it. Maddy Beckett, had you kissed me like that when we'd been alone, say, somewhere like a kitchen . . .' He moved towards her. 'Things might have been very different.'

Drew stroked her hair away from her face. The touch of his fingertips on her heated skin was like dripped trails of iced water. She shivered. He kissed her with the same slow expertise, opening her lips with his own, using his tongue. The kiss wasn't a prelude to lovemaking; it was the act itself.

His fingers stroked her breasts through the velvet. She had never experienced such delightful torment. She wanted him to make love to her. Not slowly and tantalisingly, but quickly and roughly, releasing and relieving the frustration.

Drew dragged away from her. 'Jesus Christ, Maddy . . . What are we doing?'

'Playing a very dangerous game. And one you obviously know the rules of better than I do. I've had too much to drink and you probably haven't had enough.'

Drew ran his fingers through his dark hair. It flopped forward silkily, making him look very young. 'I haven't had enough of you.'

'You're married. Married.' It was an anguished whisper. 'I like your wife. She's in the next room. For God's sake, Drew – it's just lust or something.'

'More or something. Although I think there was an element of lust there.' He was breathing more easily. 'What do you want me to do?'

Maddy took a verbal cold shower. 'Take the bread through, please. I – I do look like a tart now . . .' She glanced down. Her nipples were protruding through the velvet like acorns.

Drew picked up the baskets of bread and smiled. 'You look absolutely gorgeous.'

The pasties were enthused over. Everyone ended up eating them with their fingers, breaking off hunks of bread, washing it down with copious swigs of whatever alcohol came to hand. Luke and Suzy were feeding each other. Maddy shot covert glances at her parents but they were both squiffy and hadn't noticed.

'We were talking about children while you were in the kitchen, Maddy.' Mrs Beckett's voice was rich with sherry. 'I said I'd given up hope of ever being a grandmother.'

Give Suzy and Luke a few more minutes, Maddy thought sourly, and I'm sure they'll sort that out for you.

'I was saying we've got seven,' Bronwyn Pugh trilled. 'Four boys and three girls and our Natalie's expecting again.'

'Really?' Fran was supporting Richard as he chomped through his pasty. 'We're hoping to add to the family. Chloe and Tom are desperate for a baby brother or sister. We're hoping we'll be able to afford it now Richard's with Diana and Gareth. Maybe next year . . .'

'Shooner.' Richard jerked upright and nearly tumbled from the ottoman. Maddy felt she should have given him something with a back. 'If I win The Derby. We'll have the money then, y'see. Fran can give up work.'

'Still, next year will be soon enough.' Fran's eyes were bright with desperation. 'I enjoy my job and—'

'No chance of winning the fucking Derby with fucking Delaney sniffing round Diana Cow-Face-Bloody-James-Jordan.' Richard took solace in another pasty.

'Well, really!' Bronwyn Pugh bridled. 'Language!'

Maddy bit her lip and didn't dare to look at anybody. Drew's thigh pressed reassuringly against her own.

'I'm sorry.' Fran's voice was small. 'So sorry.'

'Actually,' Luke surfaced from Suzy's neck, 'it isn't me you want to have a go at, Rich. It's Mitchell D'Arcy. He owns Saratoga. He picks the jockey. I'd stand down if he'd put you up.'

'Oh, would you?' Suzy's eyes were wide at this magnanimous gesture. 'Really?'

'Yes.' Luke returned to working his way under the polo neck. 'It's the owner's decision – and I'd feel the same way as Richard does in his situation.'

'Don't want no shyph . . . shymph . . . shymphany . . . from you.' Richard glared. 'You're a shit.'

'We'd hoped that Maddy might marry her last boyfriend.' Mrs Beckett's voice soared above the embarrassed murmurs. 'And of course, she would have had babies by now.'

'I don't want babies.'

'Of course you want babies, Maddy, love. Every woman wants babies. You and Peter made a lovely couple.'

'Oh, Peter?' Caroline glanced across the table. 'He was the one I met yesterday, wasn't he, Maddy?'

'Yes.'

Fran was glaring. So was Suzy. Drew had withdrawn his thigh.

'He was here yesterday when I called in,' Caroline continued, tightening the noose around Maddy's blushing throat. 'He's very handsome. Like a young Robert Redford.'

'He and Maddy were together for years.' Mr Beckett helped himself to another pasty. 'They met at our place, you know?'

'No. I didn't.' Drew looked at Maddy. 'I don't think you ever explained how you met?'

'We keep a little hotel,' Mr Beckett ploughed on. 'Peter was staying with us for a few days. He was on one of his business trips. Maddy had just finished university and was working for us as a cleaner. She was cleaning Peter's room when they met and—'

Maddy staggered to her feet. 'I'll just go and warm the apple pie.' Any minute now her parents were going to reveal that she'd lost her virginity in their front bedroom. 'If everyone will excuse me.'

'So that's where you learned your skills.' Drew's voice sliced like a laser. 'Your cleaning skills, of course. That's why you're so wonderfully efficient at running Shadows.'

'Yeah.' Suzy regarded her sister through narrowed eyes. 'But I always said she should call it Scrubbers.'

Seven

'Goodness!' Mrs Beckett looked up from the table as Maddy re-emerged from the kitchen bearing the apple pie and jugs of cream on an unsteady tray. 'What took you so long? Ooh, Maddy, two pastry courses? Are you sure that's suitable with all these jockeys?'

Maddy gritted her teeth, and did a quick recce round the table. They all looked blissfully happy; manically drunk, but happy. Luke and Suzy still appeared to be fully dressed. Richard was asleep.

'Yes, Mum. Richard and Suzy can eat anything and stay like sticks. Luke,' she shot a glance across the table, 'I'm sure, will work his off.'

Luke grinned at her and she was blushing as she sat down. Drew had still withdrawn the reassuring thigh, and accepted his pudding with a nod. She wanted to take his face in her hands and kiss the anger away.

'Your dress is nice, Maddy.' Bronwyn Pugh leaned across the table. She had a double cream moustache. 'I was just saying to your mother, what a pity you don't wear girly things more often.'

'I'm not very fussed about clothes, really. I never have been.'

'Oh, I adore them.' Caroline laid down her spoon.

'Yes, dear.' Bronwyn nodded. 'You can tell. That dress you've got on – is it knotted or crocheted?'

'It's hand-knitted. In silk.'

'I think I saw the pattern.' Bronwyn helped herself to another hunk of pie. 'Wasn't it in last month's *People's Friend*?'

Drew was laughing. Maddy could feel him. She moved her leg closer and he stopped. Fran had suddenly found something interesting in the bottom of Richard's pudding dish which made her shoulders shake.

'No.' Caroline was straight faced. 'Actually it's by one of Drew's owners, Kit Pedersen. He's a designer. In Jersey.' She smiled across at Maddy. 'I nearly always shop designer.'

'Oh, of course,' said Maddy, who nearly always shopped in Oxfam. 'Who doesn't?'

She almost squeaked out loud when she felt Drew's thigh returning like a homing pigeon. She dropped her spoon.

'Let me.' Drew had dived under the tablecloth. Maddy leaned down as well. It was very dark. His face was very close.

'Don't fall out with me,' she whispered. The blood was rushing to her head. 'Not over Peter. Please.'

Drew handed her the spoon, his fingers brushing against hers. She wanted to taste him.

They straightened up. Dishes were being scraped. Glasses were being topped up. Richard was slumped sideways on the ottoman.

'Mad?' Suzy managed to prise her mouth away from Luke's. 'Are we going to play games now?'

'This isn't a children's tea party, Suzy,' Mrs Beckett chided with a ladylike hiccup. 'I don't think anyone wants to play hunt the thimble or hide the slipper . . . no, I mean hide the thimble or—'

'I wasn't thinking of—'

'I know exactly what you were thinking of.' Maddy tried to glare but couldn't quite get the expression right. 'If you help me clear the table, Suzy, perhaps someone could put some music on . . .?'

'That's the ticket.' Maddy's dad got unsteadily to his feet. 'A nice bit of soothing music to help the food down. Have you got any James Last?'

They seemed to have settled for Nirvana as Maddy and

Suzy refused all other offers of help, and carried the dishes into the kitchen.

'You should have said Pete the Perv had been here.' Suzy clattered the pudding spoons into the sink. 'Why didn't you tell me?'

'Because it wasn't important.' Maddy wiped cream from her fingers.

'Sorry I said that about Scrubbers.' Suzy gnawed her ebony fingernails. 'I just didn't want him to hurt you again.'

'He won't – and I'll forgive you this time.' Maddy smiled. It didn't matter now. 'After all, you're a star today, aren't you?'

'This has been the best day of my whole life.' Suzy's eyes were crossed in rapture. The polo-necked jumper had ridden up and Maddy was glad to notice that she was at least wearing knickers. 'I've never been so happy.'

'It has been pretty wonderful,' Maddy agreed, looking at the piles of dirty crockery. To hell with it. She'd do them in the morning. 'Is that a love bite on your thigh?'

'Probably.' Suzy stroked it lovingly. 'He's amazing. I'm in love, Mad.'

'How can you be in love? You haven't known him five minutes.'

'I've known him for ever. We were born for each other. Luke Delaney is my destiny.'

'Good God. You didn't eat anything at the pub, did you?' Maddy looked at Suzy's suspiciously dilated pupils. The chef at the Cat and Fiddle reputedly garnished selected dishes with his finest cannabis plants.

'I don't need dope. I'm high on love. You wait, Mad, one day you'll meet someone and – wham! That'll be it.'

'Really? Do you believe that love can happen like that? I mean, that quickly?'

'Isn't that how it happened with you and Pete the Perv, then? Or can't you remember that far back?'

Maddy shook her head. It hadn't felt like this with Peter.

Not at the beginning, or in the middle, and certainly not at the end.

'Well, that's how it happened to me.' Suzy hugged her sister. 'Cheer up, Mad. One day it'll happen to you. There's someone out there, just waiting . . .'

Mr Beckett had dug out Harry Connick when they got back to the sitting-room and the atmosphere was soft and schmaltzy. The sofa and chairs had been pushed back against the walls and Bernie Pugh was on yet another drinks circuit.

Caroline was sitting alone on the arm of the sofa watching Fran and Richard stumbling round in a circle. Maddy sat beside her. 'Are they dancing? Or has Richard fallen over?'

'They're dancing.' Caroline turned her exquisite face to Maddy in the candlelight. 'This has been lovely, Maddy. We so rarely do anything like this. You were very kind to invite us. It's reassured me that Drew will be happy in Milton St John. I'd hate to think he was lonely while I'm in Jersey.'

'We'll do our best to make him feel at home. Caroline . . .' She had to say something. She had to. 'This afternoon, at the racecourse, when I kissed Drew . . . I just wanted to say sorry.'

'Drew probably enjoyed it.' Caroline's eyes were gentle. 'He likes kissing. I don't.'

Maddy shut her mouth with a snap. Caroline studied her fingers. Her hands were slender, her nails perfect. 'I'm not very keen on kissing or touching. It seems so pointless. Drew is –' she shrugged '– a very tactile person. I'm sure he was dying to kiss you. He likes cuddles and hugs and talking about how he feels. I don't, as I said. We understand each other.'

She was being warned off. In a very friendly and adult way, but warned off nevertheless. She watched Drew laughing across the room with her mother. He was so gloriously sexy. It seemed such a waste that he should have chosen to spend his life with the ice-cold Caroline.

'But aren't you ever afraid that he'll – well, you know?

Meet somebody else? Somebody who does like kissing and being cuddled? He's an attractive man and—'

'Goodness, no!' Caroline looked shocked. 'Oh, I accept that he kisses people, and cuddles them and touches people when he talks – that's the way he is. But I can't imagine Drew wanting to do . . . well, that . . . with anyone else either. It's so very over-rated, don't you think? Messy and boring and embarrassing. We've never bothered much. Neither Drew nor I are particularly interested in that side of things . . .' She giggled. 'Goodness, I must have had too much to drink! I wouldn't dream of talking like this otherwise.'

'People always seem to talk like this at my parties.' Maddy patted Caroline's hand then remembered that Caroline didn't like touching and hastily withdrew it. 'Perhaps it's better not to say anything else.'

Maddy looked across the room at Drew again. He was talking to Fran now. Either she was even more inexperienced than she'd thought, or Caroline really didn't know her husband very well. Drew Fitzgerald had practically seduced her in the kitchen. Drew Fitzgerald made love with his kisses.

'Maddy.' Bronwyn Pugh edged herself down on the sofa. Suzy had just replaced Harry Connick with Metallica. Bernie Pugh was still waltzing with Maddy's mum. 'I'd like to have a little word on the QT.'

'Do you want me to leave?' Caroline asked.

'No, dear. This might concern you, too. Now you're part of the village, so to speak. I wasn't going to say anything about it tonight. I was going to put a notice up in the shop and call a meeting, but now I've got a captive audience I really think I should put you in the picture. Then we can decide what should be done.' Maddy's heart sank, as Bronwyn wriggled comfortably. 'I've heard that they're going to destroy Goddards Spinney and Maynards Orchard. Bulldoze the lot! And for why? A golf course! A damn golf course! Now, what do you say to that?'

'Are you sure it's not just another rumour, Bronwyn? Like the ones about the laser thingy and the McDonald's Drive-Thru?'

'Not this time, Maddy. I've heard from Councillor Campbell that there's a planning application in. The offer to Maynards is spectacular and Goddards Spinney is part of Diana and Gareth's land. They're all for it, so I've been told.'

'But they can't bulldoze all that beautiful countryside.' Maddy was appalled. 'It's immoral. The village is so peaceful – what on earth would it be like with a golf course bang in the middle of it? There'd be cars all the time and a club house. All that noise . . . God knows what it would do to the horses. Surely it won't get any further?'

'I'm afraid it might.' Bronwyn straightened her paisley frock. It still had a slight whiff of Glenfiddich. 'You see, Peter Knightley is behind it, and we all know how chummy he is with Diana, don't we?'

Maddy didn't, but she was beginning to understand quite a lot.

'And, of course, little Stacey's father is extremely wealthy. Little Stacey's father is going to be Peter's partner . . .'

And little Stacey was going to be Peter's wife! Maddy could have cried. It all made sense now. Peter would seduce Diana for the land – and marry Stacey for the money. He hadn't changed a bit.

'But what can we do?'

'Plenty.' Bronwyn nodded fiercely. 'We'll set up an action committee and fight them every inch of the way. And I mean fight, Maddy. People are rising up and fighting all over this country against developments like this. Houses, roads, golf courses – anything that leads to the decimation of our heritage! We must fight for the preservation of Milton St John!'

Maddy looked at Bronwyn Pugh with admiration. 'Count me in, then. As soon as you have your first meeting, let me know. I'll be there.'

'Will you speak to Suzy? And Fran and Richard?'

'Yes, but Fran and Richard are going to be a bit torn. With their connections with the James-Jordans, I mean.'

'Do your best.'

'I'd like to join in.' Caroline turned her slanting eyes to Maddy. 'When I'm here. And I'm sure Drew will support you. He's very keen on the countryside.'

'Good girl,' Bronwyn said approvingly. 'The more people we can get, the louder our voices will be – and the stronger our clout!'

Maddy was amazed. Bronwyn Pugh must have been a flying picket in a previous incarnation.

'We won't say any more about it tonight, Maddy. I don't want to spoil this lovely evening. But I'll try and book the village hall for as soon as possible. And I'm so glad you're on our side. I wondered if perhaps your, er, relationship with Peter may make you a bit doubtful.'

'Absolutely not. No wonder he's buying up the Old Manor. That would suit him down to the ground. Lord of the Manor and running a golf course. Oh no, it would give me great pleasure to fight Peter on this one.'

Bernie Pugh ambled across and asked Caroline to dance. Maddy noticed the start of panic equally masked by a small smile of acceptance. Caroline held herself stiffly away from Bernie as they marched round the sitting-room to a Led Zeppelin melody. She must be frigid. Maddy didn't think she'd ever come across the condition before. It was really quite interesting. She'd have to discuss it with Suzy later.

'Maddy, quick!' Fran's face was anguished. 'I think there's a bit of a fracas in the bathroom! I can hear swearing and—'

Maddy hurried across the hall and hurled the door open. Richard had his hands firmly round Luke Delaney's throat.

'Jesus Christ!' Fran barged past Maddy and tugged at her husband. 'What the hell are you doing?'

'Getting the ride on Sharatoga Shun,' Richard slurred. 'Leave us alone!'

'Oh, Richard,' Fran groaned. 'This is crazy. It isn't worth it.' She hauled him backwards until he collapsed against her.

Maddy shook her head. Gentle, easy-going Richard had been driven to this by Diana's greed. If there was anything between Diana and Peter Knightley – as Bronwyn had suggested – then it was a match made in heaven.

Luke straightened up. 'And I only come in for a pee . . .'

'You're not hurt?'

Luke shook his head. 'A bit surprised, that's all. I thought it was Suzy at first, messing about.' He looked at Richard. 'If you feel that strongly about it, I'll go and see Mitchell D'Arcy tomorrow, and Mrs James-Jordan. I'll step down.'

'No you won't,' Fran said angrily. 'Richard rides Saratoga because he's been chosen to – on his merits – or not at all.' And dragging Richard by his sleeve – just as she would Chloe or Tom – she marched out of the bathroom.

Maddy perched on the edge of the bath. It was a tricky situation, and one she'd feel better able to deal with if she hadn't had quite so much whisky. 'You want the Derby ride as much as Richard, though. You don't really want to step down, do you?'

'Of course not.' Luke shook his head. His black hair was silky. She'd kill for his cheekbones. 'But I'm twenty-three – Rich is in his thirties. I know how much this means to him. He's been a middle-ranker for all his career. I've got far more Derbys ahead of me than he has.'

Maddy sighed. Luke was nice, as well as beautiful. It was a heck of a combination. She could understand Suzy's euphoria. 'Do you think Mitchell D'Arcy would replace you?'

'Not at the moment. He's screwing Diana. They both want me to ride. It hasn't got anything to do with Richard not being good enough. He's a great horseman and a first-class jockey. It's—' He gave an embarrassed shrug. 'It's the publicity thing. They think I've got this image, and racing is really hard up. The more media attention they can attract the better.'

'Well, you are,' Maddy agreed, 'good looking. You'd look super on the telly. And you'd probably replace all those footballers and racing drivers on teenage girls' bedroom walls. No one is going to turn away that sort of money-making package. Apart from that, you're a brilliant jockey. It's a bit tough though – Richard can't ride because he's got ginger hair and freckles and a lived-in face.'

'That's about it,' Luke said gloomily.

'Leave it then.' Maddy prised herself away from the bath. 'I don't see that there's anything you can do.' But there was plenty she could do, she thought. Starting with Diana James-Jordan. If she was having a fling with Mitchell D'Arcy there might be a bit of leverage there. 'I'll go and pacify Richard . . .'

'You're even nicer than Suzy said you were.' Luke leaned forward. His eyes were on a level with hers. 'And she said you were bloody fantastic. Thanks, Maddy.'

He kissed her on the forehead, turned, and walked straight into Drew.

Drew looked at Maddy. 'Am I interrupting?'

'No. It's business.'

'You're forgetting I know Luke well. Luke and a gorgeous lady alone in any room at a party usually only means one thing.'

She glowed. He'd called her gorgeous . . . Still, he was probably as free with his compliments as he was with his kisses.

'You're not leaving yet?' He couldn't go. 'Caroline isn't bored?'

'Caroline seems entranced by the whole thing. Your dad's teaching her to play poker. No, I wanted to talk, and I thought we could do that less conspicuously if we danced.'

'I'm not dancing to Motorhead or whatever Suzy's found now.'

'It sounds like Luther Vandross to me. Quite suitable for the more mature members of the party to stagger around to.' He smiled at her and the world tumbled upside down.

They danced in the space in the middle of the room, surrounded by furniture and shrill laughter, but as far as Maddy was concerned they were alone in a sumptuous mirrored ballroom beneath a thousand chandeliers. No one else existed. She was only aware of his body brushing hers, of his hands branding her flesh through the velvet, of his breath warm on her cheek.

They talked about the proposed golf course; of the action committee; of the tussle for the Derby ride. They giggled about Mrs Pugh and Maddy's mum who were both pie-eyed. They said nothing about Caroline.

'I behaved badly,' Drew murmured, 'about Peter. Stupid of me, I had no right.'

'No, you haven't.' Maddy smiled into his shoulder.

'I was jealous.' She could feel him smiling in return. 'Jealous, for God's sake. It annoyed me to think he could just waltz back into your life and disrupt it all over again.'

'You and Suzy both,' Maddy muttered, then said more loudly, 'He's not going to. And it shows that you don't know me very well.'

'No, I don't.' He moved his hands to the small of her back. 'We know so little about each other. Do you think we'll ever know enough?'

She stopped dancing and looked up at him. His tawny eyes were asking a million questions. Caroline's warning screamed in her brain. She stood on tip-toe and kissed his cheek. 'Yes, I think we will.'

She longed to kiss him. Properly. But the chandeliered ballroom dissolved and she moved away from him in the cluttered sitting-room.

The party was coming to an end.

'We'll be making an early start in the morning, Maddy.' Mrs Beckett swayed unsteadily. 'We've left Carl and Marcie in charge, but we must get back. We'll just slip away without disturbing you.' She hugged her daughter. 'We have had a wonderful time. Wonderful. I'll ring you when we get home.'

Maddy promised to visit them as soon as possible. She kissed them both goodnight, and smiled as they supported each other towards her bedroom.

Fran, tight lipped, had already left, practically carrying a green-faced Richard, and the Pughs, with much uncharacteristic hugging and kissing, stumbled out of the door.

'It's been great.' Caroline pressed her cool cheek fleetingly against Maddy's flushed one. 'I can't remember a more entertaining evening. I've said to Drew, we must have a return match. Maybe when I'm next over.'

'You're going back to Jersey soon, then?' Maddy tried to keep the hope from her voice, but she was too tired to pretend.

'Pretty soon. I'll have to. It's coming up to our busy season – tourists and everything.'

Maddy nodded, realising that she had no idea what Caroline did in the Channel Isles, also realising that she didn't care. However wrong it was, she just wanted it to take Caroline back there. Quickly.

'Thank you for a delightful evening.' Drew leaned towards her. He brushed her cheek with his lips, leaving a hollow of desire in the pit of her stomach. 'I'll never forget it.'

Miserably, Maddy watched them cross the road and disappear into Peapods' dark drive. Drew was going home to bed – albeit a cold and chaste bed – with Caroline.

She closed the door and closed her mind to the devastation of the cottage. It could all be faced in the morning. All she wanted to do was sleep. Only pausing to snuff out the grotesque stubs of the candles and ease off her shoes, she padded across the hall and opened Suzy's bedroom door.

'Shift up, then, Superstar. Make room for your favourite sister. Oh . . .'

Luke and Suzy looked like Profane and Sacred Love. Young, slender and utterly beautiful, Luke's dark skin was merged with Suzy's pale fragility against the tangle of bedclothes.

Not sure if she was trembling with indignation, jealousy, or both, Maddy quietly closed the door and grabbed a spare blanket from the airing cupboard. Clearing away bottles, ashtrays and glasses, she curled wearily on the sofa.

Eight

It rained. Steadily. The village dripped beneath its canopy of chestnut trees, and the stream alongside the main road gurgled and churned with fat brown bubbles. It made Maddy's work twice as long, as every house seemed to have at least three Labradors with constantly muddy feet.

The deluge followed one of the hottest Guineas festivals on record. Maddy had accompanied Suzy to Newmarket at the last moment. Having made a valiant effort to avoid Drew in the week since her dinner party, she had hoped that he might be there. She felt it would be all right to talk to him in a crowd of thousands. However, according to the grapevine, he and Caroline were driving up to Yorkshire to meet with potential owners, and by the time she found out, it was too late to alter her plans. So, with bad grace, she too had abandoned Milton St John for the weekend.

'We could do with it.' Kimberley Weston stood mournfully in her rain-lashed yard, wearing the gabardine mac she must have had at school, and watching Maddy pack various cleaning paraphernalia into her bicycle basket. 'The ground's like concrete, and it might wash some of the bugs away. Talking of which, Maddy, you look pretty awful. Is it overwork? I sometimes feel so guilty when I watch you trying to divest my carpets of ingrained dog hair.'

'It's lack of sleep,' Maddy said, leaning against her bike in the rain. 'Newmarket was wild. I'm getting too old for weekend-long partying.'

'Don't tell me – I'm already jealous. It's yonks since I had any fun.' Kimberley wiped her face with a large red handkerchief. 'I wish I could have been there.'

'So do I.' Maddy could feel the rain penetrating her cheap cotton jacket. 'I could have done with a friend. I felt very much the odd one out. Fran was with Richard, and Suzy was all over Luke like a rash.'

'Serious, is it?' The raindrops on Kimberley's round face looked like tears.

'Sickeningly so. Not suitable viewing for unattached ladies like us, I'm afraid. We have to gain our fun from things like Bronwyn's meetings. You will be there this evening?' Maddy shivered. 'Apparently, she's commandeered the village hall.'

Kimberley nodded. 'Definitely. Unlike a lot of the others, I actually grew up here. I climbed trees in the spinney as a girl, scrumped apples from Maynards Orchard. It's a beautiful area of natural woodland and I'll fight tooth and nail to keep it. Bloody Peter Knightley won't get his hands on it if I can help it!'

'Oh good.' Maddy grinned, flicking rain from her bicycle saddle. 'We can expect a few fireworks, then.'

'Just a few. Oh, my head's like the proverbial sieve. I knew there was some snippet of goss I had to tell you. Apparently Caroline Fitzgerald went back to Jersey last night.'

Maddy cycled out of Kimberley Weston's yard wearing a broad smile, all the loneliness of the Guineas festival swept away in an instant.

As she skidded to a halt outside her cottage, Drew was walking head down against the slanting rain, across Peapods' cobbled yard. Maddy watched him covetously through the raindrops. Even from a distance he made her stomach turn over. Unlike the other trainers in Milton St John, Drew didn't wear the uniform of Barbour and chequered cap. His hair, sleekly black in the rain, was plastered to his forehead, his long legs were encased in tight faded denim, and the collar of his battered brown flying jacket was turned up against the storm. Maddy thought he looked glorious.

He glanced up, and spotting the bicycle, changed direction.

'You've been avoiding me since the party.' His eyes flashed as he approached her. 'Haven't you?'

'Of course not,' she lied, smiling. 'I suppose our paths haven't crossed, that's all. We've both been busy. You went up to Yorkshire, so I believe. I've been to Newmarket, and—'

'Crap. You were supposed to be cleaning Peapods on Friday afternoons. I waited for you last week. I got a skinny blonde.'

'Jackie.' Maddy nodded. 'She casuals for me. I, er, couldn't fit it in. She was all right, wasn't she?'

'Excellent. But she wasn't you. I don't want substitutes.' He looked up at the steely sky. 'This weather looks like it's set in for the day. Come and have a coffee – or are you too busy for that, too?'

'Well . . .' Maddy spent ages straightening the bicycle's handlebars. Her hands were shaking. 'I've only got a few minutes. One of Kat's children is ill, and I'm covering for her this afternoon, and I really—'

'And you've come home for lunch. My coffee pot is on and I've got a cupboard full of Mars bars.'

She looked at him and laughed. She couldn't resist him.

They hurried across the road, the rain lashing in a relentless drive from the misty downs. This wasn't how she'd planned it, Maddy thought, as she squelched through the puddles. In her Drew Fitzgerald fantasies it was all sunshine and roses, and she would look ravishing in something floaty and ethereal.

After the dinner party Caroline had slipped an expensive card of thanks through the letter box. Maddy had put it on the mantelshelf alongside Bronwyn's Waverley notelet of kittens and wool, and Richard's Far Side apology.

'Kimberley says that Caroline has gone.' She kicked off her boots in the porch and left her Oxfam jacket in a sodden heap on the floor. 'I meant to ring her, after she'd left the card . . .'

Drew held the door open for her and she took a deep breath before stepping inside Peapods.

'Oh!' She looked around with pleasure. 'It's lovely, Drew. I never imagined it could look like this.'

On the rare occasions she'd visited Peapods in its previous incarnation as the Knightley Health Studio, it had been a mass of glass and chrome, of mirrors and lights and vivid blue paintwork. Now it had been lovingly restored to a Victorian farmhouse.

'It didn't take long.' Drew led the way through to the kitchen. 'Peter hadn't destroyed any of the original structure, merely covered it. It was more a case of stripping away the façade and returning the rooms to their original purpose.'

'And did you bring all this with you?' Maddy indicated the elm dressers, the walnut chiffonier, the oak tables, and the masses of watercolours which adorned the walls. 'From Jersey?'

'Most of it. This all belonged to my parents. Caroline didn't like it anyway. She prefers more modern furniture. She was glad to see the back of it. Take a seat . . .'

But Maddy was far too impressed with the kitchen to sit down. She always lusted after people's kitchens, hers being so peculiar. It was cosy with its wood-burning stove, its stripped pine table with huge carvers, and a mass of old French cooking utensils hanging from hooks and beams.

'All for show.' Drew poured two mugs of coffee. 'I defrost in the microwave and eat from a tray in front of the TV. I can never raise any enthusiasm in cooking for one. Sugar?'

'Two – er, one, please.'

He heaped two spoonful's into the mug, added cream and stirred it for her. She sat down to drink her coffee and watched him as he stacked several items of dirty crockery into the dishwasher. There was something endearingly sexy about a man being so at home with domesticity. A shiver of awareness prickled her spine.

'Are you cold? Do you want to sit nearer the stove?'

She shook her head. He pulled up the chair opposite her. 'Actually, I lied about the Mars bars. It was the only way I could think of to lure you into my home. I've got chocolate Digestives . . .'

'Just coffee is lovely.' Maddy's throat had constricted again. 'Er, are you settling in OK?'

'Fine. I've got most of my staff over from Jersey and recruited one or two local lads. A nice lady from Wantage – Holly – is starting as my secretary next week.'

They sat in silence for a few minutes. She knew he was looking at her so she studied the whorls and knots on the table's surface.

'Maddy . . .'

'Have you sold your house in Jersey?'

'No. Maddy . . .'

'So, is that where Caroline is living while she runs her business?'

'No. Maddy, listen . . .'

'Oh, so you've got two houses, have you? And now Peapods? Goodness, how—'

'Maddy!' This time it was a roar. Drew leaned across the table and grabbed her shoulders. His dark hair had dried feathered across his forehead. 'Maddy, for God's sake shut up about my horses and Caroline! I want to talk to you.'

'We are talking.' She didn't even try to pull away from him.

'After a fashion. But not how we used to. You've been avoiding me, and now you're ducking and diving and asking questions that make you sound more like Bronwyn Pugh. Look at me.'

Maddy looked. And her heart turned over. She couldn't disguise the longing in her eyes. Drew relaxed his grip and sat back in his chair. 'That's better. I think we ought to get a few things clear.'

'Set the ground rules?' She sipped her coffee. 'Good. You're married, I'm friendly with your wife. I let myself get carried away a couple of times – a situation that won't be repeated. We're neighbours, and friends, and business colleagues

87

because of Shadows. It all seems pretty clear. Was there anything you wanted to add?'

Drew looked at her steadily. There was a hopelessness in the shrug of his shoulders. 'Is that really how you feel?'

'Yes.'

'Fine, then.' Drew pushed his chair back so that the legs screeched across the newly exposed flags. 'Bring your coffee. We'll do a tour of inspection. I assume that you'll be taking over the cleaning now that you know I'm not going to leap on you?'

Maddy stood up miserably and followed him out of the kitchen. She wanted him to leap on her very much indeed.

The rest of Peapods was equally glorious. The furnishings were old and well loved, the drapes hung in pale profusion, the paintings were originals. The whole house looked like a comfortable family home. It was sad that it housed this one solitary man, Maddy thought, when it should ring with laughter.

'So?' They'd finished the tour in the sitting-room. Drew sat on the edge of a worn dark green sofa. 'Do you still consider your rate for the job adequate? I know Caroline was happy with it, but if you think you under-quoted . . .'

'No. It's perfectly fair. You haven't added more rooms or anything.'

She walked across to a walnut display cabinet. Anything rather than sit primly facing the temptation of Drew Fitzgerald. The cabinet was bursting with trophies. Maddy read the inscriptions. The rain slashed against the windows. She turned to face him. 'You won a lot. I didn't realise . . .'

'A long time ago.' Drew stood up. 'Ten years and more most of them. When I was riding as an amateur. I gave it up soon after I married Caroline.'

'Why? Didn't she like you being a jump jockey?'

'Not really. It wasn't very glamorous. It meant being apart a lot because she had her own business. It was only just starting then. And I'd broken so many bones I knew it was time for me to settle for something more sedate. So, I became a small-time trainer.'

'And now you're becoming a big-time one?'

'Well, not in Diana or John Hastings' league – or even Kimberley or Barty's. But, yes, I do hope to have some successes when I start in earnest next season. My owners are very loyal and I've had enquiries from new ones. I should have the stables full by the autumn.'

'Good.' Maddy turned back to the trophies. 'What's that one?'

He looked over her shoulder. She could smell him. If she moved less than an inch she would touch him. She heard his intake of breath.

'Oh, I won that in 1985. The same year as Caroline and I were married. It was my swansong.'

'It's not an English trophy. I mean, I don't know all that much about racing, but—'

'It's for the Pardubice. The Czechoslovakian Grand National . . .'

'Jesus!' Maddy forgot that she was supposed to be distant. 'That's the race that goes on for about three days and you have to jump mountains, isn't it? Is that why Peter and everyone said you were famous?'

'I consider it my allotted fifteen minutes of glory, yes.' Drew had moved away. 'I was delighted with the win at the time, of course. It all seems such a long time ago now. So many things have changed.'

Maddy looked at him, this strong, athletic man with depths that could be trawled for ever. 'Caroline must have been so proud of you. God, I'd have been floating on reflected glory for months.'

'Caroline was glad that I won because she knew I'd hang up my saddle. I'd promised her that.'

'Then she must have been mad!' It was no good. she couldn't carry on with this pretence. 'She should have encouraged you to capitalise on it. To have gone on to greater

89

things – if that's what you wanted. Isn't that what marriage is all about?'

'And it's easy to see that you've never been married. Being married to someone doesn't alter them – no matter how much you think in those first heady days that it will. By the time you find out differently it's too late . . . My relationship with Caroline has never run on supportive lines.' His face was bleak, remembering. 'Oh, hell, Maddy. If we're just going to be friends, we can't talk about things like this. It's disloyal to Caroline and unfair to you.'

Maddy knew that she was being told something very important. She knew she had to tread carefully. 'Doesn't she mind you being unfaithful to her? Is that part of the game?'

To her surprise, Drew laughed. 'I don't play games – and since you ask, I've never been unfaithful to Caroline.'

Maddy looked down at the carpet. She didn't believe him. 'I'm sorry. You're right. This is none of my business. Look, I ought to be going.'

Drew looked at his watch. 'You've still got fifteen minutes of your lunch break. I wish we'd never had this conversation. I want to go back to where we were.'

So do I, thought Maddy sadly. She didn't want to leave him, but she couldn't stay in this room when she wanted him so badly. 'Would you show me round the stables?'

'Now? Are you sure? It's still chucking down.'

A cold shower of biting English rain might just dampen the lust that had risen hotly inside her. She nodded. Drew gave a puzzled grin. 'Very well. I'll fetch my coat.'

The horses looked sleek and snug and well cared for. Drew had nicknames for each of them and they whickered with pleasure as he approached. The stable lads scuttled in and out of boxes, grinning at him and greeting Maddy. The local boys were Suzy's friends and seemed to be completely at ease with Drew. Peapods was a very happy yard.

'Do you ride?'

They'd paused at the end of the cobbled stable block and were sheltering from the gusting rain beneath the clock arch.

'No. I don't think there's a Clydesdale big enough.'

'Don't fish for compliments. I'm not going to tell you what effect your curves have on me. Would you like to learn? To ride, I mean?'

'Oh, I can ride. It's just that I haven't for so long. And no one in Milton St John is going to risk me crippling one of their expensive babies.'

'Well, if you ever change your mind, I've got a horse that would suit you. Solomon. I brought him over with me. Would you like to?'

'Yes,' she nodded, 'very much. But on a warm summer's day – I'm a fair-weather horsewoman.'

'OK, it's a date.' Drew squinted at the ceaseless rain. 'I don't think I've missed a day's riding – apart from the compulsory side-lining when my bones were broken of course – since I've been old enough to walk.'

'Were you born in Jersey?'

'Yeah. My father went over to the island from County Mayo to work. He met my mother, who was an islander, when he was taken on for the potato harvest on her parents' farm. They inherited it and added the stables.'

'And did you inherit it from them?' Maddy wanted to know everything about him.

He nodded. His eyes were sad. 'My mother died five years ago. She had Motor Neurone Disease. It was appalling.' He paused and looked at Maddy. 'No one should be forced to suffer that sort of torture. She died trapped in her own body. She was only fifty-three . . .'

Maddy's eyes filled with tears. She reached out a cold, wet hand and touched Drew's arm. 'I'm so sorry. I do know about MND . . . though I can't even begin to imagine how awful it must have been for you. You must have felt so helpless.'

'Dad and I did everything we could, but I got so angry. It

shouldn't happen to anyone, and certainly not to Mum. She loved living. Dad never came to terms with it . . . He couldn't live without her. He drank himself to death eighteen months after she died.'

There was nothing but the blustering rain and the howl of the wind sweeping from the downs; the mournful sounds mingling obtusely with the cheerful shouts of the stable lads and the rustling of the horses in their boxes.

'Oh, Drew . . . I wish I'd been there.'

'So do I, Maddy.' He looked down at her, the tears of reawakened grief glistening in his eyes. Swallowing, he turned his head away. 'I really needed a friend.'

'But surely, Caroline –?'

'Caroline couldn't cope with emotion. Not any sort of emotion.'

'But they were your parents! Surely, she could understand?'

'Not everyone is like you, Maddy. People gravitate to your warmth. Caroline freezes people off.'

'Even you?'

'Even me.' He looked down at her again. 'It's the way she is.'

Then you should have left her years ago, Maddy thought hotly. She shook her head. 'I really don't understand why you're still married. Oh, I know it isn't my business but . . .'

'No, it isn't.' But the words were spoken gently. 'Maddy, there are a million things about my marriage that you don't know.'

'No. Sorry.'

He stared at her hand on his arm for a second, then covered it with his own. The gentleness of the contact made her shiver.

'One day I'll tell you.' He tightened his grip on her fingers. 'Maybe when we're out riding I'll pour out my heart – will that suit your romantic soul?' His eyes were teasing again, and the sadness was fading.

'That'd be ideal.' She kept in step with the mood. 'Every

time I fall off you can tell me another sordid snippet.'

She'd made him laugh again. It was probably all she could do.

'Did you close everything down when you moved here?'

'I've kept the house in Bonne Nuit because it was all I had left of my parents. But I rent out the land and the farm buildings.'

'And is that where Caroline is now? Running her business from, er, Bonne Nuit?'

'No. Caroline had her own place even when we were in Jersey. She works with her parents in St Lawrence, and lived there most of the time. It was more convenient. Bonne Nuit is pretty remote. Do you know Jersey?'

'No. Mum and Dad had holidays there, but I was at university. I never went. I know it's beautiful.'

'It's heaven.' The warmth had returned to Drew's voice. 'You should see it. I'd love to show you.'

Maddy closed her eyes. She couldn't think of anything she wanted more. She sighed. 'So what does Caroline actually do?' They'd started to walk back towards the house.

Drew raised his eyebrows. 'You mean she didn't tell you? You were talking a lot at your party, I was sure she'd have mentioned it.'

Maddy shook her head. She wasn't going to say that she and Caroline had been delving into the depths of the Fitzgeralds' sex life – or rather, the shallows.

'Caroline is the managing director of the De Courcey Vineyards.'

'Heavens!' Maddy was impressed. 'That sounds very high powered.'

'Oh, it's a fairly small concern, but growing rapidly. A lot of farmers had to rethink their lives when the Channel Islands opted out of the EEC. They all had glass houses and only limited markets where they could sell their tomatoes and other produce. Some went into flowers – Caroline's family went into grapes. It's quite a tourist attraction and the wine is surprisingly drinkable. She's doing very well. Oh, shit!'

Maddy followed his eyes and silently echoed his curse. Bronwyn Pugh, muffled against the elements, and looking for all the world like the Wicked Witch of the West, was pedalling furiously across Peapods' cobbles.

'I'm so glad I've caught you two together,' she trilled, dismounting into a flurry of spray. 'Just canvassing for tonight's meeting. You'll both be there, of course?'

Maddy nodded. Drew smiled politely. 'Yes, of course. What time is it?'

'Eight o'clock. Village hall,' Bronwyn puffed. 'We've got a lot of support. I've issued an invitation to Peter and Stacey and Stacey's father but they haven't replied.'

'It's probably better if they don't turn up at the first meeting.' Maddy wiped the rain from her face. 'Perhaps we should sort out a few things without them.'

'I'd rather they were there.' Bronwyn bristled. 'Let 'em know what they're up against. Will you be giving, Maddy a lift, Drew?'

'Oh, no. I, er . . .' Maddy blushed. 'I can walk if the rain stops, and if not I'll take the car if Suzy's home.'

'There's no point in clogging up the street with lots of cars, is there?' Drew smiled winningly. 'That's a good idea, Bronwyn. Yes, I'll pick Maddy up at about quarter to eight.'

Nine

The village hall was flatteringly full. A wide cross-section of Milton St John had squeezed itself into the stacking chairs, and was sitting, damply steaming, awaiting the main event. Maddy, beside Drew in the third row, gazed around in open astonishment. She hadn't expected anything like this turn out, especially as all stables were gearing up for The Derby. It was a testament to Bronwyn's organising powers that she had managed to prise so many away from their work.

Kimberley Weston and Barty Small were in the front row, with several other trainers. Diana and Gareth James-Jordan were not in evidence. Neither were Peter or Stacey.

'They probably haven't had this sort of turn out since the last public hanging,' Drew whispered. 'And some of them look as though they've been around ever since.'

Maddy giggled. 'This probably affects the older villagers more than anyone. After all, they've got no use for a golf course, and they probably did their courting in the spinney.'

'They possibly all started their families there too, from what I've seen of the unleashed libido in the village.'

Maddy went hot. She didn't want to think along those lines. Not with Drew's denim-clad leg rubbing against hers. It was the seating arrangment conspiracy again.

'I thought I'd missed it.' Fran pushed along the row towards them, muttering apologies for trodden-on toes. 'Has it started yet?'

'No. Bronwyn's obviously waiting 'til the last minute.' Maddy was delighted to see Fran. 'I didn't think you'd come, what with Richard riding for Diana.'

'Richard won't come because of that.' Fran was removing her coat. 'But he feels very strongly about it. I said I'd represent us both. Anyway, one of us had to stay with Chloe and Tom. Barty and I have talked about nothing else but this all day. You wouldn't think it was The Derby in – oh, hello, Drew.'

Drew beamed back along the row. Fran leaned towards Maddy. 'I thought you'd decided to steer clear? You told me at Newmarket you were just going to be friends. I thought you'd avoided him since the party?'

'I had,' Maddy whispered back. 'We've sorted out ground rules. We're just friends.'

'And I'm Joan Collins' granny,' Fran snorted. 'You're both grinning like Cheshire cats. Remember what I said. He's married, and you'll get hurt.'

'Possibly.'

'Probably. Definitely. Stone-cold certainty.' Fran peered at Drew who was studying the empty stage with apparent innocence. 'You lucky cow.'

'He's had a really sad life,' Maddy hissed. 'I'm not going to add to it.'

Fran laughed. 'So Drew Fitzgerald is your charity of the month, is he?'

'Of a lifetime,' Maddy muttered, wriggling back into her seat.

Drew leaned closer. 'Tell Fran she's got a very loud whisper.'

'Oh, God.' Maddy felt the blush spiral up her throat. 'You heard?'

Drew's grin was ear to ear. 'You lucky cow . . .'

Fortunately the Pughs chose that moment to make their entrance. They shuffled on to the stage, swollen with self-importance, and took up positions behind the microphone as though they'd been doing it all their lives. Bronwyn, in a brown corduroy pinafore dress, carried a clipboard; Bernie, in his Best Suit, was armed with buff folders. And they weren't alone.

'Dear God!' Fran snuffled into her hand. 'They've brought entertainment.'

Drew was laughing. Quietly. Maddy stared straight ahead, not daring to meet his eyes. Milton St John openly gawped at the rag-tag trail of colourfully dressed individuals who accompanied Bronwyn and Bernie on the stage.

'Who the hell are they?' Drew hissed. 'They look like Adge Cutler and the Wurzels.'

'I really wouldn't know about that.' Maddy was biting her lips. 'But then I'm so much younger than you.'

Drew's hand snaked across the seat and gripped her wrist. Their fingers entwined and Maddy gave an ecstatic shudder.

Fran looked scathingly at their linked hands. 'Well done, Maddy. Ten out of ten for staying power.'

'Ladies and gentlemen,' Bronwyn bellowed down the microphone. 'We're all here tonight to unite in a common cause. To protect the beauty and tranquility of our village. To prevent the rape of Milton St John!' The village stamped its collective feet and whistled its approval.

'Nice start,' Drew whispered.

''ello, Maddy.' Brenda and Elaine were sitting in the row behind and had leaned forward still clapping. 'Old Bronwyn's a bit of a puckie, ain't she? Bloody marvellous, the way she shouts.'

Maddy nodded. Drew looked confused. 'A bit of a what?'

'Puckie – it means . . . oh, a dark horse.'

'And she's not the only one.' Drew wriggled the brown leather flying jacket closer to Maddy's shoulder. She leaned against it with a contented sigh.

'Before we progress,' Bronwyn yelled, 'I'd like to introduce my friends.' She turned to the dishevelled bunch beside her. 'This is Sandra and Barry from the Twyford Down protesters, Joe and Nicky from the Batheaston site, and Peanut, who I'm sure you'll all recognise from News at Ten.'

Milton St John craned their necks and peered. He didn't look anything like Trevor McDonald.

Bronwyn bellowed again, 'Peanut has been frequently televised at the Newbury bypass protest. He holds the record for chaining himself to a tree. Six days, wasn't it, dear?'

Peanut nodded his dreadlocks. Milton St John whooped and cheered its support. There were very strong feelings about the Newbury bypass in the village.

'The old girl's done her homework.' Drew's voice rang with admiration. 'She's brought in the heavy mob.'

'I fancy the one in the bobble hat,' Fran whispered. 'Is that Peanut?

'Sandra,' Drew informed her.

The talk was rallying; a call to arms. Bernie quoted other similar cases, and how they would learn from those successes and failures. It was all very stimulating. Sandra and Barry, Joe, Nicky and Peanut, all pledged their expertise and support. A committee, as such, was decided against at this stage. Instead it was suggested that the village used its collective muscle. The Pughs would confront the Maynard family and try to persuade them not to be swayed by vast sums of money.

' . . . And,' Bronwyn had at last got the hang of the microphone, 'I suggest that Maddy Beckett approaches the James-Jordans regarding Goddards Spinney.'

All eyes turned to Maddy. Crimson faced she shook her head. Drew squeezed her fingers. 'You can do it, Maddy. Diana likes you, and Gareth would be putty in your hands.'

'Well, Maddy?' Bronwyn was beaming.

'Er, yes . . . well, yes.'

There was more clapping and foot stamping and whistling. The villagers of Milton St John didn't get out much.

'So, we'll meet again in a fortnight's time – just before The Derby.' Bronwyn was in complete control now. 'If peaceful negotiations have failed, we know what we have to do, don't we?'

Milton St John didn't. Sandra and Barry, Joe, Nicky and Peanut raised clenched fists and yelled, 'Fight! Fight! Fight!'

Milton St John was quick to catch on and echoed the battle cry. Fran blew her nose loudly. The Pughs and their rag-tag army left the stage, and chairs were scraped back as the village filed out of the hall into the damp night.

The atmosphere in the dusky street was euphoric. Knots of people stood around, laughing and talking, all inspired by Bronwyn's diatribe.

'Would you like to come to the Cat and Fiddle?' Drew asked Fran. 'It seems too early to go home, and I could do with a drink – especially after all that emotion.'

'No thanks. It's a great idea, but I'd better get home. Richard tends to become another kid when he's left alone with them. The house will be awash with Scalextric and Sindy's Magic Castle, and Tom and Chloe will be glued to the adult channel.'

'Is there still no news about the Derby ride?' Maddy squeezed Fran's arm. 'Is he still down in the dumps about it?'

'Down and staying down. Not even the fact that he did so well at the Guineas meeting can lift him, mainly because Luke won the blue riband on Saratoga – the bastard.' She sighed. 'I don't really mean that. I know it isn't Luke's fault, but there's really no time at all before The Derby, and the papers are already full of Saratoga being the hottest favourite for years – with the hottest jockey.'

'That's Suzy's opinion of him, definitely.' Maddy grinned. 'I haven't spoken to Diana yet – she's not been at home when I've been cleaning – but now Bronwyn has volunteered me to plead the cause for the spinney I might as well mention the Derby ride.'

'Don't bother.' Fran unlocked her car. 'It's sweet of you to offer, Mad, but there really isn't any point. Richard is just going to have to face it. Anyway, if Diana is having an affair with Mitchell D'Arcy, I can't see anything changing her mind.' She slid into the driving seat. 'You go and have a drink for me, and enjoy yourselves. Don't worry about The Derby or the bloody golf course tonight. Just enjoy yourselves.' Fran

99

started the car and leaned from the window. 'I still think you're playing with fire, Mad. You know that. But I'm your friend – I'm pretty good at bandaging burnt fingers.'

She drove away with a wave, and Drew unlocked the Mercedes. 'Will you risk a drink at the Cat and Fiddle, or is that stretching the friendship too far?'

'To breaking point, but what the heck.' Maddy climbed into the passenger seat. 'We've been seen together all evening, I don't see what harm it'll do.'

They drove along the wet road in convoy, everyone else having the same idea. Maddy was pleased that Fran and Richard's marriage seemed to be back on an even keel. They had always been her rock, her little bit of stability, in their togetherness. It had upset her dreadfully to witness the anger and bitterness at her party.

Her own proposed confrontation with Diana and Gareth made her squirm. She wasn't looking forward to it. Naturally peaceable, she disliked any sort of argument, and Diana was going to argue about the spinney, she knew she was. If Bronwyn Pugh had grasped the right end of the stick, and Diana was embroiled in some sort of relationship with Peter Knightley, then it was going to be nearly impossible. And she was sure she'd caught the vibes of something between them at that drinks party . . . But would Diana be playing fast and loose with Peter *and* Mitchell D'Arcy?

'You're very quiet.' Drew steered the Mercedes expertly into a gap in the Cat and Fiddle's car park. 'Are you having second thoughts?'

'And thirds and fourths. But not about this.' She smiled at him. 'We both deserve this.'

The pub was packed but they managed to find a table poked away in the corner at the furthest end from the juke box. Drew bought her a double whisky.

'Are my drinking habits that renowned?'

'You seemed to enjoy it at your party.' Drew drank half his beer in one draught. 'Maddy, will you come out with me?'

She looked around the Cat and Fiddle. 'We are out.'

'Out. Properly. For a meal, or to the theatre or the cinema.'

'A date?' She giggled through the whisky. 'You're asking me for a date?'

'Yes, I suppose I am. Don't laugh.'

'I'm not. Not at you. Just at the idea. I haven't been asked out on a date for, oh, years. Not since university.'

'But surely, Peter Knightley . . .'

'He never actually asked me out. We were sort of together. We went out together. He didn't ask me.'

'And since then?'

'No one.' Maddy shook her head. 'Honestly. In the last year I've thrown myself into Shadows and no one has asked me out – and if they had I wouldn't have gone.'

'Why?' Drew had emptied his glass.

'Because I had to prove to myself that I could be a person on my own. It was important. I'd gone from being looked after at home, to being chivvied around at college, and then straight into the relationship with Peter. I'd never been allowed to be me.'

'And now you are. And making a bloody good job of it. So, will you come out with me?'

'No.'

Drew stood up, picking up the glasses. 'I'm going to get refills. I want your answer by the time I come back.'

'I've just given you my answer—' She stopped as he leaned over the table towards her. 'Drew, don't – not in here . . .'

He kissed her. As his hands were occupied with the glasses, the whole weight of his body seemed to be balanced on his lips. Neither of them closed their eyes.

'When I come back.' He straightened up and edged his way to the bar. Maddy gulped. He was absolutely lethal. She cast furtive glances round the pub, but in the shoving, pushing, smoky haze, no one seemed to have noticed that Maddy Beckett had just been wildly turned on by a married man.

'You're smirking,' she accused him as he sat down again. 'And is that another double?'

'I'm not and it is. So, what's your answer?'

'Still no.'

'Why? Because I'm married?'

'Exactly. For God's sake, Drew. You know what you do to me. If we went out together—'

'I cross my heart that the evening wouldn't end up in bed.'

She sat and stared at him. To spend an evening with him would be bliss. To leave him alone at the end of that evening would be impossible . . .

'Maddy! Drew! Just the people!' Kimberley towered over the table. Maddy heard Drew's groan and wondered if Kimberley had. 'Splendid meeting, wasn't it?' Obviously Kimberley hadn't. 'Let's hope we can stymie the blighters. If Bronwyn can do her stuff with the Maynards and you can use your influence with Diana and Gareth, I reckon we'll have Peter Knightley and his confounded golf course on the run.'

Drew stood up, offering Kimberley his chair. She shook her head, smiling at him girlishly. She obviously still had a major crush on him.

'No, I won't stop. I just popped across to invite you to a little function I'm having. Oh, nothing lavish like Diana and the others put on. That's not my style, as you well know, Maddy. But I thought I'd have a barbecue. Well, I'm doing bloody nothing with my horses because of the damned virus, and everyone else is so busy. I thought next Wednesday evening . . . providing that it doesn't rain of course.' She laughed loudly. 'If it does we'll all be huddled together in my lean-to! Will that suit?'

Maddy said that it would suit very well, and Drew nodded his thanks. Kimberley beamed. 'Super, then. I'll pencil you in.'

Drew waited until she had powered her way across the pub to rejoin Barty and the other trainers who were doing serious drinking propped against the bar, then took Maddy's hands in his.

'Maddy Beckett, spinster of this parish, would you consider it an affront to your maidenly virtue if I asked to escort you to Kimberley's barbecue?'

'And no bed afterwards?'

'Jesus, Maddy. You know how to bring a man to his knees, don't you?' Drew was grinning. 'Very well, and no bed afterwards.'

'Then I'd love to.'

Drew stopped the car outside her cottage. It was in darkness. The rain had faded into a misty drizzle. She turned to him. 'Thanks. It was a lovely evening. I really hope we'll be able to stop the golf course.'

'So do I, though I'm surprised that Peter didn't turn up.'

'I'm not. Peter hates confrontation. He'll be working away in the background, greasing palms and offering sweetners. Peter would have been very embarrassed to have the village baying at him like a pack of wolves.'

'Not to mention the contingent from Twyford Down and Bath, or the Newbury tree-hugger.'

They laughed together at the memory, then Drew stopped. 'So your fight against the golf course isn't a personal one, then?'

'No. I would have opposed it whoever was behind it. In a way it makes it more awkward because it's Peter and Stacey. What about you?'

'Deeply personal.'

'I thought it might be.' Maddy opened the door and stepped out. 'Come on, then.'

'What?' Drew ducked his head down to look at her.

'I'm inviting you in for coffee. That's the way it goes, isn't it?'

'God knows.' He shut the door. 'I'm as rusty on these things as you are. In my youth, being asked in for coffee was a gold star invitation, as I recall.'

'Well, this isn't your youth – or mine – and we're not in the carnal wilds of Jersey. Anyway, you've been in for coffee before.

And I'll scream for the neighbours if you step out of line.'

'I am the neighbours.'

Maddy unlocked the front door with a grin. 'So you are. I won't have to scream very loud then, will I? Go through to the sitting-room. I won't be a tick.'

When she carried the mugs through, Drew was lounging on the sofa between two piles of washing.

'God! Sorry!' She put the mugs on the floor and scrabbled the clothes into a bundle. 'I'll just get rid of these.'

She curled beside Drew on the sofa. It was very intimate with the soft glow of the standard lamp. As usual, this intimacy lasted less than a millisecond. The door crashed open and Suzy, wearing a T-shirt emblazoned with 'Luke Delaney Rides Winners – I'm A Winner', stood in the doorway.

'I thought I heard you. Hello, Drew. Am I interrupting anything?'

'Just coffee, unfortunately. I like your hair.'

'Ta. I had it done in Newmarket. Out of my winnings. What do you reckon, Mad?'

Maddy surveyed the white-blonde crop, brushed smoothly around Suzy's elfin face.

'It looks lovely – better than the spikes – and I like the colour. How many bottles of bleach did it take?'

'Oh, masses. Luke thinks it makes me look sexy.'

'Luke would think anything made you look sexy. Where is he, anyway? He's not, um, in the bedroom?'

'Nah, unfortunately. Still in Newmarket. I got back about an hour ago.'

'And you've been on the phone for an hour?'

'How did you guess? Actually, I didn't come charging in here to louse up your love-life. I came to give you this. It was on the mat when I got in. I thought it might be important.'

Maddy took the envelope with a sinking heart. It just said 'Maddy – Urgent' on the front in a bold black scrawl. She looked at Drew.

'It's from Peter.'

Ten

'Holy hell, Mad.' Suzy pulled a face. 'I didn't know it was from Pete the Perv else I wouldn't've given it to you – not while Drew was here.'

'It's OK.' Maddy tore open the expensive envelope. 'Drew and I don't have any secrets. Much.' She skimmed through the single sheet of paper and handed it to Drew.

'Well?' Suzy was hopping from foot to foot.

'He says he wants to talk to me. Re the golf course. Urgently.'

'And that's all?' Suzy wrinkled her nose. 'What a weirdo. Why couldn't he just ring like a normal person – and what does he think you can do anyway?'

'God knows.' Maddy took the note from Drew and scrumpled it into a ball. 'He probably wants as many people on his side as possible. He'll probably try the "for old times' sake" routine again.'

'So, will you contact him?' Drew picked up his coffee.

'No chance. I'm firmly on the side of Bronwyn and Bernie.'

'And Peanut.'

Suzy shook her head. 'You're both as crazy as each other. It must be senile dementia. Who the hell is Peanut?'

'Fran fancied him.'

'No she didn't,' Drew corrected. 'Fran fancied Sandra.'

'Jesus!' Suzy swung round in the doorway, displaying fingertip bruises polka-dotting her thigh. 'I'm going to bed, and if I have nightmares it'll be your fault.'

They sat grinning at each other while Suzy thundered around in the bathroom, then Drew picked up the discarded note. 'You really don't want to talk to him?'

'Of course not. It's typical of Peter to approach me like this. He thinks he can charm me like he used to. But he can't. I don't see what sort of influence I can wield, anyway. If he's got the might of Diana and Gareth, why the hell does he need me?'

'Because the village likes you.' Drew studied her face. 'Because they listen to you. You're far more part of them than the James-Jordans are. If you said that the golf course was a good idea they'd listen.'

'Oh, rubbish. No one listens to me.'

'Don't underestimate yourself, Maddy. Because you're kind and friendly and you listen to people, they listen back. Peter knows that probably better than most. He's not stupid. He knows that you could be very important.'

Drew stood up. 'I'd better go now. The alarm'll go off at five and it's getting fed up with being bounced off the walls. Anyway, this was part of the arrangement, wasn't it? Coffee and separate beds?'

She walked the few paces across the hall with him. Not, she told herself, to be able to cling to him romantically in the doorway, but she had to be there to free the hall rug.

Suzy's bedroom light was on. Michael Bolton had replaced AC/DC. Suzy was seriously in love.

'So?' He turned to her. 'You survived an evening in my company without the village tattooing "harlot" across your forehead. Congratulations.'

'I've enjoyed it. Very much.' She stared up into the wide tawny eyes. 'Good night, Drew.'

'Good night, Maddy.'

He kissed her demurely on the cheek, and turning the flying jacket's collar up against the gusting wind, hurried to the Mercedes. Maddy watched until the tail lights had been swallowed up by Peapods' drive, then dreamily closed the door.

*

The ringing of the phone pierced a very strange dream in which she and Kimberley were throwing golf clubs like spears at Fran and Bernie Pugh in some sort of Mad Max desolated landscape. She opened her eyes momentarily, registered that it was only just light, and hunched contentedly beneath the duvet again.

''S for you.' Suzy kicked the door open with a riding boot.''s Drew.'

'God.' Maddy sat up blinking, running her fingers through her hair. 'What time is it?'

'Half-five.' Suzy was munching a bacon sandwich. 'I'm just going to work – and you don't have to do your hair, Mad.'

She stumbled from the bed, pulling down the nightshirt that Suzy had given her last Christmas. It had a lascivious-looking rabbit on the front and the words 'Midnight Swinger' in purple along the hem. She picked up the discarded receiver.

'Drew? What's wrong?'

'Nothing.' His voice made her toes curl. 'I just wanted to say goodbye.'

Her heart stopped beating. She felt sick.

'Maddy? Are you still there? I'm leaving for Jersey in about an hour. I wanted you to know.'

She shook her head. This was even more awful than the spear-throwing nightmare.

'There was a message on my answering machine last night,' Drew continued, oblivious to her pain. 'I've got to go back straight away.'

'You can't—'

'I must. It's brilliant. Maddy, what's wrong?'

'Nothing. Are you selling Peapods?'

'What?' He was laughing. 'Maddy, I'm going back to meet with one of my owners for a few days. I didn't want you to think that I was avoiding you – I know how that feels.'

She missed the irony, clinging only to the 'few days'. You – you're coming back?'

'Of course I'm coming back. Probably the day after

tomorrow if all goes well. Kit Pedersen has got a horse he wants to run at Epsom. He wants me to bring it back. It's not going to be entered for The Derby of course, probably the Woodcote Stakes, but it'll be my first runner of the season and at Epsom.'

'Oh, Drew, that really is wonderful.'

'I'll be back for Kimberley's barbecue if I possibly can. If not, we'll have to fix another date.'

'And – and will Caroline come back with you?'

There was a silence. Then she heard him sigh. 'I honestly don't know. I wouldn't have thought so. She didn't think she'd get back over here until the middle of June at the earliest. Maddy, I'll have to go. I've got to drive to Southampton. I'll ring tonight.'

'Drew . . .' She swallowed. 'Take care of yourself.'

'You too.'

She replaced the receiver. She was missing him already.

The morning dragged. Maddy had polished muddy footprints from so many parquet floors that the novelty had worn off along with the grime. She didn't want to go back to the cottage for lunch. She had absolutely no appetite. If she didn't watch it she'd be pinching Suzy's Michael Bolton tape.

The rain had stopped and the puddles were evaporating in the combination of a brisk breeze and strong sunshine. Deciding to grasp the nettle, she pointed her bicycle in the direction of Diana and Gareth's yard. She'd almost reached the tunnel of lilac trees when a white Porsche swirled round the bend. Maddy wobbled. The car screeched to a halt.

'Maddy! Maddy! Just a minute.'

The car reversed until it was alongside her and she felt a surge of annoyance as Stacey beamed out of the window. 'Sorry if I startled you. I always drive too fast. I was just coming to see you.'

'Why?'

'We came round last night. Peter left you a note. He thought you'd call him first thing.'

'I can't imagine why.' Maddy, in her Oxfam jacket and leggings, her hair tied back with a scarf, felt ten stones heavier and twenty years older than the bimbo stick-insect in her bone-tight jeans and silk shirt.

'It was about the golf course.' Stacey pouted. 'Peter was ever so disappointed that you'd gone to the meeting.'

'For God's sake, Stacey. What Peter does or thinks is of no interest to me at all.'

'But it's so silly. I mean, what can a lot of old ducks do to stop it? And why should they want to? It'll make more jobs and bring in more money and—' Stacey had obviously been subjected to a huge dose of the Knightley rationale.

'I'm sorry,' Maddy interrupted, 'but I can't agree with you. I know Peter and your father are prepared to sink a lot of money into this, but Milton St John just doesn't need it. We're surrounded by golf courses, for heaven's sake. Tell Peter that I won't be changing sides, and the only reason I want to hear from him in the future is if he needs a quote from Shadows.'

'I think you're jealous.' Stacey fluttered her false eyelashes. 'You're doing it out of spite because Peter preferred me to you. I don't bear any grudges, Maddy, but you don't seem to be able to accept that he left you for me. I told Peter that you couldn't stand seeing us together. Especially now we've bought the Manor. After all, what have you got? A little cottage that you don't even own, and no man. I don't blame you for being just the teensiest bit jealous.'

Maddy had never hit anybody in her life – she had never even felt remotely stirred to raise a hand in anger – but at that moment she would have liked to have wrenched Stacey's head from her shoulders in a blood-letting that would have made Quentin Tarantino squirm.

'Don't bloody patronise me, you stupid child!' She clenched her handlebars until her knuckles were translucent. 'I'm not jealous of you, for God's sake! Peter and I were washed up – dead and buried – long before you shimmied your bloody kiddie-hips and your non-existent chest at him! Jealous? You must be joking! On the contrary – you have my deepest sympathy. You and Peter deserve one another. And –' she glared into the car – 'I hope you'll tell him so. You can also tell him not to contact me again, unless it's about work. And as you've probably discovered he's crap in bed. Tell him that, too. Goodbye.'

It was hardly the most dignified exit, wobbling away on a secondhand bicycle, but Maddy felt proud of herself. Her anger seethed so fiercely as she pedalled into the James-Jordans' drive, that she didn't even see Richard walking towards her.

'Jesus, Maddy!' Richard leapt out of the way just in time. 'Luke Delaney trying to destroy my future is bad enough – I don't need you to nobble me completely by breaking my legs!'

'God, sorry.' She dropped the bike. 'I wasn't concentrating. I've just had a shouting-match with Stacey.'

'In the street?' Richard sounded surprised. 'That's not your usual style. Fran does that kind of thing, not you.'

'I didn't stop to think. She just annoyed me. About the golf course. She said I was opposing it because I was jealous of her and Peter.'

'And you're not?'

'Of course I'm bloody not! Don't you start—' Just in time she saw that Richard was laughing and she grinned. 'Don't wind me up just because Suzy's walking out with Luke Delaney.'

'More lying in, I'd heard.'

Maddy picked up her bicycle and leaned it against the stable wall. 'Anyway, Stacey's put me in just the right frame of mind to scream at Diana about the spinney. Is she in?'

'I haven't seen her. Gareth's in the yard somewhere. We've been working Saratoga Sun. I'm still allowed to do that while Luke is otherwise engaged in Newmarket.'

'Oh, Richard.' Maddy was instantly sympathetic. 'It's a lousy situation. Maybe things will change. There's still time.'

'Not a hope.' Richard shrugged. 'I'm good enough to ride all Saratoga's work. Good enough to ride him to victory as a two-year-old. Good enough to look after him like he was my baby. But when it comes to The Derby it's Luke that will get his leg over.'

Maddy winced at the bitterness. Richard's usually sunny face was lined with anger, and there were dark shadows beneath his eyes. She wished there was something she could do.

'I'll try for you, you know that.'

'It's a complete waste of time. Gareth might be persuaded to change his mind, but then he's not having a fling with Mitchell D'Arcy, is he?'

'Doesn't he know?'

'He never knows about Diana's men – and if he did, what could he do? Diana owns the yard. Heck, Maddy, you're not going to tell him?'

'Of course not. For the same reason that you haven't. He's a nice man who would be very hurt. I did think at one time that I might be able to use it, but I don't think it would solve anything. Oh, bloody hell!' She looked at Richard. 'What are you down to ride in The Derby?'

'Jefferson Jet. He's pretty good, but nowhere near Saratoga. I would just love to win this year. It would mean that Fran and I could afford to start a family. She says it's OK, but she's thirty-seven. We can't really wait much longer . . . Oh, life's a shit!'

Maddy watched him climb into his car and felt helpless. Richard was probably right. Life was a shit. She was in love with a married man; her best friends' lives were being ruined by Diana's excesses; Peter Knightley was hell-bent on carving up the village; and the bimbo stick-insect felt sorry for her. Jesus!

'Hello, Maddy.' Gareth sauntered round the corner. 'Why the frown?'

'I was thinking about the meaning of life.'

'Oh dear. That sounds too profound for me.' Gareth pushed his trilby to the back of his head. 'Can I help?'

'I don't think so. Not unless you'll jock Luke off and put Richard up on Saratoga for The Derby.'

'No can do, my dear. I'm sorry. Mitchell is adamant. It has to be Luke Delaney. Bit of a bugger, really. Richard is a damned fine horseman. I'd be more than happy to see him ride. I don't doubt his ability. Still, next to the Arabs, Mitchell D'Arcy is the wealthiest owner around. Diana won't risk losing him.'

In more ways than one, Maddy thought sourly. 'Is Diana in? I need to speak to her anyway – well, to both of you, but I'd rather start with Diana.'

'Most people would.' He shrugged. 'Hell of a handicap having a bankrupt family and being totally reliant on my wife. I'm lucky that we've got such a strong marriage. God knows what I'd do without her.'

Maddy gave a small smile. 'Can I talk to her?'

'If you can find her. I've just come back from the gallops with Richard. Her car is outside so she must be around somewhere. Go and have a look, my dear. I'm going down to the Cat and Fiddle for some serious drinking.'

Waiting until Gareth had ambled out of sight, Maddy walked up to the brass-studded door and pulled the bell. There was no reply, so she stepped into the hall. 'Diana?' Silence. Just the ticking of the grandmother clock. She called again. The house was empty. 'Damn.' And just when she'd stiffened the sinews and summoned the courage, too.

She sighed. Stacey's words still rankled. She was in the mood for a confrontation. Maybe Diana was in the office.

She removed her trainers in the hall – there was no point in making extra work for herself come Tuesday – and ran up the twisting staircase. Diana's office was at the end of the minstrels' gallery, tucked away out of sight. Gareth worked downstairs in full view of all visitors. Diana was more selective, and also more secretive. She quite often had her office door locked, and when Maddy had enquired about cleaning it, had been told not to bother, Diana would give a little flick round when necessary. She and Fran reckoned Diana had got a selection of the Chippendales stashed away in the filing cabinets.

'Diana? Are you up here?' There was still no reply. She was just about to retrace her steps when the faintest noise made her pause. There was somebody in the office.

'Great. I'll beard the lioness in her den, always supposing she'll open the door.' But the door wasn't locked. The handle turned silently. The door swung open on well-oiled hinges. Maddy's jaw dropped.

She'd have recognised that bum anywhere. Neat and tight muscled, with a star-shaped mole just above the cleft. She'd seen it plenty of times. Likewise the caramel-coloured tanned body; the even coloration screaming 'sun-bed'. She even recognised the athletic thrust.

What she didn't recognise was Diana. Spreadeagled on the desk beneath Peter, Diana was stark naked except for a pair of riding boots. She had a birthmark on her thigh, and her eyes were tightly closed. Her head threshed from side to side in time with the thrusts. Maddy knew she was faking.

Biting her lips, she stepped outside and pulled the door closed as silently as she'd opened it. Her blush was all over, and her first coherent thought was one of pity for Gareth. She didn't give a thought to Stacey. Stacey deserved it.

She took a deep breath and leaned back against the linen fold panels. It was like holding four aces – the trouble being that she didn't have a clue how to play them. If she was the nice well-brought-up girl that her mother hoped she was, she would creep away downstairs and pedal home and never mention it again. If she was a conniving bitch who desperately wanted to lever both Diana and Peter Knightley into complying with her wishes, she'd pick up the camera which was always in the cupboard along the landing with field glasses and spare mackintoshes, and happily blackmail the pair of them. But Maddy was neither of these things.

She smiled and opened the door again. Peter was still thrusting. Diana had given up the pretence and had her eyes open.

'Get out!' Diana sat up so quickly that Peter almost slid from the desk. 'Get out!'

She turned wild eyed to Peter, and screamed, 'I told you to lock that fucking door!'

Peter, totally confused, grabbed a sheaf of paper to cover his nakedness, and gawped at Maddy in the doorway.

'Don't worry about me,' she said quietly. 'I've seen it all before.'

Diana was struggling into her eau-de-Nil skirt and cream shirt, stumbling as she did so. 'Fuck off!' she shrieked at Maddy. 'What the fucking hell do you think you're doing?'

'Looking for you, actually. Gareth told me to come in.'

'Gareth?'

'Your husband.' Maddy continued to smile. 'Remember?'

'Of course I know who bloody Gareth is. I mean, where is he? He's supposed to be up on the gallops.'

'He was. He isn't now.' Maddy wondered if she could push it any further but decided against it. 'I'll, er, wait downstairs, shall I?'

'Just get out!' Diana was trying to kick off the riding boots. 'Go away! How dare you!'

Peter had put his trousers on inside-out and wouldn't meet Maddy's eyes as he staggered about the office.

She smiled. 'So sorry to have disturbed you. It was obviously an inopportune moment. I'll be back.' And leaving two frantic faces behind her, she quietly closed the door.

Running downstairs, she felt violently sick. God, she'd have to go into the cloakroom and throw up. She clapped her hands over her mouth. She only hoped she'd make it.

She did. Just. She splashed icy water on her face and leaned back amongst the shelves of books and bottles, gulping for air. Peter and Diana . . . Oh, God.

Feeling shaky, she opened the cloakroom door. There was no sound from upstairs. She'd never be able to face either of them again.

'Hi! Di, Baby! Are you at home?'

A shadow loomed in the arch of the front door. Maddy shrank back into the cloakroom, but just a fraction too late. The shadow stepped into the hall and became reality.

'Hi. I'm Mitchell D'Arcy. Saratoga Sun's owner – or perhaps you know that. Are you staff?'

'I'm, er, the cleaner . . .' Maddy gasped, shaking the out-stretched hand. 'Maddy Beckett.'

Mitchell D'Arcy lifted her hand to his lips and kissed it. Maddy prayed it didn't smell of sick.

'Nice to meet you. Is Di at home?'

'No . . . yes . . . I'm not sure. Was she expecting you?'

'No.' Mitchell D'Arcy smiled a smile that was the epitome of cosmetic dentistry. 'I was supposed to be in Newmarket. I think I might come as a bit of a shock.'

'Oh, a pleasant one, I'm sure.' Maddy wondered how many shocks Diana could take in one afternoon. 'If she was in, that is . . . which she isn't, I don't think.'

Mitchell D'Arcy nodded. He was very dashing, in a gangsterish sort of way. Little bits of him glinted in the sunlight: the exceptionally white teeth, the heavy gold orna-ments on his tie and cuffs, the chunky bracelets on each wrist.

Maddy backed away. 'I'll be on my way, then.'

'Tell you what, poppet . . .' Mitchell D'Arcy had the mid-Atlantic voice of a disc jockey. 'You couldn't just run and check her out for me, could you? I'm on a bit of a tight schedule, and if she's not at home I won't hang around.'

'Um – well, Gareth's in the village,' Maddy gulped. 'If you wanted to discuss Saratoga, that is. I'm sure he won't be long.'

Mitchell D'Arcy shook his head, grinning dazzlingly. 'No, I don't want to see Gareth, Marnie, poppet.'

'Maddy.' She was feeling truculent now. 'I'll just go and see if Di, er, Diana's upstairs, shall I?'

'Yeah, sure. I'll wait here.'

Maddy walked slowly up the stairs, hoping that Diana and Peter had got their clothes sorted out by this time. They met halfway along the minstrels' gallery.

'Get out,' Diana snarled. 'Stop prowling around my house. Just go home. Now!'

Peter grinned sheepishly.

'Mitchell D'Arcy's downstairs.' Maddy looked at Diana's feet. The riding boots had been replaced by a pair of pale kidskin Adriano Rizzos. 'He thinks I'm staff. He sent me to find you.'

'Jesus Christ!' Diana fluffed at her hair. 'What did you tell him?'

'Nothing of course. What do you want me to tell him?'

'Nothing.' Diana's lips were snapping open and shut like a frenzied gin trap. 'I'll see him.'

Maddy turned tail and trooped downstairs again with Diana and Peter behind her. Mitchell D'Arcy was looking very Rhett Butlerish leaning on the newel post.

'Here she is!' Maddy said brightly, sounding like Joyce Grenfell. 'She was here all the time!'

'Di – angel!' Mitchell D'Arcy pulled Diana against his Jean-Paul Gaultier jacket. 'I thought I'd missed you.'

'I was just, er, discussing some village business with Mr Knightley.' Diana indicated Peter. 'Let me introduce you. Mr Knightley lives in the Manor, and he's involved in a business project that I'm backing.'

Peter and Mitchell D'Arcy were shaking hands. Maddy smiled sweetly at Diana. 'As you're so busy, our little talk can wait, Diana. No doubt I'll see you again soon. Goodbye, Mr D'Arcy, Peter . . .'

Diana and Peter glared. Mitchell D'Arcy beamed. 'Bye, then, Marnie. It was nice to meet you.'

Maddy was humming happily as she removed her bicycle from the stable block. It was a song from Suzy's Michael Bolton tape. Maybe life wasn't such a shit after all.

Eleven

Kimberley phoned to discuss the barbecue, Fran called round for coffee, Suzy drifted in and out of the cottage, but Maddy told no one about Peter and Diana. The loveless coupling had disturbed her deeply.

She had done her Tuesday stint at Diana's only after serious deliberation. She had considered asking Jackie to take over, not wanting to face either Diana or Gareth, but luckily neither was at home.

'Gone to Newmarket,' Belinda, their secretary told her. 'A spying trip to the Heath as far as I know. That unpronounceable horse of Henry Cecil's is threatening to take some beating in The Derby according to the *Sporting Life*. I think they want to make sure that Saratoga is still number one.'

Without Drew to talk to, Maddy mooched aimlessly round the cottage, picking things up and putting them down, and spending ages just staring out of the window at Peapods. If Drew had been there she would have told him about the scene in Diana's study. She would have made it funny for him and they would have laughed. It was the laughter she missed. The laughter and talking and the sharing. She sighed. Her happily rounded contentment had a huge chunk missing.

By Wednesday, the day of Kimberley's barbecue, Drew still hadn't returned home.

'I'll try to get everything arranged for tomorrow,' he'd told her. 'It's just some delay in shipping the horse. I'll be there if I can, you know that.' He hadn't said he'd missed her, and she hadn't asked about Caroline.

'Luke's going to try and get here tonight for the barbie.' Suzy danced round the hall in her knickers. 'He's riding in the last race at Lingfield – so's Richard. He's going to try and beg a lift in the helicopter.'

'Richard'll throw him out over the M25,' Maddy grinned. 'There must be a safer way for him to travel.'

'He'll never make it in time if he drives, though. It's OK if he stays here tonight and goes back in the morning, isn't it?'

'Is he riding tomorrow?'

'Yeah, at Brighton. He can fly back. Emilio won't mind.'

Emilio Marquez was Luke's trainer. Burstingly proud of his stable jockey, he allowed Luke to get away with murder.

'OK.' Maddy disappeared into the bathroom. 'But if Luke doesn't make it tonight, we'll know what happened, won't we? You'll have to start looking for bits of him along the Surrey border.'

She managed to close the door just before Suzy hurled the hairdryer at it. At least if Luke didn't turn up he'd have death as an excuse. Drew would only have his wife.

It was such a glorious evening that Maddy decided to walk to Kimberley's. She fell into step with the Pughs just at the corner of the main road where it lurched unsteadily towards the gurgling stream.

'Any joy with Diana and Gareth?' Bronwyn strode so briskly that Maddy had to jog to keep up. 'Have you mentioned it to them? About Goddards Spinney?'

'No. There hasn't been the opportunity yet.' She blushed. 'How about you with the Maynards.'

'Old Bert Maynard is digging his toes in,' Bronwyn growled. 'Silly old sod. They've offered him a six-figure sum for the orchard. And of course, now we're only supposed to be buying French apples, his profits have been practically nothing for the last two years. You can't blame him, I suppose. Mind, his sons aren't so sure. They want to keep the orchard, as it's their inheritance, and grow English apples for an English market. For once, the younger generation seems to have more sense than the older one.'

'Bert's the one we've got to persuade, though.' Bernie trotted on the other side of Maddy, surreptitiously glancing at her cleavage. She'd ransacked her wardrobe and found a pale blue top that tied at the waist. She'd worn it with the baggy black trousers. It had the same uplifting effect as a Wonderbra. 'The Maynard boys say they'll come along to the next meeting. I hope we haven't started a family feud.'

'I hope we have.' Bronwyn's voice was fervent. 'I can see it all slipping away from us. Maybe you could speak to Diana tonight, Maddy.'

'She won't be there, will she?' Maddy was horrified. It hadn't occurred to her that Diana would attend anything quite so 'council estate' as a barbecue.

'Oh, she's bound to be. She's got Mitchell D'Thing as a house guest, so the grapevine says. Brought him back from Newmarket last night. She'll have to find some way of entertaining him.'

Oh, God, Maddy thought, having a sudden vision of the form of entertainment Diana would provide. Maybe she'd stay at home with Mitchell D'Arcy and send Gareth to the barbecue alone.

They turned the corner and crossed the cattle grid at the end of Kimberley's drive. There were cars everywhere, and a thin plume of smoke from the rear of the house indicated the barbecue was well under way. Barty Small, his trilby replaced by a Panama, was ladling out drinks from a trestle table.

'There's fruit punch with gin, fruit punch with vodka, fruit punch with brandy, fruit punch with rum,' he recited, indicating four massive cauldrons awash with fruit salad.

They opted for the rum, and Barty dipped three Ovaltiney mugs into the cauldron with a grubby hand.

'Fran's here, Richard isn't.' He winked at Maddy. 'There'll be fireworks later when he shows up, you mark my words. I've saved him some special gin under the counter. Get him nicely fired up. Then he can have his say with Diana and D'Arcy, can't he?'

'Do you think that's a good idea?'

'Look,' Barty leaned forward across the cauldrons, 'I've always maintained that the owner has the final say. It's always been the case. But Fran works for me and it breaks my heart to see her so upset. I don't reckon there's much to choose between Richard and Luke, and playing it straight hasn't helped so far, has it? All on your own tonight, then?'

'Not exactly.' Maddy gave a little laugh. 'I'm with lots of people in general and no one in particular.'

Luckily, the queue behind was growing restive, and Barty had to dive back to his cauldrons. He fingered the Panama. 'I might catch up with you later.'

Maddy was still smiling as she walked quickly away. Were things really so bad that she'd end the evening fighting off Barty Small? He'd been married three times already. His wives had all sued for divorce on the grounds of exhaustion.

The Pughs had disappeared into the mêlée, and Maddy hung back, breathing in the scents of the lilac trees and the shadowy chestnuts with their waxy candles spiked against the flaxflower sky. Kimberley's garden was like a country cottage explosion, with tumbles of old-fashioned flowers, tunnels of towering bean sticks, and honeysuckle-covered trellises surrounding the lawn. Kimberley refused to employ a gardener, and apart from the horses, it was her only passion. Maddy loved it.

She wanted Drew with her to share the pleasure. There was something so sexy about the smell of the charcoaling food mingling with the rich soapy perfume of the garden.

Kimberley, munching a hot-dog, strode across the lawn towards her. Maddy smiled. 'You look nice. What a lovely outfit.'

Kimberley had made an effort. She was a generous and popular hostess, but very rarely dressed up, and was barely recognisable now in a pair of navy trousers and a long white overshirt with her shoulder-length bobbed hair caught back in a navy and white scarf.

'Ta. I thought it was about time I spoiled myself,' she said. 'And you look super, too. We're both very done up tonight. Er, are you alone? Drew not with you?'

Maddy shook her head. Kimberley had probably dressed up for Drew. As she had. 'He said he thought he'd be back some time today, but there have been delays with the horse he's bringing over.'

'He'll have to be getting himself a stable jockey, unless he's going to employ freelancers.' Kimberley swallowed the remains of the hot-dog. 'He could do worse than Charlie Somerset for his jumpers, especially now old Pettigrove is retiring. I must mention it to Drew.'

'Yes, do.' Maddy wasn't really listening. She had just spotted Peter and Stacey through a gap in the roses. 'I'm sure he'd be interested. Kimberley, will you excuse me?'

'Yes, of course. And Maddy, if Drew does turn up, you will ask him to talk to me, won't you? About Charlie Somerset, of course?'

Poor Kimberley, Maddy thought sadly. Like the overgrown schoolgirl she was, she wore her heart on her sleeve. She dived behind the honeysuckle. Peter was wearing the cream trousers again. She hoped Drew would turn up. They could laugh about it. Stacey, with her blonde curls on top of her head like a poodle, was wearing a white mini-skirt and a black top that ended just beneath her non-existent chest. Maddy didn't want to face either of them.

Ducking down, she made her way round the outside of the lawn and reached the barbecue through a gap in the runner-bean sticks. Several people looked at her in surprise as she emerged, picking bits of twig out of her hair.

''ello, Maddy!' Brenda yelled, clutching hold of a curly-haired child in each hand. 'You been doing a spot of gardening?'

'I got a bit lost. Are you in charge of the food?'

'Me an' Elaine,' Brenda beamed, letting go of the children just long enough to run a vicious knife expertly through a dozen rolls. 'Watcha want to eat?'

'Oh, nothing, thanks.' The fried onions were making Maddy's mouth water, but she couldn't risk them. 'I'll get something later. There seems to be plenty.'

'Loads,' said Brenda. 'You know Kimberley, she don't stint 'erself.'

There were rows of sausages and burgers, chicken legs and steaks, salmon and tuna, all shimmering deliciously over the red-hot glow, and three side tables piled with salads, pickles and breads. Maddy's stomach rumbled.

'Oh look, there's Peter and Stacey.' Brenda nodded her perm over Maddy's shoulder. 'They're all got up like dog's dinners, aren't they, Maddy? I said—'

But Maddy, feeling like an extra in a Carry On film, had dived back into the runner-bean tunnel.

'Jesus! Where did you come from?' Barty Small nearly tumbled into the fruit punch and gin cauldron in surprise as Maddy emerged from the herbaceous border behind him. 'Not trying to queue-jump, are you?'

She shook her head. 'I had no idea that Kimberley's garden was like a maze. Did you know that there are little paths through all the flower beds?'

'Old Mrs Weston, Kimberley's mother, had them put in.' Barty ladled out a dozen rum punches into a selection of Tom and Jerry beakers held out by Diana's stable lads. 'She was a right old devil. She used to use one lot of paths to ferry her lovers into the house, and the other lot to avoid her creditors.' He turned back to the bemused youngsters in front of him. 'There you are, lads. That'll make you big and strong. Although you don't want to be too big, do you, else you'll be out of a job.'

He roared with laughter at his own wit, and the crowd around the table tittered with him. He must have been helping himself liberally all evening. Maddy thought, as she accepted a refill. The punch was very strong. Another mugful and she might just be able to take on Diana . . .

She wandered back towards the main lawn by the conventional route. It was a truly glorious evening, with not a breath of wind, and a still-strong sun shining low in the west. The mingled scents of food and flowers was now a voluptuous assault on the senses. It seemed as if the whole of Milton St John was partying on Kimberley's lawn. Maddy sipped the punch through a tidal wave of fruit salad. Was she brave enough – or, come to that, nasty enough – to blackmail Diana over the golf course? Could she really use her knowledge of her affair with Peter to persuade her to change her mind? Could she do anything at all without hurting Gareth? She wished Drew was here. Drew would know what to do.

'Maddy!' Fran forced her way through a munching bunch of burger-eaters. 'I've been looking for you everywhere. You haven't seen Richard yet, have you?' Maddy shook her head. Fran was grinning. 'I went into the bookie's to watch the last race at Lingfield on SIS. Richard won! It was brilliant.'

'Richard often wins races.'

'Yes, but, he beat Luke Delaney in a photo finish. You could almost see them snarling at each other. Thank God there's going to be at least a hundred miles between them tonight. Maddy, what's up?'

'Luke was going to beg a ride in the helicopter tonight.'

'The same helicopter that Richard . . ?'

'He probably didn't,' Maddy said hopefully. 'If the atmosphere was that bad between them he wouldn't risk it – would he?'

'Christ knows. What's the penalty for a punch-up in a helicopter?'

'Death, probably.'

'Cheers.'

They lapsed into silence. They were like two women at the pit-head after a mining disaster, Maddy thought hazily, neither of them knowing if their man would return safely.

Except, of course, that her man was somebody else's.

'Good God! Is that Suzy?' Fran squinted across the lawns. 'What on earth is she wearing?'

'It's called a dress.' Maddy peered. 'Is Luke with her?'

'No. Not that I can see. Suzy doesn't wear dresses . . .'

'She does now she's in love.' Maddy smiled fondly at her sister, fleetingly visible across the crowded garden. Suzy was wearing a red and white polka-dot dress that skimmed the top of her thighs. She was also wearing the red Doc Martens. With her newly bleached elfin hair-do she looked like a young Paula Yates.

Fran screwed her eyes up against the bright evening sun. 'I can see at least two of everybody. What has Kimberley put in this stuff?'

'No idea,' Maddy took another mouthful, 'but I'm praying that it loosens inhibitions. Bronwyn's relying on me to talk to Diana about Goddards Spinney.'

She drained her beaker and placed it upside down on a gnome. She'd come back for it later. Right now she was going to speak to Diana while the punch still pumped valour through her veins.

'Wish me luck.'

'I'd come with you to hold the handbags,' Fran said, 'but I've left Chloe and Tom with Brenda and Elaine's kids and they've probably disembowelled each other. Catch you later.'

Maddy picked her way through the villagers who were lying about the lawn in untidy heaps. The punch had made everyone extremely friendly. Maddy hoped Diana would have drunk a gallon of it before she reached her.

Richard suddenly appeared through the lupin border and Maddy felt a surge of relief. At least he was OK. She waved. 'Fran's over there with the kids. By the barbie. Congratulations on your win.'

Richad threaded his way through the throng. His lip was swollen and he had the beginnings of a black eye. Maddy's heart sunk.

'I hate him!' Richard winced. 'Luke Delaney is a shit!'

'He did that to you? In the helicopter?' Maddy was beginning to panic. If Luke had violent tendencies would Suzy be safe?

Richard shook his head again. It was agony to watch. 'I wish he had. I could have floored the bastard. No, I tripped on the step getting out.'

Maddy was very relieved. 'So why are you so angry? If he didn't hit you?'

'He helped me up!' Richard exploded. 'I had to say fucking thank you!'

Twelve

The bacchanalian revelry roared on. Everyone was hugging everyone else and agreeing that it was Kimberley's best party ever. The sun was setting over the Downs, smearing the sky with pink and orange. Drew wasn't coming.

Maddy, wanting to be alone just for a moment to let this awful truth sink in, rounded the lilacs and came face to face with Diana.

'Maddy! Darling!' Diana's brittle smile didn't reach her eyes. 'Lovely to see you!'

Maddy gave an inward groan. Gareth looked at her down his long nose and grinned. He'd obviously had more than one helping of the punch. He was wearing a sprig of lilac in his buttonhole that reached just under his ear. Mitchell D'Arcy, completely overdone in heavy jewellery for such an informal occasion, gave a small frown and then a toothpaste adman's dream of a smile.

'Marnie! Nice to see you again.'

Maddy twitched her face in reply.

Diana put an elegant, scarlet-nailed hand on her arm, 'A little word, Maddy . . .'

Oh, shit, Maddy thought, she's going to sack me. Even with the new contract at Peapods she couldn't afford to lose Diana's business. Shadows ran at a profit – just – but Diana was one of her best customers. She was damned if she was going to beg Peter and Stacey if she could scrub the floor at the Manor.

'In private, Maddy.' The scarlet nails had dug their pointed tips into Maddy's arm. Diana threw a laugh carelessly across her shoulder. 'Won't be a moment, boys.'

Gareth beamed. Mitchell looked a little puzzled. Diana practically dragged Maddy back into the bushes.

'I think we have to say this now, don't we?' Diana's teeth were almost as white as Mitchell's. They must share the same dentist, Maddy thought. 'What do you want from me?'

'Nothing . . . oh, well, Bronwyn did ask me to speak to you about Goddards Spinney. To see if you'd reconsider your decision to sell it to Peter and Jeff Henley for the golf course, but I'm sure we can talk about it some other time.'

'No, we can't.' Diana's eyes were like flint. 'We'll discuss this now. Once and for all. I don't want you skulking round my house – knowing what you know – threatening to spring it on me.'

'You mean, you still want me to work for you?'

'Of course I do,' Diana snapped. 'You're a damn good cleaner. Anyway, if I got rid of you I'd have to dredge up some excuse why – and I couldn't. And we've always been friends.' She tried to smile. It was a pretty good attempt under the circumstances. 'Maddy, you know better than anyone just how, er, persuasive Peter can be. We were discussing the golf course and we' – she gave a little laugh – 'just got carried away. Well, he's a very attractive man and he seems to find me irresistible. It was completely impromptu.'

So impromptu, Maddy thought, that you had time to remove everything and slip into a pair of handy riding boots. She looked at Diana. 'I don't want to talk about my relationship with Peter – or yours, come to that. All I need to know is whether you're prepared to change your mind about the golf course.'

'Absolutely not. We're going to be shareholders. It's what Milton St John needs. Something to give it a bit of class, for heaven's sake. I mean, Maddy, look at this tonight. A *barbecue*. It's so tacky. No, I'm firmly behind Peter on the golf course.'

'And under him on the desk.'

'Oh, well, if that's your attitude, I'm sorry, Maddy. You must do your worst – I will not budge.'

'You haven't even mentioned Gareth.'

Diana flicked at her cream jacket and laughed. 'Darling, Gareth wouldn't believe you in a million years. And I'm sure dear little Stacey wouldn't either if you told her. You can't prove anything. All I want is your assurance that you accept the incident for what it was. A couple of like-minded people who got carried away in the heat of the moment. Something you stumbled upon, and, as a lady, will not breathe a word about to anyone else.'

'Why should I keep quiet?' Maddy really didn't care very much about anything any more. 'And how can you be so sure that no one would believe me? Stacey's father, for instance.'

'Because, darling, you know exactly what Peter looks like in the buff. Everyone knows that. You couldn't prove a thing.'

Maddy had a sudden vision of Peter and Diana. Of Peter's all-over tan and the star-shaped mole. Of Diana's spreadeagled legs . . .

'Very true. But would either Gareth – or Mitchell D'Arcy –be interested in my description of the riding boots and that port wine stain just below your hip?'

Diana blanched and swayed. Maddy felt sorry for her. A thrush sang merrily just above them. Her lips tightened. 'You wouldn't? Not to Mitchell . . .?'

Maddy shook her head. She couldn't continue with this. She didn't want to hurt Diana. 'Oh, forget it. We'll carry on with the battle to save the spinney. I'll tell Bronwyn Pugh that you're still intending to sell it to Peter and Jeff Henley. I'll forget what I saw, and we won't mention it again. Is that what you want?'

'And you honestly won't say anything to Mitchell?'

She looked so terrified that Maddy wanted to hug her. She must really love Mitchell D'Arcy. Maddy, hurting from loving Drew so much, felt nothing but sympathy. 'No. I'll leave that to you.'

'What?' Diana frowned. 'If you know I won't give up the sale of the spinney, I don't know what else you think I can do . . . oh! Yes, of course. That won't be a problem. Thank you, Maddy – oh, yes, thank you!' And kissing Maddy's cheek she almost skipped out of the lilac bushes.

Maddy followed, not understanding. The whole situation was bizarre. She felt that she was in a play and had got the wrong script. Still, Diana seemed more cheerful, and she wasn't going to sack her, so she must have said the right thing somewhere.

Gareth was ambling away towards the bar, and Diana had linked her arm through Mitchell's. She smiled brightly, and tapped the side of her nose. 'Mitchell and I will just go and have a little talk while Gareth's getting some more drinks.'

'See you around, Marnie.' Mitchell glinted, snuggling up to Diana.

Maddy stood forlornly in the middle of the merriment. Kimberley was talking to Barty; Bernie and Bronwyn were deep in discussion by the rose border; Richard and Fran, with Tom and Chloe hanging on to their hands, were laughing with a group of jockeys by the rockery; Suzy was chatting animatedly with John Hastings. Even Stacey and Peter were smiling, although Peter's smile was wary. Everybody had somebody.

'Do you want a drink, Maddy?' Charlie Somerset, jump jockey and ladykiller, was grinning at her. 'Or are you waiting for someone?'

'No. I'm just sort of milling.'

Charlie was wearing grubby white jeans and a navy shirt, and his hair was the colour of a fox's pelt. He and Suzy had fallen on each other when she'd first arrived in Milton St John. Maddy liked him.

'I'd love a drink, thanks.' She fell into step beside him. 'I think Kimberley was aiming to champion your cause tonight.'

'Yeah, with Drew. Shame he hasn't turned up. Kimberley said she'd mention that I'd like to ride for him next season.' He paused. 'Rumour has it that you and Mr Fitzgerald are doing a number.'

'Goodness, no!' Maddy laughed. She was becoming so adept at hiding her true feelings. Except, of course, with Drew – and, unfortunately, Caroline. 'We're just friends. He's married.'

'So?' Charlie grinned, showing crooked teeth that had all been chipped by collisions with hurdles across the country. 'Since when has that been a handicap in this place?'

Maddy grinned back. Charlie had been to bed with nearly every female over sixteen in the village. With the exception of her and probably, although it was by no means definite, Bronwyn.

He shouldered his way expertly through to the bar and returned with two brimming Batman beakers. He took a mouthful of punch. 'Hell's teeth! This must be a hundred per cent proof. No wonder Kimberley manages to stay so cheerful. She ought to give it to her horses – that would stop them coughing.'

'It'd probably stop them breathing.' Maddy's eyes were watering. 'What's this one supposed to be?'

'Gin, Barty said. With a fruit base . . .' He fished into his beaker and produced a piece of apple. 'This must be it.'

It really wasn't that funny, but overcome by the mixture of drinks and desolation about Drew, Maddy began to giggle. Charlie laughed with her, slipping his free arm around her shaking shoulders.

'So sorry to break up the party.' Drew's voice would have sliced through the Rock of Gibraltar. 'Charlie, when you're free, could I have a word?'

'Oh, yeah, sure.' Charlie slowly disentangled himself, letting his fingertips slide idolently over Maddy's breasts.

Stunned by Drew's arrival, Maddy's mouth dropped open. 'When, er, I mean, how long have you been here?'

'Long enough.' Drew's brows were drawn together. 'I was looking for you.'

Oh, joy! Maddy wondered if Drew could hear the delirious thumping of her heart. 'And now you've found me. And, um, Caroline?'

'Is talking to Kimberley.' He turned to Charlie. 'If we could have that chat?'

'I'll leave you alone, then,' Maddy said, trying to control her lips. 'If you're going to talk horse.'

He was here! Caroline was here too, but it really didn't matter. Drew was back in Milton St John. With a beatific smile, she made her unsteady way back towards the lawn. Colours seemed brighter, noises seemed louder, her tongue was far too big for her mouth. She was in danger of becoming very drunk.

Diana drifted past with Mitchell and waved coyly. 'It's all sorted Maddy, darling.'

'Goody.' Maddy was aware she was waving back and had to make a conscious effort to restrain her hand. 'What is?'

'Our bit of business.' Diana was winking. 'Mitchell is an angel. An absolute angel.'

'Never think you can better a woman, Marnie.' The smile almost blinded her. 'Especially not a woman like Di, here. Di knows her stuff. I always listen to her.'

Maddy watched them drift away again, not having an inkling what they were talking about. The barbecue would probably be raided by the Drugs Squad at any moment, and the cauldrons impounded. Rumour had it that Kimberley's mother had been a bit of a herbalist. Maybe Kimberley had family connections with the chef at the Cat and Fiddle.

Emptying her Batman beaker, Maddy sat heavily on the rockery next to a morose-looking stone badger. What with Caroline and Drew being together, it was probably the best she could hope for tonight.

'Do you want to make it a threesome?' Luke plonked down beside her. 'We could call it suicide corner. I don't know which one of us looks most pissed off, but I think the badger has got a slight edge.'

'Have you had a row with Suzy?' Maddy had never seen him look so miserable. 'Luke, what's wrong?'

'Oh, it's not Suzy. At least, I don't think it is. I mean, I haven't even seen her yet and I've been here for ages.' He sighed. 'I've been jocked off.'

Maddy tried to focus. 'Jocked off what?'

'Saratoga Sun.' Luke sucked in his breath. 'I know I told everybody it wouldn't matter, but it still bloody hurts.'

'When? Who told you?'

'Mrs James-Jordan and Mitchell D'Arcy. Just now. They said they'd been thinking things over and that maybe Richard's age and experience would be better. They've offered me Jefferson Jet.'

'Oh, God. Luke, I'm sorry – but I'm so pleased for Richard. And you did say you'd have plenty more chances at The Derby. Jefferson is second favourite anyway.'

'Yeah, I know. Oh, Christ. I know how bad Rich felt now.'

'I'm sure he felt a lot worse than you do.' Maddy's head was reeling. Fran and Richard would be ecstatic. 'I wonder what made them change their minds?'

'God knows.' Luke turned and stared into her eyes. 'I feel like a kid who's just lost his best toy.'

'Suzy's your best toy, and there's no danger of you losing her. And Jefferson could easily win The Derby.'

'Not against Saratoga.' Luke's eyes had brightened. 'But you're right about Suzy. If I lost her I don't know what I'd do.'

Maddy smiled fondly. If she couldn't have a love affair of her own this was the next best thing. She felt quite motherly.

'Have they told Richard yet?'

'No. Mrs James-Jordan says she'll tell him tomorrow. He'll be over the moon. I am pleased for him, honestly.'

'You're nice, Luke. Suzy's a lucky girl. Why don't you go and find her and get roaring drunk together?'

Luke grinned. He really was impossibly handsome, with those chocolate eyes, and those cheekbones. 'OK. And if I can't find Suzy, can I come back and get roaring drunk with you?'

'Any time.' Maddy gave him a hug. She was heavier than

him, and far more squiffy. With a giggle, they toppled backwards over the badger.

'I seem to have arrived in the middle of your jockey period,' Drew's voice barked from somewhere above them. 'When you've finished test driving them, perhaps you'll let me know.'

Maddy scrambled into a sitting position. Luke got to his feet and wandered away to find Suzy.

'Don't shout.' Maddy was removing bits of aubretia from her hair. 'You can't talk.'

'I merely brought my wife.' Drew's voice was icy.

'You sound jealous. Charlie was being nice to me because I was on my own, and Luke's been jocked off Saratoga so I was being nice to him.' She squinted up at him. 'That's what we're like in Milton St John. Nice to each other.'

'So I've noticed.' Drew sat beside the badger. 'And yes, I am. Jealous.'

They stared at each other. Drew slowly reached out and pulled her into his arms. He smelled of horses and sunshine, of heat and hay.

'Caroline,' Maddy squeaked. 'We can't. Caroline—'

'Is now discussing paramilitary operations with Bronwyn and Bernie. Oh, Jesus, Maddy . . .'

He kissed her with long, slow, expertise. Again it had all the undertones of log fires and fur rugs, and all the overtones of pent-up passion. It was not the kiss of a man who found sex repulsive.

'You look gorgeous and I missed you,' he said simply. 'And I'm so glad to be back. I'm sorry Caroline came with me. Oh, God. Is the whole world here tonight? Isn't there anywhere we can have some privacy?'

The laughing, noisy crowds seemed to be spewing from every corner of the garden. Maddy was aware of several villagers gazing at them with open curiosity.

'They think we're the floor show.'

'Not a hope.' Drew slid his arm round her shoulders. 'I'm

knackered. They won't be getting an encore.'

Nor will I, Maddy thought drowsily, but the overture had been absolute bliss.

'Do you want to eat?' She watched her own fingers clenching and unclenching themselves on the sleeve of his black sweatshirt. 'The food is wonderful – not that I've tried it, I mean.'

'You haven't?' He raised a dark arched eyebrow. 'Are you ill?'

They walked apart towards the barbecue. Drew told her about the horse, Dock of the Bay, that he'd ferried from Jersey and who was now eating his head off at Peapods. He told her about the house at Bonne Nuit which looked out over the sea and how he'd sat there alone in the moonlight and watched the headlights of the cars on the French coast. He told her about Kit and Rosa Pedersen, his friends and the horse's owners, who would be coming over to see him run at Epsom. He said nothing about Caroline.

'Drew, please talk about her. We can't pretend she doesn't exist just when it suits us.'

'OK, then. We had dinner each evening, we gossiped about our respective businesses, I had drinks with her parents and spent one morning sweating in the glasshouses while she and her mother had a meeting with a potential customer. We behaved exactly as we have for the last ten years.'

'Oh.' The bitter knife of jealousy was twisting its blade in Maddy's stomach. 'That's nice.'

'You wanted to know.' Drew reached for her hand. 'Caroline and I are very good friends. This is the way our life has always been, ever since—' Maddy held her breath. He sighed. 'Well, the way our life is, you know?'

He wasn't going to tell her anything. Maddy, not quite sober enough to err on the side of caution, wanted more. 'And did you – well, after dinner, at the end of the evening . . .?'

'Sleep with her?' Drew's eyes were veiled. 'Does it matter?'

'Of course it bloody matters. Oh, I know it's none of my business, but yes, it matters.'

'Yes, then. Not at Bonne Nuit. At her flat at the vineyard in St Lawrence. There, is that what you wanted to hear?'

Maddy's eyes filled with tears. She tugged her hand away from him.

Drew shook his head. 'We slept together. We didn't make love.'

'I don't believe you.'

'Jesus, Maddy, I'm too tired for this. I thought you understood.'

'I don't understand anything. How can you kiss me like you do, behave the way you do, and still sleep with Caroline?'

Drew stopped on the edge of the swaying crowd round the barbecue, and pulled Maddy round to face him.

'I have never lied to you. You've always known I was married. I've tried to explain my marriage to you. Oh, Maddy. I missed you so much. I thought you just accepted me, warts an' all.'

'Wife an' all,' Maddy muttered. 'I do. I'm sorry – I didn't mean to behave like a mistress.'

'I've never had one, so I wouldn't know.' Drew's eyes were teasing again. 'All I know is that much as I adore Jersey I was counting the damn hours until I could see you again. Every delay with Dock of the Bay's shipment was driving me crazy. When Caroline told me she was coming with me I could have throttled her. Now, are we going to eat or spend the rest of the evening sniping at each other like school kids?'

Maddy's stomach rumbled. Drew laughed and pulled her into his arms. 'Well, that's one decision taken care of.'

They piled their plates with something from every section of the barbecue and sank down on the grass beside the rockery. Balancing their plates on their knees, they smiled at each other. The crisis was over. This time.

'So, what's been happening while I've been away?' Drew

forked up a delicious pink mound of salmon. 'You've told me nothing on the phone.'

'It's been fairly quiet. Oh, I met Mitchell D'Arcy . . . which was just after I'd discovered Diana and Peter making love in her office . . .'

Drew choked noisily on his chicken leg. A family from the new bungalows looked across and tutted. 'Bloody hell!' His eyes were wide. 'Well, go on . . .'

She told him. He sat with a forkful of salad suspended in mid air. 'I'm sure Peter thinks I'm going to blackmail him,' she finished. 'But there's no point. I couldn't. I've been avoiding him and Stacey all night.'

'And Diana?'

'Diana and I had a little chat earlier this evening. We know where we stand. At least she's not frightened of me. I need her business.'

'And how did you feel? Seeing them together, like that?'

'Sick. I threw up. I haven't told Fran or Suzy or anyone. I wasn't jealous. Just sick . . . It was horrible.'

'And she was just wearing riding boots? Does Peter have a thing about boots, then?'

'Not as far as I know. Oh, you mean, did I have to put on wellingtons and a balaclava when we were together?' She laughed. 'No, not at all. Maybe it's Diana's fetish.'

'You could use it, you know.' Drew bit into a burger. 'You could get Peter to back off the spinney and probably stop the golf course in its tracks. Bronwyn would love you for ever.'

'No, I couldn't. I wouldn't. And anyway, it would be their word against mine. I just want to forget it. I wouldn't even tell Stacey, much as I dislike her. She'll have to discover for herself that Peter is a rat. Like I did.'

'You're too nice, Maddy.' Drew inched closer. 'I'm pleased you told me. I'll never look at either of them in the same light again. I'm so glad I came to Milton St John.'

Maddy snuggled against him and started eating his salad. 'So am I . . .'

Barty had handed over his makeshift bar to Brenda and Elaine's husbands and was doing the rounds of the barbecue with a big metal jug full of punch. Seeing Maddy and Drew without mugs he beavered across to them and ladled out two huge drinks.

'Going well, isn't it?' His Panama was at a rakish angle and his eyes blinked rapidly as he tried to focus on Maddy's cleavage. 'This has got everyone in the party spirit.' He tapped the jug and winked at Maddy. 'Especially Richard – he's had three pints and thinks he's Mike Tyson.'

Maddy looked up in alarm. 'Where is he? I thought he was with Fran and the kids? He's not fighting with Luke Delaney?'

'God, no!' Barty rocked on his heels. 'Luke's in no condition to fight with anyone. He's with your Suzy in the greenhouse. No, Richard is prowling the grounds looking for Diana. I wouldn't give much for her chances. Enjoy yourselves.' And he staggered away to the next customers.

'Should I go and throw a bucket of water over Luke and Suzy?' Drew grinned. 'Or – Christ, Maddy, where are you going?'

She staggered to her feet. 'We've got to find Richard before he finds Diana. She's put him back up on Saratoga.'

'So?' Drew stood up. 'Maybe he wants to thank her.'

'He wants to kill her.' Maddy looked over her shoulder. 'He doesn't know he's got the ride back. He'll blow it completely. Come on!'

Thirteen

They emerged on the far side of the garden behind the greenhouse. Charlie Somerset was giving Fran a piggy-back round the ornamental pond, with Kimberley and John Hastings taking bets from a crowd of stable lads.

Drew looked in horror. 'I've just taken him on as my jump jockey. I hope Fran doesn't hurt him. And what are John and Kimberley doing? Trying to stop it?'

'Probably laying odds of three to one on about whether one or both of them fall in,' Maddy told Drew. 'Kimberley and John both run gambling yards – they'll take money off anyone. Where the hell is Richard?'

'There.' Drew pointed. 'Just coming through the rockery. Who hit him?'

'No one. He fell out of the helicopter.' Maddy looked at Drew's face, 'when it was on the ground, I mean. Oh, damn! He's making for Diana and Mitchell D'Arcy. You head them off.'

'Maddy.'

'Yes?'

'Is life always like this with you?'

'Odd, you mean? Yes, mostly.'

'Good. At least I won't die of boredom.'

Richard was roaring, fighting, drunk. Maddy made sure that Drew had sauntered smiling towards Diana, then took a deep breath. Richard, like all jockeys, had a strength far outweighing his size. She hoped she could handle him.

'Richard! I've been looking for you!'

His reply was unintelligible. It would have been bad

enough with the punch, but with his enormously swollen lip, it was impossible to understand him. His eyes glittered. Maddy caught a lot of f-words linked to Luke and Diana and Mitchell with a lot of spitting. She grabbed his shoulders.

'Richard. You're going to ride Saratoga Sun. In The Derby. *You*. Not Luke. You, Richard!'

'Going to kill Diana.' He smiled suddenly. 'And Luke. Now.'

'Richard. They've changed their minds. They've jocked Luke off. They want you to ride Saratoga!'

'Uh?'

At last. Maddy sighed and tightened her grip. Slowly, she explained it again.

Richard gave a lop-sided smile. 'Honeshtly?'

'Honeshtly – I mean, yes, really.'

Richard pulled Maddy tightly against him. 'And Fran can have a baby?'

'Well, probably not straight away. Maybe it'd be better to wait 'til you got home. Or after you've won The Derby if you want to be really sure.'

Richard swayed, still clinging to her. 'I'll win.'

As he threaded his way unsteadily towards the stables, Maddy heaved a sigh of relief. She felt quite grown up. And was becoming rapidly stone-cold sober. She'd have to find Barty for a refill of punch. At least the punch blurred the edges. Sadly, Caroline found her first.

'I've just seen Drew with Diana James-Jordan and that awfully attractive suntanned man. The one who looks like a gangster. This is such fun. Your friend is in the pond with a really sexy-looking man. They seem to be taking each other's clothes off.'

Maddy was thankful that Richard had bypassed that little scenario. 'I'm glad you're enjoying yourself.'

Caroline had got her fruit punch in a glass and sipped it delicately. 'Oh, yes. I had a feeling that Drew didn't want me to come back with him. Now I can understand why. We just don't do this at home.

'Actually, I've got a proposition to put to you.' She raked her fingers through the shining fall of her hair. 'Please say no if you don't want to. I'm going back to Jersey the day after tomorrow. Being over on the mainland is such a treat and I'd love to go to London, but I hate to shop alone. Would you come with me?'

Whatever Maddy had been expecting, it certainly wasn't this. She wanted to laugh. Caroline had to be crazy. She had one more day she could spend with Drew and she wanted to go shopping.

'Even if you don't actually want to buy, I would welcome your advice. And I'd love your company. After all, we have so much in common.'

Only one thing, Maddy thought. Still, she could ask Jackie to take over for her tomorrow. Kat could help out on the lighter jobs – she was pregnant again. It seemed to be common among jockeys' wives – proving their stud value. It was ages since she'd had a day off, and she might learn some more about Drew – or, at least, his marriage. Oh, what the heck.

'Yes, all right, I'd love to. Are you going to drive?'

'As far as Didcot station. We'll travel in comfort from there. Oh, Maddy – it'll be such fun.'

Fun, it wouldn't be. Maddy wondered how her bank account would stand up to an assault on Oxford Street. It could hardly cope with Oxfam.

'Hello, darling.' Drew appeared at Caroline's side. Maddy and Caroline looked at him, then at each other, and laughed. Drew shook his head. 'Mission successfully accomplished, I think. Richard has fallen on Diana with cries of gratitude and Mitchell is flashing his teeth, so I presume they're all happy. I'm a bit concerned about my new jump jockey, though. I just hope Fran leaves him in one piece. Are they, er, you know?'

'No! Fran is very much in love with Richard. Charlie's just a flirt.'

'Oh, that's flirting, is it?' Drew looked doubtful. 'Anyway, whose reputation are you two ripping to shreds?'

'Don't be sexist, Drew.' Caroline flashed her eyes. 'Maddy and I were talking about tomorrow. We're going up to London together. For a shopping spree.'

Maddy heard Drew's sharp intake of breath. Caroline obviously didn't. She was smiling. 'It's such a shame I can't stay any longer. Bronwyn has called an emergency meeting of VAGs for the following night. It's all so exciting here.'

Oh, please don't let her want to come here permanently, Maddy prayed.

'VAGs?' Drew looked at Maddy who shook her head.

'Villagers Against Golf,' Caroline informed them. 'Bronwyn reckons it's time the village showed its muscle.'

'I thought they were having a meeting next week? Before The Derby?'

'Apparently, Bronwyn thinks it'll be too late. She thinks there should be more action and less talk.'

'Sounds like one of Peanut's edicts.' Drew smiled at Maddy. She wanted to kiss him so badly that she had to grit her teeth.

'You two will be able to go along, won't you?' Caroline said happily. 'And don't forget to ring me afterwards, Drew. I shall want to know what happened. Bronwyn is a fearsome old lady. I wouldn't like to get on the wrong side of her.'

'Was Diana surprised to see you just now, Drew?' Maddy asked, deftly steering the subject away from shared experiences. 'Didn't she wonder what was going on?'

Drew's eyes creased at the corners. 'Diana was full of stories about how wonderful you are. I couldn't imagine why. She told me that it was because of you that she and Mitchell had decided to reinstate Richard.'

'Me?'

'Apparently so. She owed you a massive favour, so she said.'

'Oh – she thought that was the price I wanted for my silence?' Maddy laughed in realisation. 'Maybe I should go into blackmailing with kid gloves. I never even thought about asking her to reinstate Richard.'

So Diana had a conscience after all? And Mitchell D'Arcy must be very smitten to have acquiesced so readily. It only added to Maddy's sudden despondency, and to the loneliness she'd felt earlier. Everybody had somebody . . .

The light was fading. The sky was streaked with navy and lilac, and Caroline, obviously feeling left out of the conversation, shivered slightly. 'If you're ready to leave, Drew, I should like to go home now.'

Drew looked reluctantly at Maddy who had just discovered something fascinating in the grass. She couldn't look at him. She didn't want him to see the hopelessness in her eyes.

'Yes, well, I suppose I really ought to see how Dock of the Bay's settling in. Maddy? Can we give you a lift?'

'No, thanks. I'll stay a bit longer and wait for Suzy and Luke.' Who probably wouldn't want her either. 'Thanks for asking, though. Caroline, I'll see you in the morning.'

Caroline smiled. 'About eight, and then we can have a lovely long day in town. Good night, Maddy.'

Maddy watched the Fitzgeralds walk away across the lawn in the twilight. It only gave her the merest spark of satisfaction to notice that they were walking at least six inches apart.

Fourteen

'What do you think, Maddy?' Caroline swept out of the fitting room and executed a twirl of scarlet and black. 'Is this one me?'

Maddy sighed. There were at least a dozen similar outfits discarded across chairs. They were all Caroline. Neat, elegant, and wildly expensive.

'It's lovely. They all are. Is it for a special occasion?'

'Entertaining clients, mostly. And I just love buying clothes.' Caroline looked at Maddy in the black trouser suit. 'You haven't tried anything at all yet and it's nearly lunchtime. Go on, there must be something that you like.'

There had been plenty. Even in Oxford Street they had been beyond her dreams, and now Caroline had started an assault on Knightsbridge, the prices were almost obscene.

'I'll have this one, then,' Caroline beamed at the assistant, whose working clothes must have cost more than Maddy's entire wardrobe. 'And the turquoise – oh, and the little lilac suit. I'll think about the green and cream over lunch . . .' And she dived happily back into the fitting-room. 'You ought to be thinking about The Derby, Maddy,' she called from behind the curtain. 'Surely you'll get a special outfit for that?'

'Maybe.' It depended what Oxfam had to offer. 'I don't usually dress up that much, even for Epsom.'

'Oh, but you must.' Caroline whisked the curtain aside and stood smiling unselfconsciously in her underwear. 'Go on, spoil yourself.'

Maddy felt sick. Caroline was wearing a black lace teddy with dark stockings and suspenders. Her figure was exquisite,

143

with creamy breasts accentuating a slender waist, a flat stomach, and firm, unmarked thighs.

That was what Drew had seen this morning as Caroline had dressed. What he'd seen last night when they went to bed at Peapods. What he slept with those nights in Jersey. Drew's wife had a perfect body.

'I'll go and have a look.' Maddy turned her back on the fitting-room. Tears were burning her eyes. How could she have been so stupid? How could Drew, used to that sort of perfection, ever find her curves attractive? Caroline must be at least ten years her senior, yet her body was as trim and toned as that of a teenager.

Maddy tugged a green dress from the rails and held it against her.

'Lovely with your hair and your colouring,' the assistant nodded. 'And very flattering. Why don't you try it on?'

'I – oh, no, I couldn't . . .'

'While your friend is getting dressed.' The persuasion was inches thick. 'I'm sure you'll be surprised how well it suits you.'

Frowning, Maddy carried the frock into the cubicle. She peeled off the trouser suit. The lights, designed to flatter, could do very little with her cotton bra and supermarket knickers. With a sigh, she slid into the dress.

Elegantly tailored, it buttoned down the front into a neat waist and flared out to just above the ankle in sensuous soft folds. The sleeves came to the elbow. The curve of her bosom stopped it looking matronly. She gazed at herself in the mirror. The green was like the oily, swirling, patterns on a peacock's tail, merging and changing beneath the light, making her eyes emerald green, her tumbled hair russet. It was simply the most beautiful thing she had ever worn.

'Come on out, Maddy,' Caroline called. 'I'll give you my honest opinion.'

Feeling beautiful for the first time in her life, Maddy stepped out into the shop.

'You've got to have it,' Caroline said. 'It is simply divine. Maddy, you look terrific.'

'Wonderful, madam.' The assistant was smiling genuinely for the first time. 'A complete transformation.'

'With the right shoes, Maddy,' Caroline was saying, 'maybe green suede courts, and opal jewellery . . . oh, yes. It's absolutely fantastic. Do you like it?'

'I love it but—'

'That's settled then. Oh, I wish Drew was here. He'd tell you just how gorgeous you look. Men are so good at knowing what suits one, aren't they?'

Maddy didn't know. She'd never consulted Peter over her mainly secondhand wardrobe. And she certainly didn't want Drew to be there, drawing comparisons between Caroline's racehorse slenderness and her own voluptuous body.

'I don't think . . .'

'Don't be silly.' Caroline was already fishing in her handbag for her credit cards. 'Go and get changed, then we'll zoom off to Harvey Nick's for lunch.'

God, Maddy thought, as she pulled the fitting room curtains again. Could she afford Harvey Nicholls for lunch? Would she ever be able to afford lunch again? She looked at the price ticket on the dress and nearly fainted. It was more than she allowed herself out of Shadows for two months. She let the soft folds trail through her fingers and looked in the mirror again. Maybe Drew would love her if she dressed like this. Maybe that was what he wanted, someone who dressed as Caroline did. If she wore it to Epsom . . .

She did lightning calculations. It would mean no Hobnobs, no visits to the Cat and Fiddle, no spare bottles of Glenfiddich for desolate moments, and probably no electricity, gas or telephone.

She sauntered up to the desk as though she'd been shopping in exclusive boutiques all her life and smiled at the assistant. 'Yes, thank you. I'll take it. Is Visa all right?'

They only just made it back to Paddington in time. Caroline, high on her mammoth spending spree, collapsed in a corner of the first-class carriage surrounded by bags. Maddy, having also used her credit card for green shoes and mock opal earrings, slunk in behind her feeling the guilt that always comes in a hot rush after foolish overspending. She'd have to ring the bank manager first thing in the morning. Caroline had insisted on paying for lunch, and for the taxi back to Paddington, which Maddy thought was a frightful luxury when the Tube was so handy.

Caroline leaned back in her seat, easing off her shoes. 'What a wonderful day. I can't wait to show my mother that outfit I bought in Harrods. We're trying to interest some Spanish holiday complex in taking our wine. That should sway the deal. European men always notice how one is dressed.'

'What about Drew?' Maddy's feet were killing her but she couldn't remove her loafers because her toenails needed cutting. 'Will he like what you've bought?'

'Probably. He never comments very much. I sometimes drag him with me when I shop because I think it does him good to realise that not everything revolves around horses. He's usually quite complimentary.'

'Why don't you live with him?' The train was rattling out of London, past grimy rows of houses and high-rise flats. 'How can you bear to be apart from him?'

Caroline stretched like a cat. 'I know you're smitten with Drew, Maddy. But honestly, you don't know him. I told you before, Drew and I are better at a distance.'

'And you've never wanted to leave him permanently?' Maddy's head was thumping. She had to know. 'It just seems such a peculiar arrangement. Yes, I do like him, Caroline. Very much. I'm sure that if he were my husband, I wouldn't risk losing him.'

Caroline leaned forward. 'I've never considered leaving him – as he's never considered leaving me – because our relationship works so well. Everyone has a different idea of marriage. Drew and I don't happen to believe that you need to live in each other's pockets.' She sighed. 'There have been other girls, Maddy, who, like you, have thought that Drew was fun to be with and maybe more . . . Drew, again like me, isn't particularly interested in the physical side of things.' She stopped and gave an embarrassed laugh. 'Neither of us rates sex very highly on our agenda. And, of course, there are other, deeply personal reasons, why Drew and I stay together.'

Maddy bit her lip. The heartache was clouding her eyes. Just how much more deeply personal could you get?

'It would be foolish of you to think that Drew will become your lover,' Caroline spoke the words as calmly as she'd ordered lunch, 'because, among other reasons, Drew is hopeless in bed. That's why our marriage and our friendship works, Maddy. Because I have absolutely no reason to think that he'll stray. I don't like sex and Drew can't do it. We suit each other admirably. Now,' she smiled happily, 'show me those earrings again. You honestly can't tell that they're costume, can you?'

Fifteen

Bronwyn had been busy. The entire window of the Village Stores was taken up by a flourescent orange poster exhorting everyone opposed to the golf course to meet at the site at seven on Friday evening. Maddy surveyed it worriedly on Friday morning. It all seemed to be getting out of hand. She rested her bicycle against the window, and pinged open the door.

'Everyone's mentioned it,' Bronwyn said happily, smoothing down her floral crossover pinafore, and raising her voice against the hubbub of the stable lads who were clustered round the sweet counter. 'I reckon when Diana and Gareth and Bert Maynard see the opposition they've got, they'll change their minds.'

'I'm not sure.' Maddy picked up the cheapest packet of washing powder she could find. 'Shouldn't we just have stuck to our original plan, and had the meeting next week? I don't think Milton St John is ready for the militia.'

'Nonsense.' Bronwyn popped the washing powder into a bag. 'If we're not getting anywhere with collective bargaining, then we've got to fight. No one wants to see the village desecrated.'

'But who are we fighting, exactly?' Maddy was alarmed to hear such aggression from Bronwyn. 'Only the people who own the land and have an absolute right to sell it, surely?'

Bronwyn took Maddy's money. 'A legal right, maybe. But certainly not a moral one. A strong show of people power is what we need.'

Maddy winced. The Twyford Down and Batheaston

people had fought their fight on a massive scale. The bloody battles over the Newbury bypass had attracted nationwide coverage. Milton St John golf course was very small beer by comparison. She only hoped that Bronwyn wasn't getting too carried away.

Bronwyn paused before ringing up the washing powder. 'Is this all? No Hobnobs? No chocolate?'

Maddy shook her head. The previous day's extravagances had put paid to luxuries. The green dress and shoes would take care of sugary treats for many weeks to come.

Bronwyn peered across the counter. 'You're not changing your mind? About the golf course?'

'No, of course not. I just think there must be some other way. I think we're in danger of making fools of ourselves. Bert Maynard wants to sell the orchard because he can't see it ever making a profit for him again, and Diana is adamant that she'll sell the spinney because she and Gareth will become shareholders in the golf course. Neither of them will change their minds, not even if we build treehouses and fire Exocets at the JCBs.'

'Which can be arranged,' Bronwyn said darkly, ignoring the clamour from the stable lads who were desperate for a calorie rush. 'You had such a success with getting Richard reinstated on Saratoga, I thought maybe you would have been able to persuade Diana—'

'Not a hope,' Maddy put in quickly. 'The Derby ride was something completely different.'

Bronwyn gave in to the stable lads and bagged up dolly mixtures at the speed of light. 'So, will you be coming to the protest tonight?'

'Yes, of course.' Maddy tucked the washing powder under her arm. 'But I still think we're going about things the wrong way.'

She cycled home slowly, wobbling alongside the stream and gazing at the glorious spread of the spinney and the orchard as it rolled away from the village in a billow of green.

Trust bloody Peter to want to turn such natural rural beauty into yet another sop to Mammon. She'd fight him every inch of the way, but in her heart she felt that the battle had already been lost.

She reached the cottage, and fed the washing powder into the machine. The morning stretched idly ahead, because for once all her normal Friday paperwork had been completed before the end of the *Breakfast Show*. Unable to sleep, Maddy had risen before Luke and Suzy, and tackled the invoicing and the wages. It had absolutely nothing to do with the fact that the office window looked out on to Peapods' drive, and she had been able to watch Caroline's departure at just after seven.

Her leggings needed washing. In her haste to make an early start, she'd pulled on a grubby pair. She tugged them off and then pulled her T-shirt over her head. The washing machine could take a bit more if she leaned on the door. After all, she had to economise now. The first repayment on the credit card would bring anguished screams from the bank manager.

Padding across the oblong bit of the kitchen in a pair of disreputable pink knickers and a blue bra, she filled the kettle. This afternoon she'd be cleaning Peapods for the first time, now that Jackie was helping out the visibly pregnant Kat. This afternoon she'd wear the red satin bra and knicker set that Fran had given her last birthday. It was wildly frivolous and she'd kept it in the drawer of her dressing table still in its lilac and gold carrier bag. One day, she knew, there'd be an occasion to wear it. Not, of course, that she expected Drew to pounce on her this afternoon. But if he did . . .

She'd watched him ride out of Peapods on Dock of the Bay within minutes of Caroline leaving, leading his small string of horses up on to the gallops. She'd shivered, watching the mere movement of his thighs controlling the big bay horse, his slender hands gently coaxing on the reins, the lean strength of his body rocking rhythmically in the saddle. She refused to believe Caroline's assertion that Drew wasn't interested in sex. It simply wasn't possible.

'No one answered the letter box and the back door was open so I thought I'd just—' Drew stopped in mid-flight. 'Good God!'

Maddy screamed and dived for cover.

'I've closed my eyes,' he lied, laughing. 'You're quite safe.'

'Go away!' she backed into the square bit of the kitchen, desperately trying to find the door and consequently jarring herself against the cooker.

Drew, his shoulders shaking, turned away from her. 'Maddy, go and get dressed. I'll go out and come in again.'

She hurtled across to her bedroom, and tugged on a pair of jeans and a navy sweater. Why hadn't she chucked out all that ghastly underwear? Why didn't she have a toned, tanned body? Why hadn't she at least shaved her legs? Because, she admitted sourly to herself as she dragged her hair from the neck of the sweater, as no one was going to see it, it hadn't mattered.

Drew had poured two mugs of coffee and was sitting at the kitchen table, his eyes deceptively innocent.

She looked at him reproachfully. 'You should have knocked.'

'I did. You didn't answer. I knew you were home because it's Friday. I didn't expect you to be undressed.' His eyes sparkled. 'That was a bonus.'

'Don't lie.' She picked up her coffee with shaking hands. 'I'm surprised you're still here. You must be very brave. Seeing me like that probably took more courage than participating in the Pardubice.' Drew laughed. It seemed she could always make him laugh.

He met her eyes. 'Actually, I didn't come round here to play at peeping toms. I came to ask you if you'd like to come out on Solomon. You said you'd like to ride. I need to take Dock of the Bay for a gallop, I only hacked him out with the first lot. He needs a lot more work before Epsom and the gallops should be fairly quiet now. I just wondered if you'd like to come with me. Of course, if you're too busy . . .'

'No, I'm not. I was up early this morning.' She wasn't going to tell him why. 'I haven't got anything to do until I clean for you this afternoon.'

He frowned slightly, then smiled. 'Great. Finish your coffee and I'll see if I can hire a block and tackle.' He grinned at her perplexed expression. 'To haul your mammoth bulk into the saddle.'

Throwing the tea towel at him, Maddy made a grab across the table. Drew caught her flailing hands and pulled her towards him. 'You're lovely, Maddy. I have never met anyone like you. I had no right to walk in here unannounced, but I'm glad I did. You're adorable.' He released her hands and sat back in his chair. 'Your only problem is that you've got to learn to adore yourself.'

Solomon was placid, and stood looking round with only the merest curiosity as she pulled herself up on to his back. She gathered the reins between her hands, sliding her feet into the stirrups. Drew swung himself into Dock of the Bay's saddle with ease and Maddy's stomach contracted with desire, watching his muscles tightening beneath the denim. They walked sedately across the cobbles, the horses' hoofs creating ringing echoes that hovered beneath the lichen-covered walls, and out into the street.

Maddy soon became accustomed to the rolling gait, loving the oily, dusty feel of Solomon's mane brushing her hands and the warm fusty smell rising from his gleaming coat. Milton St John was practically deserted. Maddy would have liked the streets to be lined with people to witness this epic event. She smiled to herself. This was the third time she'd felt this surge of elation since Peter Knightley had walked out on her; first there had been Shadows, then Drew, and now this rediscovery. Her self-esteem edged up a notch.

Drew pulled Dock of the Bay alongside her as they approached the gallops. 'You ride beautifully. No wonder

Suzy's so successful. It must be in the blood.'

She glowed under his approbation, but shook her head. 'Not as far as I know. Dad's addicted to betting shops but I think that's as close as anyone in our family got to the turf. I learned to ride when I was a kid. My parents had a deal with the people who kept the local stables – they sent people to our bed and breakfast and Mum and Dad pointed guests in their direction. They gave me, and later Suzy, free riding lessons.'

'Obviously successfully. Why on earth didn't you keep it up?'

'Other things got in the way, I suppose.' Things like puppy fat that stayed put. There was something sad, Maddy had always thought, about a lumpy teenager jolting about on the back of an elderly pony. 'And then I went to university.'

'And?' Drew's eyebrows rose quizzically.

'Another disastrous area of my life. I went to Brighton to read Humanities. I spent most of my time sitting on the cliffs at Peacehaven watching the sea and dreaming. I scraped a third.'

'That's very impressive to a boy who left his secondary education with dismal qualifications and dire warnings of nothing ahead but impending failure.'

'Still, you proved your doubters wrong. I didn't.'

'Oh, I think you did, Maddy.' Drew leaned across from Dock of the Bay and brushed his lips against her cheek. 'In fact, I know you did.' And wheeling the horse round, he kicked with his heels and sped towards the brow of the hill.

Maddy sat on the sleepy Solomon and watched in admiration as Drew, crouched low over Dock of the Bay's neck, became one with the animal in a flowing movement of controlled power. Why on earth hadn't Caroline persuaded him to continue riding? Maybe there had been broken bones, but all jockeys accepted them as part of the job. Drew had sacrificed the chance to become a professional for Caroline. He must have loved her very much.

All her earlier confidence ebbing away, Maddy adjusted

her toes in the stirrups and kicked Solomon into life. There was nothing but the roaring wind in her ears and the rhythmic thunder of the hoofs on the softness of the peaty turf. Solomon was nowhere near as fast as Dock of the Bay, but the gallop was steady. Maddy felt as light as thistledown. The sky, the trees, the whole world, were kaleidoscoped into a dizzying landscape that effortlessly carried her with it. She pulled up just as Drew wheeled Dock of the Bay round and was hacking him back along the track. Solomon was hardly sweating. Maddy was exhausted.

'I'm very out of condition . . .' The ride had been exhilarating and she hadn't fallen off. 'That was, oh . . .'

'Orgasmic?'

'Not unless orgasms make your arms feel like they've come out of their sockets, your legs feel like they belong to someone else, your whole body crumple from exhaustion, and make you sweat so much that you think you've just spent three days in a sauna.' She caught his eye and flushed crimson. 'Oh! I don't mean . . .'

'You'll have to tell me one day, won't you? And before you become all po-faced and puritanical again, you rode like an angel.' He swung his legs out of the saddle and slid to the ground. Dock of the Bay immediately started cropping the scrubby grass. 'Come down here . . .'

Maddy dropped to the ground. The sudden return to gravity made her stumble. Drew steadied her. 'Caroline warned me not to hurt you.'

Maddy said nothing. Her heart was thumping from the exertion of the ride. His body was warm.

'She said that she'd told you there had been other girls – women – who thought they could come between us.'

'I wasn't particularly interested. Drew, don't let's talk about this. Don't spoil this moment. I'm feeling proud of myself for once.'

'I just wanted you to know that I'm not a womaniser. I'm not a Peter Knightley, or a Charlie Somerset. I didn't want

Caroline to have given you the wrong impression.'

'Caroline is your wife. She has every right to warn me to stay away from you.' Maddy wanted to stamp her foot. 'But she did say that because you kissed people and were friendly that maybe you gave off the wrong signals.'

Drew frowned. He looked up at the sky and then back at Maddy's face. 'And do I?'

'How would I know? I liked you at the start because you were funny and friendly and because you came to my rescue even though you didn't know me.' She dragged air into her aching lungs. 'I thought you were very attractive . . . I liked you even before we became friends.'

'And now?'

'And now I still like you. But you're married. You and Caroline stay together because you love and trust each other. If you weren't married it would be different, but we'll never know, will we?'

She grabbed Solomon's reins and hauled herself back into the safe distance of the saddle. Drew was still on the ground looking up at her. She gave a small smile.

'Don't complicate things, Drew. We know how we feel, but I'm not going to be the one to end your marriage. And I'm not prepared to screw up my life again. Not even for you.'

'Caroline doesn't want us to separate.'

'No,' Maddy said bleakly. 'I gathered that.'

'Will that make a difference to us?'

She looked down into his face and shook her head. 'How would I know? I'm hardly an expert on love and relation-ships, am I? Is this why you brought me up here? To discover if you could make me a bit on the side?'

'Jesus!' Angrily, Drew swung himself on to Dock of the Bay's back. 'If I'd wanted to do that, I'd have done it a long time ago.'

Would you? she thought, as Solomon started his rolling walk back along the gallops. Or was Caroline right, and was Drew merely contented with flirting and kissing? And if so, where did affairs start? Did you have to actually make love to be having an affair, or was being in love equally immoral? If so, she realised, she was already an adulteress.

Drew had overtaken her and was tugging off Dock of the Bay's tack when she rode into Peapods' yard. He'd pulled off the crash hat and his dark hair was plastered to his forehead. 'I'll see to Solomon as well. Just leave him. I'll sponge them both and see to the rugs.'

He was bitingly angry. She closed her eyes and cursed herself. She wanted to recapture the laughing friendly flirtatiousness. If only it could stop at that – for both of them.

'I might as well do the cleaning while I'm here.' She dragged off the hat and shook her curls free. 'Where did Jackie put the stuff?'

'Cupboard under the stairs. You don't have to—'

'Of course I have to. It's what I'm paid for. By your wife.'

She turned on her heel and practically ran underneath the clock arch towards the house. Their relationship was like a seesaw – with far more downs than ups. And it was probably permanently down now.

She pulled the cleaning paraphernalia out from the cupboard and had a sudden vision of herself as a lonely, lumpy child. She'd been eight or nine, before Suzy was born, and her parents had taken her on holiday to a small village on the Norfolk coast. It had been a grey and blustery week and they were sheltering in a recreation ground. She'd sat on one end of a wooden seesaw in her shorts and blazer, her legs purpling in the wind, while her parents took turns to push down the other end. Eventually, both of them tired of the game and left her sitting there, firmly anchored to the tarmac, tears streaming down her cheeks.

That was how it was now, she thought, blinking back grown-up tears, as she bumped the vacuum cleaner up Peapods' exquisite staircase. And how it was probably always going to be. She'd insulted him once too often. He really had been furious. She, Maddy Beckett, who would never knowingly hurt anyone, had hurt the man who least deserved it.

Totally depressed, she couldn't even take any comfort from the fact that two main bedrooms had been made up; and that as she cleaned, it was obvious that Drew's belongings were all in the master bedroom with the magnificent brass bed and the cream drapes, and Caroline's were arranged with almost antiseptic neatness in the smaller room at the end of the passage.

They probably galloped along the landing between bedrooms, she thought angrily, knocking the vacuum cleaner viciously against the antique skirting boards. Maybe Drew snored. Maybe they made love in one room and slept in the other. Maybe they really didn't make love at all, but drifted off to sleep in each other's arms as loving companions. Whatever the reason, Caroline slept at Peapods with Drew, while she slept across the road in the cottage. And nothing would change it.

Sixteen

The main street was crowded. The villagers jostled, laughing and talking in the misty evening sun, at the entrance to Maynards Orchard. Hordes of children swung from the boughs of Goddards Spinney, and Bronwyn and Bernie were handing out leaflets. Several protesters waved placards with felt-tipped messages like 'Hands Off Our Heritage', 'Trees Have Feelings Too' and 'VAGs Will Win'. Maddy, who had walked from the cottage with Suzy, bit her lip. There were far too many people.

'Holy hell!' said Suzy. 'This is serious.'

'Too serious.' Maddy's stomach had tightened in dismay. 'Bronwyn is going about this all the wrong way. I tried to tell her this morning.'

This morning seemed like three years ago. This morning she'd still had Drew's friendship.

'Look! There's Central telly! And Thames Valley Radio! Bronwyn must have tipped them off.' Suzy was jigging up and down. 'And are they newspaper reporters over there?'

'She should have thought about some sort of security as well as media coverage.' Maddy felt like a real wet blanket but the size of the crowd was quite daunting. 'There's not even a token police car. God knows what'll happen if there's any trouble.'

Suzy had no such fears. Her eyes shone with excitement. 'It's such a shame that Luke's at Lingfield. He'd have loved all this. Still,' she shot a questioning look at Maddy, 'we're both deserted women tonight. Where's Drew?'

'He couldn't make it,' Maddy said flatly. 'He had something else on.'

'Do I detect a bit of a rift between you and the divine Mr Fitzgerald?'

'No, you bloody well don't! To have a rift you have to have a join in the first place.' She glared at her sister. 'And if you draw any sexual connotation from that I'll hit you.'

'OK. OK. Keep your knickers on. Mind you, that's probably half the problem. If you'd . . .' She ducked the swipe of Maddy's hand. 'Sorry. But if you need any advice, I'm always here. Sod it, Mad. It isn't that bad, is it?'

'No, of course not.' Maddy tried to smile but her teeth seemed to have gummed themselves together. 'And if Luke can rise above the disappointment of not riding Saratogo Sun in The Derby, I'm sure I can rise above a night without Drew Fitzgerald.'

'Luke can rise above anything.' Suzy's grin was lascivious, and once again she side-stepped Maddy's hand. 'He's happy just to be riding in The Derby. God, I wish I could.' Suzy blinked into the distance, her face full of dreams.

Despite her misery at the row with Drew and her misgivings about the ever-swelling crowd, Maddy hugged her sister tightly. 'You will one day. And win it. Wait and see.'

'Yeah, the first woman to do it.' Suzy's eyes widened amongst the kohl. 'Suzy Delaney – Champion of Epsom.'

Maddy looked at her quickly. 'Suzy? Luke hasn't proposed, has he? You're far too young. You haven't known each other long enough.' She stopped abruptly. There was a real danger that she was turning into her mother.

'God no! If only. I was just trying it out for size, the way you do. You know?'

'No, I don't actually,' Maddy lied. She'd covered her notepad that morning with a hundred Maddy Fitzgeralds. She'd screwed up the sheet and poked it to the bottom of the bulging rubbish bin as soon as she'd got in from Peapods. 'I'm far too mature for that sort of thing.'

Suzy was jigging up and down again. 'There's Mr Twice-Knightley and the bimbo stick-insect. And who's the fat geezer with them?'

'Jeff Henley, I should imagine. Stacey's father.' She sighed. 'This could get out of hand.'

'Oh, I do hope so. Bags I get first punch at Stacey.'

Diana and Gareth were also on the outskirts of the crowd which seemed to be swelling by the minute. Bert Maynard's dissident sons, Paul and Phil, had joined the Pughs at the head of the throng. Balding, stocky, and dressed in cords and knitted pullovers, they looked out of place amongst the rabble-rousers. A chant of 'Ban the course!' thumped through the air as Barry and Sandra, Nicky, Joe and Peanut quietly walked towards Bronwyn and Bernie. Maddy was troubled to notice that even they looked concerned at the size of the crowd.

'Will you be all right here if I go and talk to Jason and Olly?' Suzy asked. 'I'll stay if you want.'

'No. I'll be fine.' Maddy waved back at the knot of apprentices and stable lads sitting beside the stream. 'Are they having a party?'

'Just a few lagers. They'll get withdrawal symptoms otherwise – they're usually in the Cat and Fiddle by this time. Don't look so worried, Mad. It's not going to turn into a riot.'

Maddy hoped not. She watched Suzy thrusting her way through the crowd and wished Fran was there. But she'd telephoned and said she wouldn't join in because of Richard's being reinstated on Saratoga. Neither of them wanted to cross Diana.

'I've come to say sorry.' Stacey, who always seemed to appear like a shimmying zephyr from nowhere, touched Maddy's arm. 'I think we both said things in the heat of the moment.'

'I'm sure I didn't,' Maddy said coldly. 'In fact, I can't even remember what was said, but I'm sure I meant every word of it. Did Peter send you over here? What's he trying to do? Canvass support at the eleventh hour?'

Stacey obviously didn't understand this. She wrinkled her

retroussé nose. 'No, he didn't. Daddy and Peter are just horrified by all this. It's so stupid. After all, what on earth does that silly old woman from the shop think she's doing?'

For once, Maddy found herself in agreement with Stacey – but she'd die before she let her know it. 'I think it's just to show how much the villagers are against the idea of ploughing up the orchard and the spinney for a golf course that is neither needed nor wanted. Surely, Peter and your father could plan their golf course somewhere else?'

'Why should they?' Stacey pouted. 'All the trainers play golf, and most of the jockeys. They'll all join, Peter says, and it'll make a lot of jobs. Anyway, Peter and I are getting married in September. And we'll be moving into the Manor and—'

'I know all that,' Maddy snapped. 'Peter came round to the cottage to tell me himself.'

'Did he?' Stacey's full lips trembled slightly. 'Oh, yes, he told me . . . Anyway, it'll be so handy for us living in the village with Petie running the golf club. You're just being an old stick in the mud.'

'No, I'm not. God, Stacey. Look at this.' She waved her arms wildly. 'These trees are glorious. It would be a desecration to tear them all down. There are enough golf courses in the area already – and enough people ploughing up what's left of this country to build houses and industrial estates and, yes, bloody golf courses. If you want to live happily in Milton St John you'd better persuade Peter and your father to change their minds.'

'Daddy won't do that and neither will Peter. Anyway, golf courses are ever so pretty and green. I've seen the plans. They're going to put lakes in and—'

'Don't go any further,' Maddy stormed. 'Yes, I'm well aware that golf courses are beautifully landscaped, but what do we need with manmade beauty when we've got the real thing right here? Oh, run off back to Peter and Daddy and tell them you failed – on all counts. I will not change my mind about the golf course, and I'm bloody well not going to apologise to you for anything I said or did – now or ever. Understand?'

'You're weird.' Stacey turned away. 'I don't know why anyone should get so upset about a few old trees. And –' she looked slyly over her thin shoulders – 'I told Peter that you said he was crap in bed – which he isn't – and he laughed and said that was rich coming from you. He said you just used to lay there. He said you didn't know what you were supposed to be doing. He said he had to show you how to do *everything*.'

Maddy wanted to shout every obscenity she had ever heard. Suzy would have reacted in that way – Fran, too. That was what Stacey expected. So instead, she smiled. Slowly and knowingly.

'Stacey? Does Peter like you to wear riding boots in bed?'

'What?' The slender young-old face was scornful. 'Don't be silly. 'Course not.'

'Then ask him if you should. You never know, he might be delighted . . .'

Maddy turned away to hide her grin. That should rattle him sufficiently to keep him and the bimbo stick-insect from pestering her in future. There was a stirring at the entrance to the orchard as Bronwyn took the microphone. Maddy frowned. She'd thought it was just a gathering to display mass protest; she hadn't realised it was going to be a rally.

'Villagers!' Bronwyn bellowed. 'Thank you for turning out in such large numbers tonight to show our unity in saving our natural heritage.'

There was a roar of support. The cameras trained first on Bronwyn and then panned across the crowd. People waved at them. Reporters from the local press scribbled diligently.

'The purpose of this meeting is to demonstrate to those who want to destroy our village, that we – the people who matter – will not allow it!'

Another roar. Maddy watched the faces. They were enjoying

themselves. Diana and Gareth moved towards Peter, Stacey and Jeff Henley. Bronwyn pointed towards them. 'I'm pleased that Mr and Mrs James-Jordan, Mr Knightley and Mr Henley are with us tonight. I think that now they may begin to see how unpopular their proposal is.'

The crowd hissed and booed. Diana and Peter remained boot faced. Gareth smiled winningly at the crowd.

Bronwyn coughed into the microphone. 'Paul and Phil Maynard are here with us to lend their support. They don't want to see Maynards Orchard destroyed. They are prepared to stand up to their father on this vital issue. Are *you*?'

A volley of hand clapping suggested that they were. Paul and Phil blushed like twin orbs. Diana shook her head. Stacey was whispering something to Peter and had managed to worm her way between him and Diana. Maddy felt quite sorry for him. A thorn between two other thorns.

Bronwyn held up her hand. 'Would anyone from the proposed golf course like to say a few words at this point?'

They wouldn't. Gareth beamed at everyone again and waved at Maddy. Diana glared at him and wriggled herself back to Peter's side.

'Very well.' Bronwyn looked quickly at her supporters from Twyford Down, Batheaston and Newbury as if asking for their backing for the next step. They looked uncertain. She sucked in her breath. 'I think it is fair to say, then, that we will not let this proposal go ahead. We will fight. We will intercept all machinery and personnel. The villagers of Milton St John will not be brought down!'

This brought an ear-splitting roar of support. Diana was turning pale. Maddy felt that in her place she'd give in now. So far so good. Bronwyn had handled it well. The points had been made: the village was against the desecration; the village didn't want the golf course.

Then suddenly Peter took the microphone from Bronwyn. A hush fell as his persuasive voice swirled over the crowd. 'I think now is the time for me to say something.' He scanned the villagers with his oh-so-blue eyes. 'You are my friends. Friends are supposed to stick together. I can understand your point of view, but I feel that you have been misinformed. Mrs Pugh,' he inclined his golden head to Bronwyn, 'has been very persuasive, but I am here to give you facts. The land in question is owned by two parties. Both these parties are more than willing to sell it to provide a golf course. That is their right. They would like your support, naturally, but with it or without it, the golf course will go ahead. And any talk of destroying equipment or attacking personnel will be met with the full force of the law.'

He stopped. The villagers were silent. They were weighing this up. Peter smiled. Some of the younger women patted their hair.

'I met certain opposition when I first came to Milton St John and wanted to set up my health studio in an established stable. I overcame it. People – you – came to the gyms and the saunas and the solariums in droves and enjoyed yourselves. You were against it at first because you didn't want change, but in the end you were more than happy. Now, isn't that true?'

There was a murmur of assent. Bronwyn looked murderous, but having protested loud and long for democracy, she could hardly snatch the microphone back. Maddy nodded ruefully. Peter was eloquent and charming. It all sounded so plausible. He spoke again and this time his voice was caressing and persuasive.

'I am going to be living in the Manor. In the heart of Milton St John. I, as much as any of you, love the beauty and tranquillity of this village. I, like you, would do nothing to destroy it. The golf course will be an enhancer, not a desecrator. It will give work in an area which has a lot of unemployment, and bring visitors to our village. Visitors who will spend money at the shop, at the pub . . .'

'What about cars, though?' Barty Small piped up from the front. 'We don't want a lot of imbeciles tearing through the village, scaring the horses and causing mayhem, do we?'

The villagers shook their heads. Peter smiled at Jeff Henley and the James-Jordans and Maddy's heart sank. She knew that smile. Peter played poker like a demon.

'If you – especially Mrs Pugh – had troubled to check the plans, which are available at the council offices, you will see that there is to be no access to the course in Milton St John.'

Bronwyn was almost puce at this oversight. Maddy wanted to put her arms around her to protect her, because, knowing Peter as she did, there would be a next bit. There was.

Peter ladled on the charm. 'It is part of the planning permission proviso that we build the access road to the golf course directly from the motorway slip road, on the other side of the gallops. Four miles away from the village, and nowhere near any houses or stables. There will be no golf course traffic anywhere near the village.'

There was a stunned silence.

'But the trees.' Kimberley had her hand in the air. 'You're still going to bulldoze all these wonderful trees.'

'Not at all.' Peter was oozing syrup now. 'Yes, of course there will be some uprooting needed, but I have taken conservation advice. Each tree removed will have a sapling planted in its place. And there will be no trees – none at all – taken from the first half mile of the village boundary. We intend to keep the spinney and the orchard as a backdrop to the course. It will look no different from Milton St John. You won't even know it's there.'

The stunned silence gave way to murmurs which ballooned into a roar. Sandra and Barry, Nicky, Joe and Peanut were glaring at Bronwyn. They had been badly misinformed.

Maddy swallowed. It was typical of Peter. He could have stopped all this a long time ago, but he enjoyed seeing people stirred up. The media were packing up, deprived of anything but a filler item. Diana and Gareth were shaking hands with Peter and Jeff Henley. Bernie Pugh had disappeared. If only

Bronwyn had looked at the plans first, Maddy thought sadly, then all this would have been unnecessary.

'Ladies and gentlemen . . .' Bronwyn's voice wavered. 'I suggest that we call a halt to this evening's protest. In the light of Mr Knightley's information –' she shot Peter a glance that should have shrivelled him on the spot – 'I will take it upon myself to inspect the plans. We will still have the meeting in the village hall next week, as planned, to discuss our next move.'

But people weren't listening. The impetus had gone. Peter was as bloody-minded as ever. Maddy watched him kissing Diana's powdered cheek. He knew exactly when to play his trump card. Everyone had begun to drift away from the orchard.

Having been robbed of any further free entertainment, the stable lads started lobbing lager cans at each other.

Diana, sweeping regally away from the throng between Peter and Jeff Henley, stopped. 'I trust none of you works for me.'

They shook their heads. Most of them had done at one time, but Diana was notorious for shedding her stable staff as regularly as she shed her lovers. She was not a popular employer. Ignoring her, they continued to play catch-ball with the empty cans.

Diana peered at them. They all looked the same to her. 'If any of you works for me, you can pick up your cards in the morning.'

'Well, we don't.' Jason, Suzy's friend, smiled amiably. 'So, sod off.'

'Excuse me,' Diana bridled. 'What did you say?'

'Sod off,' Jason repeated, still smiling. 'We're not doing any harm.'

'Just enjoying ourselves.' Olly backed up his room-mate. 'Like you do, Mrs J-J, except we do it with our clothes on.' This caused uproarious laughter. The stable staff were well aware of Diana's predilections.

Suzy was sniggering. Diana, her face scarlet, grabbed her shoulder. 'And just what do you find so funny, Suzy Beckett? What has your sister said to you?'

Suzy looked at Diana in astonishment. 'Nothing. I don't know what you mean. And let go of me, please.'

Maddy had watched with amusement until then. Somehow, Suzy shaking Diana's hand away resulted in a bit of a scuffle. Jason and Olly, Suzy's long time defenders, leapt to their feet. Maddy took two steps forward.

'Oh, I say!' Gareth brayed, just as Diana, smartly dressed in a taupe trouser suit, toppled into the stream.

It was bedlam. People pushing from the back to see what was happening, shoved those on the edge into the water. Fists started to fly. The TV cameras were immediately brought out again. Suddenly everyone was hitting and grabbing, kicking and shoving.

Diana, drenched and muddy, clambered to the edge of the stream, grabbed Gareth's proffered hand and immediately pulled him in on top of her. The media were going mad. Maddy bit her knuckles in horror and tried to get to where Suzy had been standing.

'I shouldn't, Maddy,' Barty Small panted, trying to fight against the crush. 'You'll only end up in there, too.'

'Suzy!' Maddy shrieked. 'Suzy!'

'She's OK,' Kimberley, her hair awry, gasped. 'It wasn't her fault.'

'I know,' Maddy, absolutely terrified, ducked a fist. 'I just hope she's – ouch!' She turned and glared at Stacey. 'You hit me!'

'Accident.' Stacey looked like a petrified rabbit. 'Really . . . Oooh!'

Slithering, trying to grab hold of anything solid, Stacey splashed satisfyingly into the stream. Kimberley looked at Maddy with admiration.

'It wasn't me! I didn't—'

'No, I did.' Bronwyn Pugh smirked. 'Little madam. She

won't call me a daft old bat again in a hurry.'

Maddy tried to fight her way out of the mayhem. The noise was unbearable. She had dreaded this happening. Somewhere, sirens echoed eerily above the shouts and screams. It didn't deter the battlers. They hadn't had anything like this since the last inter-village cup final when Milton St John were robbed by an iffy penalty in the last minute. The police cars screeched to a halt, and blue uniforms swarmed amongst the mob. Maddy felt a hand on her arm and failing to shake it free, bit it.

'Shit!' Drew swore at her. 'Thanks a lot! Come on, unless you want to get arrested! Maddy – now!'

He hauled her out of the throng and glared at her. People were pushing and shoving all around them.

She glared back. 'I didn't need rescuing.'

'Yes you did.' Drew examined his hand. 'You were right in the thick of it. I think I'll need a tetanus jab.'

Maddy was shaking. 'I was trying to get to Suzy.'

'Suzy is well able to look after herself. I'm not so sure about you.'

'I've always managed before,' she spat. 'I don't need anyone to fight my battles. Especially not you.'

'And I thought you'd be grateful—'

'Why the hell should I be grateful?' She sidestepped the Maynard brothers who were fighting with each other. 'I didn't ask you to play Sir Lancelot!'

'Galahad,' Drew corrected. 'He was the shining-armour one who rescued damsels in distress. Lancelot was the lover.'

She looked at him mutinously and then laughed. He didn't. Drew Fitzgerald was still very angry.

'Have you been here all the time?'

'Most of it – bugger!' A lager can caught his shoulder. 'Who ever told me that Milton St John was the peaceful heart of rural England should be sued under the bloody Trade Descriptions Act! I really think you should get out of here.'

'I'm not leaving Suzy. And why didn't you make your presence known earlier?'

'Because I didn't think you'd want to see me. After all, according to you I'm only interested in you as a dalliance while my wife's away.'

'It came out wrong. That wasn't what I meant – oh, help!' A little knot of scufflers bowled into them, bounced off, and splashed into the stream.

Drew fastened his hand round her wrist and was tugging her towards the road. 'Maybe we can talk about it later. Not now. We'll be arrested if we stay here.'

The police were hauling dripping villagers out of the stream and shoving them into the back of cars. Maddy wriggled in his grasp. She wasn't leaving without Suzy.

'Have you seen Stacey?' Peter loomed up out of the crowd, still managing to look cool and elegant despite the fracas raging around him. 'We seem to have lost her, and Diana and Gareth.'

Drew tightened his grip on Maddy. She frowned at them both, then pointed at the stream. 'They were all in there just now – and no, I didn't push them. Just what the hell did you think you were doing, Peter? You could have prevented this, couldn't you?'

'Not this,' Peter said. 'I didn't think it would turn out like this. But, yes, of course I knew that the golf course wouldn't be a problem to the village. Nobody listened.'

'Because you deliberately didn't tell anyone. You just loved seeing them getting all stirred up and Bronwyn making a fool of herself, didn't you?'

'It was rather amusing, yes.' Peter's smile was so smug that Maddy longed to smack his face. He shrugged. 'I did try to tell you, though. I didn't want you to be mixed up in this. I sent you a note. I tried phoning. I asked Stacey to get you to speak to me. You didn't bother. And then—'

'And then when we did come face to face – or rather face to buttock – you weren't really in any position to discuss anything, were you?'

Peter glared at Maddy, and then at Drew who beamed back innocently and merely tightened his grip on Maddy's hand. Suddenly, completely overwhelmed by desire, she leaned against him. Peter looked murderous.

Maddy shook her head. 'You were always a manipulative bastard, Peter. Maybe you would have told me, but I doubt it. You like to see people making fools of themselves. You've probably broken Bronwyn's heart by witholding that information until the last minute.'

'She should have checked. You're all so gullible.'

'I think they've just trawled your girlfriend out of the stream,' Drew said.

Peter swung round. Stacey, Diana and Gareth, along with at least two dozen villagers, were being wrapped inside a collection of hastily assembled coats. Jeff Henley was ineffectually patting his daughter's sodden shoulders. Maddy was delighted. Stacey looked like a weasel that had been dunked in a bucket.

'I must go and see if she's all right.'

'They'll probably have to send in frogmen to recover the false eyelashes,' Drew said, straight faced, 'but I would think the wig has gone for ever. It'll probably end up housing a family of water voles.'

Snarling, Peter stumbled down the bank towards the sobbing Stacey. Diana, her teeth chattering with rage, was jabbing accusing fingers at the crowd. The media had homed in. Those policemen who were not involved in separating brawlers, were listening intently.

'What a perfect end to a so-so day.' Drew was laughing as he pulled Maddy against him. 'Oh, I feel sorry for the Pughs', and for anyone who got caught up in the scuffle – but it was surely worth it to see Diana's ardour cooled so eloquently, wasn't it?'

'Definitely.' Maddy snuggled against his sweater. 'And to see Stacey without her artificial bits. I wonder if she wears them in bed?'

'Along with her riding boots . . .' Drew grinned.

Laughing, Maddy hugged him, then his face moved down to hers and he was kissing her hungrily. He kissed her with his lips, his tongue, his teeth.

Maddy's body was no longer her own. It was only the sound of her name that brought her toppling back to reality. Reluctantly she pulled her lips from the onslaught.

Barty Small, his face puckered, was shouting at her. 'Maddy! For God's sake! They've arrested Bronwyn! And your Suzy!'

Seventeen

Wantage Police Station seethed. The Duty Officer, used to fairly peaceful evenings – at least until the pubs turned out – was marshalling groups of angrily protesting people and wearing a perplexed frown. No one had explained to him the numbers involved, or that so many of them would be wet.

Maddy, still holding Drew's hand, shoved her way through to the desk. 'My sister – Suzy Beckett – is she here?'

'I'll look in a minute.' The policeman was trying to fill in forms that had been dripped on. 'Just sit down over there. With everyone else.'

'But you arrested her,' Maddy insisted. 'She didn't do anything. She—'

'Madam, no one who ever walks through these doors has ever done anything. Please just sit down. Everyone will be sorted out in a minute.' He turned back to the Maynard brothers, who both had bloody noses and wanted to bring charges against each other. 'So you admit to hitting him first, do you?'

'Come on, Maddy.' Drew took her arm. 'Come and sit down. There's nothing we can do at the moment.'

She sat alongside a selection of villagers who had also come to collect miscreants.

'Hiya, Maddy!' Brenda waved along the row. 'They've got my Wayne. The little bugger. And Elaine's Gavin. Still, they're used to 'aving 'im 'ere. 'E's got 'is own cell.'

Maddy smiled faintly. The overhead lighting did nothing to improve the ambience. Harrassed policemen and women were scuttling about, the phone rang incessantly, and clumps of morose villagers were beginning to smell mildewy as damp clothes dried on muddy bodies.

Drew slid his arm round her shoulders and pulled her head down. Maddy closed her eyes. She knew Brenda was watching them beadily but she didn't care.

'I hadn't envisaged the day ending like this.' Drew spoke into her hair. 'In fact, I thought I'd probably never see you again.'

'Difficult, when I live across the road.'

'You know what I mean. I thought we'd just exchange polite nods.'

'I didn't even think we'd do that. I'm sorry that I spoiled this morning. I think we just ought to steer clear of mentioning Caroline.'

'So do I.' Drew was stroking her hair now, making her feel quite dizzy with longing. 'At least for the rest of the day. This is fraught enough. Eventually though, we're going to have to talk about her.'

She sighed. 'Yes, I know. Have you ever been arrested?'

'No. Have you?'

'No. It's nice to have a shared new experience, isn't it?'

'I could think of better ones . . .' His head lowered, and remembering just in time, he turned away. 'Sorry. Wrong time. Wrong place.'

The doors swung open. Peter and Jeff Henley strode in, talking animatedly with a policewoman and a rather scruffy man with a pot belly and a drooping moustache.

'He's probably the Chief Commissioner,' Drew said. 'Trust Peter to go to the top.'

'I want them charged with assault!' Jeff Henley bellowed as they forced their way through the crowded office. 'Bang 'em up!'

'We'll have to take statements first,' the policewoman was saying, glancing at Peter and moistening her lips. 'I understand both Miss Henley and Mrs James-Jordan have been checked over in hospital. We've sent someone to speak to them.'

'But we know who did it! It was common assault! My little Stacey's only a child! I want justice!' The policewoman ushered him into an interview room.

Peter was still talking to the pot-bellied man. Maddy leaned forward and called him.

He looked at her blankly. 'What on earth are you doing here?'

Pushing through the crowd, Maddy smiled at the plainclothes policeman. 'Could I just have a word with Mr Knightley? In private?'

'Yeah. Sure. You the duty solicitor?'

'No, just a friend – of sorts.' She pulled Peter into a corner. They were sharing it with a very drunk lady carrying six shopping bags, and a young couple in tears. It was extremely depressing.

'Have you been arrested?' Peter shuddered, visibly holding himself away from the other occupants of the corner. 'If so, there's nothing I can do.'

'No, I haven't. But Suzy has. And Bronwyn. They had nothing – absolutely nothing – to do with what happened to Stacey and Diana, did they?'

'I wouldn't know. And that's best left to the police. They're taking statements at the moment.'

'Listen to me. They had nothing to do with it. They're going to be released without charge. They just got caught up in the mêlée, didn't they?'

'How would I know? All I know is that Jeff Henley wants justice – and so do I.'

'Good. So you will just go and tell Jeff and your friendly fat policeman that Suzy and Bronwyn were innocent bystanders –' she paused looking at his blank face – 'or I will tell Jeff and Stacey and Gareth and this whole bloody police station about the riding boots and Diana's birthmark.'

They stared at each other. Maddy wondered if she had ever loved him. He seemed so pale and insubstantial compared to Drew. Realisation dawned in the cornflower-blue eyes. 'You wouldn't, would you?'

'Absolutely. Diana was scared enough to reinstate Richard as Saratoga's jockey. I'm sure she'll be equally understanding over this little matter. I'll leave it with you, then, shall I?'

'You've turned into a conniving bitch,' Pete hissed. The old lady with the carrier bags clapped her hands. The young couple had stopped crying.

Maddy nodded cheerfully. 'Oh, I do hope so. I'll be waiting over there when they let Suzy go. OK?' Not looking at him, she forced her way back to the bench and Drew.

She was trembling when she sat down. Drew covered her hand with his. 'What was all that about?'

'Riding boots.'

'Oh, brilliant!' He kissed her. 'You are amazing. No one else would even dream of blackmailing someone in a police station full of people.'

'It wasn't blackmail. It was just a trade-in.' She turned to him and sighed. 'I know this isn't the right time to mention it, but I'm starving.'

Drew kissed her on the forehead and stood up. Two stable lads immediately slid into his place.

'Nathan Gardner and Joseph Dougan!' the Duty Officer roared. The two stable lads stood up again.

''E gone to the lav?' Brenda leaned along the row again.

'I don't think so.' Maddy smiled dreamily. 'I think he's gone to get me a Mars bar.'

'Bleedin' 'ell Maddy! You ain't never been in a cop shop before, 'ave you? It's not a bloody cinema!' Brenda shook her head at such innocence. 'Still, 'e's a bit of all right, that Drew. Shame 'e's married.'

'Isn't it?' Maddy knew she was smiling like an idiot but could do nothing about it. 'Anyway, his wife doesn't live with him all the time.'

'More fool 'er.' Brenda nodded. 'I wouldn't let a man like that out of my sight.'

Nor would I, Maddy thought to herself.

Brenda stretched noisily. 'Jackie said they've got separate bedrooms at Peapods. Is that right?'

'You know we're not supposed to discuss anything we see or hear at the customers' homes. That's a really important part of Shadows, being discreet, and—'

'Cobblers!' Brenda rocked with laughter. 'You're as nosy as the rest of us, Maddy. 'Ow the 'ell would we know what was going on in Milton St John if we didn't discuss things, eh? It's all in the public interest. So, is that right about Drew's bedrooms?'

Fortunately Maddy was spared having to voice her thoughts on the Fitzgeralds' sleeping arrangements by Drew's return. Forcing his way through towards the bench, his face wreathed in smiles, he held a paper package above his head.

'Oh!' Maddy sniffed in rapture. 'Fish and chips!'

Brenda settled back in her seat. 'Bloody 'ell! That's better'n a diamond ring under the circumstances. I wish someone cared that much about me.'

Maddy scrabbled at the paper, aware that every head in the police station had turned in envy as the delicious smell of hot, spicy vinegar wafted upwards in a mouth-watering cloud.

'You're brilliant,' she laughed in unashamed delight at Drew. 'Where on earth did you conjure these from?'

'I noticed the shop when we parked. I was hungry, too.' He glanced at the bare white washed walls. 'I can't see any notices banning eating, so I presume we won't be arrested.'

'Mobbed, probably.' Maddy bit into a succulent chip. 'Drew, you are incredible.'

'I know,' he mumbled through a mouthful of fish. 'I've been telling you that for ages. I hoped you wouldn't have any objections to eating chips from the paper. I've always thought it was the best way.'

Maddy was licking her fingers just as Peter and Jeff Henley emerged from the interview room. Peter looked at her in horror. He would never dream of eating chips in public. He pushed his way towards her.

'You'll be pleased to hear that there doesn't seem to be any charge for Suzy or Bronwyn to answer as far as I can gather. The police seemed quite relieved – they've got more than enough to be going on with. Jeff, after some persuasion, now accepts that it was an accident, that everyone was pushing and pulling and there was no intended assault on any one person.'

'Good.' Maddy offered him a chip, delighting in the revulsion on his face. 'So, we needn't mention any of this again, need we? I think honour is now satisfied.'

'Aren't you even going to thank me?'

She broke off a chunk of flaky white fish, shaking her head. 'No, Peter. Why should I? For once in your life, all you did was tell the truth. You should try it more often. It might make you a nicer person.'

He glared at her. 'You've changed. You used to be—'

'Meek and mild and frightened to step out of line? I know. You'd better go and rescue Stacey from the hospital, hadn't you? After all, she needs you – I don't.'

He looked at her again, almost sadly, then marched out of the police station, twitching irritably each time he cannoned into the mass of humanity which refused to stand aside and let him pass. Jeff Henley, looking apologetic, strode after him like a tug bobbing in the wake of a stately galleon. Peter was gloriously handsome when he was angry, Maddy thought, but the blond beauty no longer touched her. She was now completely cured of Peter Knightley. She looked sideways at Drew. It was just such a shame that she'd become so hopelessly addicted to the antidote.

'That was the best meal I have ever had in my life,' she said. 'Thank you so much. Although this wasn't quite the way I'd imagined our first date.'

'We haven't had that yet.' Drew took the paper from her and lobbed it neatly into a wastepaper basket. 'I said I'd take you out, and I will. It was supposed to be Kimberley's barbecue, and that didn't work out either, did it?'

'No. It's fate conspiring against us. Fate is probably

moralistic and disapproving.' She sighed. 'Maybe we'll never actually go out together.'

'Yes, we will.' Drew took her greasy hand in his. 'You know it as well as I do.'

Suzy, looking furiously dishevelled, and followed by Bronwyn, fought her way through to them.

'Holy hell! I thought I'd be in there for ever! Bloody cheek – arresting me!'

Maddy jumped up and hugged her. 'Are you all right? Was it really awful?'

'I'm fine. Just angry. Bronwyn enjoyed it, though.'

Bronwyn was beaming. 'It made me feel like Emily Pankhurst. The cell was a bit cramped, but everyone was very nice. Where's Bernie?'

'Safely in the Cat and Fiddle with Barty and Kimberley and John Hastings.' Drew also stood up. 'I told him we'd drop you off. Are you sure you're feeling OK?'

'Never better.' Bronwyn's eyes were bright, and two spots of colour glowed on her sallow cheeks. 'And it hasn't made me change my mind. Quite the opposite, in fact. I still don't see why Peter Knightley and his cronies should steamroller over the rest of the village.'

'I think you'll have to tread carefully,' Drew said as they walked outside. 'After all, the golf course isn't going to be a threat to the tranquillity of the village, is it?'

'Maybe not.' Bronwyn jerked her chin in defiance. 'I won't run the risk of repeating tonight's fiasco, but I still want to see Peter Knightley get his come-uppance. No one,' she said darkly, scrambling into the back of the Mercedes, 'makes a fool of Bronwyn Pugh and gets away with it.'

Maddy and Suzy exchanged amused grins as they joined Bronwyn in the car.

'All on again, is it?' Suzy hissed as the car purred away from the police station. 'The little rift healed?'

'He bought me fish and chips.' Maddy smiled across at Drew in the darkness.

'Oh, Jesus.' Suzy shook her head. 'That's like putting an announcement in *The Times*.'

The Cat and Fiddle roared with the aftermath. Everyone had a story to tell, and every story grew taller with the telling. Bronwyn was fêted as something of a heroine for having provided so much impromptu entertainment.

Suzy and Maddy squeezed into seats around the table with John Hastings, Kimberley and Barty. There were a few notable absentees, but no doubt all the revellers would be returned to the village by morning. The advisory committee from Twyford Down, Batheaston and Newbury had surged around Bronwyn and Bernie and Maddy hoped they wouldn't be needed for any of Bronwyn's future plans. She, too, would still be delighted to see Peter stymied, but felt that after this evening anything else would be something of a damp squib.

Drew placed glasses in front of them and eased himself between Maddy and Suzy. He looked at the three trainers. 'I needed to talk to you. I have a proposition to put to Suzy, but I'll need you to OK it first.'

The raised glasses were held suspended in three hands. Suzy looked at Maddy who shrugged. Drew drank half a pint in one go, obviously needing to wash down the fish and chips, and then spread his hands on the table.

'In ten days' time it'll be The Derby.'

'Gold star. Go to the top of the class,' Suzy intoned quietly. Maddy kicked her under the table.

'Sorry, that was stating the obvious. What I really want to know is if any of you intend putting Suzy up in the Woodcote Stakes?'

'I would if I could, but I haven't got a fit runner in the yard,' Kimberley said sadly.

John Hastings shook his head 'My two are already booked. Owners didn't want an apprentice – unfortunately.'

'I haven't got a runner in the Woodcote this year,' Barty said.

'Great.' Drew turned to Suzy. 'Then I'd like you to ride Dock of the Bay.'

Suzy dropped her Bacardi. 'Really? Honestly?'

'Really honestly. I've spoken to Kit and Rosa – the horse's owners in Jersey – and they'd be delighted. So – will you?'

'Oh, yes, – thank you. Oh, shit . . .' Tears sparkled on Suzy's thickly mascaraed lashes and she threw herself at Drew.

Laughing, he held her away from him. 'It's going to mean some pretty hard work. As soon as you've finished at John's yard each day I'll need you to ride him out. I want you to do all the work on him between now and Epsom.'

'I'll do it in my sleep if I have to. I'll never be able to repay you.'

'Just give him a good ride,' Drew said. 'I'm not expecting him to win, but he's well bred, and should get a place. I've got faith in you, Suzy. I know you'll do well.'

'Can I tell everybody? Jason and Olly and the others?'

'All those who aren't still floundering in the cells at Wantage, yes, of course you can.' Drew laughed at her excitement. 'I'll get Holly to do the entry tomorrow.'

Watching Suzy being swamped in congratulations, Maddy snaked her hand into Drew's. 'That was a wonderful gesture. And very brave of you. I only hope she'll be up to it.'

'She's very, very accomplished. I'm sure she'll give a good account of herself and the horse. And of course,' he stared deep into Maddy's eyes, 'it wasn't entirely without an ulterior motive.'

'It wasn't?'

'No.' He stroked her fingers with his thumb, sending dancing waves of lust washing through her body. 'Because, as Suzy's mentor and guardian, you'll have to come to Epsom with me, won't you?'

Eighteen

The days preceding The Derby were frantic with activity. There was a sort of election fever crossed with carnival atmosphere in Milton St John, as the Press converged on the gallops for last-minute spying, and the Channel Four racing team holed up in the Cat and Fiddle to present their pre-Epsom coverage. This nervous excitement was repeated in racing communities across the country; and from Newmarket to Lambourn, Ilsley to Arundel, horror stories spread and rumours were spawned.

Suzy worked Dock of the Bay with almost religious fervour, listening intently to Drew's instructions and obeying without demur. Maddy, who accompanied Drew's small string occasionally on the plodding Solomon, watched Suzy – flying along the horizon in the early morning mist, crouched low over Dock of the Bay's neck – with a lump of pride in her throat. There was only one drawback to all this frenetic preparation: despite Caroline's absence, it meant she had had no time to see Drew on his own.

As a result of the media coverage of the skirmish, Bronwyn had decided to adjourn further meetings of VAGs until after The Derby. It was felt that Milton St John had had its fair share of invasive television for the time being.

'Luke'll be here tomorrow,' Suzy beamed two days before The Derby. 'Emilio is letting him off to ride out Jefferson Jet for Diana. He can stay, can't he?'

'Of course.' Maddy was distractedly wandering round the oblong bit of the kitchen trying to make a fish pie and wondering whether she dare ask Drew if Caroline was coming over for the Epsom meeting. 'Although we'd better put him in my room. I'll go in with you.'

'No you bloody won't.' Suzy tugged off her boots and jeans on the kitchen floor. 'I haven't seen him for five days.'

'Poor old you,' Maddy mocked. 'I just thought that athletes were supposed to refrain from energetic romping prior to a major event.'

'Sex is now considered therapeutic.' Suzy, stripped down to minuscule white bra and knickers, looked like a superwaif.

'Who says?'

'Luke does.' Suzy danced into the bathroom, singing along with the Michael Bolton tape as she turned on the taps. 'Anyway, Mad, there's something I wanted to ask you . . .'

Maddy looked at her sister's pert face framed by the white-blonde bob and shook her head. 'Don't bother. I don't think I'll be able to help you. I think you're way ahead of me.'

'Not about sex. It's about the other night, when I got arrested.'

Maddy paused in the middle of chopping parsley. Suzy had emptied half a bottle of Badedas into the bath and the wafts of woodland-scented foam clashed with the cod halfway along the hall.

'I've been thinking.' Suzy was peeling off her underwear with no signs of inhibition. 'Before Diana fell into the stream, she said something about you. She said you'd told me something. I didn't know what she was on about. Do you?'

'Yes.' Maddy scraped the parsley into the white sauce. 'But I'm not going to tell you.'

'Oh, Mad! Go on!'

'No. Definitely not. At least, not yet. After the Derby I will . . . it won't matter then.'

'You are bloody irritating.' Suzy wrapped a towel round her nakedness as she waited for the bath to fill. 'I'll keep you to that, though. As soon as Luke has won The Derby and we've finished celebrating, then you can tell me.'

'You'll be waiting a long time then.' Maddy mashed

potatoes with vigour. 'Because Richard is going to win The Derby.'

'I've had a tenner on Luke.'

'You can't. Jockey's aren't allowed to bet.'

'John put it on with his. Anyway, you're splitting hairs. Whoever wins The Derby, you'll tell me about Diana then?'

'Yes,' Maddy sighed, ladling potato on to the creamy cod. 'It won't matter any more. Now, go and have your bath. This won't be long.'

Suzy scuttled away, and as Maddy stood up from sliding the pie into the oven the letter box rattled. Wiping her potatoey hands down her jeans, Maddy kicked the rug away and opened the door.

Drew stood on the doorstep. It was a dank, grey evening and his dark hair was studded with raindrops. As always, he looked gorgeous, and Maddy's stomach dissolved. He smiled. 'Is it a bad time?'

'Of course not.' Maddy wanted to die. Her jeans were almost as scruffy as her sweatshirt, and her hair, unwashed for three days, was tied in an unbecoming ponytail. 'Come in.'

'God, that smells wonderful.' Drew sucked in his breath. 'What is it?'

'Suzy and three gallons of Badedas.' Michael Bolton was warbling at full tilt from behind the bathroom door.

'The food, idiot.' Drew laughed.

'It's only fish pie. Would you like to stay for supper? I've done loads – or weren't you stopping?' Please let him say he had somewhere else to go just for half an hour, she prayed. Just to give her time to tart herself up a bit. Again, capricious fate wasn't on her side. He was already tugging off his leather jacket.

'I was going to have a word with Suzy and then invite you to the pub. However, as I've been living out of the freezer, a real meal would be wonderful. If you're sure . . .'

'Positive.' She hung the jacket on the bathroom door. 'I

always do too much. There's broccoli and carrots, too. What would you like to drink?'

'Anything. We can still go down to the Cat and Fiddle later. You'll have to let me repay you for supper.'

She splashed the remains of a bottle of Lambrusco into two glasses and handed one to him. Her fingers brushed his and she snatched them away in case they were encrusted with cod.

'I hope the weather improves before the weekend.' She watched the soft grey rain sweeping from the downs. 'It would be such a shame to have a soggy Derby.'

Drew was watching her face. 'The forecast is hot and sunny, which will be great for Dock of the Bay. He acts well on fast ground. Jesus!' He slammed the Lambrusco on to the table. 'I can't stand here and talk like Michael Fish! Come here, Maddy . . .'

He pulled her into his arms and found her lips, his tongue plundering her mouth, his teeth closing gently over the sensitive flesh. Maddy tried to pull away. She hadn't even cleaned her teeth. Drew didn't seem to notice, or if he did, it didn't matter. Her body dissolved against his.

'We can't stay here,' he murmured against her neck. 'Not in the kitchen . . . Not with Suzy in the bathroom.'

'Not anywhere . . .' She was finding breathing difficult. 'We can't . . . you can't . . .'

He kissed her again, then picked her up as though she was as light as thistledown and carried her into the hall. Looking round, he kicked open the bedroom door.

'No, Drew,' she squeaked. 'It's all—'

But again, still holding her, he silenced her protests with his lips. Opening her eyes, she saw the tumbled unmade bed, the clothes in untidy heaps, the dressing table cluttered with debris. Drew obviously didn't. Gently he laid her on the bed and stood looking down at her.

'You are the most beautiful woman I have ever met.' His eyes glittered in the dusky light. 'And the most desirable, funny, crazy, and infuriating one. You have driven me mad from the moment I first saw you.'

He tugged the scarf from her hair, allowing her tangle of curls to fall to her shoulders. She never knew which one of them disposed of the sweatshirt and jeans.

'Oh, God . . .' she groaned, burying her face in the pillow, trying to cover her body with her hands. 'I'd always planned to do this in red satin.'

Drew grinned. 'I'd planned to do it in the bedroom at Bonne Nuit where the window opens out on to the balcony and the cliffs drop away to the sea.'

They looked at each other and laughed. Somewhere amidst the laughter, Drew had removed all his clothes, and her bra and knickers. She stared at him. His body was golden, hard muscled, incredibly fit.

Gently, he sat on the edge of the bed, and traced his hands across her body with wonderment. She reached for him as he lowered himself beside her, allowing her mouth to taste his sweet clean flesh. Oh, God, she thought drowsily, how could he even want to seduce her?

'Jesus,' Drew breathed. 'You are gorgeous . . .' She *felt* gorgeous. He looked at her again. 'What are you doing?'

'Holding my stomach in.'

'Bloody don't. I love every inch of you.'

Drew's head moved downwards as he kissed each breast in turn, flicking his tongue across the thimbles of her nipples, using his long fingers to explore and arouse. Instinctively, Maddy caressed and teased him, the sensations creating a growing volcano inside her.

Whatever she had dreamed he would be like, it hadn't been this. Not this explosive, savage, uncontrolled desire. He made love with lethal expertise. Her body rocked with his relentless onslaught until she knew she would scream unless the swelling crescendo was released.

Sensing her frustration, and driven by his own needs, Drew took her upwards with his body. She clung to him, aching, until his low-throated shout of release triggered her own melting, swirling, explosion of passion. Clinging together, shuddering, they floated down, their sated bodies drenched in sweat.

He held her close to him, rocking her, smoothing her hair. Maddy had never experienced anything so wonderful; had never realised that anyone could give so much pleasure; or that there would be this soporific, languid sense of drifting happiness. It had never been like this with Peter.

'Are you OK?' His voice was drowsy in her ear. 'Maddy?'

She swallowed, her cheek sticking to his shoulder. 'I'm an adulteress.'

Drew sat up, still holding her, his eyes gentle. 'No you're not. You're not married.'

'But *you* are.' Suddenly the appalling truth hit her. 'Oh, God, what have we done?'

'Something I haven't done ever before in my life.' He smoothed the curls away from her damp face. 'Made love.'

'Rubbish. That wasn't in the least virginal.'

'I said, "made love". Which is what we did.' He rolled over on the bed. 'It was – all right?' His eyes were concerned. 'I mean, it felt as though you . . .'

'Had an orgasm?' She breathed deeply. 'Oh, yes. For the first time in my life. I used to pretend . . . But, then, with you, it was just difficult trying to stop it happening too soon.' Her eyes filled with tears as she pulled him towards her again. 'Drew, you were sensational. It was amazing.'

'For me, too. I was frightened that I couldn't . . .'

Maddy sat up in the rumpled bed. She knew her thighs were dimpled against Drew's legs, but she had never felt so beautiful. 'I thought I was the only one with self-doubt.'

'Men have pressures, too.' Drew was kissing her neck. 'Bloody awful pressures. About performance and size and being able to do it at the drop of a hat and all night long and—'

'I get the picture. But Caroline said . . .'

'This hardly seems to be the right time to talk about Caroline.' Drew released her fingers, walked over to the wicker chair and picked up her quilted dressing gown. He looked magnificent naked, Maddy thought, dreamily. He wrapped the dressing gown round her shoulders and held her again. 'Caroline was never very keen on sex. At first, I thought she was just naive, and that I would be good enough to teach her to enjoy it. I wasn't.'

'Of course you were good enough!' Maddy said hotly. 'It can't have been your fault! I mean, there must have been girls before Caroline.'

'Yes. But once I realised how distasteful Caroline found it, I began to wonder about the others. After all, I've seen *When Harry Met Sally*. Meg Ryan must have worried a lot of men. I thought I was useless, that everyone must have faked their pleasure.'

'I didn't.'

'No, sweetheart. You didn't. And it had to happen like that. If we'd planned it, I would probably never have done it. I would have been too scared of failure.'

'So why do you stay with Caroline.'

'Because I have to.' He was staring over her head. 'Because although I know we'll never have a proper marriage, I can't leave her. She still wants me in her life. There are reasons . . . Oh, I gave up trying to make love to Caroline years ago because I didn't want to upset her. I even forgot about sex for weeks at a time. Then, I met you.'

Maddy wiped her eyes and stuffed the tissue back beneath the pillow. 'But I'm overweight and disgusting.'

'You're adorable. Beautiful. Warm, cuddly, loving, funny. The sexiest woman I've ever met.'

'I've never thought of myself as therapeutic.' She grinned, then stopped. 'Do you feel guilty?'

'No. Blissfully happy. What about you?'

'The same. Except I really would have liked to have been bathed and scented and made up and wearing decent knickers.'

Drew bundled her over on the bed, making her gurgle with laughter. If it wasn't love, it was a pretty close thing.

An hour later she tip-toed out into the hall. Suzy zoomed from the sitting-room. 'I've put the dinner on a low heat. I've topped up the bath water. You can even play my Michael Bolton tape if you want.'

'Thanks.' She grinned sheepishly at Suzy. 'I'm so sorry. I must have fallen asleep.'

'Crap, Mad.' Suzy smiled fondly. 'I know you and Drew have got it together at last – and about bloody time.'

'You weren't listening?' Maddy was appalled.

''Course not.' Suzy wrinkled her nose. 'It was the little things that gave it away. The glasses of wine un-touched. His jacket on the door handle. No sign of either of you. The bedroom door closed. And now – well, you've only got to look at you.'

Impulsively, Maddy hugged her sister. 'It was the most wonderful, amazing experience of my whole life. God, Suzy, you won't tell anyone, will you?'

'Nah.' Suzy shook her shorn head. 'I won't need to, Mad. Your smile says it all.'

By the time she'd had a bath and washed her hair and, again wrapped in the quilted dressing gown, had staggered back into the kitchen, Suzy and Drew were setting the table. She felt slightly embarrassed, but extremely relieved that he was still there. He smiled at her. 'Feel better now?'

'Cleaner. Not better. You can't improve on perfection.'

'I'll clear off, if you like,' Suzy offered. 'After all, this healthy eating is getting pretty boring.'

'I wondered why there weren't any Mars bars on the menu.' Drew paused in dealing out the oddments of cutlery. 'It's my fault, is it? You're getting Suzy into racing fitness?'

'Plenty of protein,' Maddy said dreamily, heaping fish pie and vegetables on to three mismatched plates and not adding that the economies were necessary because of her overspending with Caroline. Caroline! She blushed. 'I thought we could both do with a change of diet.' She turned to Suzy. 'And you'll stay and eat it. Otherwise you'll be eating crisps at the Cat and Fiddle.'

'As long as that's all she eats at the Cat and Fiddle.' Drew sat down beside Maddy, rubbing his long denim leg against her naked one, and making her drop her broccoli. 'Holly popped in there for lunch the other day. She giggled all the afternoon.'

They ate cosily, with the rain sliding softly down the windowpane like silent tears. Maddy felt happy. Drew helped to wash up, despite their protestations that everything could be left to soak. It all felt so right. So perfectly right.

Sitting idly at the kitchen table with cups of strong coffee, they talked about The Derby, about Drew's strategy for Dock of the Bay, about Luke and Richard's battle to become Epsom's supremo. They didn't talk about Caroline.

Suzy stood up and grinned at them. 'Well, if I can trust you two alone, I'm going to the Cat and Fiddle. I can't stand you looking all dopey-eyed at each other while I'm manless. And –' she pirouetted out of the door '– I do hope you took some sort of precautions. "Auntie" is such an ageing title.'

Maddy threw the tea towel at her then sank back into her chair. They looked at each other sheepishly.

'Are you . . .?' Drew stroked her fingers. 'On the pill or anything?'

Maddy shook her head, 'No need. I've been celibate for over a year. And of course, you didn't . . .'

'No, I didn't. I hadn't planned it.' He lifted her hand to his cheek. 'Maybe we were a bit irresponsible.'

'Just a bit. I've always screamed at Suzy to make sure about these things. I just never thought. Oh, hell. I'm so out of touch. I suppose these days people ask each other about AIDS and things before they go to bed.'

'I suppose they do. It all seems so very unromantic.'

'But necessary. You're all right because you've been with

189

Caroline for years. I've never even thought about me. But there was only Peter, and I know he had a test just before we split up, for insurance purposes.' She made patterns in the spilled salt on the table. 'That side of it is OK. It's just . . .'

'Pregnancy.' Drew rolled the word round his tongue. 'I've always wanted children.' His eyes were suddenly bleak. 'Caroline was pregnant once.'

'What?' Maddy felt suddenly cold. 'When? What happened?'

'It was early in our marriage. She lost the baby at six months. She was told there couldn't be any more. I was devastated, of course, but Caroline –' Drew swallowed – 'she never came to terms with it. That was when our sex life stopped altogether.'

'Oh, God.' Maddy's eyes welled with tears. 'Oh, poor Caroline – and poor you. Oh, Drew, I've been so unfair. I just thought she was frigid. I never stopped to wonder why.' Maddy was stricken. 'Jesus, Drew. What if—'

'Our whole life is "what if", Maddy. There's no point in worrying about it. I have no regrets about making love with you at all.'

'Nor have I,' Maddy said honestly. But at the back of her mind, there was a stirring of doubt. If, just if, she was pregnant, what would happen to her? What on earth would happen to Caroline?

'Shall we go and have that drink?' His hand was caressing her cheek. 'Or do you want to stay here?'

She moved her lips to the palm of his hand. 'I want to stay here, but until one of us has sorted out some sort of, er, arrangement that I won't get pregnant, I don't think that's a good idea.'

'Probably not.' Drew stood up. 'Anyway, I'm waiting for a call from Kit and Rosa in Jersey to tell me when they'll be over for The Derby. If I give you fifteen minutes to get ready I'll just go and check my answer machine.' He pulled her to her feet, sliding his hands inside the quilted dressing gown and cupping her breasts. 'Please don't think about Caroline. Not tonight, anyway. Not now. Caroline is my problem, not yours. I am in love with you, Maddy. Hopelessly in love.'

She bit her lip as he closed the front door. The emotions seesawed again. She loved him, too, but now she was the other woman, the mistress. All ugly, disgusting terms for what she and Drew shared – and the very thing she'd vowed she would never be.

She wrapped her arms tightly round her waist, remembering how it had felt when Drew had touched her. He was married, and because of her he'd been unfaithful to his wife. The loss of the baby must have been appalling for them both.

The phone rang, making her jump. She wanted it to be Drew's voice telling her that he'd missed her. It was her mother.

'Maddy, love. I won't keep you a minute. Did Suzy tell you I'd called earlier?'

'No, I don't think so.'

'Well, we've got everything sorted out. Carl and Marcie are angels. They said of course they'd stand in. Isn't that wonderful?'

'Wonderful,' Maddy echoed without understanding.

'Yes, so we'll be down tomorrow evening, then we can all make our way to Epsom together, can't we? I mean, I know our Suzy's not actually riding in The Derby, but as good as. We're so excited. Do you want me to bring anything?'

'N-no,' Maddy stammered. 'That'll be lovely, Mum. I'll see you tomorrow. Give my love to Dad.'

Bugger! She dropped the phone back into place. Tomorrow was when Luke was staying. She'd end up sleeping on the sofa again. If she could even sleep. She'd probably never sleep again. She'd just lie awake and think of Drew.

She wandered into the bedroom and pulled on clean underwear and the black trousers, then dived across the hall and fished beneath Suzy's bed until she found a suitable top. For good measure she used Suzy's make-up, and was in the middle of drawing black lines under her eyes when Drew once again rattled the letter box.

Pulling the door open she slid into his arms.

He kissed her hungrily. 'You look lovely. I can't stand being away from you.'

'Fool.' She stroked the silky hair at the nape of his neck. 'Anyway, it looks as though we'll have loads of guardians of our virtue from now on. My mother phoned. She and Dad are coming down for Epsom tomorrow and Luke is staying too.'

'I'm going to have a houseful as well,' Drew groaned into her neck. 'Kit had left a message on the answerphone. He and Rosa are flying into Southampton at midday. They're bringing Caroline with them.'

Nineteen

Maddy stared at Drew. She had been a mistress for merely hours. It seemed like a career that was destined never to get off the ground.

'I could put her off.'

'Of course you couldn't. She'd know then, or at least suspect. And I like her. Oh, God.'

She turned back into the hall. Drew kicked the door shut and pulled her against him. This was awful, she thought, as she snuggled into the soft flying jacket that smelled evocatively of Drew and horses and damp meadows. She had always known she wasn't cut out for infidelity.

'It doesn't matter,' Maddy sniffed into his shoulder. 'Maybe we should just forget what happened and behave as we were doing before.'

'Could you?' Drew pulled away and looked at her. 'Because I bloody well couldn't. I want to touch you, to be with you, to talk about you all the time. I want to behave like some besotted schoolboy and scrawl your name on every wall in the village.'

Maddy understood but she wasn't going to tell him about all the 'Maddy Fitzgeralds' she'd scribbled on her pad.

'How long will she be here for?'

'No idea.' Drew picked up Maddy's black jacket from the pile of coats beside the front door and wrapped it round her shoulders. 'As soon as I got Kit's message, I rang him and Caroline, but they both had their answering machines switched on.' He looked at her gently 'Are you still OK for the Cat and Fiddle?'

She nodded, 'Under the circumstances I think it's the best place to be. At least I won't disgrace myself in there by trying to remove your clothes.'

Drew's eyes sparkled as he opened the door. 'Pity.'

The pub was packed. Because of the fretful night, the atmosphere was warm and damp, rather like a conservatory. The whole village seemed to be squashed around the tables or standing three-deep at the bar. It was the last opportunity they'd have before tomorrow's Epsom exodus. Most of the trainers and jockeys travelled to Surrey at least a day before the meeting, to walk the course, settle the horses, and generally pick each others' brains.

Suzy was chatting up one of the Channel Four presenters and gave Maddy a huge wink as she and Drew walked in. Maddy gave a rictus smile in return and scuttled to a table in the far corner which was usually unoccupied because it was reputed to be haunted or something.

While Drew barged his way through to the bar, Maddy peered at her reflection in the steamed-up window. Would everybody know? Wasn't there something about a woman's eyes being different after making love? Or was that after losing one's virginity? It didn't really matter. It seemed to Maddy that her eyes, alternating between feverishly glittering happiness and abysmal sadness, screamed mistress.

Even Diana and Gareth were in the Cat and Fiddle tonight, talking animatedly to John Francome about the joys of having The Derby first and second favourites in their yard. Mitchell D'Arcy, wearing an extra helping of heavy gold jewellery, was beaming with the complacency of one who expected to be even more disgustingly wealthy than he already was within forty-eight hours. Owning both Saratoga Sun and Jefferson Jet, his bets seemed to be well and truly hedged.

Maddy hoped that Diana wouldn't want to discuss the incident at the stream, or anything else. She sincerely hoped that Diana wouldn't speak to her at all tonight. If Diana was Milton St John's scarlet woman, then Maddy must be at least a carmine apprentice.

'I got a quadruple whisky.' Drew placed a half pint glass in front of her. 'Psychologically, it's the same as four singles, isn't it? I just thought it would save time trying to fight my way through to the bar again. Anyway, all the staff are pie-eyed. I think they must have eaten on duty.' He took her hand across the table, caressing her fingers with easy familiarity. Luckily, the villagers were all too wrapped up in horsy talk to take any notice of this intimacy.

'Suzy is holding forth on Luke versus Richard to the guy from Channel Four.' Drew's eyes were definitely not talking about Suzy. 'I was listening in. They want to interview them both tomorrow before they leave for Epsom.'

'They'll be able to bill it as "The Big Fight", then.' Maddy giggled. 'I still can't see them shaking hands and behaving like gentlemen. The papers were full of speculation this morning.'

Drew scanned the bar. 'I'm surprised Fran and Richard aren't in here tonight. Everyone else is. Well, with the exception of Peter and Stacey, of course. I'd have thought Fran would have enjoyed all this.'

'I'm sure she would, but she phoned me this morning. It appears that when Richard isn't working Saratoga he's concentrating on becoming a father.'

Drew drank half of his lager and laughed. 'Lucky Fran.'

'I wouldn't have thought Richard was your type.'

'Absolutely not.' He picked up her hand again and gently kissed her fingers. 'You are.'

She shivered with lust. It was even worse now, because there was no speculation. She knew how glorious his love-making was.

'Good evening, Maddy. Hello, Drew.' Bronwyn took in the feverish colour, the linked hands, the body language, and adding them up made a very neat four. 'You're something of a regular couple now, aren't you?'

'Just being neighbourly. My wife will be here tomorrow.'

'And probably not before time.' Bronwyn was wearing her righteous hat.

'Won't you sit down?'

'No, thank you all the same.' Bronwyn's lips were pursed. 'And I'm surprised at you, Maddy. Sitting at this table.'

'It was the only one available.'

'And that's not surprising, is it? After all, you know what they say, don't you?'

'That it's haunted?' Maddy rattled her half pint of whisky against her teeth. 'I don't believe that.'

'It's not haunted. It's the baby table. Everyone who sits here seems to fall pregnant. Surely you know that? That nice girl who worked for John Hastings, three or four girls from the new estate, young Kat, even my Natalie. And,' she looked meaningfully at Drew, 'some ladies from Wantage and area who are having trouble in that department, come here deliberate.'

'Oh.' Maddy bit her lip. 'I knew there was something.'

'You'd do better standing at the bar.' Bronwyn frowned at Drew. 'Young Maddy's got enough problems.' She hustled away to remove Bernie from the attentions of a mini-skirted stable girl, leaving Drew and Maddy helpless with laughter.

Maddy wiped her eyes on the back of her hand. 'Oh well, if I am pregnant, we'll know who to blame, won't we?'

'It'll look good on the birth certificate, I must say.' Drew grinned. 'Father – teak veneered circular table.' He suddenly became serious. 'Maddy, if you are—'

'Don't!' Maddy raised her eyes in horror. 'I'm not superstitious, but even so . . .' She swallowed. 'Look, I won't be, so don't talk about it, Drew. Please.'

So he didn't. He talked about horses, and The Derby, and briefly about travel arrangements.

'The village hires an open-topped bus,' said Maddy. 'Everyone who isn't actually involved, travels down on Derby morning. Bronwyn makes egg and bacon rolls and we have buck's fizz.

Drew frowned. 'So is that the way you normally go to The Derby? On the bus? I would have thought that when you and Mr Knightley were together he would have chauffeured you in whichever penis-substitute car he happened to own at the time.'

Maddy giggled. It was a combination of three quarters of the whisky and being in love and the joy of Drew's description. 'Peter never went to The Derby, but I suppose he might this year, if he's intending to impress Stacey and Jeff Henley with his social standing.'

'I invited you to come with me, but now I don't think that would be a good idea. I just wanted to make sure that you would be there.'

'Oh, yes. Definitely. I couldn't miss it, could I? Don't worry, Drew, Caroline will be your partner, not me.'

He looked at her bleakly for a moment, then sighed. 'I've asked you out twice, and each time Caroline has got in the way.'

'Hello, both.' Kimberley beamed hugely through a schooner of gin. 'That's the baby table, Maddy. Did you know?'

'Bronwyn's just reminded me, thanks.'

'Good-oh.' Kimberley leaned forward in a cloud of Rive Gauche, which was completely out of character. Maddy wondered if she'd doused herself in it for Drew's sake and hoped not. 'Maybe I ought to sit there myself, what with the old biological clock ticking away and all that. I've just been talking to Suzy, and she tells me—'

Maddy shot Drew a frantic glance. Kimberley didn't seem to have noticed and carried on blithely. 'We were talking about clothes for Epsom. Quite girlie talk for Suzy.' She smiled wistfully. 'I believe she is really in love with young Luke Delaney. Anyway, I was telling her that as I haven't got any runners because of the damn virus, I shall be going with Barty, and I've bought myself a frock and a hat. She tells me that you've got a simply stunning new outfit, Maddy dear, but you haven't got a hat. I wondered if I could help?'

'Oh, I never wear hats,' Maddy said quickly. Kimberley's hats were dung-coloured felt trilbys or upside-down flower pots in shiny straw. 'I haven't got the right sort of head.' Drew and Kimberley looked at her in joint non-comprehension. She shrugged. 'With all this hair, and I've got such a round face. I'm not a hat person.'

'Nonsense.' Kimberley noisily drained her gin. 'A gal simply must wear a hat for The Derby, mustn't she, Drew?'

'Oh, absolutely.' Drew was chuckling. Maddy threw him a murderous glance. 'I'm sure Maddy would love your hat.'

'It probably wouldn't go with the outfit,' Maddy began.

'Ah, that's where you're wrong.' Kimberley beamed. 'Suzy says that your frock is green. I've got this simply stunning hat in green. Belonged to my mother. She always defied convention and wore it racing in Ireland. Green's not considered unlucky over there, of course. I'll pop it round tomorrow, shall I?'

'Lovely,' Maddy said weakly. 'It's very kind of you.'

'No problem at all.' Kimberley waved at Barty and indicated her empty glass. 'It'd be lovely to see it put to use again. I'll be round in the morning, then.'

Maddy watched her weave her way towards Barty and decided to kill Suzy all over again. Firstly for nosing in her wardrobe, and secondly for telling Kimberley. Kimberley's mother – the one with the lovers, the creditors, and the very dubious herbal remedies – had probably had the hat in the 'twenties. It was bound to be a cloche.

'You'll look lovely,' Drew spluttered into his drink. 'She's very kind, isn't she?'

'Very. But I won't bloody wear it.'

'Oh, but you'll have to. You can't hurt her feelings. And this green frock – it's not the one you wore to your dinner party? Because if it is I definitely won't be able to keep my hands off you.'

'I'll wear it, then.' Maddy was still feeling irritable.

'Actually, no. It's the one I bought when Caroline and I went to London.'

'Oh, good. I do like my mistress to have my wife's approval on her wardrobe.' He caught her hand in mid-punch and pulled her towards him across the table. His kiss was lethal and far more arousing than was acceptable in a crowded pub.

Maddy sank back in her chair. 'I think you've got completely the wrong idea about how the baby table works. Sitting at it is apparently sufficient. Copulating on top of it isn't necessary.'

'Spoil sport.' Drew stuck his tongue out at her, just as the Channel Four team's cameras whizzed round the bar.

Maddy woke alone. As she'd gone to sleep alone, it wasn't surprising. But she'd dreamed vividly about Drew and woke with a jolt of despondency to find that he wasn't beside her. She rolled her face into the pillows, trying to recapture the smell of him.

After they'd woven their unsteady way back from the Cat and Fiddle, accompanied by Suzy, Jason and Olly and most of the stable lads from Peapods, he'd left her at the cottage door with a decorous kiss on the cheek. It was the best they could manage with that sort of audience.

Maddy stretched drowsily. It was her last day of work for three days. Normal life was suspended in Milton St John during the Derby period. Lazily, she watched the dappled leaf patterns dancing on the sun-washed bedroom walls and realised that it had stopped raining. She also realised that her parents and Luke would be arriving before long, and that Caroline Fitzgerald would be taking up residence at Peapods. Groaning, she staggered out of bed.

She cleaned with almost demonic fervour. She wanted to get back to the cottage and spy on Caroline's arrival. Midday, Drew had said. She kept checking her watch. The hands seemed to be going backwards. Everyone was unbearably cheerful, the excitement spreading like a particularly virulent virus from yard to yard. She wouldn't have been surprised to see bunting.

It was just after half past eleven when she crashed the bicycle against the cottage gate. Pink-faced with exertion, her flapping black T-shirt and tatty leggings dust-smeared, she almost expected to see Drew waiting for her. After all, he'd never caught her on a good day yet. In fact it was Kimberley who was standing smiling beside the front door, a huge box in her hands.

'Mother's hat.' She gestured towards the box. 'As promised.'

'Lovely.' Maddy unlocked the door and shouldered her way into the hall. 'But you are sure you won't want to wear it yourself?'

'Quite sure,' Kimberley beamed, taking the yellowing lid from the box. It smelled of damp and gin. 'I'd never wear green. It's like actors saying "Macbeth", or anyone having peacock feathers in the house. And anyway, I've bought my entire outfit in pink.'

Maddy winced. 'That's nice. Is it pale or fuchsia?'

'It's the same colour as a stick of rock.' Kimberley lifted the hat from its folds of tissue paper. 'I don't know what you'd call it.'

Frightening, Maddy thought, but Kimberley looked so delighted that she didn't have the heart to say anything. As the hat began to appear from the box, Maddy closed her eyes in an act of complete cowardice.

'There, Maddy,' Kimberley enthused. 'It's as good as new. Try it on.'

Maddy opened one eye. 'Well, maybe not with my leggings – oh!'

It was beautiful. Even to Maddy who wasn't a hat person. It was huge brimmed, and made in bottle-green brocade. Fronding green ostrich feathers floated down like a veil all round the brim and a wide dark green velvet ribbon encircled the crown.

'Will it suit?' Kimberley anxiously gnawed her full lips. 'I thought with your colouring . . .'

'Kimberley, it's perfect!' Maddy hugged her. 'Oh, let me try it on.'

Squinting at her reflection in the dusty mirror, Maddy grinned. She looked like Scarlett O'Hara. With the green dress it would look exquisite. Her abundant hair, usually so unruly, fell from beneath the brim in a profusion of curls.

Kimberley clasped her hands in rapture. 'Oh, Maddy, you look lovely. Drew won't be able to resist you.'

'Dangerous ground, Kimberley.' Maddy lifted the hat carefully from her hair and put it reverently back into its box. 'Especially with Mrs Fitzgerald being *in situ*.'

Kimberley leaned against the bathroom door. 'We've been friends ever since you came to the village, haven't we? Oh, I know not best buddies like you and Fran, but good friends. I always disliked Peter Knightley. I found Drew Fitzgerald very attractive myself.' She blushed. 'I soon realised that his attention was drawn elsewhere. Look, I know it's an absolute bugger that he's got a wife, Maddy, but I really don't think you should let that stand in your way. Life is too short not to grab happiness when it looms. And when it looms gorgeously like Drew Fitzgerald . . .'

Maddy hugged her again. 'Oh, Kimberley. Thank you for understanding. It's just that I can't be brazen. I don't want to be the other woman.'

'We'll just have to hope that Drew leaves her, then, won't we?' Kimberley headed towards the front door.

'I don't think that will happen somehow.'

'It might – especially if you wear that hat. My mother swore by it. She said it never failed.'

What with the hat and the baby table, Maddy thought as she waved Kimberley goodbye, the folklore of Milton St John could have her married and pregnant pretty quickly – but not necessarily in that order.

She stood on a chair in her office and watched Caroline's

arrival. A luxurious black hire car swept into Peapods' drive just before twelve o'clock. By standing on tiptoe and using a pair of binoculars, Maddy watched it disgorge its three occupants. The tall fair-haired man must be Kit Pedersen and the tiny girl with the ginger hair had to be Rosa. Caroline, in pale blue trousers and a cream and blue shirt, uncurled herself with habitual elegance from the back seat. Maddy felt sick with guilt. How did other people cope with infidelity? Diana and Peter seemed not to let it touch them. How on earth was she going to be able to act cool and distant tomorrow?

The arrival of her parents in their battered Capri was something of a relief. At least it took her mind off Caroline and Drew being together. Her mother had brought their Epsom outfits on hangers covered in swathes of plastic bags, and her racegoing wedding hat, and immediately commandeered Maddy's bedroom. Maddy's dad commandeered what was left of the Glenfiddich. She was delighted to see them.

So was Suzy. She had gone straight from her stint at John Hastings' to Peapods to ride Dock of the Bay's last piece of work before his departure for Epsom that evening, and came back wreathed in smiles. After greeting her parents and accepting their compliments over her new hair-do, she dragged Maddy into the kitchen.

'Kit Pedersen is gorgeous. And Rosa is so sweet. She used to be a jockey. We got on really well. They were so nice to me, Mad. I can't let them down.'

'What about Caroline?'

'Oh, she was cool, you know.'

'Cool as in super trendy laid back, or cool as in distant as befits her behaviour towards the relative of someone who has slept with her husband?'

'The former. And isn't that just the stupidest way to describe having sex? I mean, "sleeping" is the last thing you do, isn't it?'

'Hush!' Maddy flashed anguished glances towards the

sitting-room. 'We've still got to explain you and Luke to Mum and Dad. When's he arriving?'

'Oh, he's already here. He's been up at Diana and Gareth's getting his last minute work and instructions. Look.' She pulled down the shoulder of her T-shirt, displaying a whole new batch of glaring love bites.

'Jesus!' Maddy sighed. 'How did you manage that?'

'The tack room.' Suzy started hacking at the last loaf of bread and reached for a pot of plum jam. 'Where there's a will there's a way.'

Maddy raised her eyes to heaven and filled the kettle. No doubt her parents would be gasping for a cup of tea.

Drew phoned her at nine o'clock. 'We've decided to go down tonight. To get Dock of the Bay settled. I know Suzy's driving down first thing with Luke. Kit and Rosa were very impressed with her. Your parents OK?'

'Fine, thanks. Drew—'

'Good. And you'll definitely be on the bus, won't you?'

'Yes. Drew, is—'

'What was the hat like?'

'Amazing. Drew, is Caroline there with you?'

'Yes, that's right.'

She felt bitterly ashamed. It was all so underhand. She swallowed. 'Right, then. I'll see you somewhere in the grandstand tomorrow.'

'Yes.'

'I love you.'

'Likewise,' Drew said, with appalling pain in his voice.

Twenty

Derby Day dawned, as forecast, hot and sunny. Those of Milton St John who had not already departed for the Surrey Downs, were gathered outside the Village Stores.

'I wouldn't wear your hat yet, Mum.' Maddy leaned towards her mother. 'Not if you're intending to sit on the top deck for the journey. You'll lose it before we get out of the village.'

'I've got plenty of room for it in here.' Mrs Beckett patted her voluminous handbag. 'I'll pop it in when we start, but I just wanted to look the part.'

'You do, Mum'. Maddy smiled fondly. 'You look lovely.'

Mrs Beckett was wearing an aquamarine two piece, and the wedding hat had been swathed in matching chiffon for the occasion. Maddy's dad was wearing his only suit and looking nervous.

Maddy squeezed his hand. 'Suzy'll be fine.'

'I bloody hope so. I've got a hundred quid each way on her, but not a word to your mother.'

Her parents had been stunned into silence when Maddy had appeared in the sitting-room in the green dress, the green shoes, and the opal earrings. And they hadn't even seen the hat.

'Oh, what a smashing get-up, Maddy.' Bronwyn bustled out of the shop, followed by Bernie, and locked the door with a Mrs Danvers-sized set of keys. 'She looks really nice, doesn't she, Bernie?'

Bernie looked, and unable to see more than the merest hint of bosom, nodded disinterestedly. Bronwyn, in beige and orange floral polyester, bustled amongst the villagers, ticking off names on her clipboard.

'Is Fran coming with us, or did she go with Richard yesterday?'

'She's definitely with us,' Maddy said. 'She rang earlier. She was having trouble with her shoes.'

What Fran had actually screeched was, 'What sort of bloody shoes am I supposed to wear as a winning jockey's bloody wife? I mean, am I supposed to be there with him, or is he supposed to be young free and single? Do I wear heels and tower above him or stick to flats and look frumpy? Jesus, Maddy! Help me!' They'd settled on medium-heeled courts and decided she should stay in the background when – if – Richard won The Derby.

Brenda and Elaine in bright shiny dresses, and complete with husbands and children, were leaning against the shop window and laughing loudly. Jackie and Kat, both married to jockeys who weren't racing at Epsom, were sitting sedately on the wall. Maddy stared hard at Kat's bump beneath her gathered summer dress, and let her hands stray to her own stomach. It was slightly curved now; what would it be like if she was . . .? She pushed the idea quickly out of her mind.

'It's like Shadows' works outing, innit, Maddy?' Elaine called cheerfully. 'All of us going off on the same bus? Scrubbers on tour!'

Jackie and Kat, who always considered themselves above such ribaldry – especially in public – shuddered. Maddy laughed. She was very fond of them all. They were her friends and they worked with her and for her. If someone could just unmarry Drew and Caroline she'd be the happiest person alive.

'Bloody hell!' Fran appeared round the corner, looking stunning in cream silk trousers and tunic with a floor-length black chiffon waistcoat, and carrying a black and cream cartwheel hat. 'I thought I'd missed it! I'd got the shoes sorted out then I couldn't decide on the right handbag and – bugger me!' She surveyed Maddy from top to toe. 'That didn't leave you much change out of five hundred pounds, I'll bet. Maddy Beckett, you look sensational.'

'Thanks.' Maddy waved a Tesco carrier bag under Fran's nose. 'And you wait 'til you see the hat.'

'Isn't the dress an Ally Capellino?' Fran's mouth was still sagging as Maddy nodded. 'And is this all for Mr Fitzgerald's benefit?'

'No. Actually, it's not.'

'Liar.' Fran squeezed her amiably. 'Still, he loved you in Oxfam – God knows what he'll do for you in that lot.'

Nothing more than he'd already done for her in the supermarket undies, Maddy thought smugly. Because, as she'd told him, you couldn't improve on perfection.

''Ere comes the bus!' The ritual cheer went up from the thirty or so villagers who were sitting on the kerb peering along the road. 'Get the beers in the boot, Bernie!'

They hired the bus annually from Newbury, and as usual, there was a tumble of sharply jabbing elbows to secure the best places on the open top deck. Fran was brilliant at this, using her feet, shoulders and even fingernails if she had to. Maddy followed more sedately with her parents, making sure that they were seated before joining Fran up front.

The bus was decorated in ribbons and balloons, with banners proclaiming the virtues of Saratoga Sun and Jefferson Jet, and the destination board read – as it always did – Milton St John to The Derby. It was all very noisy and friendly and the excited tension was mounting as it did every year; but for Maddy, this year was even more special.

'How was Richard?' she asked, as the bus swayed away along the main street. 'Nervous?'

'Not when he left.' Fran was twisting round in her seat, and waving to the contingent from the Cat and Fiddle who were taking up the rear quarter of the deck and already rustling cigarette papers. 'This morning he'll probably be throwing up, poor love. Still, he's not riding in the Woodcote which should give me a chance to cuddle him before the telly gets hold of him.'

'And Chloe and Tom? Have they gone to Epsom with Richard?'

Fran nodded. 'His parents are keeping them for the weekend at Esher and bringing them to the course this morning. The kids couldn't be more excited if Richard was their real father. He's done a wonderful job. I just wish we could have a baby of our own. Still, after today, who knows.'

Not wanting to even think about babies, Maddy looked down on the village. Milton St John was like the *Marie Celeste*. The few who hadn't already decamped for Epsom were hard at work so that they could watch the meeting on television. It was a maze of winding sandy roads and pale grey cottages, with the yards and their red-bricked creeper-covered houses dotted amongst the frothy green trees. Deserted and drowsy beneath the strong morning sun, it was simply the most beautiful place in the world.

'Hat time, then.' Fran jammed her cartwheel on to her head, holding it in position. 'Come on, Maddy. Let's see it.'

Maddy carefully removed the green hat from its bag and lowered it on to her curls.

Fran looked at her in admiration. 'You'll be the talk of the Queen's Stand, and Drew won't know what's hit him.'

'Caroline's here. I don't think he'll be able to comment.'

'Oh, he will.' Fran patted Maddy's arm with her free hand. 'Believe me, he will.'

A shout and a lot of foot stamping from the lower deck indicated that Bronwyn and Bernie had started their circulation with the huge egg and bacon baps and cardboard beakers of bucks fizz. Maddy and Fran smiled at each other in excitement. They were on their way.

The bus pulled into position on the downs side of the racecourse just before the winning post. It was still early, but the rolling hills were covered in marquees and market stalls and travellers' caravans. In front of them, the Grandstand and the Queen's Stand, looking like an ocean-going liner, towered into the Mediterranean-blue sky, and the bright green racecourse encircled them like an undulating emerald ribbon. The fairground screamed its raucous welcome, fortune tellers beckoned, and the crowds spilled everywhere. Maddy swallowed. Somewhere, in all that mass of humanity, was Drew.

Most of the villagers were quite content to remain on the bus until the first race, or explore the downs, so Maddy and Fran, with Mr and Mrs Beckett and the Pughs, made their way to the tunnel that burrowed beneath the course.

Maddy's dad, unable to resist anyone, bought lucky white heather and dead rosebuds from every passing gypsy, and Mrs Beckett bought a whole sheaf of race cards so that she could show Suzy's name to everyone back home.

'You'll be OK here?' Maddy asked her parents at the turnstile entrance to the Grandstand. 'Bronwyn and Bernie will show you the ropes.'

'We're fine, Maddy, love.' Mrs Beckett was bristling to get in and rub shoulders with the celebrities. She was dying to see Joan Collins in the flesh, and George Hamilton was always there, and usually Roger Moore. 'We'll see you later on, won't we? For Suzy's race?'

'Of course.' Maddy kissed her parents, and hoping that Bronwyn wouldn't divulge too many details of her burgeoning and increasingly public relationship with Drew, linked arms with Fran and headed for the Queen's Stand.

Fran looked at her watch. 'Why don't we have a bit of a mingle? We've got ages yet and Richard will be closeted with the Saratoga connections for most of the morning. Do you fancy soaking up the atmosphere, or are you breaking your neck to get at Drew?'

Maddy was, but she wasn't going to admit it. 'Of course not. Caroline is most probably anchored to his side. I'm not in any rush to make up a cosy threesome. So, what do you fancy?'

'Oh, just looking.' Once again Fran linked her arm through Maddy's and turned sharply away from the grandstand area. 'And candyfloss and brandy snaps.'

'I'm not sure about the candyfloss,' Maddy said, clamping Kimberley's mother's hat more firmly on her curls. 'It'll stick to the feathers.'

Giggling like teenagers, they stumbled up the scrubby incline and wobbled unsteadily across the dusty grass of the downs. The car and coach park was crammed to capacity, with people crowding round open boots unpacking crates of beer, boxes of wine and every conceivable form of edible delicacy. Maddy's mouth watered as she watched cloths being spread with cold chicken, trays of salad, pies, pastries, and glorious gooey puddings.

There were people everywhere: men dressed in morning suits and top hats, braying loudly to well-preserved women with geometric bobbed hair and Chanel suits; pub outings with both sexes sporting perms and vest tops; families with children and grandparents. Maddy soaked up the atmosphere.

'You are not going on the dodgems,' Fran grabbed Maddy's arm. 'Look what happens when you do?'

Maddy gazed at a knot of young men clinging greenly to each other's shoulders behind a hot dog stall and reluctantly allowed Fran to lead her away from the fairground. She sniffed at the air. 'You can really smell the excitement, can't you?'

'I can smell people, diesel, fried onions and sweat,' Fran said prosaically. 'Oh, Christ! Now where are you going?'

'In here. Wait for me.'

'Maddy! No!' Fran's wail was drowned by the splintered rendition of a dozen different pop songs. She gazed at the gaudily painted caravan in horror.

Maddy blinked wildly in the gloom. It was hot inside Madame Maria's living wagon. The pink velvet curtains were pulled against intrusive stares, but it had a cosy odour of coffee and fresh bread. Maddy was somewhat disappointed. She had expected incense and roast hedgehog.

'Won't keep you a sec, my duck.' Madame Maria stubbed out a cigarette and folded the *Daily Mirror* away tidily. 'Do you want the crystal, the cards, or the palm?'

'Whichever is most accurate, please.' Maddy perched on a pile of Algarve holiday brochures. 'The palm seems more personal, doesn't it?'

Madame Maria raised a pencilled eyebrow and clanked more gold jewellery than Mitchell D'Arcy. 'It's entirely up to you, my duck. But I will tell you the truth, and your hand can't lie. Is that what you want?'

Maddy nodded, making the green ostrich feathers dance frenziedly. 'Oh, yes, please. I don't care how bad it is, I just want to *know*.'

'Fine, duck.' Madame Maria leaned forward and took Maddy's left hand in both of hers. 'But I don't do death. I can't. The hand doesn't foretell death, only destiny. Your life line doesn't indicate the length of your life, you know, only the smooth or otherwise passage of it.'

Maddy nodded again. Madame Maria scrutinised her palm closely, then raised her eyes.

'Your heart line is much stronger than your head line. You are ruled by your emotions, and not always wisely. You love without selfishness, and because of this are loved in return. I see a deep and troubled relationship with little happiness in the past and a new and complicated one in the present.'

'That's right.' Maddy's feathers bounced enthusiastically. 'Is it happy?'

'Very – in bursts.' Madame Maria returned to Maddy's hand. 'There is an obstacle to total happiness, which looks as though it is permanent.'

'His wife,' Maddy muttered.

Madame Maria jerked her head up sharply. 'Can't do nothing about that, my duck. You plays with fire and you gets burned. I can't hex his wife for you.'

'Good heavens, no! I didn't want you to. She's nice. I just wondered if she might, er, disappear somewhere along the way.'

'This is a palm reading, duck, not a Mafia contract. Do you want me to go on?'

'Please.'

'Very well. You are happy in your work and your business will prosper. You will go on to greater things.'

'Oh good.' Maddy was pleased. At least Shadows seemed to have a rosy future, even if she didn't. 'Is that the end of the romantic bit?'

Madame Maria looked at Maddy kindly. 'Your palm does indicate a very happy marriage in the middle distance and three children. And before you ask, no, I can't say who with or when. Look, duck, I can't advise you, but it's all there in your hand. Just let it run its course. The funny thing is . . .'

'What?' Maddy began to panic.

'Well.' Madame Maria heaved a brocaded sigh. 'I can see the marriage and the children very clearly, but I can't see a third relationship. I reckons you'll be wedding one of the two already there. And as this current one is already married, it looks as if you might have a reconciliation with your former beau.'

'Oh, whoopee,' Maddy groaned. 'Thanks for nothing.'

Madame Maria shook her head as Maddy scrabbled in her handbag for her fee. 'I could make a fortune if I told people what they wanted to hear, duck, but me ethics are all against it. Have a lucky day.'

'You too,' Maddy muttered, as she forced her way out of the hot gloom and blinked in the brilliant sunshine.

'So?' Fran was hopping from foot to foot. 'What did she say?'

'That I'm going to marry Peter bloody Knightley.'

'Serves you right. You shouldn't dabble in witchcraft. Can I be the one who tells Stacey?'

Twenty-One

'Make way for the rich and famous,' Fran muttered, elbowing past beautiful girls in frou-frou dresses and mile-wide hats in the Queen's Stand. 'Jesus, I'm nervous now we're in here.'

'You've been here before, done all this before.' Maddy said, looking around her, for once feeling as glamorous as every other woman stalking the gently sloping mossy lawns. 'It should all be pretty passé to you by now.'

'Richard has never been riding the Derby favourite before.' Fran's teeth were chattering. 'I daren't even think about him losing. Especially not to Luke. Let's not talk about it. Let's get our first glass of Pimms and survey the opposition.'

Some of the men, elegant in morning dress, and their partners in jewel-bright frocks, were strangers; most were at least vaguely familiar. The racing community was very insular. The lawns looked like Pygmalion come to life. Maddy realised she was holding her breath each time a lean, broad-shouldered, dark-haired man turned round.

'Over there!' Fran waved her glass of fruit and mint wildly. 'Look! Kimberley and Barty. Oh, doesn't he look sweet in his topper? Oh, and Diana and Gareth!'

Maddy looked. Kimberley, in her coral-pink outfit, could have been used for guiding planes on to the runway. She had a Pimms in each hand and was laughing with Barty who, without his top hat, only came up to her shoulder.

Gareth, who with his elongated body, looked better in morning dress than most people, was steering Diana carefully down the steps. Diana's dress was in apricot silk and so tightly fitting that she could only move one leg at a time, hence Gareth's assistance. Her hat was a mixture of apricot and black lace and veiled her expression. There was no sign of Drew or Caroline.

As the morning wore on, the Downs became a seething mass of people with not a pinprick of grass between them. The ocean of a thousand splintered conversations rose and fell. The sun climbed steadily as the grandstands swallowed yet more visitors and the bookmakers set out their pitches. Maddy found herself screwing up her eyes and counting to ten, then twenty, telling herself that when she opened them she would see Drew. Fran was gulping back Pimms like lemonade.

'Maddy!' The warm voice slithered through the crowd. 'Maddy – oh, you look gorgeous. Didn't I tell you that dress was made for you? And what a hat!'

Maddy turned and faced Caroline. 'Hello.' While her smile was for Caroline, her eyes, skimming the crowds, were searching for Drew. He wasn't there.

'You look sensational.' Caroline was wearing the black and red dress they'd bought in Knightsbridge. Her hat, in red net, sat on top of her glossy bob in variegated peaks like stiffly whisked egg whites. She really was exceptionally beautiful.

'This is wonderful.' Caroline waved her hands, encompassing the whole scene. 'Even if you don't like horses, which I don't, this is still an occasion not to be missed. I came out of the bar to watch the band and, of course, see the Royals. Have you seen Drew yet?'

'No,' Maddy said, too quickly. 'I mean, no, I haven't. I suppose he's with Kit and Rosa?'

'And the horse and Suzy.' Caroline gave a martyred laugh. 'Tactics, tactics, tactics. So boring!' She smiled politely at Fran who giggled back.

'I've been instructed to meet Drew in the paddock.' Caroline gave them both the benefit of her sleepy smile. 'For the saddling-up procedure. Until then, I'm free to circulate, which is just what I intend to do. I've got my business cards with me and I'm sure some of these people would be very interested in my wine. I told my parents to expect an increase in orders. Will you be in the paddock, Maddy?'

'Er, no . . . I shouldn't think so. I'll watch Suzy's race from the Grandstand. Why?'

'Because I want to talk to you.' Caroline's eyes were still warm. 'But I'll wait until everyone has stopped walking on eggshells over this race. We'll meet up later, then?'

'Yes.' Maddy felt sick. How could she know? Drew couldn't have told her, could he? 'I'll be around . . .'

Caroline drifted down the grassy slope to find a vantage point on the rails. Maddy discovered she'd been holding her breath.

'What the hell is wrong with you?' Fran tilted her head so that she could see under the cartwheel brim of her hat. 'You've gone really white. Do you feel sick?'

'I want a drink. And not Pimms. I want a real drink. Like half a pint of whisky.'

'You're sure you're OK?' Fran trotted behind her as Maddy hurtled through the hordes of suntanned models clinging to the arms of portly businessmen towards the Mezzanine Bar. 'Isn't it a bit early to be starting on the spirits?'

'It's far, far too late,' Maddy hurled over her shoulder. 'I knew I should have stuck to my principles.'

Fran, who didn't know she hadn't, shrugged and ordered doubles.

By the time the whisky had steadied Maddy's nerves, the band had swept up the course, resplendent in their red and gold uniforms and their towering bearskins; the Royal party had been disgorged from their limousines to tumultuous cheers; and Fran had slipped away to spend half an hour calming Richard's pre-race panic.

'We've got twenty-three minutes. What do you suggest?'

The voice laughed just behind her left ear. Maddy, on the

steps leading to the lawn, tottered slightly, but was smiling when she turned round.

Drew looked devastating in an exquisitely cut pale grey morning suit with a silk shirt and cravat. 'What a moralistic hat. I can't get anywhere near you.'

'Just as well, as your wife is circulating down there somewhere.' Maddy nodded the ostrich feathers in the direction of the banks of red and white flowers. 'Is everything OK?'

'No, it bloody isn't.' Drew took her elbow and steered her towards the rails bookmakers with their hotlines to their London offices. 'I've missed you.' He let his eyes trawl lazily over her. It was still the same. 'You look absolutely wonderful, Maddy. Like Lillie Langtry.'

'Oh, thanks. Wasn't she the best-known mistress ever?'

'Maybe, but not for much longer.' Drew laughed, then his eyes softened. 'You do look gorgeous – but then, you always do. Have you seen Caroline?'

Maddy nodded bleakly. 'She wants to talk to me. She doesn't know, does she?'

Drew shook his head, still holding her arm and caressing the inside of her wrist with the ball of his thumb. 'She's probably going to ask you to dinner.'

Maddy sagged against him. For a second she longed to be back in the relative anonymity of Milton St John, and away from all this pomp and circumstance. She wanted Caroline to be fermenting, or whatever it was she did, her wines in the wilds of Jersey. She wanted to be back in her scruffy comfortable clothes drinking coffee with Drew in her odd-shaped kitchen with the cool misty rain sweeping from the Downs.

The list of runners and riders for the Woodcote Stakes was being hauled on to the board on the far side of the course. Suzy's name and number in red on white indicated her apprentice status.

'Next year she'll have lost her allowance and be riding as a full jockey,' Drew said. 'She's so determined, that next year she could even be riding in The Derby.'

Maddy looked at Suzy's name and realised with a guilty pang that she hadn't even asked about her. 'Is she OK this morning? Not too nervous?'

'Not at all. She's very hyped up. Kit and Rosa adore her and Dock of the Bay is in love with her.' He glanced at his watch. 'I really should be going down to the paddock. Are you coming?'

'Caroline will be there, so I'd rather not. I do want to, you know that, but Mum and Dad want me to watch the race with them, of course – oh, goodness. Look.' Maddy watched the last of the runners and riders being listed. Luke's name had appeared. 'I haven't even opened my race card. I didn't know they'd be riding against each other.'

'It'll make a change.' Drew pulled her against him, making the huge green hat dip alarmingly. 'I'll give her your love, then, shall I?'

'Please.' She was very close to him. 'And I'll see you later . . .'

He kissed her, to the delight of the bookies and the Channel Four team who were just scanning the crowd and getting a distinct feeling of *déjà vu*. Several people clapped. Maddy didn't care.

She was still floating when she found her parents and the Pughs in the Grandstand. She'd put a reckless twenty pounds on Suzy at the Tote window, then a further five to win with a florid-faced bookmaker in the enclosure who was offering optimistic odds of 25 to 1 on Dock of the Bay's chances. She'd be reduced to bread and water for the rest of the month – always assuming the water board didn't cut her off.

Pressed against the rails between her parents, she cried openly as Suzy, in the Pedersens' grey and pink colours, cantered down the course to the six furlong start. The commentator barked across the downs, the bookmakers shrieked the odds – Luke was hot favourite – and the tension mounted.

Removing the hat at the request of a whiskery lady behind her who was sweating profusely inside a beige pac-a-mac, Maddy craned her neck and squinted at the Prince's Stand. Overlooking the home straight, it was the special reserve of owners and trainers. Drew would be there with Caroline. Was he scouring the crowds below, trying to pick out a dot in ludicrously expensive green?

She watched the loading into the stalls on the huge screen that spreadeagled the downs. Suzy looked so very frail, but was smiling all the time, especially at Luke in dark blue and yellow as they continually circled past each other.

The race started. Mrs Beckett was screaming encouragement long before the commentator had bellowed. 'They're off!', but this was swallowed up in the sort of tidal roar that raised goose bumps. Maddy stuffed her fingers in her mouth and prayed.

The ten runners were bunched together, moving like a multi-coloured arrow, then suddenly spearheaded by blue and yellow. The crowd were screaming for Luke. Obviously unable to let him out of her sight, Suzy, in pink and grey, zoomed forward. Dock of the Bay became a glossy brown blur. Luke and Suzy were neck and neck. Maddy's stomach had disappeared. She could feel the thundering of hoofs beneath her feet, smell the divots of turf as they flew through the air, heard her mother's yells becoming hoarser and her father's shouts becoming higher pitched. Maddy thought incessantly of Drew.

They swept past, blue and yellow and pink and grey momentarily clamped together as closely as they were off the racecourse. An explosion of sound split the air as they reached the winning post. It had been the longest minute of Maddy's life.

The commentator's voice was completely obliterated. Through swimming eyes, Maddy looked at her parents. White faced, they shook their heads. Then the announcement: 'First, number three, second, number ten . . .'

They looked at each other in speechless delight for a moment and then started laughing and crying and hugging each other. 'She's won! She's bloody won!' The whiskery lady, who had backed Frankie Dettori, snorted, tore up her betting slip, and marched away.

'Winner's enclosure,' Mr Beckett said gruffly. 'And bloody quickly.'

Having practically punched their way through the crowds, they stood pressed against the rails. Drew and the Pedersens were wearing ear-to-ear grins of delight. Caroline was looking coolly enthusiastic. Suzy, who had weighed in, appeared not to know where or who she was as the media pounced with bristling microphones. Digging her nails into the flaking white wood, Maddy shook. Drew raised his head and found her eyes. The message was crystal clear.

In racing, success lasts only until the next race, and already everyone was preparing for the Coronation Cup. Drew had disappeared to attend to Dock of the Bay, Kit and Rosa were talking to John McCririck, and Suzy had dived off in the direction of the changing rooms. Caroline swept across, her eyes shining.

'Wasn't that wonderful? We'll really have something to celebrate tonight.' She beamed at Mr and Mrs Beckett. 'I'm having an impromptu get-together when we return to Peapods. Bronwyn and Bernie have already said they'll be coming. You'll be there of course?'

Maddy's heart plummeted to the soles of her green shoes as her parents accepted. She'd never get Drew on his own, not with that sort of vigilante presence.

'We'd love to.' Mrs Beckett's voice was squeaky from so much shouting. The wedding hat was askew. 'Can we see Suzy, do you think?'

'Of course.' Caroline looked over her shoulder. 'If you speak to the steward over there, I'll pop across to meet you.'

Maddy was blatantly excluded from this invitation and

started to move away. Mr Beckett grabbed her hand. 'Don't go too far away, Maddy, love.' He'd just calculated the extent of his winnings and was sweating. 'We've got some celebrating to do.'

'Oh, save all that for tonight,' Caroline trilled. 'We've got a cellar full of Dom Perignon just in case. It's going to be such fun. Drew and I haven't entertained for ages.

That's not the only thing you and Drew haven't done for ages, Maddy thought bitchily, as she fought her way against the tide of people back towards the Grandstand. She felt strangely depressed. Delight for Suzy, and Drew, and Dock of the Bay, had splintered into a biting loneliness.

Drew would be surrounded by his entourage and his wife. Again, everyone had someone. Even John Hastings, who normally shunned female companionship, had hired himself a Page Three lookalike for the day. Maddy longed to be with Drew, to be able to congratulate him, to share his joy. The game rules of The Other Woman were becoming increasingly clear. She wasn't sure she could adhere to them.

Disconsolately, she drifted behind the stands where the caterers cursed her for getting in the way, and people stood in laughing, chattering groups. The sun, spiralling in a still-cloudless sky, hadn't penetrated between the high buildings, and it was grey and cold.

'Jesus Christ! I thought I'd never escape! And then I thought I'd never find you. Thank God for Kimberley's hat!' Drew's arms encircled her waist, dragging her back against him. 'Holy hell, Maddy—' He stopped and laughed at her. 'God, I've spent far too long with Suzy.' He surveyed her steadily. 'I have never wanted anyone more in all my life.'

Spinning her round and pulling her against the hardness of his body, he kissed her with hungry desperation. Suddenly, the chilly, dark passageway was suffused in sunshine.

Taking her hand and dragging her round tower blocks of beer crates, Drew negotiated the bustling crowds, and out across the close-cropped grass of the owners' car park.

Serried ranks of wildly expensive cars simmered in the sunshine, shielding glamorous people grouped round the open boots, all eating Fortnum & Mason picnics.

Leaning against a pale grey Rolls-Royce, Drew pulled her between his expensively clad thighs and kissed her again. 'We did it,' he whispered into the ostrich feathers. 'We really bloody did it – oh, Christ.' Spitting out feathers, he wrenched the hat from her curls and dumped it on the Rolls-Royce's bonnet along with his grey silk top hat. 'That's better. I feel as high as if I'd eaten three square meals at the Cat and Fiddle.'

'It was sensational,' Maddy croaked against his shoulder. 'How's Suzy?'

'Just coming down to earth. She and Luke had to be prised apart so that he could ride in the Coronation Cup. He was absolutely delighted for her. It's the first time I've ever known a jockey to be ecstatic at not winning.'

'But, shouldn't you be there . . . I mean, talking to people?'

'You're the only person I want to talk to. I made sure Dock of the Bay was all right, Kit and Rosa are dealing with Press, and Caroline is revelling in reflected glory. They won't miss me.'

Oblivious to everyone else, they kissed again, falling backwards on to the bonnet. Wanting him desperately, Maddy squirmed rapturously as his hand snaked up the fullness of her thigh.

'I wish all these bloody people would disappear,' Drew groaned.

'So do I.' She giggled into the silk cravat. 'I'm wearing the red satin.'

The combination of laughter and well-polished car led to them sliding inelegantly sideways and landing beside a very surprised picnic party.

'I'm so sorry.' Drew picked himself up. Ex-colonels and their ladies bristled with red-faced indignation. Maddy smiled winningly as she scrambled to her feet.

'Tonight,' Drew whispered, grabbing their hats and Maddy's

hand before the party could have mass apoplexy, 'we'll celebrate the red satin. Right now, I guess I ought to be getting back to my seriously boring duties as husband and trainer. What about you?'

'I'll have to watch The Derby with Fran to stop her biting people. And as I've just won the cost of this dress back I might have a drink or two.'

Drew kissed her thoroughly again, and removed the pink rose with its grey foliage from his buttonhole. 'One day I'll buy you an entire florist's shop.'

Twenty-Two

'Where have you been?' Fran was gnawing her fingers. 'And what the bloody hell are you wearing?'

'Green dress, green shoes, Kimberley's mum's hat.' Maddy gave a beatific smile. 'Exactly what I was wearing before.'

'And this?' Frank flicked at the pink and grey corsage. 'Gypsies don't sell flowers in the Pedersen colours, Mad. So, who, exactly, does this belong to?'

Maddy bit her lip. 'Drew gave it to me. Isn't it pretty?'

Fran narrowed her eyes. 'You mean, you and Drew were cavorting – here?'

'Well, not cavorting as such. We just fell off someone's Rolls-Royce and—'

'And missed the Coronation Cup. The two of you managed to miss an entire race.'

'Who won?'

'Michael Hills,' Fran hissed. 'Luke and Richard were nowhere. I needed you.'

'I'm here now.' Maddy squeezed Fran as close as their hats allowed. 'Sorry.'

'Oh, sod it. I'm being selfish,' Fran sniffed. 'Did you and Drew have a nice time?'

'Lovely, thanks.'

Fran surveyed her quizzically. 'Maddy, are you and Drew . . .?'

'No, of course not.' Maddy smiled.

'You lucky bitch,' Fran breathed. 'And?'

'Amazing. Magical. Out of this world – and if you mention it to *anyone*, I'll throttle you.'

'As if,' Fran said, wondering who she could tell first.

The Derby parade had started, the nineteen runners and riders stalking down the course in front of the Grandstand in race card and alphabetical order. Luke on Jefferson Jet was therefore some way ahead of Richard on Saratoga Sun, but in Mitchell D'Arcy's apricot and black colours, the only thing that distinguished them was their different caps.

Suzy must be bursting with pride, and probably frantic with nerves, Maddy thought. And what Diana was going through was anyone's guess. Both Richard and Luke, however, looked cool and imperturbable. So far so good. At least with that many horses between them and an audience of thousands, they could hardly start brawling. Clutching Fran's trembling fingers, she settled down to watch the race.

'They're off!'

The cry hung in the air alone for an infinite moment, instantly followed by a feral roar from across the downs that lifted the hairs on the back of Maddy's neck. The noise was incredible as the horses streamed forward.

'I can't look.' Fran squeezed her nails into Maddy's hand. 'Tell me when it's over.'

Maddy focused on the two apricot and black riders somewhere in the middle of the field, watching them on the screen as they flowed away in the distance. They must have already covered the first half mile and were cresting the hill. Maddy could hear nothing above the tidal wave of screamed encouragement.

'They're at Tattenham Corner,' she yelled in Fran's ear. 'For Christ's sake, look!'

'Can't,' Fran muttered, shivering. 'Who's winning?'

'No one. Well, they're all bunched up. The lead keeps changing – oh!'

'What?' Fran was practically drawing blood.

'They're racing neck and neck now, and there's two of the Arab's horses up there too . . .'

The screams were maniacal. Maddy was shaking as much

as Fran as Saratoga Sun and Jefferson Jet matched each other stride for glossy stride. Then the apricot colours parted company.

The nineteen runners streamed below them like a multi-coloured banner, the noise, the heat, the wild energy, becoming a living force. They flashed past the winning post in a blur. Top hats were thrown in the air as the crescendo of noise echoed and repeated across the downs in a nonstop ocean of sound.

'Who won?' Fran opened her eyes, rocked by the rush of people from the stand. 'Who bloody won?'

'One of them,' Maddy said, dry mouthed, drained of all emotion. She scrabbled for her race card again. 'Whoever was wearing the all-black cap . . .'

With a scream of delight, Fran vaulted the seats in front of her, and clutching the cartwheel hat, disappeared into the scrum for the Winner's Enclosure.

Maddy stood, surrounded only by those who had lost a serious amount of money on the other horses, and wiped away her tears on the back of her hand. Saratoga Sun had won The Derby.

Maddy watched the presentation on the screen. Diana and Gareth were delirious, and Mitchell D'Arcy clanked his jewellery and flashed his teeth in delight. Richard, interviewed by Channel Four, was incoherent, and Luke, bravely agreeing to talk about the jocking off, was philosophical.

As the atmosphere began to calm, and the racegoers realised there were still three races to go, Maddy drifted towards the Champagne Bar.

Amidst the silks and satins and sea of morning coats, the Milton St John trainers were out in force. Some jockeys, their duties over, were recounting to their connections how they lost. Both Luke and Richard were riding in the rest of the afternoon's races, so weren't in evidence.

Scanning the bar for Drew, Maddy accidentally caught Diana's eye. 'Congratulations.'

'Maddy, darling!' Diana hobbled towards her as fast as the skin-tight dress would allow, and clashed cheeks. 'You were right all the time. Richard was pure perfection. I'm so glad I listened to you.'

'Oh, I hardly think—'

'Nonsense!' Diana's eyes glittered. 'I've had the winner of The Derby, thanks to you. You put me on the right track. I should have realised that no one knew Saratoga better than Richard.'

How conveniently people turn things round, Maddy thought. Saratoga Sun would have probably won anyway. Still, if Diana had convinced herself that she had made the training decision of the century, who was she to argue? And of course, it was absolutely wonderful for Fran and Richard.

'Marnie!' Mitchell D'Arcy swayed towards them, shining brightly. 'This is a day in a million, and it's all thanks to this lovely lady.' He gave Diana's tightly clad silk bottom a pat. 'I love this lady, Marnie. Di is my princess.'

'I must find Caroline Fitzgerald. Anyway, congratulations to you both – and of course, Gareth.' There was a braying laugh and all eyes turned towards the bar. Gareth had emptied an ice bucket over his head.

As Maddy hurried away, she heard Mitchell D'Arcy saying, 'That's a seriously expensive outfit Marnie's wearing, Di, poppet. Don't you think you might be over-salarying your domestics?'

She met Caroline on the lawn just as the horses skittered down the course for the fourth race.

'Hello.' Caroline smiled her pussycat smile. 'Oh, is that Drew's buttonhole?'

'I asked for it . . . as it's in the Pedersen colours. For Suzy . . .'

'Oh, I see.' Caroline's face showed no hint of doubt. 'Actually, I want to go home. I've had enough. I think they should end this as soon as The Derby's over. It's all such an anti-climax, and it's ruined my plans for this evening.'

'Oh?' Maddy felt a surge of hope.

'I had no idea that so many people would be staying over for the rest of the meeting . . . Or that they'd have so many prior invitations to attend functions.'

Maddy, nodded. 'Well, you couldn't be expected to know all the horsy protocol. No one really does, except the chosen few. Sometimes it gets horribly cliquey. Does this mean you'll cancel for tonight?'

'Oh, no. I never actually cook myself, but I've already ordered the food from a catering service in Oxford. Diana James-Jordan recommended them to me. So it'll still go ahead. I'll just have to revise my guest list.' She looked interested for a second. 'Do you have anyone you want to bring? A partner?'

Maddy shook her head.

'That's good.' Caroline looked suspiciously pleased. 'Because I've got an extra man. Maybe I can play Cupid.'

And maybe you bloody can't, Maddy thought angrily. 'And who is this extra man? Someone I know?'

'Yes.' Caroline's laugh was tinkly. 'That gorgeous young man that Drew has engaged to ride his National Hunt horses.'

Charlie Somerset! Bloody hell!

'Oh, nice,' Maddy said bleakly. 'And you've invited my parents and the Pughs, who will obviously come. And Kit and Rosa Pedersen are staying with you anyway.' This was getting worse and worse. 'Anyone else?'

Caroline screwed her eyes up and winced against the noise as the fourth race finished with Frankie Dettori three lengths clear. 'All the trainers seemed to have cried off with prior engagements. But I have invited Peter and Stacey.'

'What on earth for?' Maddy didn't have time to be polite. 'Drew doesn't like them, and they're on the opposite side to everyone else regarding the golf course. Bronwyn will throw a fit.'

'I'm sure she won't,' Caroline said placidly. 'The golf

course thing seems to have been amicably settled. And Drew doesn't mind Peter, does he? I thought he quite liked him really.'

Maddy closed her eyes. This was going to be the dinner party from hell. She'd have to catch something like bubonic plague on the bus going home.

'So,' Caroline beamed, 'I'll see you at about nine, then?'

'Yes, of course.' Maddy's face ached from the forced smile. 'I'm really looking forward to it.'

The bus journey back to Milton St John was riotous. Everyone had backed Richard and Suzy, and most of them had had something on Luke since he'd become so much part of the village, and he had conveniently won the last race. Brenda and Elaine were leading community singing on the lower deck, while the Cat and Fiddle passed joints round upstairs.

Maddy, sitting with her parents because Fran had opted to stay overnight with Richard, felt cold and deflated. She hadn't seen Drew again, and dreaded having to ward off Charlie Somerset at the dinner party. And how could she spend an entire evening with Peter and Stacey?

'What's up, love?' Mr Beckett patted his daughter's hand. 'You look sad, and no one should be sad today. Our Suzy did us proud.'

'She did, Dad.' Maddy flickered a smile. 'I think I'm just tired.'

'You'll liven up tonight.' Mr Beckett grinned knowingly. 'Mrs Fitzgerald is putting on a real spread. It should be one heck of a celebration. She's such a nice lady. Me and your mother were trying to persuade her to move over to Milton St John permanently.'

'Oh,' Maddy went even colder. 'I don't think she'll do that. She's got her business to run in Jersey and—'

'That's what she said.' Maddy's mum leaned across. Her pupils were slightly dilated. Maddy hoped it was just excitement and not passive dope smoking. 'But I told her, it's no way to run a marriage, being apart like that. You and she seem to get on well, Maddy, love. Maybe you could persuade her. Why don't you suggest it to her tonight?'

Twenty-Three

They had all managed to bath and change and even snatch a few minutes' sleep before they trailed across the road to Peapods at just after nine o'clock. Maddy still felt suicidal. She would have cried off, but her parents were so excited about the whole day, and especially Drew's part in Suzy's triumph, that it would have been unthinkably cruel.

It was a glorious evening, still and warm, scented by old roses and freshly cut grass. St Saviours' bells were rolling melodiously around the downs in a celebration peal, almost drowning out the party raging at the Cat and Fiddle which could be heard on the far side of the village. Maddy wished fervently that she was there. She wished she was anywhere other than walking up Peapods' cobbled drive to spend an evening with the Fitzgeralds.

'Oh, you've changed.' Caroline pulled open the door. 'Aren't you good. I simply didn't have time.'

Maddy was wearing the dark green velvet dress she'd worn for her own dinner party. Now that she could pay her credit card off from her winnings she didn't feel it was necessary to wear the Knightsbridge outfit to every function.

Caroline ushered them into the dining-room. Mr and Mrs Beckett enthused wildly over the furniture and the drapes and the paintings. The french doors were opened on to the lawn, and a drinks table had been set up on the terrace. It was all very tasteful.

Bronwyn and Bernie were standing, drinks in hand, by one of the old-fashioned flower borders, nodding over lupins and foxgloves and honesty.

'Why don't you go and join them,' Maddy suggested to her parents. 'I'll see if Caroline needs a hand.'

Caroline didn't. The caterers had delivered everything, and it only needed popping in the microwave just before serving.

'I've gone for a very basic menu.' Caroline stroked a stray lock of hair away from her unlined cheek. 'I thought everyone would have had enough of the high life for one day. Let me refill your glass. I can't think where Drew's got to . . .'

Without realising, Maddy had already gulped back one glass of wine. She'd have to be more careful.

'Oh, look, here's Kit and Rosa.' Caroline made brief introductions. Maddy smiled at the tall fair-haired man and his delicately pretty wife and congratulated them on their win. They held hands all the time, Maddy noticed, just as they had all day. It was sickening to see such devotion. Caroline beamed. 'Maddy is Suzy's sister – not that you'd think so, would you? She cleans Peapods.' Kit Pedersen frowned slightly and Rosa shot Maddy a look of sympathy. Maddy was too dispirited to explain about Shadows, and was about to make a fatuous remark about Dock of the Bay when the doorbell rang.

'I'll go.' Caroline swept off in a swirl of black and red.

'Drew's in the stables,' Kit Pedersen said quietly. 'He said to tell you.'

'If Caroline asks,' Rosa grinned, 'you've gone to the loo.'

Maddy stared at them both. Their eyes sparkled. 'You'll have to be quick.' Rosa leaned forward and took Maddy's glass. 'She'll want to have us sitting down with paper hats and crackers in a minute.'

With a look of absolute gratitude, Maddy sidled out of the french doors and flew across the lawns to the stable block.

Drew, still dressed in his morning-suit trousers and silk shirt, was in Solomon's box. 'What kept you?' He pulled her into his arms, burying his face in her hair. 'God, I've missed you.'

'Kit and Rosa . . .?'

'Are my friends.' Drew was stroking her neck.

'They *know*?'

'Of course they know. Kit and I have been mates since school. He said he only had to look at me the first time I went back – when I collected Dock of the Bay – to know.'

Stumbling back against the flaking woodwork, he kissed her, moving his hands gently and caressingly over her body. She clung to him, trembling.

'This will probably be the only time we'll have alone,' he said softly. 'The rest of the evening you'll be flirting outrageously with Charlie and I'll be growling at Pete the Perv . . .'

'You've definitely spent too much time with Suzy,' Maddy reproved with a giggle, then yelped as Solomon, who had been ignored for long enough, nudged her in the back. It pushed her even closer to Drew, leaving her in no doubt that his desire for her was as strong and urgent as ever. She curled against him, breathing in the warm, clean smell of him.

'Even Solomon is on our side.' Drew smoothed her curls from her cheeks. 'Oh, this is crazy. I'm not cut out for deceit and infidelity. I want to be with you all the time.'

'No!' Maddy jerked away from him. 'It's impossible.'

'Isn't that what you want?'

'Of course it is. But not at the expense of Caroline's happiness. I couldn't live with myself – or you – knowing that we'd caused someone else's unhappiness.'

Drew moved away, his feet rustling in the shredded paper bedding on the stable floor, then turned and faced her. 'So what do you suggest? That I wait for Caroline to leave me? Because if so, I think we'll both be waiting a hell of a long time.'

'I don't know. And don't glare at me. Everybody, everywhere, is being unfaithful with no qualms at all, and we have to have bloody consciences. Oh, Drew, something'll work out.'

'I bet you still believe in Father Christmas, too.' He held her again. 'You're lovely, Maddy.'

'I'm not really. I'd love Caroline to leave you. Maybe we could get Charlie to seduce her.'

'Caroline is non-seduceable.'

'I know. She told me.' She sighed and laced her fingers in his hair. 'I think we'll just have to go on like we are. Sort of slotting ourselves into your Caroline-free moments.'

'And if you're pregnant?'

'Of course I'm not pregnant. Don't talk about it.'

He didn't. He kissed her instead, and it was only Kit's cough of apology that prevented it from degenerating into something far more steamy.

'Sorry to be a bore, but the rest of the guests have arrived. Caroline's waiting to serve the soup.' He smiled at Maddy. 'She's really worried about your stomach upset. Rosa has allegedly been sitting in the upstairs bathroom with you for the last twenty minutes.'

'You're both wonderful,' Drew laughed, straightening his cravat and grabbing Maddy's hand. 'Come on then, Ms Beckett. Let's face the music . . .'

The food was delicious. Caroline accepted fulsome praise from those who didn't know about the caterers, without ruffling one immaculate hair. The seating curse was operating well. Maddy was between Charlie and Peter. At least she had her mythical stomach upset to explain away her loss of appetite. Not that it mattered: Charlie happily ate everything she left. Peter held himself away from her, and Stacey ignored her completely. However, the Pughs and Maddy's parents, who were by now firm friends, kept the conversation flowing.

'Syllabub, Maddy?' Caroline offered pudding across the table. 'Or will it be a bit too rich for you?'

'I'll try a little, thank you,' she answered as Charlie nudged her. Living alone he very rarely got this sort of meal and didn't want to see anything go to waste. 'It looks scrumptious.'

'Scrumptious?' Stacey's pencilled eyebrows drew together like two thin caterpillars. 'What an old-fashioned word.'

'It's a nice word,' Charlie said quickly. 'But you probably wouldn't know any of those.'

'Was that meant to be insulting?' Peter leaned across Maddy.

'Not at all.' Charlie grinned broadly, showing his crooked teeth. 'It wasn't *meant* to be anything. It *was* insulting.'

Drew was laughing quietly. So were Kit and Rosa. Caroline had missed the undercurrent.

The conversation centred naturally on The Derby, and Maddy, despite getting frantic nudges from Charlie, forgot that she was supposed to be ill and spooned up all of her syllabub.

'We'd like to have a Derby runner next year,' Kit said looking at Drew. 'We're hoping to buy one of Moon Dancer's offspring and race him as a two-year-old. You'll train him, of course?'

'Try and stop me. I'll need to have a flat jockey by then, too. A good one. I'll have to cast around.'

'What about Luke Delaney?' Rosa asked.

'He'll never leave Emilio.' Drew stood up and filled glasses, spending just too long at Maddy's side. She wanted to stroke his long pin-striped leg. 'I'd like Suzy to ride for me as a casual, but I know she won't leave John Hastings. I'll have to give it some thought.'

Caroline served cheese and fruit and port – luckily not suggesting that the ladies should withdraw. It was all so calm and orderly and grown-up. 'I do hope you enjoyed the wine tonight.' She waited for the response, which was quick in coming. Everyone murmured enthusiastically. 'Oh, good. It's some of mine – and I'm certainly hoping that after today, I shall have captured a bigger chunk of the English dinner party market.'

'You weren't touting for business at The Derby?' Drew looked appalled. 'I asked you not to.'

'And since when have you a say in the vineyard? Either the production or the marketing?' Caroline's eyes flashed.

'Really, Drew. Do I tell you how to train horses? Of course not. And everyone that I spoke to was extremely keen.'

'But it was The *Derby*.' Drew pulled a knife through the luscious tenderness of a peach. 'You really shouldn't—'

'I think it was a great idea.' Peter's voice was rich with admiration. 'I always try to promote my business wherever I go. You simply have to these days.' He smiled at Caroline. 'I think it was very enterprising of you.'

Drew stabbed a grape. Maddy tried to remove her thigh from the attentions of Charlie's left hand. He grinned at her. 'Can't blame me for trying.'

'At least I have some support.' Caroline turned her pussycat smile to Peter. 'Which makes a pleasant change.'

Bronwyn Pugh, sensing an impending row, cut huge chunks of cheese for everyone and dished them out, more or less the same way that she did in the shop. Maddy's parents were talking about Suzy to Kit and Rosa, and didn't seem to notice the plunging temperature.

'How about some music?' Charlie smiled lopsidedly along the table at Caroline. He was a nice man who didn't like friction – at least, not when it wasn't instigated by him. 'After all, this is supposed to be a celebration, and it's in danger of turning into a wake. Have you got something lively?'

Drew shot him a grateful glance and there was a lot of chair scraping as everyone moved away from the table.

'Show me what music you've got,' Charlie was saying to Caroline. 'That's a seriously impressive sound system. Have you got CDs or tapes?'

'How was Diana today?' Peter stood beside Maddy, ostensibly gazing out over the dusky gardens. 'Pleased.'

'Delirious,' Maddy said shortly. 'And you've got a nerve. I wouldn't have thought you'd ever mention her name to me after—'

'You are so sweet, Maddy.' His voice oozed insincerity. 'I don't know why you get so hung up about sex. Anyway, if it makes you happy, Diana and I are no longer, um, friends.

There is no danger of you catching us in *flagrante* again.'

Maddy blushed. It still embarrassed her. 'So you're being faithful to Stacey, are you?'

Peter's eyes strayed across the garden to where Stacey and Bronwyn appeared to be arguing. 'Jesus, she's probably going on about the golf course. I told her to leave it tonight.' He turned his head and looked at Maddy for a long time. 'Sometimes I realise what a mistake I made. Stacey is such a child . . . I don't suppose there's any chance that we could go out for a meal some time, Mad? Just for old times' sake?'

'Not a hope in hell,' Maddy spat under her breath. 'And if you're intending to dump Stacey I should do it now – before the preparations for the wedding get under way – otherwise you'll have Jeff Henley and his twelve-bore to contend with.'

'I can't dump Stacey. I need her father's money.' His eyes were bleak.

'God, Peter. You can't do that. Not even you can do that.'

'No, I suppose I can't.' He shrugged. 'You're too nice, Maddy. You always were. Stacey and I are right for each other. I suppose we'll probably make a go of things. Anyway, if you and Charlie are getting together I hope you'll be happy. You deserve it.'

She was about to say that there was nothing at all between her and Charlie Somerset, and then stopped. It might prove a useful smokescreen.

Charlie and Caroline had selected Gershwin. The music flooded the headily scented garden. Everyone was dancing on the crew-cut lawn. Drew took her hand and led her towards a secluded corner.

They danced as they had in her cramped sitting-room, swaying together, not moving their feet.

'This is probably why we'd be wrong for each other.' She laid her cheek against his shoulder. 'This is all so elegant and right. This is what you're used to.'

He lifted her head up. 'This is what bores me rigid. I hate all this pretence and social snobbery. Having nine sets of cutlery and eighteen glasses and polite conversation at dinner. I want to be swigging whisky out of beakers and eating Mars bars and not being nagged if my boots are dirty or my jeans are torn. And I don't want this bloody music any more.'

'But Gershwin is fabulous.'

'For you and me – alone.' He looked at her. 'When we're cuddled up with the aforementioned whisky and Mars bars on your sofa. Charlie was right. This is supposed to be a celebration, and that's what it's bloody going to be!'

And it was. With the help of Eddie Cochran, Bill Haley and Thin Lizzy, aided and abetted by Charlie dispensing the best of Caroline's wine with equal measures of vodka, the previously decorous dinner party degenerated into a ballroom blitz. The Pughs and Maddy's parents proved ace jitterbuggers. Caroline, holding herself stiffly as always, danced with Peter while Stacey and Charlie skittered across the terrace. Kit and Rosa, as ever, were so entwined that it would have taken a crowbar to separate them.

'That's how I'd like to be,' Maddy sighed enviously, when she and Drew paused in the middle of an energetic jive for a further swig of Charlie's cocktail. 'And that's how we won't be. Ever.'

'Yes, we will.' Drew touched her cheek in the darkness. 'One day, we'll – God almighty!'

The party was suddenly interrupted by the entire Cat and Fiddle conga-ing out on the terrace from the dining-room.

'You left the door open!' whooped the chef. 'We came to suss out the competition! Join on to the back – we're going to do the whole village!'

The dinner party rushed to participate, clinging to waists and kicking their legs in wild enthusiasm. Caroline, tentatively clutching Peter and laughing, was bringing up the rear as the tail of the conga whiplashed past Drew and Maddy on the terrace.

Maddy closed her eyes. It looked as though Caroline Fitzgerald was here to stay.

Twenty-Four

There was hardly time to draw equine breath between The Derby and Royal Ascot, but for the less horsy inhabitants of Milton St John, life had returned to normal. For Maddy, whose life in the village could never have been described as mundane, normal was a thing of the past.

Kit and Rosa had returned to Jersey. Caroline hadn't.

'Mrs Fitzgerald moved in permanently, then?' Bronwyn asked two weeks after The Derby as Maddy, craving chocolate, made a lunchtime stop at the Village Stores. 'She's going to move her vineyards over here, is she?'

'I don't think it's as easy as that.' Maddy dug deeply into her purse. 'I don't know what her plans are. She hasn't told me.'

'She wouldn't though, would she?' Bronwyn looked beady. 'I mean, you and Drew were getting a bit too pally by my way of thinking.'

'No we weren't.' Maddy blushed. 'We were just friends – still are. I suppose Caroline will go back to Jersey eventually and then—'

'You ought to take up with young Charlie.' Bronwyn was ripping open cardboard containers. 'Especially now he's moved into Peapods. I thought you were getting on so well at their party.'

'We've always got on well.' Maddy wanted to stuff a whole Mars bar in her mouth and was itching to get out of the shop. And she didn't know Charlie had moved into Peapods. 'But he's hardly my type. He's far too flighty.'

'Takes one to know one,' Bronwyn muttered, ducking

237

down behind the counter to arrange meat pies and sausage rolls temptingly for the ever-starving stable lads.

Maddy flushed angrily. Her head ached. So did her back. She was in no mood to fight with Bronwyn. 'Look, I'm not having an affair with Drew Fitzgerald. I do not want to become the next notch on Charlie Somerset's bedpost. In fact, right now, I'll be very happy to become a spinster with cats and spend my dotage nodding in a rocking chair and dribbling. OK?'

Bronwyn straightened up and smoothed her overall. 'And there's no need to take that tone. Your parents are very worried about you. They told me.'

'My parents think I should be married with at least four children.' Maddy snapped. 'My parents, thankfully, live far enough away not to stick their noses into my business every thirty seconds.'

'They were delighted to see Peter at Caroline's party,' Bronwyn trundled on. 'Your mother said she was hoping for a reconciliation. She said—'

'Shut up!' Maddy screamed. 'Mind your own business!'

She slammed out of the shop and leaned against the window, scrabbling at the Mars bar wrapper and cramming the whole gooey delight into her mouth. Bronwyn flung the door open.

'You want to see a doctor, my girl. You got trouble with your hormonals?'

The door crashed shut again. Maddy gulped down the Mars bar and immediately felt sick. She'd seen a doctor. She wasn't pregnant. The news, which she had been praying for, had perversely reduced her to tears. Dr Hodgson had been more than happy to prescribe the pill to prevent further problems of that nature. Maddy had the little foil envelopes in her handbag. She'd start taking them next week.

Listlessly, she pushed her bicycle away from the shop's window. It was pathetic, really. What was the point of knocking back contraceptives when the nearest she'd get to sex in the future was stuffing her fingers in her ears every time Luke came to stay?

The front door to the cottage was wide open. Had she forgotten to shut it? Probably, she thought, dropping the bicycle on the path. She was forgetting everything else. For a moment she wondered if she'd been burgled, then immediately discounted it. Any self-respecting burglar would sniff round the cottage and leave a note saying: 'Not today, thank you,' and then send a food parcel. And burglars wouldn't be playing Def Leppard at a hundred and thirty decibels, would they?

Come to that, Maddy thought, kicking away the hall rug and shutting the door, neither would Suzy. Recently she'd swapped Michael Bolton for groin-tingling smoochiness from Roberta Flack. Def Leppard was not a good sign.

The noise jarred her headache into her teeth as she opened the sitting-room door. Suzy, her face pale, was hunched on the sofa. Forgetting her pains and her menstrual spots, Maddy switched off the stereo. Suzy didn't move.

'What is it, love? Is it Luke?' She gathered Suzy into her arms. She was so thin it was like cradling a baby bird. Her body seemed to have no substance. 'What's he done?'

Hurting so much from not having Drew, Maddy could feel Suzy's pain. A sigh shuddered through the fragile frame. ''S not Luke.'

Thank God for that, Maddy thought, smoothing the white-blonde hair away from Suzy's troubled eyes. She wasn't sure she could cope with any more heartbreak. 'What, then? Come on, Suzy. Tell me.'

''S Kimberley.'

'God! What's happened to her? Has there been an accident?'

'No.' Suzy shook her head. 'She's selling up . . . Selling the yard . . . The virus has knackered her this season. Owners are pulling out because there's no prize money. Oh, Mad!' She turned her woebegone face to Maddy. 'It's so sad. Kimberley's lovely. She doesn't deserve this.'

'No, poppet, she doesn't.' Maddy smiled at her sister in admiration. The hard and streetwise Suzy was hurting for Kimberley. 'When did you hear? Did Kimberley tell you this morning?'

Suzy shook her head. 'Nah. I haven't seen her today. It's all round John's yard, though. Holy hell, Mad. It's her whole life. Jason and Olly told me that she'd gone bust and she didn't want to say anything until after The Derby.'

'Maybe it's not true, then.' Maddy didn't hold out a lot of hope. Stable gossip was usually horribly accurate. The grapevine knew what was going on long before it happened. 'And even if it is, the lads and the jockeys should be OK, love. There are lots of yards. Drew is looking for a flat jockey for next season and—'

'Oh, I know they'll get fixed up.' Suzy scrubbed her eyes with her bunched fingers. 'I'm just upset about Kimberley. I mean, where will she go? It's her home, Mad.'

'I know. I know.' Maddy cradled Suzy again. 'Look, I've been meaning to take her hat back for ages. I'll pop in this afternoon, shall I? Kimberley and I are good friends. I'll see what I can do to help.'

'Don't tell her I said,' Suzy sniffed, anxious to retain her street cred. 'Just see if she tells you.'

'Yes, of course.'

Maddy had been going to ease her stomach and head and back with a hot bath and a dose of Anadin. She stood up. She really couldn't face the bicycle again. She'd have to take the car. Poor, poor Kimberley.

She knocked on the heavy door with trepidation. It was ajar, and immediately Kimberley's pack of mongrels streamed yapping towards it, jamming wet noses through the gap.

'Who is it?' Kimberley's voice echoed down the stone-flagged passage. 'I'm in the kitchen. If you don't like dogs come round the back, otherwise just push your way through the little blighters.'

Maddy pushed, with a dozen pairs of excited feet scrabbling at her leggings. At least Kimberley didn't sound suicidal. 'It's me. Maddy,' she called. 'I've returned the hat.'

Kimberley was by the Aga, simmering entrails for the dogs. She looked over her shoulder and smiled broadly. 'Won't keep you a jiff, Maddy. And you needn't have bothered with the titfer. I won't wear it, and you did look a treat in it.' She straightened up. 'Ta, anyway. Have you got time for a cuppa?'

'Er, yes, thanks.' At least she could take her Anadin with a cup of tea. She sat at the table which was even more cluttered than her own. 'Are you all right?'

'Never better. Why?'

'Oh, nothing, really . . .'

'C'mon, Maddy.' Kimberley clashed around with a giant teapot and mugs. 'You're the worst fibber in this village. What's up?'

'Nothing . . . oh, I just heard, on the quiet, that you've, . . .'

'Bloody hell!' Kimberley sloshed boiling water into the teapot. 'A girl can't have any secrets, can she? Who told you?'

'Suzy said it was all round John Hastings' yard this morning.'

'Little bastards!' Kimberley said happily. 'How the devil do they find these things out? Well, aren't you going to congratulate me?'

'It doesn't seem the right sort of thing to congratulate you about, really.'

'Christ, Maddy!' Kimberley pushed a mug of luminous orange tea through the debris on the table. 'We're in much the same boat. I know Barty's not the catch of the century, and he's not Mel Gibsoney like your Drew, but after all—'

'What?' Maddy choked on the Anadin. 'I think we've got crossed wires. I'd heard you were selling up because of the virus.'

'Yes, I am.' Kimberley heaped sugar into her mug and rattled the spoon. 'But also because I'm marrying Barty.

We're going in together. Seemed eminently sensible to me. The worst of the bug is over, most of my owners will hang on – but Barty's place is so much bigger than this. We thought we'd run a combined yard – and he asked me to marry him.'

'Oh, Kimberley. That's wonderful.'

'Glad you're pleased.' Kimberley blew noisily across the top of the mug. 'I'll take all my staff with me of course. I'll need 'em for my horses. No one will be out of a job. Is that what Suzy was worried about? Her pals being on the scrap heap?'

'Apparently, no. She was worried about you.'

'She's a good kid.' Kimberley's voice was gruff. 'It runs in the family. At least you haven't said I'm stupid for becoming the fourth Mrs Small.'

'Why should I?' Maddy squeezed Kimberley's large hands. 'You didn't lecture me over Drew. I'm delighted for you, Kimberley. Really. When's the wedding?'

'September. Wantage Registry because of Barty being divorced. Then a bloody big reception for the entire village back at Barty's place. Didn't seem any point in hanging about too long.'

'That's lovely. I really am pleased. But won't you miss your garden?'

'Yes. That was the only thing that delayed me. Still,' she brightened, 'you know what Barty's garden is like – very municipal parks. It'll be a challenge to make it all cottagey, won't it?'

'And have you got a buyer?'

Kimberley nodded briskly. 'All but in signature, and I won't say any more until it's settled legally – not even to you. So don't ask. But it's a trainer. The place won't be turned into a gigolo's parlour like Peter did with Peapods. Speaking of which, are you going to Bronwyn's meeting at the village hall?'

'Doubtful. Bronwyn and I aren't speaking again. Anyway, it's a waste of time. The golf course will go ahead now.'

'I'll probably show my face.' Kimberley drained her mug. 'It'll give me a chance to invite everyone to the shenanigan, won't it? And why are you and Bronwyn not speaking?'

'Drew.'

'Silly old besom! She really should MHOB. I should think it's hard enough for you with that cold fish of a wife of his hanging around, without nosy parkers like Bronwyn Pugh sticking their oar in. I don't know why Drew doesn't leave her.'

'He said he would but I told him not to. I can't wreck a marriage.'

Kimberley poured another mug of tea. 'Some marriages are wrecked already. They don't need outside influences. If you're prepared to wait, I'm sure it'll all work out in the end.'

'I'd wait for ever, Kimberley. But I don't think Drew will. Caroline is running her business by fax from Peapods at the moment and showing no signs of budging. I haven't seen Drew to talk to for days.'

'I'll ask her to provide the wine for the reception, and tell her she's got to brew it in person. That'll get rid of her for a few weeks. Give you and Drew a chance to roll in the hay.'

'You're terrible. A complete reprobate.'

'I know.' Kimberley's large face dissolved into a smile. 'I got expelled from Cheltenham Ladies' College for it.'

The Anadin had worked well, easing the worst of the pain by the time Maddy got home. She thought it was a pity someone couldn't dispense an analgesic to cope with heartache. They'd make a fortune.

Having told Suzy Kimberley's news, the cottage once again throbbed Roberta Flack. It was very soothing.

'I'm just going to tell Jason and Olly and the other guys. That'll be OK, won't it?' Suzy was tugging on her Doc Martens.

'Yes. Kimberley said it was better to keep the record straight. This is one secret I don't mind you sharing.'

243

'I never breathed a word about the other . . .' Suzy's tongue protruded as she kohled her eyes in the skew-whiff window.

'I should hope not.' Maddy went scarlet. 'That was private.'

'Not you and Drew, stupid.' Suzy tugged her T-shirt down to groin level. She didn't appear to be wearing a skirt. 'I'd never say anything about that. No, the other-other. About Mrs J-J and Mr Twice Knightley. I can keep a secret. I'm not a child.

'No, you're not. I'm sorry. And anyway, Peter and Diana are now history. I suppose Mitchell D'Arcy is flavour of the month. Peter and Stacey are getting married – definitely a match made in hell.'

'You should be getting married, Mad. You're too lovely to be on your own.'

'I'm not on my own. I've got you, haven't I?' Maddy hugged her, loving her dearly. She really was becoming revoltingly broody. 'I'm very proud of you, Suzy.'

Embarrassed, Suzy wriggled free, and picking up the car keys, slammed out of the cottage. Roberta Flack was still crooning about making love.

Unable to do that, Maddy made a spaghetti bolognaise instead. She was just sloshing red wine into the sauce when Drew walked into the kitchen.

He leaned against the refrigerator. 'It's like a dream come true. You, the music, delicious food . . .'

Maddy quickly wiped her lips on her sleeve. 'How did you manage to escape?'

'Nefarious means.' Drew pulled her into his arms. 'You smell of herbs and garlic and red wine.'

'Good enough to eat?'

'Definitely good enough to kiss.' He did. 'Oh, Christ. I miss you. I wish you'd let me tell Caroline. If I did—'

'I wouldn't see you again.' Maddy turned back to stirring the sauce. 'How is she?'

'Happily flooding the whole of southern England with

wine.' He sat at the table. 'And showing no signs of going home. Ever since Derby night when she actually enjoyed herself for once, she's seemed to want to stay. I wish she wouldn't. Hell, this is terrible. I shouldn't even be saying this.'

'No, you shouldn't. Did you know that Kimberley and Barty are getting married?'

'No! That's wonderful. When?'

'Some time in September. They're merging their yards. I don't know who's buying Kimberley's, but no doubt the grapevine will tell us soon enough. Do you want a drink?'

'No time, unfortunately. We're eating out tonight and I've still got evening stables to do. September is going to be a hell of a time for weddings, then. Isn't that when Peter and Stacey have planned theirs?'

Maddy dived into the larder and rummaged around in the muddle for the pasta jar. She didn't want him to see her face. Drew and Caroline were going out to dinner. She'd eat spaghetti bolognaise on her lap in front of the television.

'Mmm, I think so. Drew, I'm not pregnant.' He didn't answer. She found the jar and re-emerged. 'I said—'

'I heard you.' His face was stony. 'When did you know?'

'This morning.' She wasn't going to tell him she'd been prescribed the pill. She'd probably never need it. 'So, at least that's one thing you don't have to worry about.'

'I wasn't bloody worried about it. Quite the opposite in fact. I'd convinced myself that if you were then I'd leave Caroline and—'

'Make an honest woman of me? No, Drew. If I had been pregnant, I would have been a single mother. I still wouldn't have come between you and Caroline.'

'But you have, Maddy. Can't you see that?' He stood up, still looking bleak. 'Whether she knows or not, the situation is still the same. I love you. I want to be with you.'

'You're married!' She hissed the words at him. 'End of bloody sad story!'

'Christ!' His face was drained of colour. 'Sometimes you can be so bloody stubborn! What are you doing tonight?'

'Why? Are you going to ask me to make a cosy threesome at your dinner table?'

'No. I just wanted to know. I need to know. I'm pathetic enough to want to know what you're doing so that even if I can't be there doing it with you, at least I can imagine.'

She shrugged. She did exactly the same thing. 'Well, if you and Caroline are going to be out of the village I'll probably go to Bronwyn's wind-up meeting at the village hall. It'll be a good idea to be seen without you. I'll sit at the back and knit mittens with the other old ladies. And Bronwyn told me that Charlie Somerset is living at Peapods. You never said.'

'I've hardly seen you. And Charlie's living arrangements are honestly not uppermost in my mind when we do meet.' He sighed. 'He's moved into the stable flat. It seemed more convenient. OK?'

'Fine.'

He smiled then and reached for her. 'I'm really sorry you're not pregnant.'

'So am I.' She sniffed. 'Stupid, isn't it?'

The village hall was only a quarter full. The excitement had gone. Bronwyn and Bernie were alone on the stage; the professionals had deserted them now there was no battle to fight. Maddy slunk in at the back and sat behind Kimberley and Barty who were holding hands. Surprisingly, Peter, Stacey and Jeff Henley were sitting in the front row.

'This won't take long.' Bronwyn beamed out across her depleted audience. 'And I am glad that at least some of you were brave enough to turn up tonight after the fiasco of our last meeting.'

There were a few muted giggles. Stacey stared straight ahead.

'Anyway, the stage tonight really belongs to Peter Knightley. He spoke eloquently last time, and I did in fact check up on his statements. They were quite correct. The access road would not affect the village.'

The clapping was very half-hearted. Maddy wondered if Drew and Caroline had started their first course.

'Anyway, I think it is high time that I let Peter address you.' She gestured towards him. 'Peter Knightley . . .'

The applause was even less enthusiastic. Peter didn't smile. There was no honey in his voice as he surveyed the room. 'I felt I should tell you all this, because if I don't, then the gossips will have blown it out of all proportion by the time you do get to hear.'

Maddy frowned. He really looked very crushed. Maybe he was missing his romps with Diana. She wondered if Drew and Caroline had candlelight.

'There will be no golf course in Milton St John.'

There was a mass intake of breath. Kimberley turned round and grimaced. Maddy raised her eyebrows. Peter shuffled his feet.

'As you know, it was imperative that we purchased both the spinney and the orchard. It seems that the orchard is now no longer for sale.'

The audience rumbled. The grapevine had missed this one. Paul and Phil Maynard were standing at the back of the hall. All heads swivelled to stare at them.

'Bert Maynard,' Peter went on, 'has, in fact, sold his orchard to a private purchaser for an undisclosed sum, but one that we –' he gestured towards Jeff Henley – 'are apparently unable to match. 'Paul and Phil are going to be joint-managers of the orchard. And that's about it. Without the orchard we cannot go ahead. I'm sorry that the village has been robbed of this leisure facility.'

'And more sorry that you've been done out of a nice little earner!' Kimberley roared. 'Who's bought it, then?'

'I really don't know.' Peter looked very harassed. 'Bert refuses to tell me, and so do his sons.' Again, all eyes turned to the back of the hall.

Paul shook his head. 'We dunno, do we, Phil?'

'Nope. Dad won't say nothin'. Just told us we're to run it and he'll take instructions from the new boss. Suits us.'

Peter walked disconsolately from the stage and Bronwyn clapped her hands. 'I still feel that it's a victory for the village,' she bellowed. 'We showed solidarity, and if the need arises, we will do the same again. Anyway, let's give three cheers for freedom and for triumph.'

There were two and a quarter very half-hearted hurrahs, then everyone shuffled out into the street.

'Lot of damn fuss about nothing,' Kimberley snorted. 'Still, I did enjoy the fracas by the stream. I wonder who's lined Bert Maynard's pocket?'

'Not got a clue.' Barty was practically hung round her neck. 'But whoever it is must have a hell of a bank balance. I felt quite sorry for young Peter. I wonder where that leaves him?'

Maddy shook her head. 'God knows. I suppose he'd relied on the golf course to fund his standard of living at the Manor. Still, knowing Peter, he'll have some other scheme up his sleeve. I'm pleased that the spinney and the orchard will stay untouched, though.'

'Me too.' Kimberley pulled Barty's hand through the crook of her arm and nearly yanked him off his feet. 'I'd love to be a fly on Diana's wall. I bet she's spitting blood.'

'Serves 'em all right,' Barty said smugly. 'Now, are you going to join us for a quick drink, Maddy?'

She shook her head. 'I'll leave you lovebirds alone, thanks all the same.'

Her stomach ached again. She just wanted to go home and put her feet up. Suzy would be at the Cat and Fiddle. Drew was out at his cosy dinner *à deux*. It would be nice to curl up in her quilted dressing gown with a cup of chocolate and some more Anadins.

The walls were rocking when she unlocked the front door. Led Zeppelin's greatest hits could have been heard clearly in

Newbury. Feeling lousy, she threw open the sitting-room door.

'Hi, Mad.' Suzy sat up on the sofa wearing nothing but a smile. 'You're back early.'

Luke gave his usual heartbreaking grin and strategically placed a cushion to cover his nakedness. It was fairly ineffective. 'I thought I'd surprise you, but it seems like you've surprised us.'

'Yes, it does rather,' Maddy said weakly, and turned the stereo down. 'Don't mind me, children. I needed an early night.'

Suzy tugged her T-shirt over her head. 'Shall I bring you a hot water bottle? And some cocoa?'

'I could read to you if you liked.' Luke was trying to put both his legs into one of his jeans. 'I know some really good bedtime stories.'

'I bet you do.' Maddy smiled at them both. 'I'll pass on the stories, but the rest sounds lovely.'

She'd got as far as the bedroom door when the phone rang.

'Maddy? Hello, it's Caroline. I've been itching to ring you all evening but Drew said you'd probably gone to the meeting. How did it go?'

'Quietly.'

'Oh, good. Maddy, I have a proposition. Could I come and see you?'

'What, now?' Maddy's heart plummeted.

'Not now.' Caroline's laugh tinkled. 'We're still in the restaurant. Drew's practically chewing the table because I've commandeered the phone trolley all evening. Still, you know what it's like, you being a businesswoman.'

Maddy didn't.

'Tomorrow evening?' Caroline continued. 'I really do need to talk to you and something's come up at home – oh, Jersey, I mean. I may have to go back much sooner than I'd anticipated.'

'Oh, that's a shame.' May God forgive her. 'Yes, I'll be here tomorrow evening. Is Drew coming with you? Do you want a meal?'

'No. No, I wouldn't put you to that trouble. I just think you're the only person who can help me on this one. Oh, Drew wants a word. I'll hand you over. I'll see you tomorrow, then.'

'What the hell is going on?' She whispered. 'Is it, you know? Us?'

'No.' Drew's voice was edgy. 'We'll see you tomorrow. Was the meeting OK?'

'Fine. Drew, you haven't bought Maynards Orchard, have you?'

'No.' He sounded puzzled. 'I think I'd have noticed. Why?'

'No reason. I'll see you tomorrow evening. It'll be better than nothing. Good night.'

'Good night, Maddy.' It sounded like goodbye.

Twenty-Five

Fortified by Anadins, Maddy tidied like a dervish. She wanted the cottage to look its best when Caroline arrived. It seemed important.

The simmering day had melted into a pink marshmallow evening, and even with all the cottage windows open, it was still suffocatingly stuffy. If she'd had a proper garden she could take Caroline out there, as they did in all those Merchant Ivory films. They could link arms and stroll leisurely amongst fragrant flower beds while Caroline exclaimed rapturously over the vista. As it was, thirty strides forward would bring them slap up against the water butt, and twenty the other way would find them amongst the dustbins and back-door debris.

'This is a flying visit, the kids are in the car so I can't stop.' Fran crashed into the kitchen. 'Have you got the Health and Safety people coming round?'

'Caroline.' Maddy paused in the middle of scrubbing the draining board.

'Oh? Can I stay and watch?'

'No, you can't. It's a social visit.'

'Not a "keep your hands off my husband" visit? Are you sure?'

'Positive. You look very done up. Are you going out?'

'The evening meeting at Windsor. Richard's got four rides.'

'Luke and Suzy have gone, too.' Maddy rinsed the dish-cloth and picked at a lump of congealed bolognaise on the tap. 'Did you want anything in particular, or was this a scouting party for the jungle drums?'

'You have such faith in your friends,' Fran laughed. 'Yes and no. I'd heard about the orchard and wondered if Mr Fitzgerald had bought it.'

'No, he hasn't. And don't ask me who has because I don't know. Next?'

'What do you reckon to Kimberley and Barty?'

'Fantastic. I'm pleased for them, even if it isn't the love-match of the century. Aren't you?'

'Yeah. It'll just mean having to share my office with Violet, Kimberley's old bag of a secretary. She sucks aniseed.' She glanced out of the skew-whiff window. 'Oh, look, Maddy. You've got a visitor, and they're using the back path.'

'Drew usually does.'

'It isn't Drew.' Fran glanced at her watch. 'I would have loved to stay for this – I'll ring you. No, I'll see myself out.'

She clattered towards the back door and Maddy sighed. She wasn't anywhere near ready. She was just hiding the dishcloth in the saucepan cupboard when she heard Fran's raised voice from the back garden. It was laughing.

'One in, one out. It's like a weather house. No, go in. She's in the kitchen, Peter!'

Christ! Maddy dived towards the door. She'd have to tell him it wasn't convenient. She simply couldn't see him now.

'Peter, I'm really sorry, but—' She stopped. His face was utterly woebegone. He looked tired and rumpled and not at all like Peter. She sighed. 'Come in.'

He slumped at the table. His blonde hair fell forward and the cornflower eyes were red rimmed.

'I'm sorry to dump on you, Mad.' He looked up at her. 'I didn't know where else to go.'

'Go on.' She pulled up a chair opposite him. 'Is it because of the golf course? Surely you can find another site?'

'Stacey's left me.'

She fought down the urge to say 'now you know what it feels like, you heartless bastard.' 'Why?'

'Because Jeff has pulled out of the golf course. He only

came in with me because I was so sure that with my connections with Milton St John getting hold of the land would be a doddle. He was absolutely furious about the punch-up, and then, finding that we couldn't get the site after all, well . . .'

'But surely Stacey doesn't have to leave you because of that?'

'Stacey . . .' Peter swallowed. 'Stacey was apparently more in love with the idea of becoming Lady of the Manor than with me. No golf course, no Manor, no Stacey.'

'Oh, Peter.' She was genuinely sorry for him. 'I don't think there's anything I can do. I mean, if she's still in the village, I'll certainly speak to her, but—'

'She's gone. Packed. Left me a note.' He looked deep into her eyes. 'Just like I did with you. Christ, Mad, I'm so sorry. I didn't know it hurt so much.'

'Oh, come on. You were screwing around like a rabbit.'

'Mad!' He seemed quite shocked. 'OK, I might had had one or two harmless flings—'

'Huh! Anyway, you said at Caroline's party that Stacey embarrassed you. You even asked me out. I don't believe you're that heartbroken.'

'But I've always been the one to end my relationships.'

First Diana and now Stacey. Maddy tried not to smile. 'So it's your pride that's hurt, not your heart?'

'Both. Have you got a drink? I feel terrible. I've invested all my money in the golf course and the Manor, and nothing was finalised. I suppose I might get some of it back, but not much.'

Maddy poured him some of Bronwyn's sweet sherry in a cup. Everything else had been tidied. 'So does this mean you're penniless, jobless, and homeless?'

'Basically, yes.' Peter swigged the sherry. 'Shit! I don't like sherry. Still, I suppose I'm not in a position to refuse anything now, am I?'

'Don't exaggerate. You'll hardly be reduced to cardboard city, will you?'

'No, but—'

'Look, see what you can recoup first. You'll be able to stay on at the Manor for a while. You've got loads of contacts. You'll pull through on the material side with no problems. You're probably not even down to your last thousand, are you?'

'God, no! I'm not that broke!'

Maddy laughed bitterly. 'Wait until you have to choose between toothpaste or soap in one week. Or whether you can face beans on toast ten days in a row.'

'I didn't think you were that skint. God! I couldn't live like that.'

'Compared to a lot of people, I'm rolling in it. At least I've got a roof and food and I'm warm. Welcome to the real world, Peter.'

He reached across the table and took her hands. It did nothing to her at all. He smiled. 'I should never have let you go.'

'I'm very glad you did.'

Sadly, when Drew and Caroline passed the open skew-whiff window, that was what they saw. Maddy, scruffy and dishevelled, holding hands across the table with Peter Knightley and staring at him with deep compassion.

'Can we come in?' Caroline trilled, already in. 'I do hope we're not interrupting?'

'Not at all.' Maddy almost threw Peter's hands across the table. 'Peter's just leaving.'

Drew's lips were drawn in a tight line.

'So nice to see you again.' Caroline was gushing all over Peter. 'You and Stacey must come for drinks really soon.'

'I'd love to.' Peter's voice was choked. 'But I'm afraid Stacey and I are no longer together.'

'Oh, dear, I am sorry.' Caroline bit her lip. 'I didn't mean to be insensitive. How very sad.'

'Maddy has been consoling me,' Peter gave a wan smile. 'She's so good at it, and we're such old friends . . .'

Drew had reached boiling point. Maddy knew it without even looking at him. She sucked in her breath. 'I don't want to seem rude, Peter, but I did invite Caroline and Drew.'

'Yes, of course.' He leaned towards her and kissed her cheek. She heard Drew's intake of breath. 'I'll see you very soon. And thanks for everything.'

'Such a handsome man,' Caroline sighed as he closed the back door. 'What on earth happened with him and Stacey?'

'I've no idea,' Maddy said shortly, cursing Peter Knightley to hell. 'I'm sorry, but I've had several unexpected visitors and I'm a bit disorganised. If I pour drinks will you excuse me while I get changed?'

'Please don't change on our behalf.' Drew said quietly. 'I'm sure whatever is good enough for Peter Knightley is good enough for us.'

Maddy narrowed her eyes at him.

'As you wish. I thought we'd go out into the garden. It's so hot. I'm sure there's going to be a storm.'

'I'm sure there is.' Drew stalked out through the kitchen door.

Owing to the absence of garden furniture they sat on the fallen tree trunk.

Caroline sipped her gin and tonic. 'This is very pleasant. What a sweet little garden, Maddy. So rustic. Actually,' she leaned forward in a wave of Joy, 'I'll come straight to the point of this visit. I wanted to ask you about marketing my wines.'

'Me? I know absolutely nothing about wine. I only buy what I can afford. I prefer white to red, and only enjoy it if it sparkles.'

'Wonderful.' Caroline seemed impressed. 'That's just what I need. So many people are such snobs, I find. It's so refreshing to find someone who tells the truth.'

'Maddy always tells the truth,' Drew said, examining a molehill with the toe of his desert boot. 'Even when it hurts.'

Caroline shot a look of anger towards her husband. 'Take

no notice of him. He's sulking because I've pulled off the deal with the Spanish holiday complex. He told me it was coals to Newcastle. I knew differently. You see, if they're going to be catering for the British holidaymaker, I knew they'd be interested in British wines. People are so afraid when they go abroad, and this place does English breakfasts and roasts on Sundays. It was perfect. That's why I'm going home. I have to be in Alicante on Monday.'

Maddy would have inwardly whooped at this information if Drew hadn't been so po-faced about Peter. She smiled. 'Congratulations, but I still don't see what I can do to help.'

Maddy looked fleetingly across at Drew. If he was ever going to draw comparisons it was going to be now. Caroline, tall, slender, elegantly groomed, in pale pink trousers and a white broderie anglaise blouse, and Maddy in cut-off leggings, a blue T-shirt splashed with Flash, and a tangle of curls. He met her eyes for a second and looked quickly away.

'This is a pretty clematis. You must give me a cutting.' Caroline reached up and let the fronds drift through her fingers. 'I would have preferred to come alone this evening. Drew is so negative about my business, and had I known Peter was going to be here I would have definitely left him at Peapods.' She made Drew sound like an untrained Labrador.

'Why?' Maddy, shocked by Caroline's dismissive words and aware of Drew's hiss of breath, wasn't sure she wanted to know. 'What's Peter got to do with it?'

'He's got such style. And he's very astute, business-wise. I could have asked his advice, too. Still, maybe another time. Now, Maddy, I'm thinking of expanding. The money from the Spanish deal will help tremendously. I want to open wine bars.'

Drew snorted.

'Aren't they very 1980s?' Maddy was vague about these things. 'Do people still go to wine bars?'

'Oh, absolutely. I've already made enquiries in Jersey and Guernsey and got some super feedback. And while I've extended my visit here I've scouted round the area. It's crying out for that sort of thing. Not just wine bars but an eaterie as well.'

Maddy flinched at eaterie. She still looked blank.

'If I opened one in Milton St John – which is very likely – there's an empty shop along by Bronwyn's that used to sell photographs or something . . .'

'It got raided by the Vice Squad last August.'

'Yes, well, that one. Maddy, what I want to know is, would you run it for me?'

'You want her to what?' Drew rocked forwards. He obviously hadn't been consulted. 'I've never heard anything more ridiculous.'

'Drew, please.' Caroline's lips were a tight line. 'When have I ever interrupted a business meeting of yours?'

Maddy wanted to laugh. She stared at Caroline. Was the woman mad? 'Why on earth me?'

'Because you're warm and friendly and people flock to you. Because you can cook. Because I think you should be doing something other than cleaning for a living.'

Fury spiralled up in a white-hot volcano, Maddy choked it back. Drew stared at his wife in disgust. 'For Christ's sake, Caroline! Maddy isn't—'

'It's OK, Drew.' She spoke evenly, looking at Caroline. 'I am more than happy with Shadows. It's very kind of you, Caroline, but no, I couldn't possibly.'

'Please think about it.' Caroline's voice was still light. 'I do need someone of your calibre. I want you to work for me.'

'I work for myself.'

'Yes, but it's not really work, is it? Cleaning? Anyone can clean. I'm offering you managerial status.'

'I'm sure she doesn't want your charitable offerings,' Drew snapped, looking at Maddy for the first time. 'Do you?'

'Absolutely not. I don't want charity, managerial status, or an employer.' Maddy's eyes glittered. 'Thank you again, but no. Anyway, you'd be in direct competition with the Cat and Fiddle.'

'Oh, no. I've talked to the landlord. We wouldn't be doing the same thing at all.' She snapped off a piece of the clematis. 'I shall be spending less and less time with Drew, Maddy.' She cast slanting eyes along the tree trunk. Drew was staring at the ground. 'Our lives aren't even parallel any longer. I won't want to be having to check up on my establishments every five minutes. With you in charge here, I wouldn't need to. I trust you.'

Maddy closed her eyes, counted to ten, then opened them again. 'Well, don't. I'm the most untrustworthy person in the whole world!'

Caroline dropped the clematis on the grass. Maddy knew Drew was humming with anger. The glasses were empty. Maddy sighed.

'Let me get you a refill. Look, Caroline, I'm not being rude. It was very kind of you, but for any number of reasons, I must say no.'

'And is Drew one of those reasons?'

'What?' Maddy almost stopped breathing.

'I know how you feel about Drew, Maddy. I've always known. We've talked about it often enough. But I've explained the situation to you.'

'Can I have a say in this now?' Drew was almost incandescent with anger. 'I don't know why you've asked Maddy to work for you – Christ knows, I'm the last person you consult these days – but, she has a company of her own to run. How Maddy and I feel about each other simply doesn't come into it.'

'I disagree.' Caroline was still completely composed. Maddy looked at her in admiration. Was there nothing that would ruffle that ice-cold exterior? Caroline smiled. 'But before we say anything else, shall we have that drink?'

They were all on their feet now. Maddy filled the three glasses, her hands shaking.

'That's better.' Again, Caroline was cool. 'Now, your relationship . . .'

'We don't have a fucking relationship!' Drew yelled. 'We like each other. We've become good friends. Jesus, Caroline, it was you who didn't want to move to England with me.'

'And with good reason. Drew, darling. We've lived together and apart and always managed to be friends. I merely thought that if Maddy was in love with you, she may feel awkward working for me. I just wanted to reassure her that I wouldn't mind at all.'

'I don't understand you.' Maddy shook her head. 'Look at him, Caroline. He's wonderful. How can you say that you don't care if other people love him?'

'Because he has to stay with me.' Caroline stirred a rather grubby piece of lemon round with an elegant finger. 'He needs me. Not sexually, of course. We both find that distasteful—'

'No, he doesn't!' Maddy clapped her fingers over her mouth in horror. 'Oh, God, I mean . . .'

Twenty-Six

'You've slept together?' Caroline's eyebrows imitated the Clifton suspension bridge. 'Well, well. This is quite a development.'

'We haven't – slept together,' Maddy said truthfully. 'Have we?'

Drew looked at her, than at Caroline. 'No, we haven't. But we have made love.'

'You can't have.' Caroline made it sound like he'd just confessed to being Jack the Ripper.

'I can and I did. And it was wonderful.'

'Really? How nice for you.' Caroline's face was ashen.

Maddy wanted to die. This was horrific. 'I told you I was untrustworthy.'

'At least you've only stolen my husband,' Caroline said frostily. 'It's not quite the same as being caught with your fingers in the till, is it?'

'It's exactly the same.' Maddy blinked back her tears. 'I'm really, really sorry, Caroline. I can't help loving him.'

'As no doubt he can't help loving you.' Caroline's tone was as cold as her eyes. 'You're both warm and loving people, while I'm not. I don't see that we have to let this blip make any difference.'

'Of course it'll make a bloody difference,' Maddy shouted, feeling sick. 'And it wasn't a blip! It was the most wonderful experience of my life.' She swallowed, remembering. 'Caroline, I live in a world where fidelity and truth and trust are all part of love. I can't have anything to do with *ménage à trois*, or open marriages. I've never done anything like it before. I love Drew very, very much. But he's married – to you. I hope you'll forgive him, because I won't see him again.'

'That'll be difficult as you live so closely together.'

'You know what I mean.' She choked on her grief and looked at Drew. 'She doesn't deserve you. She doesn't understand you.'

'And you do?' Caroline tossed back her glossy hair. 'On the strength of your brief acquaintanceship and a sexual encounter? I don't think you know Drew at all, Maddy.'

'Oh, but I do. You told me Drew wasn't interested in sex. You told me he was impotent. He's nothing of the sort. Why did you tell me lies, Caroline?'

'Maddy . . .' Drew shook his head wearily.

'You told him he was useless in bed so often that he believed you?' Maddy stared at Caroline's calm face. 'Jesus, you're cruel.'

'Maddy.' Drew stepped between them. 'Don't say anything else.'

'Why not?' She glared at him, then turned again to Caroline. 'Drew is amazing in bed. He needs a normal physical relationship – not with a mass of mistresses, Caroline, with you. His wife. You don't know what you're missing.'

Gulping in a shuddering breath, Maddy stared at them both. She was practically begging them to stay together.

'I think we have a lot of things to discuss.' Caroline made it sound like she was opening a board meeting. 'Perhaps we could talk about them later, Maddy?'

'You don't need to talk to me about them at all. You need to talk to Drew. God Almightly, Caroline! Take him home and drag him into bed! You say you love him, then for God's sake show him before it's too late!'

'Actually—' Caroline started, but Maddy never heard the rest of the sentence.

Charlie Somerset, hair flaming in the setting sun, appeared round the side of the cottage. He looked at the angry faces, shrugged helplessly at Maddy, then crossed the grass quickly to Drew. 'Phone call. Urgent.'

'Shit.' Drew's shoulders were hunched in anger. 'Won't it wait?'

''Fraid not. It's not something I can deal with.'

'OK.' Drew looked at Caroline. 'Are you coming?'

'In a moment. I haven't quite finished.' She waited, her face composed, until Drew and Charlie had disappeared, then smiled. 'I suppose you do know why Drew and I will never separate?'

'The baby . . .' Maddy bit her lip. 'He told me. It must have been awful, but—'

Caroline laughed harshly. 'The baby! My convenient miscarriage! He's been trotting that one out again, has he? Dear, dear. You really mustn't believe everything Drew tells you, Maddy. I'm afraid he's been playing for sympathy. Oh, yes, there was a miscarriage, but Drew doesn't stay with me because of that.' Her eyes flashed. 'Drew stays with me, Maddy, because I own him. I own Peapods. I'm financing his little venture. He couldn't be a trainer without my money. It all comes down to cash in the end. As does everything. So, I'm not the only one who doesn't always tell the truth. I'm afraid, my dear, that Drew has been lying to you all along.'

Charlie appeared round the side of the cottage again and motioned to Caroline.

'Bugger off,' Maddy snarled, hating Caroline, loathing Drew, and taking it out on Charlie. 'We're busy.'

'Sorry.' Charlie shook his head. 'Caroline, the phone call – it's your mother ringing from Jersey.'

'Oh, I do hope there isn't a problem with the Alicante deal.' Caroline sighed crossly. 'Very well, I'll come now. I don't think there's any more to be said here.'

'No, there isn't.' Maddy's teeth were chattering. 'You've made everything very clear, thank you.' She raised her eyes as Drew appeared again behind Charlie. 'And you'd better go as well!'

'Maddy!' Charlie hissed as Drew took Caroline's arm. 'For Christ's sake! Her mother's on the phone because her father has had a heart attack. He died fifteen minutes ago.'

Drew led Caroline gently away, turning bleak eyes to Maddy almost as an afterthought. 'We'll be going to Jersey on the next flight out of Southampton. I don't know when we'll be back. Charlie, we'll need to talk about Peapods. Goodbye, Maddy.'

They trailed desolately away between the dustbins. Feeling more sick than she ever had in her life, Maddy crashed blindly into the kitchen.

She must have cried for hours. She was sure she hadn't fallen asleep hunched over the kitchen table but when she opened her swollen eyes the room was eerily dark and raindrops drummed against the windows.

Oh, God. All the horror came flooding back. And she'd left the windows open. She staggered round the cottage, jarring her legs on shadowy furniture, slamming out the storm. If only it was as easy to slam out the memories.

The phone rang. She lifted the receiver and crashed it down again. It immediately rang once more. She snatched it from the hook and left it dangling, trying to ignore the nasal voice squawking: 'Sorry – please replace the handset and try again. Sorry – please replace the handset . . .'

'If only I could,' Maddy whispered, smothering it with the oven gloves.

When Suzy and Luke came in, laughing, triumphant and soaking wet, she was curled on the sofa in the darkness.

'What's happened? Has the electricity gone off? Why are you sitting in the dark?' Suzy switched on the table lamp. 'Holy hell, Mad! Who hit you?'

'No one,' Maddy snuffled. 'And turn that light off.'

'But your face is all swollen.'

'She's been crying, love.' Luke looked quickly at Maddy

and switched off the light. 'I'll go, Maddy. I can always scrounge a bed at the James-Jordans'.'

'No you bloody can't,' Suzy snapped. She sat down beside Maddy. 'Do you want to talk about it, or are you best left alone? I feel a bit useless . . . You never cry, Mad. You always cheer everyone else up.'

Luke had gone into the kitchen. Maddy could hear him making cup of tea noises. He was lovely. She gulped back her tears and wiped her eyes on her sleeve. 'I'd like to talk about it. If you can bear it.'

''Course I can.' Suzy curled her damp, skinny body next to Maddy's and held her hand. 'Start at the beginning . . .'

It took them four cups of tea. Luke sat on the floor, idly stroking Suzy's leg. Neither of them interrupted her. When she'd finished she felt completely drained.

'Well, it's one king-sized balls-up,' Suzy said. 'Poor Caroline – losing her dad and her husband.'

'She hasn't lost her husband,' Maddy sighed. 'I have.'

'He won't give up.' Luke spoke in the darkness. 'I know Drew too well. He's never even looked at anyone else before. It was so special, you and him. Jesus, Maddy. I know it's the wrong time to say it, but Caroline is a frigid bitch who only cares about her business. You made Drew so happy – the happiest I have ever seen him.'

'But he lied to me. He told me that he only stayed with Caroline because he felt so guilty. It wasn't true. He stayed with her because she's got the money that keeps him going. He's not only a liar, he's a gold-digger. He's married and I should never have got involved. I should never have believed him.'

Suzy stroked Luke's black hair. 'But if they split up now? Where's the problem?'

'They'll never split up,' Maddy croaked. 'He won't leave her because Peapods is all he's ever wanted. No Caroline – no Peapods. It's like bloody Peter and the bimbo stick-insect in reverse.'

'It isn't and you know it!' Suzy stormed. 'You love each other!'

'Correction. I love Drew. Drew loves being a trainer. Without his wife's financial backing he'll lose it all.'

'So what are you going to do?' Suzy frowned through the streaked kohl. 'When he does eventually come back to Milton St John?'

'Pretend none of this ever happened. Let Drew and Caroline get on with their sad and financially knotted marriage and smile politely if we happen to meet. Turning Peapods into the best yard in Milton St John is all Drew wants. And that's what he's going to have. I always thought I couldn't compete with Caroline. Now I know I can't. I'll probably never speak to him again.'

'You can't!' Suzy narrowed her eyes.

'Watch me,' Maddy groaned, shakily getting to her feet and tottering towards the bathroom. 'Just bloody watch me.'

It was long after midnight when the phone rang. Luke had retrieved it from the oven gloves on his way to Suzy's bed.

'Can we talk?' Drew's voice hissed through the darkness. 'Your phone has been off the hook.'

'I know. There's nothing to say.'

'There's a hell of a lot. Don't you dare hang up on me.'

'Don't bark orders at me.' Maddy winced at her bloated face in the hall mirror. 'How's Caroline?'

'Sleeping. The doctor gave both her and her mother a sedative. I'm ringing from Bonne Nuit.'

'Oh.' Maddy would never see Bonne Nuit now. 'Tell her how sorry I am. I'm sure she won't want to hear it, but tell her anyway.'

'I will. Maddy—'

'Don't bother, Drew. Please don't insult my intelligence any more.'

'I never have. I just wanted to talk to you. It's all so incredibly sad over here. I want to know what you intend to do.'

'Me?' Maddy stared incredulously into the telephone. 'I don't intend to do anything. I shall live here and work and be part of the village – everything that I was and did before you came on the scene.'

'I see.' Drew swallowed. It was probably whisky. 'And what about us?'

'We haven't got an "us". Caroline has made it very clear that you and she will stay together. You know why. I'm not going to be part of it. Drew, I fell apart after Peter. I picked up the pieces. I can't do it again. I – I don't want to see you again.'

'I love you.'

She gulped back the tears. 'And I thought I loved you, too. But I didn't really know you, did I? That's why I'm saying goodbye. Go and patch up your marriage, Drew. It's over.'

'Very well.' Drew's voice had subsided to a whisper. 'Then it makes the next bit slightly easier.'

'What next bit?' Maddy felt sick.

'While Charlie is living at Peapods he can keep an eye on things. I don't know how long I'll be needed over here. Maybe months.'

She whimpered. 'And are you coming back?'

'Eventually. I don't know when. But when I do, I trust we'll be able to behave like adults. Maybe even friends.'

Friends! How could they ever be friends? 'Why not? Stranger things have happened. Good night.'

For the second time that night, Drew said sadly, 'Goodbye, Maddy.'

Twenty-Seven

Dragged down by despair, Maddy was determined to survive. She still jumped every time the phone rang, but it was never Drew. Everyone in the village knew that Drew had flown to Jersey, and everybody knew why. All sympathy was with Caroline. With her smile painted on brightly, and her eyes hidden behind dark glasses on the worst days, Maddy fooled most of Milton St John.

Most, but not all.

'You can't keep on doing this,' Fran said as they sat in Maddy's kitchen drinking coffee. 'He's been gone for three weeks. The poor guy is probably suffering the worst kind of hell trying to forget you and going slowly crazy. And –' she took in Maddy's listless expression and dull hair – 'you've already gone.'

Suzy draped her arms round Maddy's shoulders. 'She won't listen. She says it was for the best. Bloody funny best, if you ask me, booting out a man like Drew Fitzgerald.'

'Leave me alone. I know what I'm doing.' Maddy glared at them both.

'Really?' Fran pulled a face. 'I don't think you do, Maddy. Caroline and Drew have gone back to Jersey. Together. And are showing no signs of returning. He loved you but how much longer did you think he'd keep battering his head against your bloody ridiculous moralistic brick wall? There are women, beautiful, available women, on the racing circuit, slavering. Don't you think he's given up on you and already gone for one of them?'

'It's not like that,' Maddy intoned through clenched teeth.

'Why will no one listen to me? He lied to me! He let me believe that they stayed together because he felt sorry for her! It wasn't true! He only stayed with her for the money!'

'I still refuse to believe that Drew is totally dependent on Caroline – and even if he is, at least give him the choice. You love him, don't you?'

'Yes.' Maddy raised her head. 'Desperately. But I am too afraid of being hurt again. Anyway, I do have principles, and I had to give his marriage a chance.'

'His marriage hasn't had a bloody chance for years!' Suzy was doing her make-up in a smeared mirror at the table. 'Stop being so bloody silly, Mad. He was in a no-win situation. If he left Caroline you said you wouldn't have anything to do with him because you'd have wrecked their marriage. If he stayed with her you wouldn't be his mistress.' She spat on her mascara wand. 'It seems to me that you didn't want him as much as you said.'

'I wanted him more than anything ever in my life.' Tears burned Maddy's eyes. 'But properly. For myself. If he was free to be mine, which he'll never be. So,' she shuddered, 'I'll live without him, which is why I'm being taken out tonight.'

Fran shook her head. 'You should have been a nun in the Middle Ages. You'd have had a whale of a time with self-flagellation. Anyone hopelessly in love with Drew Fitzgerald does not go gallivanting with Charlie Somerset!'

'And you've changed your tune just a bit, haven't you?' Maddy hissed at Fran. 'You were the one who told me not to get involved with Drew because he was married.'

Fran's eyes softened. 'Shit, Maddy. That was before I knew him. Before I realised how perfect you were together, and certainly before I discovered just how much he loved you. I thought he was just going to take you for a ride.'

'He did. On Solomon.' Maddy started to laugh, then burst into tears. 'Oh, God, what have I done?'

'Screwed up your life, his life, our life . . .' Suzy smeared her full lips with glossy scarlet. 'While, no doubt, Mrs

Fitzgerald, the ice queen, when fully recovered from her no doubt profit-making bereavement will be making wine and money and laughing her frozen socks off.'

'I liked Caroline,' Maddy sniffed. 'I should never have told her . . .'

'No, you shouldn't,' Fran agreed. 'But you did, because that's how you are. And she should never have told you about their financial set-up. But she did because she knew that if you really loved him you'd never let him risk losing his stables. The cow. Maddy, when Drew comes back to Peapods, at least be friends with the guy.'

Maddy wiped her eyes. How could they just be friends? They'd shared everything. She loved him to distraction. She couldn't treat him the way she treated Luke or Richard – or even Peter. They were her friends. Drew was – had been, so briefly – her lover.

Fran stood up, feeling useless. 'I take it you will still be coming to Kimberley and Barty's reception? Barty said they hadn't had your reply yet. Or are you going to be totally bloody selfish and avoid that too?'

'It's ages yet. Months. I hadn't replied because Drew might be there.' She scrubbed at her eyes with a piece of kitchen roll. 'I can't bear being there when he's not with me. Not after all the other functions we've been to together.'

'Of course he won't be there. No one knows when he'll be back. And if he was he'd probably ignore you.' Suzy jammed her make-up into its hold-all. 'I would if I was him. Mad, you can't let Kimberley down'.

She sighed heavily. She knew they were right. 'OK. I'll send my acceptance. But if he's there . . .' She knew she was fooling herself. He wasn't going to be there.

Fran and Suzy exchanged martyred glances over her head. It wasn't the breakthrough they'd been hoping for, but it was a start.

The Cat and Fiddle throbbed moistly. As July had followed

June's example by scorching into the record books, the evenings showed no signs of respite from the heat. The back of Maddy's neck itched damply, and the long cotton floral frock which had looked so cool and enticing in Oxfam was already clinging to her ribs.

'Shall we sit outside?' said Charlie Somerset, juggling two lager shandys in cold cloudy glasses. 'I've never got to grips with drinking in a sauna.'

She followed Charlie into the pub's garden. He really was devastating with his russet hair and his strongly athletic body displayed to advantage in tight jeans and T-shirt. Maddy sighed sadly as she lowered herself into a rustic chair opposite him. She felt not the merest twinge of lust.

'Drew's delighted with the horses.' Charlie gulped his shandy, leaning back in his chair. 'He rings every evening to approve the entries and ask after their progess.'

'Really?' Maddy wished he'd check on her progress. 'And how are things going in Jersey? With Caroline, I mean.'

'Slowly and sadly, I gather. Drew seems to think he'll have to stay out there for most of the summer.' Maddy's heart plummeted.

Charlie carried on, happily. 'Her father did most of the travelling and the selling. I fancy that he's something of a hard act to follow. Drew seems set to stay out there until they've found a replacement. Are you missing him then, Mad?'

Shaking her head and almost spilling the shandy, Maddy attempted a laugh. 'Of course not! Goodness, no! And I'd prefer it if we didn't talk about Drew any more. There are far more interesting topics . . .'

Charlie, never one to delve beneath the surface, seemed quite happy to do just that and spent the rest of the evening regaling her with scurrilous racecourse stories. Maddy half-listened. She was getting very used to only half doing anything.

They walked back through the village in the sweltering

darkness. It was very reminiscent of all those old Rod Steiger films set in the Deep South where people had back porch swings and listened sweatily to the alligators croaking in the bayou.

'Am I coming in for coffee?' Charlie asked cheerfully, his arm draped casually round Maddy's shoulders, as they reached the cottage.

'Is that euphemistic coffee, or real?' Maddy fumbled for the door key.

'Whatever you're offering.'

'Instant in a mug. Maddy grinned at him. 'On opposite sides of the kitchen table.'

The telephone rang just as she was sloshing water on to the granules. Charlie loped across the hall and lifted the receiver. 'Oh, hi.' Maddy could hear him chatting. It was probably Suzy ringing from Newmarket. 'Yeah, sure. No problem. I'll get her.'

'Coffee's on the table.' Maddy took the phone. 'Make yourself at home.'

'I'm sure he will,' Drew's voice growled in her ear. 'I'm sure he already has.'

Maddy closed her eyes. Drew's voice had aroused all the desires that Charlie's body had failed to do. For the thousandth time she marvelled at the appalling timing of sexual attraction.

'We've, er, just been to the Cat and Fiddle,' she mumbled. 'You know . . .'

'Only too well.'

'It's very hot here,' she gabbled lamely. 'Is it hot out there?'

'Yes.'

'Oh, good.'

There was a ringing silence. She could hear Charlie mooching through her food cupboard. Drew sighed. 'Maybe I should ring some other time. When you're not so busy.'

She longed to be off-hand. It was difficult when she was practically kissing the phone and her toes were curling inside her sandals. 'Why did you ring?'

'Because –' his voice softened for a moment, then remembered and resumed its harshness – 'because I'm coming back to Milton St John at the end of the week.'

'Oh. And, er, Caroline?'

'No. Caroline is trying hard to take her father's place. She won't be coming with me. I just wanted to tell you myself. I didn't want to bump into you in Bronwyn's shop without you knowing I was back.'

'Thanks.' Maddy swallowed. She wanted to ask him so many things, but there wasn't any point. Not now. Not ever. 'I'll tell Charlie, shall I?'

'I already have,' Drew said tersely. 'Although he seems to be managing very well without me.'

'Mad!' Charlie's voice echoed from the kitchen. 'Hurry up! Drew knows what jockeys are like – quick to rouse and even quicker to pleasure! I'm sure he wouldn't want you to miss it!'

Maddy screwed her eyes tight shut. Drew sounded as though he had dropped the phone. His voice was distant. 'I may see you later in the week, then. Goodbye.'

'I hope I didn't say the wrong thing.' Charlie grinned over the rim of his mug as she walked back into the kitchen. 'Still, Drew has a sense of humour. Great news, huh? Hey, Mad, why are you crying?'

They met outside the Cat and Fiddle four days later. Maddy, on her way home from cleaning at Diana and Gareth's, had propped her bicycle against the wall of the public bar, and removing her trainers, had hobbled across the road to the stream.

The sun scorched and spiralled above her head and the cold brown water bubbling between her toes was, as Suzy would have said, orgasmic. Padding back through the dust, her eyes on the ground to ward off stray bottle caps and broken glass, she didn't notice the solitary figure sitting beneath the brewery parasol.

'Is this your contribution to water conservation? Bathing in the stream?' Drew's voice sliced through the pulsing midday heat. 'Very laudable.'

'Jesus!' She stumbled over her trainers. 'Where did you spring from?'

'My fridge seems devoid of anything cold to drink. In fact it seems full of very little. I came for a gallon of anything. I settled for lager.' His voice was as icy as the stream.

They gazed at each other. He looked older and thinner. There were dark shadows of sadness beneath his eyes, and hard lines on either side of his mouth. Maddy knew she looked much the same.

She finished lacing her trainers and blew damp wisps of hair away from her glistening cheeks. 'I've been cleaning Peapods. While you've been away. Only once a week because it doesn't need very much. It's just dust, really.'

'Fascinating. I love hearing about your business.'

'Bastard.' She knew she was blushing. 'I just thought you'd like to know. At least I haven't been taking money under false pretences.' She grabbed angrily at her bicycle.

Drew stood up. 'And what's that supposed to mean?'

'Nothing.' She jarred the pedal against her leg and wanted to cry. 'I'll send Jackie in again now that you're home.'

'Don't bother. I'm not intending to stop for long. Certainly not long enough for it to interfere with your roster.'

Oh, God. Maddy gripped the handlebars. Obviously the death of his father-in-law had depleted the family coffers. Caroline would want the money from Peapods to shore up the vineyard. He'd only come back to put the yard on the market.

'I needed to reassure myself that Charlie could cope long term. Naturally, I don't need to tell you that he can. There were just one or two things I had to sort out before I left,' he said as he walked towards her.

'Left? Are you going straight back to Jersey?'

'No.' He swallowed. He was close enough now for her to

see the dark bruised shadows under his tan. 'I'm not. Caroline is coping well with her mother. The vineyard is running smoothly. They no longer need me. Peapods no longer seems to require my residency. And you . . .' He looked into her eyes. 'I doubt if you ever needed me, Maddy.'

She wanted to cry in his arms. She jumped on to her bicycle. It wobbled unsteadily. She couldn't see through the mist of her tears. 'So where are you going?'

'America.'

He might as well have said the moon. She'd never see him again. 'For ever?'

'No. Maddy, are you happy?'

Bloody, bloody stupid question. She glared at him. 'I'm always happy. You don't have to worry about me, Drew.'

'I never did. Maddy—'

'Don't say anything.' She pushed a wodge of J-cloths more firmly into the bicycle basket. 'We both know it was a mistake. That night, Caroline told me all of it. I know you won't leave her. And I know why.' She lifted her head and stared into his bleak eyes. 'I wouldn't even ask you to. I hope things work out well for you, Drew. And one day maybe we will be friends again.'

'Friends?' Drew spat the word like discarded bubblegum. 'I've got all the friends I'll ever need!'

'Oh, good.' Maddy wobbled unsteadily from the car park and on to the dusty curve of the main road. 'I'm so glad.' She turned her head only when she reached Bronwyn's shop. Drew was still standing on the grey car park, the sun dazzling round him. Too sad to cry, Maddy cycled round the corner.

The summer stretched scorchingly ahead like a penance.

Twenty-Eight

Kimberley and Barty had a glorious September day for their wedding. They'd chosen a Wednesday as it was less busy for the racing fraternity than a weekend, and with Suzy and John Hastings as witnesses had sailed off to Wantage Register Office in a cloud of good wishes and early confetti.

Maddy, having lost over a stone in weight, put on the Knightsbrige dress, the shoes and the earrings, and surveyed herself in the mirror. She looked terrible. Her skin was lifeless, her eyes lacklustre, and her hair refused to do anything except hang. The dress, so voluptuous when she'd worn it to The Derby, now simply skimmed past what was left of her curves, and draped shapelessly against her legs. The dull green matched her complexion.

She shuddered and walked to the window, lifting the merest edge of the curtain. Peapods was deserted. Charlie would be getting dressed in his party finery. The stable lads, encouraged by an entire day's free food and drink, already had.

Drew still hadn't returned. She knew from Charlie that he'd telephoned regularly, but whether from Jersey or America, she hadn't enquired. Living without him had not become any easier. It was more than six weeks since she'd seen him. It seemed like sixty years.

Fran's car pulled up outside in a cloud of dust. The weather had been scorchingly barren for weeks, too. Closing the front door behind her, Maddy scurried down the path, feeling as though she were going to a funeral.

'Lovely day for it,' Richard said conversationally as they

drove along the main road. He looked, as did all flat jockeys, like a child dressing up when he wore a suit. 'You look nice, Mad.'

'No she doesn't,' Fran snapped. 'She looks just as she deserves to.'

'Let me out of the car!' Maddy hissed scrabbling at the side of her. 'Stop the car and I'll walk. I won't stay in here if you're going to be bitchy. I just don't need it. Oh, where's the bloody door handle?'

'It's a two-door,' Fran said smugly. 'So sit there, shut up, and listen.'

Glowering, Maddy sat. Fran looked stunning in burnt-orange chiffon. She stared at Maddy over her shoulder.

'You do look awful. If you smiled it would be a hundred per cent improvement. Don't you dare sulk today, Maddy. It's the biggest day of Kimberley's life and you're going to enjoy it. The whole village is going to enjoy it. You will not be a death's-head. Understand?'

'Yes, Mum.'

Fran and Richard both stiffened. Maddy frowned. 'What now? I was trying to be funny – as ordered.'

'I'm pregnant.' Fran's smile was wall-to-wall.'

'Oh!' Maddy hugged what she could reach of her, her misery momentarily forgotten. She tried to hug Richard too. 'Oh, I'm so pleased! When's it due?'

'The end of March.' Fran's eyes sparkled. 'Dr Hodgson confirmed it this morning. We'd been hoping and praying it wasn't a false alarm.'

'And it's all down to you.' Richard steered the car into ranks of other cars all jamming Barty's drive.

'Why me?' Maddy tried not to look for Drew's dark blue Mercedes. It was a habit she couldn't break. 'I wasn't even there, was I?'

'You might have been. It depends which party we were at. No, idiot – because of The Derby.' Richard laughed as they all scrambled from the car. 'You did that for me, Maddy.

God knows how you managed to persuade Diana, but you did. It gave us the financial stability we needed.' He slid his arm round her waist. 'You persevered for me even when I'd behaved like a complete prat over Luke. You're the best friend anyone could wish for, and this,' he kissed Fran's cheek, 'is better than winning a million Derbys.'

'Oh, Christ!' Fran scrabbled in her handbag. 'Now you've made her cry again. She'll look worse than ever.'

Maddy blew her nose and giggled and walked straight into Drew.

'Oh, yes. We meant to tell you he might be here. It must have completely slipped our minds, what with the news about the baby and everything. So sorry we can't stop. We'll see you in the marquee.' Fran grabbed Richard's arm. 'Good afternoon, Drew.'

He smiled fleetingly as Fran and Richard hurried away to join the rest of the villagers. Maddy thought he looked awful.

'Oh, er, hello.' She attempted to walk past him, her whole body having turned to jelly. 'I can't stop. I'm with Fran and—'

'Who said she'd see you in the marquee.' His voice was dead. 'So you can spare me a minute, can't you?'

Oh, God. Maddy looked at his bleak, grey face. That was what she'd done to him. 'Have you had a nice time wherever you've been?'

'That's a fucking stupid question.'

She winced. He didn't swear except when he was really angry. It sounded coarse and harsh.

'We haven't spoken civilly for three months,' Drew spat at her. 'Unless you count that charade outside the pub as a reasonable conversation. I arrived in England yesterday morning, and at Peapods in the middle of the night. I thought there might be some message from you.'

'I told you it was over.'

'Oh, yes. So you did.' Drew's pallor made his eyes paler, his hair darker. He'd lost weight too. 'I just expected more from you.'

'You had everything from me.' She looked across the neat gravel and the clipped lawns towards the billowing pink and white marquee, her heart breaking. 'There isn't any more. Is Caroline here?'

'No.'

There were a million other things she wanted to ask him, but more than any of them she longed to throw herself into his arms. She swallowed. 'I'm really sorry . . .'

'So am I.' The voice was still bleak. 'I loved you very much.'

Maddy's heart plummeted at the past tense. Fran and Suzy were right. She'd lost him. She took a step forward. 'Maybe if we talked it over . . .'

'Now you're beginning to sound predictable. You were never that. But, yes I agree that we should talk. Not here though.'

'Why not? I'm not with anyone. You're on your own.'

He gave a harsh laugh. 'I naturally expected you and Charlie to be together, and you're just assuming that because Caroline isn't with me that I'm on my own, are you?'

Maddy rocked on the spot. Drew's eyes drifted over her head. 'This is why today wouldn't be right . . .'

'Drew! Goodness, that bar is crowded! If I'm going to be living in Milton St John, I'm going to have to get used to their drinking habits! Oh, hello . . .'

Maddy stared in absolute misery at the girl carrying two glasses of champagne. Tall, slender, extremely pretty, she was wearing pale blue to match her eyes. Her hair was streaky blonde and moved silkily in the warm breeze.

'This is Maddy.' Drew smiled the warm devastating smile he used to smile for her. 'Maddy lives in the cottage opposite Peapods. You might have noticed it. Maddy, this is Angie.'

Her smile was frozen. Her lips were numb. If she stayed there a moment longer she'd disgrace herself. She nodded her rigid neck like an automaton. 'I'd better go. Fran and Richard will be waiting.' She looked at Drew and the pale and pretty

Angie and stifled a sob. 'It's been very nice . . .'

She flew towards the marquee, her head thundering, a gnawing pain spreading under her ribs. The villagers called greetings. She might have answered them. She didn't know.

Inside the marquee it was pink and warm and as highly scented as a florist's shop. Huge banks of lilies and roses wafted sensuously, music played discreetly, Milton St John, arrayed in their very best, were out in force. Maddy stopped short at the edge of the cork dance floor, looking helplessly at the array of tables. The noise of happy talk was a roaring ocean that threatened to engulf her.

She didn't know what to do. In total misery and confusion, she shook her head. She didn't want to stay here and witness Drew and Angie's togetherness, but equally, the thought of returning alone to the cottage was just as frightening. She was shaking. She couldn't help it. He couldn't have loved her at all. He was no different to Peter.

Fran was waving. 'Over here, Maddy! You're with us and Suzy and Luke – oh, and Charlie when he comes back.'

She tottered towards the flailing burnt-orange arm and sank into a pink and white chair.

Fran pushed a glass of champagne towards her 'There. The first of many. Have you seen Kimberley yet? She looks stunning, and Barty is – Jesus! What's wrong? What did Drew say?'

'Not a lot.' Maddy couldn't stop her hands or mouth trembling enough to get the glass to her lips. Richard leaned across and helped her. 'He's with someone else.'

'Not Caroline?'

'Someone very pretty called Angie.' Her tears rolled down her cheeks and she dashed them away with a napkin emblazoned with wedding bells. 'Oh God, Fran. What am I going to do?'

'Get very drunk and have the best time you've had in your life.' Fran's voice was grim. 'Don't you dare let anyone see how you're feeling for once. Smile for Kimberley's sake even if it kills you. And Suzy and Luke will be here in a moment. They've gone to get some food for all of us. Don't let them know. Promise me?'

Gently, Fran dabbed at Maddy's eyes with the napkin. Maddy gave a tremulous smile.

'That's better.' Fran squeezed the napkin back into Maddy's hand. 'We'll worry about Drew and . . . Angie . . . later. You can do it, Mad. Remember how you fell apart after Peter?'

'That was nothing like this,' Maddy sniffed. 'I didn't feel this pain.' She punched her ribs. 'I didn't feel this frightened.'

'No. But then you only thought you loved Peter.' Fran poured more champagne. 'Today you're going to sparkle and scintillate and knock 'em for six. OK?'

'OK.' Maddy clattered the champagne flute against her teeth. She had never felt less like scintillating in her life.

Kimberley looked fantastic. Her cream silk suit had been tailored to make the most of her large, shapely figure; her hat, a massive brimmed confection in cream lace, perched on her glossy bobbed hair. She'd even had a professional make-up. Barty looked like he'd just won the lottery.

'You're quite a skinny ribs these days.' Kimberley held Maddy's hands. 'Oh, have you seen my ring?' She displayed an engraved gold band. 'I am so happy.'

'It shows,' Maddy whispered, kissing her. 'You look beautiful.'

Kimberley leaned forward. 'I'm so sorry about Drew, my dear. I don't suppose you want to talk about it?'

'No.' Maddy gave a little laugh. 'And certainly not today. I've met, er, Angie. She's very pretty . . .'

'Very. And she seems a nice intelligent girl. No bimbo.' Kimberley sighed. 'I've no idea who she is. It's a bugger, Maddy love. He rang this morning and asked if he might bring a guest. I assumed it would be Caroline.'

Maddy lifted her chin. 'Yes, well, it isn't. Are you and Barty having a honeymoon?'

'Yes. Right in the middle of the season, too. I thought he'd make me wait. He's arranged for his assistant to take over the yard and we're going to cruise on the *Oriana*. The high life, or what?'

'God.' Maddy was impressed. 'You lucky thing!'

'Anyway, we've got to circulate.' Kimberley grinned down at Barty. 'But you take care my dear. Enjoy the rest of today, and don't brood on Drew. Miracles do happen.'

Not in Milton St John, Maddy thought sadly, watching Kimberley and Barty swallowed up by more wellwishers. Not twice. It had been a miracle that had brought her and Drew together. You didn't get a second shot.

The reception roared on. Unable to eat, Maddy drank everything that was put in front of her and stayed boringly sober. She watched feverishly as Drew and Angie talked and laughed together at their table on the far side of the marquee. They were sitting with John Hastings and Diana and Gareth.

Luke squinted across at them. 'I've seen her around the racecourses, I'm sure I have. Not for some time, but I know her face.'

'You probably know a lot more than that,' Suzy giggled, squirming herself on to his lap. As Kimberley's witness, she'd worn a short cream shift dress and cream canvas boots with red roses fastened in her short white hair. She looked gorgeous.

'Do you want me to ask, Mad?' Luke was deadly serious for once. 'Shall I find out who she is?'

'No.' Maddy shook her head violently. 'I don't want him to know that I'm interested. Anyway, it doesn't matter now, does it?'

They looked at her with sadness.

'Do you want to dance?' Charlie Somerset loomed over the table. 'I've exhausted all the girls on the other side of the tent.'

'No,' Maddy said.

Fran looked up. 'Of course she does. And try and get her to eat something.'

'Yeah, I thought you'd been on a diet.' Charlie's eyes roamed across her body. 'You shouldn't, Maddy. Your curves were the best in the village.'

She tried to smile and failed miserably. Glaring at Fran she allowed Charlie to haul her to her feet. The band was playing Gershwin. Maddy wanted to throttle all of them. Charlie moved as well when he danced as he did when he rode. Maddy stumped, stiff legged, not caring.

'Are you still going to be living at Peapods?' she asked, wanting to talk about Drew however obliquely. 'Now that Drew's back.'

'Oh, yeah. The stable flat is mine for as long as I'm riding his jumpers – which I hope will be until I'm too old and arthritic to ride anything . . .' He laughed lasciviously. 'So I'll still be nice and handy.'

He manoeuvred them between foxtrotting couples on the tiny dance floor. 'Drew and I get on great. I'd like to become his assistant when I'm too knackered to be his jockey. I learned a lot while he was in the States.'

She didn't say anything. Drew had been in America and he'd brought Angie back as a souvenir.

Charlie smiled kindly. 'Have you spoken to Mr F yet? He was not a happy bunny when he arrived at Peapods. Jetlagged to the eyeballs and storming about the house like an addict without a fix. He seemed to think I'd be with you today.'

'Is that what you told him?'

'I just said I'd have to stand in line behind every red-blooded male in the county.' Charlie gave a crooked grin. 'But I thought I was in with a chance.'

'So you don't know the girl he's with today?'

Charlie laughed in her ear. 'Ah, so that's it? No, I don't, Mad. Although I wouldn't mind getting to know her. She's a cracker. No one seems to know anything about her, although some of the boys seem to think they've seen her around.'

'Her name's Angie. Luke said he'd seen her on the circuit. I suppose that's where Drew met her.'

'I suppose so.' Charlie had lost interest. Fickle in his own love-life, he could never understand other people making high drama out of failed relationships. 'I heard that the Manor's up for sale.'

'Really?' Desperately, Maddy tried to think of something other than Drew. 'I didn't know. I haven't seen Peter since—' Since the night she'd told Caroline that she and Drew were lovers, she thought, feeling sick. Years and years ago.

'You wouldn't. He's left the village. I never liked the bloke. He's pissed off to make his fortune somewhere else. Sad really, isn't it? There's probably some quaint and peaceful little place somewhere that doesn't know what's going to hit it.'

Peter had gone again. Maddy sighed. If Peter hadn't come back to Milton St John, she wouldn't have gone to Diana's party, and she wouldn't have met Drew socially straight away. If only she hadn't gone. She swallowed. 'If only' was probably the most desolate phrase in the English language.

The band stopped playing. Charlie returned her to her table and drifted off looking for more receptive company. Fran and Suzy looked at her for signs of improvement, and finding none, poured her another glass of champagne.

Barty tapped the microphone which had been lowered specially. 'Don't all run away,' he yelled. 'I'm not making a speech. Kimberley and I just want to say thank you for turning up in such gratifying numbers. It really makes our special day even more special to be able to share it with all our friends.'

Everyone clapped. It was a very popular match.

'The one piece of news I wanted to share with you today is one that we have been keeping secret until the last minute.'

'Christ!' Suzy removed her hands from undoing Luke's shirt buttons. 'She can't be pregnant, can she? Not Kimberley? She's practically geriatric!'

Fran, who was two years older, jabbed Suzy's arm. Suzy blushed. 'Oh, sorry, Fran. You just seem so much younger.'

'It's not perfect, but it'll do.' Fran sank back in her chair, mollified.

'We just wanted you all to know that Kimberley's yard was sold yesterday, and that the new owner will be taking over at the end of the flat season, although he will be moving in gradually all through the autumn. I know you'll make him very welcome in his transition from Newmarket. Milton St John is very lucky to have him. I know Lambourn were hoping for him . . . '

'Who is it?' Bronwyn shouted, obviously praying for Henry Cecil or Luca Cumani. 'Get on with it, Barty.'

'Your new neighbour will be Emilio Marquez.'

There was a wave of excitement and speculation and laughter. Maddy just stared. The only two people in the marquee who seemed unfazed were Diana and Luke. Of course, Mitchell D'Arcy split his horses between Emilio and the James-Jordans. He'd probably pillow-talked information to Diana. It would mean he'd have all the more reason to be in the village. Maddy looked at Gareth, who seemed delighted, and felt very sorry for him.

Suzy glared at Luke. 'You bloody knew! Didn't you?'

'Well, yes.' Luke was grinning. 'But I was sworn to secrecy. I was bound to know, Suze - I am his stable jockey.'

'Bastard!' Suzy hissed lovingly. 'We're supposed to share everything – oh!'

'Yes, it does mean I'll be living here. He nuzzled her neck. 'If you can stand it . . .'

There won't be much standing done, Maddy thought, gazing at them over the table. Why did everyone else seem to be so hopelessly happy? She suddenly realised that Suzy was talking to her.

'I said, Luke can move into the cottage, can't he, Mad? Until he finds a place in the village?'

'What? Oh, yes, of course . . .' Her heart plummeted even further floorwards. How on earth was she going to cope with Luke and Suzy's exuberant loving all day every day when she felt as dried up and wasted as an empty husk?

The reception pulsed on into the evening. The band had been replaced by a disco. The flashing lights and throbbing bass found an echo in Maddy's head.

Happily drunk, the villagers were climbing over tables, screaming with laughter, not even pretending to behave any more. Kimberley, with her expensive silk skirt rucked up to show a pair of large but shapely legs embellished by an ornate garter, was dancing wildly with Barty who was wearing her hat. Maddy was suddenly swamped by absolute misery. She looked towards Drew's table. She'd been limiting herself to a covert glance every five minutes.

His chair was empty. So was Angie's. They must be on the dance floor, she thought wildly. Or getting some refreshment from the stifling atmosphere of the marquee.

'I'm just going outside,' she said to Fran. 'My head aches.'

It was even hotter outside than it had been in the marquee. She sucked in the humid air. It was like drinking bathwater. The night was dark, black clouds visible against the black sky. The air was heavy with roses and jasmine. Scuffles and muted giggles echoed from every corner of the garden. Maddy couldn't bear it. Suppose Drew and Angie had been overcome by lust and sneaked off outside? She was suddenly reminded of that awful loveless coupling she had witnessed between Peter and Diana. Would it be like that? Or would Drew make love to Angie the way he had to her, tumbling, laughing, with glorious spontaneity? Gripping her fist tightly against her mouth, Maddy gagged, and the gnawing hollow pain beneath her ribs spread up into her throat until she thought she would choke.

She fought her way back into the marquee. It was beginning to look like an animated *Karma Sutra*. Fran and Richard were dancing dreamily together on the edge of the floor.

'I'm going home,' she said in Fran's ear. 'If Kimberley and Barty are still here tell them I'm sorry to poop so early.'

'Oh, they disappeared ages ago,' Fran said. 'Mad, do you

want me to drive you? I haven't been drinking because of this.' She patted her stomach.' You shouldn't walk. It's dark.'

'It's the village,' Maddy said shortly, 'not Soho. And anyway, if anyone did jump out on me, the way I look they'd just run a mile.'

'It's not a good idea. Everyone has been drinking, and some of the lads can get quite larky. They wouldn't mean to hurt you, but they'd think it was funny.'

'There won't be anyone left in the village.' Maddy gazed round the heaving marquee. 'This is scheduled to go on all night. Kimberley's organised kedgeree and champagne for a dawn breakfast. Honestly, Fran, I'll be fine.'

Fran still looked concerned, but she hugged Maddy. 'OK. You've been very brave. I'll come round tomorrow. Just try to sleep tonight.'

Maddy smiled wearily. Sleep was another luxury she'd learned to do without.

As predicted, Milton St John was deserted. Although it wasn't yet eleven o'clock, even the Cat and Fiddle had closed its doors, its occupants all whooping it up in the marquee. There was no sound except the constant swish of traffic on the distant motorway, the occasional whinny from the stables, and the gurgling of the stream.

She had never been afraid of the dark, and tonight it moulded itself round her like a cloak, almost as if it was trying to shroud the misery. It was as hot as it had been at midday. No breath of wind stirred the trees. No hint of moisture in the air gave refreshment.

Maddy turned the corner. Lights blazed in Peapods and she felt sick. Drew must have taken Angie home. Her footsteps became slower. She suddenly wanted to run back to Barty's yard and the noise and life of the reception. She didn't want to be alone.

She paused. There was a car parked outside the cottage. It was probably one of the guests who, arriving late, hadn't been able to park any closer. As she approached, the interior light flicked on and for the first time she felt a tremor of apprehension.

The driver's door opened and a tall figure stepped out. 'Hello, Maddy,' Caroline said. 'I've been waiting for you.'

Twenty-Nine

'Drew's at home,' Maddy said, looking quickly across the road to where the lights from Peapods twinkled like stars through the lacy tracery of the ebony branches. 'He's not with me.'

'I know.' Caroline's quiet voice sounded like a shout in the silence. 'I've already spoken to Drew. He told me you were at Kimberley's reception. I waited. Can I come in?'

'OK.' She fumbled with the key and kicked the rug away. 'Would you like a drink?'

Caroline blinked in the harsh light. 'Tea would be lovely, if you don't mind.'

'No. I need one myself.' Maddy slopped water into the kettle. She had made tea on Caroline's first visit. Maybe this was symbolic. 'Do you want to talk in the sitting-room?'

'Here will be fine.' Caroline had followed her into the kitchen and pulled out a chair while Maddy rattled the cups.

'I was very sorry about your father. Are you and your mother coping?'

'Yes.' Caroline spoke stiffly. 'It was a devastating blow, but we're coming to terms with it.' She paused and examined her apricot nails. 'I insulted you by offering you that job. I shouldn't have done it. I was being insensitive. I want to apologise.'

'There's no need.' Maddy frowned. 'Surely that wasn't what you wanted to talk about?'

'No. I just wanted to clear that up. I hate ragged ends. The wine bar was just an idea I had, and one I've since dropped. You should have told me that shop was known locally as the Porn Parlour.'

'It didn't seem the right time, actually. There seemed to be more important issues at stake that night.'

'Yes, there were, weren't there?'

'I am very sorry.' Maddy's voice was a squeak. 'For hurting you. I didn't mean to, and it won't happen again. Drew and I aren't . . .' She stopped and clattered around again with the cups.

'So I gathered.' Caroline smoothed her neat peach dress. 'Maddy, before we discuss any of that, there are things that need to be said. I tried ringing you.'

'Did you?' Maddy placed two white cups and the mammoth teapot on the table. She couldn't find any saucers and anyway it was far too late to fuss about being genteel. 'I haven't answered the phone much, and I told Suzy just to say I was out if you called.'

Caroline raised her sleepy eyes. 'I was hurt, but not surprised. You weren't predatory, just friendly. Over the years I've watched other women throw themselves at Drew with fervour in their eyes. You were different.'

'It doesn't matter,' Maddy said again, feeling ashamed. Caroline was so dignified. In her place she'd have probably screamed like a banshee. 'I should never have let myself become so close to him. He was lonely – I didn't have that excuse.'

'Please listen. You didn't wreck our marriage. It was well into injury time. You weren't the cause, Maddy. You were possibly the catalyst, but definitely not the cause. If we'd had a proper marriage, Drew would never have left Jersey – or if he had, I would have come with him. Drew could have left me on numerous occasions.'

'You had *lovers*?' Maddy spluttered into her cup. 'But you said that you weren't interested—'

Caroline almost smiled. 'No, I didn't have lovers. There are other reasons for a relationship dying than the appearance of a third party.'

Maddy's head ached. The clock ticked slowly in the solid

atmosphere. She emptied her cup and poured another. Her mouth was dust dry after so much champagne.

'I was completely unsupportive during the time he was riding. I was useless when his parents died. I was utterly selfish, Maddy. I cared about my business first and Drew second. I always have. Oh, I suppose I loved him but I should never have married him.'

'So, why . . .?' Maddy was desperate to know.

'Jersey is very insular.' Caroline helped herself to more tea, adding milk straight from the bottle. Maddy had been too distraught to bother with the niceties of a jug. 'Drew and I more or less grew up together. We found each other attractive, and we'd always been friends. I think we each thought we could change the other, the way that you do when you're young. By the time we found we couldn't, and had lapsed into being so apathetic that we didn't even want to, it was too late. I used the miscarriage as an excuse. I made him sweat with guilt because he wanted children and I didn't.' She leaned forward, her eyes glistening. 'Then he fell in love with you.'

'I think he did,' Maddy admitted sadly. 'For a while . . . but I always knew I was only borrowing him from you. Anyway, you've got something that I couldn't possibly supply.'

'Oh? And what is that?' Caroline's lips curved into a smile.

'Money.' Maddy shrugged. 'I could never back him the way you have. So is he going to go back to Jersey?' She wanted to stuff her fingers in her ears, not wanting to hear the answer.

Caroline shook her head.

'So you're moving to Milton St John . . .?'

Again, the shake of the head. Maddy rubbed her face wearily. They must be planning to move away to start afresh. Together. It was all she deserved. It hurt far more than she could bear.

'He's left me. He wants a divorce.'

The words rang with hollow victory. Maddy scraped back her chair and walked to the skew-whiff window. The garden was plunged into impenetrable blackness, inky and suffocating, all life extinguished. Drew would be free. And he and Angie. Angie must have money, too. Caroline would retain what friendship she wanted from him. But for Maddy there was nothing. She turned from the window.

'When you spoke to him earlier, when you discussed all this, was A—' She gagged on the word and tried again. 'Was Angie there?'

'Angie?' Caroline's eyebrows arched. 'Who is Angie?'

Maddy closed her eyes. 'He took her to Kimberley's reception. I – we've only seen each other once since that evening.'

'Yes, he told me.'

'He introduced me to Angie.' She gulped again. 'He was with her all day. She was very pretty. They left together. I thought . . .'

Caroline looked genuinely mystified. 'I've never heard of Angie. There was an Annabelle once in St Helier who made a bit of a nuisance of herself, and Anna from somewhere on the south coast who thought she could oust me . . . but Drew was never interested. I've never heard of an Angie.'

Clenching and unclenching her fingers, Maddy sat down again. She felt very sick. 'Is the divorce why you came to see Drew tonight?'

'Yes, well, in a way. We'd discussed it on the phone. I had to come over for a meeting with a bottling plant in Birmingham, and as I'd got the initial papers from my lawyers regarding the ending of the marriage, and I knew he was back from the States . . .' She paused. 'I thought I'd call in and finalise a few things.'

'Are you citing me?' Maddy asked. It didn't matter any more. No one could hurt her any more than she'd already hurt herself.

'Good God, no.' Caroline seemed to find the idea amusing. 'Drew is divorcing me on a two-year separation basis. That way neither of us had to provide grounds.'

'And will you go on financing Peapods?'

Caroline poured a third cup of tea from the fat teapot. 'Actually, I never did.'

'What?'

'I lied.' Caroline smiled her sleepy kitten smile. 'I wanted to humiliate him. He was so sure of you, and you were so smitten. I wanted you to think he was weak and dependent. I was also pretty sure that you loved him enough not to let him lose the stables, so I lied.'

'Jesus!' Maddy could almost admire the cold calculation of it all. 'So Drew owns Peapods?'

'Not outright. His parents left him very little money, and that ramshackle place at Bonne Nuit costs more than it earns. Oh, I suppose it doesn't matter now. Peapods is backed by Kit and Rosa Pedersen. Drew is in partnership with them. It's their money, not mine.'

Maddy said nothing. She wanted to smack Caroline's serene face. The conniving bitch. Anyway, it had worked. She'd handed him to Angie gift-wrapped. She sucked in her breath. 'Did he mention me tonight?'

'No. Only to say he hadn't seen you much until today. He didn't want to talk about you.'

That was it, then. Over. Finished. Caroline gave a ladylike yawn, stifling it with a slender hand. 'I ought to be getting back or they'll lock me out. I've booked into the Regency Park in Thatcham. Maybe next time I'm over I'll be able to stay in the village. After all, I have made friends, and I do have an interest now.' She took a deep breath. 'I own Maynards Orchard.'

'Bloody hell!' Maddy couldn't stop herself. '*You* bought it? Why?'

'For Bronwyn, really.' Caroline smiled. 'I liked her, and all the other people who really cared about the village. I wanted to do what I could to halt the golf course. That was the first reason – the others came later.'

'Others?'

'Yes, well, in discussions with the Maynards, I realised that they could bulk supply me with apples and I could add to my range with apple wine, champagne, a sort of Channel Islands Calvados – and then there was Peter Knightley . . .'

Maddy shook her head. What the hell did Peter have to do with this?

Caroline pleated the skirt of her dress, not meeting Maddy's eyes. 'I liked Peter. Right from the start I recognised a kindred spirit. To cut a very long story short, Peter Knightley is now my partner.'

'Holy hell!' Maddy gawped at her. 'Not, er . . .?'

'Oh, absolutely not. No, Peter is quite free to tomcat around wherever he likes. That'll suit me nicely. But he looks superb, has a wonderful business brain, is totally ruthless, talks like an angel, isn't remotely interested in bloody horse racing, and my mother adores him.'

'Your mother has met him?'

'Yes. He's been over to Jersey a couple of times to sort things out with my solicitors. He's already introduced some brilliant schemes for marketing and new production. He's a real acquisition for the company.'

'Does Drew know?'

'I told him tonight. He reacted in much the same way as you. But you see, the vineyard will always be the most important thing in my life. Peter will take my father's place admirably.'

Maddy glanced at the clock. It was past midnight. Caroline stood up and pressed her cool cheek fleetingly against Maddy's flushed one. 'I'll have to fly now or I'll be locked out. I'm so glad we've had this talk. I want us to stay friends, Maddy, however hard you may find it to believe. I've always liked you. Good luck.'

'You too . . .' Maddy heard herself saying, kicking the rug away and closing the door.

If the fat teapot, now covered in tannin dribbles, and the two lipstick-rimmed cups hadn't still been sitting on the kitchen table, Maddy would have thought she'd dreamed the whole bizarre episode. She looked out across the dark garden. Milton St John was still revelling wildly. Caroline was driving back through the night, having tidied up the ends of her marriage in her usual cool and efficient way. And Peter bloody Knightley . . . Maddy gave a wry smile. That part of it was utterly believable.

She turned back into the kitchen. Were she and Drew the only people not happy tonight? No, of course not. He was fine. He had Angie.

She sank down at the table and cradled her head in her hands. She'd lived through pain and disillusion before. There was no reason why she shouldn't do it again . . . But there was, she thought wearily. A tall, lean, dark reason who lived across the road. Helplessly, she closed her eyes.

The storm woke her. A hail of bullets woodpeckered against the window. The wind rattled the letter box. And somewhere, rolling lazily across the downs, a low-throated groan of thunder threatened.

Maddy couldn't see anything. Had she turned the lights off when Caroline left? And when had Caroline left, anyway? How long had she been asleep? Staggering to her feet, she felt her way round the obstacle course of the kitchen, stubbing her toes. Her mouth tasted foul. Her head still throbbed. She found the switch. Nothing.

'Oh, bugger,' Maddy groaned aloud. Talking to herself didn't matter. There was no one to hear or censure. 'A bloody power cut.'

Candles. She always had candles . . . She started scrabbling for the drawers and then remembered. She *had* always had candles; she just hadn't replaced them after her dinner party. And she and Suzy had thrown the stubs out weeks ago when they'd had a cottage blitz. She shuddered. She was going to be alone. All night. In the dark.

'Oh, well,' she said with false bravado, 'I can cope. I'll just go to bed and sleep through it. After all, a storm is the least of my worries. I've still got to survive the rest of my life.'

She found little comfort in the pitch-dark cottage. Familiar objects seemed to loom up and bump into her, and every creak and groan sounded like someone testing the doors. Above the moaning of the wind and the roar of the rain no one would ever hear her screams.

She tugged off the shoes and the earrings in the dark, comforting herself with the thought that Luke and Suzy would be home soon. The power cut would surely fore-shorten the festivities, and the village would soon be teeming with drunken, noisy life.

She edged her way into the bedroom and groaned. The luminous hands on her alarm clock showed just past one, and she remembered Fran saying that Kimberley and Barty had installed a generator. As long as the marquee didn't blow down, the party would rage until dawn as planned. She shivered. There was a long, dark night stretching ahead.

When the phone rang she screamed, then felt her way back into the hall. It was probably Fran making sure she was OK. Maddy's palms were damp as she groped for the receiver. She didn't care who it was; she was just desperate for the comfort of another human voice.

It was the one she least expected.

'Is Charlie there?' Drew's voice was sharp with anxiety. He didn't even say hello.

'No. He's at the reception.'

'Is anyone there?'

'I'm on my own.'

'Shit.' The phone was slammed down the other end.

Trembling more than ever, reacting to his voice, which was harsh and abrasive instead of gentle and loving, she punched out Peapods' number. It rang for ages. Maybe he wasn't even there. Maybe he'd been ringing from his mobile. Maybe Angie was snuggled up next to him . . .

'Yes.'

'Drew? Is anything wrong?'

'Nothing you can help with. I'm in the stables. I've got a problem.'

'Can I—?'

But again the phone was crashed down and there was nothing but an eerie silence as the wind gathered its breath for a further onslaught.

Maddy glared at the telephone. 'Arrogant, bad-tempered bastard!' she hissed. 'Sort your problems out on your own, then!'

Her lips were trembling in time with the rest of her. She wasn't frightened, just angry. How dare he talk to her like that? How bloody dare he?

She stumbled back along the hall and collided with the bathroom door. Tears prickled beneath her eyelids. She'd just crawl into bed, pull the duvet over her head and pray for oblivion. That was the only sensible thing to do. Sod Drew Fitzgerald and his bloody problems. Let Angie sort them out. She, Maddy Beckett, was never going to be at anyone's beck and call ever again. She'd become an icon – or did she mean island? – and distance herself from everyone's problems in future. Milton St John could manage without her. She'd show them.

Thirty seconds later she was tugging Suzy's Doc Martens on to her bare feet and pulling her Oxfam showerproof over the crumpled Knightsbridge dress. Maybe she'd start being an icon in the morning.

She pulled open the front door and was almost knocked sideways by the storm.

'Damn and bugger, Drew Fitzgerald!' she cursed as the wind tore at her hair and the rain slapped icy knives into her face. 'I bloody hate you!' And staggering against the punching wind, she stumbled across the road towards Peapods.

Thirty

The thunder which had been growling round the hills, suddenly decided to pounce just as Maddy tottered into Peapods' drive. With a roar it reverberated overhead, followed by a jag of green-white lightning. Maddy ducked her head and ran, the unfamiliar boots skidding on the cobbles, the Oxfam jacket instantly saturated.

The welcoming lights of earlier had been extinguished. Peapods loomed gloomily through the storm, only visible each time a further fork of lightning lit the sky. The wind was clattering unseen horrors around her feet, her hair was plastered across her eyes, and all the time the thunder crashed directly above her.

The stable yard had become a torrent. Rivulets of water gushed unseen, splashed over the Doc Martens and up her legs. It was if the world had exploded.

Parting her hair with icy fingers, panting from a mixture of panic and exertion, Maddy focused on a swinging, blurred illumination somewhere through the clock arch. Head down again, she struggled towards it.

The light came from a hurricane lamp, swinging eerily against the tack-room door. The stables were all bolted and closed snugly against the storm, but Maddy could hear the shufflings and murmurings of their occupants, complaining about the disturbance. Although horses were so often spooked by thunderstorms, there didn't seem to be any immediate signs of panic. She cursed under her breath.

'Who's that?' Drew's voice echoed from the black infinity.

She was suddenly blinded by a white beam of torchlight,

and turned her head away. 'Switch it off!' she screeched at him. 'It's me. Maddy.'

The beam dipped a little as Drew, even wetter than she was, loomed out of the darkness. 'You shouldn't have come over. There was no need.'

'Thanks a bunch.' Her teeth were chattering. 'I just thought you might need some help. As you don't, I'll just go again.'

'Don't.' His voice was lost in a roll of thunder. 'Sorry. I'm just bloody wet and uncomfortable. Thanks, Maddy, but I don't think there's anything you can do.'

No, there probably isn't, she thought, flinching as a particularly wicked crack of lightning sizzled towards them. Probably Angie's already done it.

He rocked towards her, leaning backwards because of the wind. His black hair was plastered to his head. The flying jacket was the colour of jet. The rain had made ebony stars of his eyelashes. Maddy looked at him in the dipping torchlight and knew she would never love anyone else.

'Are the horses OK?'

'Yes. Except Solomon,' Drew shouted. 'The door of his box blew open when the storm started. I can't find him. The other horses were getting pretty restless. I needed someone to help.'

'I'm here. I'll help.' Maddy thought of sweet, placid Solomon, who had given her so much confidence and pleasure, and wanted to cry. 'He can't have got far, can he?'

Drew shrugged. 'He's not in any of the corners of the yard. I've been up and down the road. I don't think he could have got out – he didn't really like the cobbles. I just thought if he'd strayed towards the main road . . .'

Maddy clapped her icy hands to her mouth. 'Don't even think about it. Have you got another torch?'

Drew handed her a cudgel-sized torch from his pocket which nearly slipped from her frozen fingers. He smiled. 'Thanks – you don't have to do this, you know.'

'Of course I do.' She turned away quickly. 'I suppose Angie

didn't want to get wet . . .' She'd already moved away and his reply was drowned by a clap of thunder.

She found herself calling Solomon as you would a straying cat, and immediately stopped. Weren't horses supposed to respond to whistles? She pursed her numb lips and tried. Nothing came out.

She followed the torch's bouncing beam all round the yard. The storm was demonic and showed no signs of abating. Everything groaned and creaked and rattled beneath the onslaught. There was no sign of Solomon.

She was crying now, her tears mingled with the slashes of rain. Poor Solomon. He'd be so frightened. Gentle and trusting, he wouldn't understand. She gulped. Drew's torch beam was occasionally visible on the far side of the stable block. She knew he was heading towards the road again. Just in case. It was a nightmare.

She pushed her way through a tangle of wildly waving wisteria which had been tugged from its mooring by the wind. There were only three boxes in this part of the yard, which was separated from the main block by a five-bar gate. The gate had blown open and was crashing back against the wall with a rhythmic screaming of its hinges. Two of the boxes were empty, she knew. The third had housed Dock of the Bay when he'd first come over from Jersey. She lifted her torch and screamed.

Two huge black eyes blinked at her, showing white crescent moons at their corners. Solomon, his coat streaming, was pressed up against Dock of the Bay's box, shivering.

She lowered the torch beam and began to speak gently. He backed away from her in terror. She stood still, buffeted by the storm, and held out her hand towards him. In the alternating pitch black and sickly green light, Solomon seemed about three miles high. She swallowed. She'd ridden him, groomed him, told him all her secrets. She wasn't afraid of him . . .

Slowly, she edged towards him. His hoofs clattered on the

cobbles as he tried to press nearer and nearer to the horse box. Talking all the time, she stretched out her hand and grabbed his head collar. It was stiff and cold, drenched by the rain, and Solomon yanked away from her, almost pulling her arm from its socket. She dropped the torch with a crash and Solomon jumped backwards.

'Steady, baby . . . Steady . . .'

Gradually, he stopped backing away from her, and leaned his great head down, blowing foamy moisture from his nostrils. She wanted to kiss him.

'Come on . . .' she coaxed. 'You don't have to stay out here in the cold. You've got a nice warm bed round the corner. Come on, baby . . .'

Solomon's eyes became less hostile. His muscles relaxed. And slowly he allowed her to tug him forward.

'Please God,' she prayed, her eyes tightly shut. 'Please God, don't let there by any more thunder or lightning just for a minute.'

There wasn't. Solomon, still trembling, allowed her to lead him through the creaking gate and back into the main yard, slipping and slithering across the cobbles.

'Any luck?' Drew's voice was tossed on the wind.

She nodded and then laughed at herself. But she didn't dare shout.

'Maddy?' The beam arced through the darkness. 'Oh, Jesus!'

Drew almost threw himself on her, then prised the icy leather from her numbed fingers. He kissed Solomon but not her.

'Thanks,' he said gruffly. 'Where was he?'

'Trying to get in with Dock of the Bay.' Maddy dashed her tears away, not that it mattered. They looked like raindrops. 'I think he's OK.'

'I'll just get him into his box and check him over. He's been in love with Dock of the Bay ever since he arrived. I didn't check that part of the yard. I thought the gate was locked.

God, Maddy, I'll never be able to thank you enough.'

'It's OK.' Her teeth were chattering. 'I was just being neighbourly. I'll go now.'

'No!' Drew's shout was drowned by thunder. Solomon rolled his eyes and flattened his ears. 'Go into the house and have a shower. Get warm and dry. I'll just settle Solomon down and I'll come in.'

'I've got hot water at home,' Maddy started. 'I wouldn't want to impose.'

'You're not bloody imposing,' Drew roared. 'And if you haven't got power in the cottage how the hell do you expect to have a shower or a bath or even get warm?'

'You haven't got any power either.'

'No, but I've got a separate steam shower system – thanks to the Knightley Health Studios – and every candle in Christendom burning. You know where it all is. I won't be long.'

'What about Angie? What shall I say to her?'

'Maddy.' Drew's eyes narrowed. His face was dark. 'Sometimes I could hit you. Just for once do as you're bloody told.'

'But Angie . . .?'

'Isn't here!' Drew roared again. 'Now for God's sake go and dry yourself before I have your death on my hands. I'm prepared to feel a lot of things for you, Maddy, but guilt over your death isn't one of them!'

Grinning, Maddy slithered away towards the house.

She squelched out of Suzy's Doc Martens in the hall and dropped her soggy jacket beside them. The Knightsbridge dress clung to her like a second skin. Peapods throbbed warmly thanks to the extra water heating system, and glowed gorgeously in the light of massed candles. Maddy dived into the shower room. Drew didn't have odds and sods of candles jammed in wine bottles. He had tall elegant white wax sticks flickering in unison in various ornate candelabras.

By the time she'd returned to the sitting-room she was clean and snug and deliciously warm. She'd wrapped herself in a white towelling dressing gown and twisted a huge gold towel around her hair. The shower room had been bright blue and chrome in Peter's day, but Drew had transformed it with white tiles and gold fittings. She'd always coveted it when she'd cleaned. Fat piles of fluffly gold and white towels were always stacked on the shelf beside the door, and at least three mammoth white bathrobes hung on hooks. She thought it was the last word in luxury. When her quilted dressing gown was in the wash she had to scuttle about the cottage draped in a Mickey Mouse beach towel.

She curled up on the green sofa, tucking her bare feet beneath her and towelled her hair. Inside Peapods' solid walls the storm was muted, and the lightning jagging through the drapes was the only indication that it was still raging.

Drew dripped his way into the room. 'Solomon's fine. Dry, warm, no damage done and eating his silly head off.' He paused. 'You look a lot better, too.'

'I won't stay.' Maddy slid her feet to the floor. 'Thanks ever so much for the shower and everything. If you could just lend me some clothes so that I can get back to the cottage, I'll go.'

'Is that what you want?'

'Yes, I suppose so.' Maddy couldn't look at him.

'OK.' His face was stony. 'But just let me get dry, then I'll sort you out a pair of jeans and a jacket.' He stopped and looked at her. 'Thanks for being there tonight, Maddy.'

'It's OK. You'd have found him eventually.

'I should have realised that he'd run to Dock of the Bay, silly old sod.' Drew smiled fondly, then withdrew it. 'You're obviously itching to get away, so I won't keep you much longer.' He strode out of the room leaving wet indents on the carpet.

Maddy towelled her hair until it stood out round her head in a halo of unruly curls, wishing she had a hairdryer and make-up.

Drew came back wrapped in a matching white robe. His fitted. Maddy dragged her eyes away from his brown legs and his long bare feet. He walked across to the drinks cabinet and poured two tumblers almost brimful of whisky. Handing one to her, he dropped down beside her on the sofa.

'Thanks.' She clutched it gratefully. 'But weren't you going to find me some clothes?'

'Yes. In a minute. I think we could both do with a drink. Cheers.'

He raised the glass to her, mockery in his eyes. She clattered the glass against her teeth, spilling whisky on her fingers. Surreptitiously, she tried to lick it off. Drew noticed and laughed. 'For a cleaner – and an educated cleaner, at that – you really are the messiest person I've ever met.'

'Really?' She glared at him over the rim of the glass. The malt was already stealing warmth into her toes. 'Is this going to be a brutal appraisal of my strengths and weaknesses all of a sudden?'

'No.' Drew shook his damp dark hair so that it feathered towards his eyes. Maddy wanted to touch it so badly that she had to look away. 'But you are. Messy. And stubborn. And so bloody irritating sometimes.'

'So are you,' she retorted, and immediately wished she hadn't. He could now add childish and unoriginal too.

'Did Caroline tell you about the divorce?'

'Yes.' The criticisms still rankled. 'She said you'd left her. I suppose Angie—'

'It had nothing to do with Angie. I should have done it a long time ago. I know you didn't want me to, but I knew it would happen. Caroline and I couldn't go on the way we were. This way we'll both retain some dignity – and our friendship. Caroline seemed to accept it with her usual sangfroid, and both sets of solicitors are agreed that the split will be relatively painless.' He gave a mocking grin. 'To be honest, it won't be all that different.'

'Except you'll be free.'

'Oh, yes. There is that.'

They sat in silence, drinking, not looking at each other. The thunder crashed overhead, the lightning still poked invasive fingers through the drapes, but it held no threat now.

'Is that why you and Angie were celebrating today? Your freedom?'

'No.'

Bugger, Maddy thought. He wasn't going to talk about her. It must be serious. Oh well, she'd have to get used to it. Living across the road, she'd have to see them together all the time. The prospect filled her with such intense pain that she felt faint. She took another gulp of whisky and turned her head. His face was still, his features thrown into sharp relief by the flickering candles. Her heart turned over.

'Why didn't she stay tonight?'

'Why?' The eyebrows rose slightly. The eyes didn't soften.

'Oh, I just wondered. I mean, you'd been together all day, and you knew all about the divorce. I thought—'

'Angie's staying in Lambourn with Owen and Jessie Green. The trainers.'

'Oh.' It didn't make a lot of sense. 'But she said she'd be living in Milton St John. I heard her.'

'Yes, she did.' Drew drained his glass and stood up for a refill. 'Do you want some more?'

'No thanks. I'll be too squiffy to move.'

'Good.' He prised the half-empty tumbler from her fingers and refilled it with his own, then sat beside her again. 'Yes, Angie will be moving into the village. That's why she's here. House hunting.'

'She won't be living with you, then?' Maddy's heart was breaking. The tight knot of sorrow that had lived beneath her ribs for weeks, now threatened to rise up and choke her. 'Oh, no, I suppose not. Caroline said it was a two-year separation. I suppose you can't really live openly together.'

Drew shook his head. 'Maddy, shut up.'

'No, I bloody won't. She looked down into her lap. Her dressing gown had fallen open and she wriggled its fat towelling edges together. 'Why is Angie looking for a separate house?'

'Oh, God.' Drew sighed. 'I wish you hadn't done that with your robe. I like looking at your thighs. I suppose Charlie does, too.'

'I doubt it. They're like sausages.'

'I like sausages.'

Maddy's stomach dissolved with lust, and clutching the whisky with one hand, she edged away from him. Obviously gaining his freedom had made him aware how much time he had to recapture. He laughed and she glared at him again.

'You were saying about Angie?'

'No I wasn't. You were. I was saying about Charlie. Have you seen a lot of him? No, let me rephrase that. Knowing Charlie, you must have seen all of him.'

'Don't be disgusting! He took me out a few times while you were – I mean, during the summer. We didn't do more than kiss goodnight. Unlike you and Angie, no doubt.'

'Angie's surname is Mitchell.'

'Oh good. You're going to tell me her shoe size and her dress size and her preference in breakfast cereals, too, are you?'

'I'm probably going to slap you if you don't stop babbling.'

She sneaked a quick look at him from beneath her lashes. He didn't look as though he would hit her or any woman. Still, you could never tell . . .

'Angie is married to Perry Mitchell.'

'Good God, Drew!' she exploded. 'A married woman! I thought—'

'Oh, Christ.' He sighed again. 'Perry Mitchell. He was Champion Jockey three years running. He's been riding in Hong Kong and the States for a couple of years. He wants to come back to the UK. That's why I was in America. I've offered him a job as my stable jockey for the flat horses. He accepted last week. Angie flew over with me to look for a house for when he arrives at the end of the season.'

'Oh.' Slowly, the reality dawned. Maddy, all inhibitions

swept away by the whisky, began to grin. 'So you and Angie aren't . . .?'

'No. We aren't. And if you'd stayed around longer this afternoon I would have introduced you properly, but of course, you no longer wanted to talk to me, and you were draped all over Mr Somerset, and as you'd already jumped to all your usual wrong conclusions—'

'I do not jump to conclusions.'

'You do. All the time.' He unhooked her tense fingers from the tumbler and put it on the floor beside his own. 'It's another one of your many faults.'

She wriggled away from him again until she came up against the arm of the sofa. 'Stop criticising me.' She tried to stare angrily and failed. 'I've been through hell for you these last months.'

'And you think I haven't?' His eyes glittered, reflecting the candle flames. 'I hadn't got a clue what was going on. I felt you knew something that I didn't.'

'Oh, that. It was a misunderstanding,' she said quickly. 'I thought that Caroline owned Peapods. I thought that you'd lose everything if—'

'Whatever put that notion into your head?'

'I've no idea. I jumped to the wrong conclusions, I suppose.'

Drew laughed then. He was very close. He looked ten years younger. 'Jesus, Maddy. I thought I was going mad.' He slid his hand inside the robe and stroked her gently. 'You've lost weight.'

Her skin burned beneath his touch. She shuddered. 'I didn't eat much.'

'Hell, it must have been serious.' He buried his face in the cloud of her curls. 'Well, start eating again. I don't want you all gaunt and boring. We'll have to put you on a diet of Mars bars and Hobnobs right away.'

'Right away?' She had untied his bathrobe and was letting her fingers caress his firm, smooth, clean body.

'No, not right away,' he groaned, kissing her face, her eyes, her neck, and lastly, lingeringly, her lips.' I love you so very much, and right now there's something far more important . . .'

He made love to her in the candlelight with an urgency born of deprivation. She clung to him, nipping his shoulder between her teeth, clenching her nails into his strong back. The crescendo grew in pace with the storm outside, and exploded with the same force.

'Oh, God . . .' Maddy lay beneath him on the sofa, loving the weight of his body, the feel of his hair falling silkily on her face. 'I love you so much . . .'

'Can you wait two years?' he whispered, sliding away from her without letting go, and pulling her against him. 'To become Mrs Fitzgerald?'

'I think so,' she murmured drowsily. 'I don't seem to have any choice, do I?'

Drew grinned at her. 'I suppose in the meantime, you wouldn't consider becoming my mistress?'

'God, no. I don't think I'd be very good at that. Anyway, you couldn't keep making clandestine trips across the road to visit me at the cottage, because Luke is moving in. We'd have no privacy.' She giggled. 'So, it looks as though we'll just have to be chaste and virtuous until you're a free man.'

'If I thought you meant that I really would slap you.' He kissed her gently. 'I suppose you'll just have to move in here, won't you?'

'I suppose I will.' She sighed happily. 'If you can put up with my faults.'

'I feel there might be compensations.'

'Such as?' She slid beneath him again, pulling his face to hers.

'Such as your cooking – oh, and your cleaning . . .'

'Pig!' She bit his neck. 'I shan't give up Shadows.'

'No, of course not.' His fingers stroked her breasts. He stopped and looked at her. 'We've done it again, haven't we?

Made love. And we'll probably be doing it all night and non stop for the next two years and we haven't been at all sensible—'

'I'm on the pill now.'

Drew smiled at her with complete adoration, and resumed stroking her breasts, teasing each nipple in turn with his mouth.

'I'll just have to trust that your precautions had nothing to do with Charlie Somerset . . .' He laughed at her furious face. 'OK. Sorry. So you just assumed we'd be making love one day, did you? Despite telling me that you were never going to see me again?'

'Absolutely.' She wriggled with total delight.

'I knew we were on the same wavelength.' He caught his breath as her fingers circled tantalisingly on his thighs. 'What were you saying about Shadows?'

'That I won't be cleaning Peapods for free.'

Drew ran the tip of his tongue along her jaw bone until it found her mouth. 'It never occurred to me that you would.'

'And,' she trailed her fingertips down the flat plane of his stomach, 'I shall still charge you the going rate.'

Drew raised his eyebrows. 'And there's no room for negotiation?'

'None at all.' She rolled towards him, and in a tangle of arms and legs and white towelling, they tumbled laughing to the floor.

'We've landed on the whisky. All the more work for your cleaner, Mr Fitzgerald. Who, I believe, is considered a treasure beyond price . . .'

'So I've heard.' Drew's voice was husky as he pulled the robes away, and moulded his body to hers. 'Which is why I shall be happy to pay her in full.'

'You will?' She shuddered in ecstasy, wrapping herself around him, never wanting to let him go.

'Oh, yes.' Drew laughed softly, loving her with his eyes, his voice, his heart. 'Frequently, Maddy, my angel. As often as required.' He paused, kissing her again. 'But definitely not in hard cash. We'll just have to find some other form of remuneration, won't we? I'm sure something will spring to mind . . .'